The Book
Of Deacon

Joseph R. Lallo

DEDICATION

This book is dedicated...

To Gary, who inspired me to start writing the books.
To Sean, who encouraged me to keep writing the books.
To Cary, who convinced me to finish writing the books.
To Mom and Dad, who are the reason there is a me to begin with.

ACKNOWLEDGMENTS

I would like to acknowledge the hard work and contributions made by the following people, without whom this book would probably never have made it into your hands:

Nick Deligaris
For the magnificent artwork.

Anna Genoese
For the help in polishing my lackluster grammar.

My fans, bloggers, and friends:
For giving me the help, confidence, and exposure to come this far.

The end of an era is always a time of great importance. Sweeping change. Advancing into a new age. These are surely things worthy of a place in the memory of a people. Too often, though, it is a single event that brings about the most direct change that receives the attention. The blow that ends the battle, the last brick to fall. In our worship of these moments, these endings, we neglect the journeys, the trials, the hardships, and the battles endured to make them possible.

Whosoever is fortunate enough to find this book shall finally hear the greatest of these tales. I have spent much of my life piecing together the words that follow. Most of what you shall read comes from the mouths of the people who lived it. It is my hope, in recording the path taken by these heroes, that those in the years to come will not be blind to the dangers that threatened this world once before. If the unthinkable is once again allowed to come to pass, perhaps the knowledge and the deeds of the heroes of old will stir others to their greatness.

The tale you shall read is of the Perpetual War. If you live in a time or a place that has allowed you to forget this dark era, consider yourself fortunate. To be ignorant of these events is a blessing. However, knowledge of the evils of old is the only protection against their return.

The Perpetual War, at the start of our tale, had been plaguing the world for one and a half centuries. It was a conflict that divided our people. The large farming kingdom, Tressor, formed half of the conflict. It was a land of fertile fields, a land of plenty, that covered most of the southern part of the continent and was home to more than half of the people of the world. They opposed a union of the three remaining kingdoms--Kenvard, Ulvard, and Vulcrest--that had come to be known to its people as the Northern Alliance, and by its enemies as the Nameless Empire. This was a land of snowy fields, dense forests, and icy mountains. Despite a vast disadvantage in strength and size, this Alliance had managed to withstand decade after decade of battle. This conflict was a constant part of the lives of all, and is the reason that what follows must be told.

My place in this tale is small. There are others better suited to put to words what came to pass, but most have taken their final steps down their own paths. Thus it falls to me, lest the tale go untold. I shall endeavor to recount the events in as straightforward and impersonal a manner as possible. Do not imagine this as a tale told by a man. It is merely a record. Words on a page. Words that tell of the most unlikely of events, beginning in the most unlikely of places . . .

#

The end of the fall had only just come, and already the air could chill one to the bone. Of course, this far north, one could seldom expect anything else. It was not the cold that bothered her, though. She'd dealt with that all of her life. Pulling the tattered remnants of her uncle's old cloak closer about her, she pressed on.

As Myranda strained her eyes against the blistering wind, she saw nothing more than horizon. It would likely be another full day of walking before she saw anything but the unbroken field ahead of her. She shook her head, a faint frown cracking her dry lips.

"I should have known," she said aloud to herself. "He seemed a shade too eager to give me directions."

Myranda had taken to talking to herself to fill the long, lonely, and all too frequent trips like these. With no companion, the only thing likely to interrupt the ceaseless howl of the wind was the periodic noisy complaints from her stomach. That much concerned her. She could afford to buy no supplies in the last town, and no tavern or inn had been willing to serve her thanks to a simple yet disastrous slip of the tongue. Anyone could have made the same mistake. In another time, it might have gone unnoticed--or, at least, unchallenged--but in the world of her birth it was inexcusable.

Two older women had been standing in the street, discussing the most recent news of the war. These days one would be hard-pressed to find a different topic of discussion. In this instance, it seemed that the Northern Alliance had pushed back a rather sizable advance. After three long, bloody days of battle, the Alliance troops had managed to take back the very same piece of land that they had started on. The cost of this maintenance of status quo was the lives of the better half of the troops in the area. In and of itself, such a tale was anything but notable. Indeed, a day without such a battle was rarer than a day with one. The difference on this day was that the Tresson army had lost even more.

The two women cackled and bragged over the victory, each telling exaggerated tales of their nearest war-going relative. "My boy promised to kill three of those swine just for me," one would say. Another would respond triumphantly that all four of her children had made the same promise. It was during this exchange that Myranda made her fateful slip.

"All of those lives . . . wasted," she had said with sorrow.

Wasted! Having your child give his or her life for the cause was the greatest honor a mother could hope for. To speak of such noble efforts as a waste was tantamount to treason. How dare this wandering woman speak ill of the war! After countless generations, it had ceased to be a simple struggle between two lands and had become a way of life. Those who opposed this sacred tradition of noble battle were unwelcome. That one word--*wasted*--may as well have sealed the poor girl's doom. It had kept her from filling her pack and from filling her belly. Worse still, it had led a seemingly good man to send her through this frozen waste, claiming it to be the fastest way to the next town.

She shook her head again. It was one lesson that she could not bring herself to learn. If someone was going to tell a lie, they would tell it with a smile. Now she found no less than a day of solid travel between herself and another human being. The cold was tightening its grip on the icy field with each passing moment. In perhaps an hour, the last glow of the sun would leave the sky, taking with it the meager warmth it had cast upon the world. The cold of the day was unbearable, but the night was unlivable. Worse, there was a darkness due to the impenetrable sheet of clouds overhead that warned of a snowfall in the coming hours. She had yet to find a replacement for her thin summer blanket, and she could neither afford nor carry a tent. If Myranda was to survive this night, she would need a fire.

Alas, there were but three types of terrain in this land: vast, treeless fields; dense, forbidding forests; and rocky, impassable mountains. She found herself in the first, an icy, barren stretch of land with not a plant to burn for warmth save some sparse grass and tough lichens. Neither would be good for producing anything more than smoke and ash. She scanned the endless horizon for a tree, a bush, anything that could yield a flame. Finding none, she made ready to bed down where she was and hope for the best.

Just as she stopped, the last rays of the setting sun peeking through a rare break in the cloud cover reflected their crimson radiance back from the east. After squinting, rubbing her eyes, and blinking only to find the fading twinkle still present in the distance, she was convinced that whatever it was, it was real.

"It was probably nothing," she said. She glanced back in the direction she'd come, then in the direction she'd been heading. "Which beats every other direction, where there is certainly nothing."

To fill the time as she approached the mystery object, and to take her mind off of the rather dire position she found herself in, she busied her imagination with thoughts of what it might be.

"Shiny . . . a mirror. Perhaps a caravan of nomads came by and dropped wares. Or perhaps it is a jewel. A dozen or a hundred jewels. And gold, too. A king's ransom left behind by some daring thief where no one would ever find it, in no man's land. Ha, that would be my luck. To find a pile of treasure when all I need is a pile of wood," she said to herself.

The time passed quickly as she dreamed up objects and ways to explain them. She'd not yet reached the object when the sun's rays failed, leaving her without a reflection to guide her. Her sense of direction was nearly flawless--a fortunate fact, as it was all she had left to lead her to the mysterious object. The sunset-painted clouds gave little in the way of light, but night brought utter darkness. Neither moon nor stars could hope to break through the solid sheet of gray overhead. That was no different from any other night, though. Even without the stars to follow, one found ways to stay on course in this land.

In the thick blackness that surrounded her, she literally stumbled over what she was looking for. There was what seemed to be a large mound of rocks surrounded by a liquid that was sticky, despite the cold that would have frozen most things. There was also a bundle of irregular metal plates that she heard clang and crunch as she stepped on them.

"What happened here?" she asked no one in particular as she tripped blindly through the obstacle course she'd found. Two more steps, though, brought a squeaky crunch that made her heart skip a beat. It was the sound of icy wood. She must have stumbled into the remains of a camp site, and now stood ankle-deep in her salvation.

She knelt by the fireplace and began to pull away the icy crust that eventually formed over anything that remained outside long enough. Soon all that remained was the powdery remains of the fire that had occupied this place not long before. It was bone dry and better than kindling. A single spark and she would have a fire in no time. The overjoyed young lady pulled her flint from one of her tattered pockets and reached blindly for one of the metal plates she'd heard clang free when she'd nearly tripped over it. She struck the flint to the metal and in moments had a warm bed of embers. A few moments more and the largest of the charred pieces of wood had caught, casting a delicious warmth and light on her immediate surroundings.

Now, with light enough to see what she held in her hand, she looked over the piece of metal. It was oddly shaped and not nearly polished enough to have caused the reflection that had led her here. On the curved interior of the metal plate, she found a few torn leather straps bolted to it. The outside bore an embossed symbol that looked to be a crest--one that she did not recognize.

"It must be a piece of armor," she decided, turning it about one last time.

Satisfied that the fire was in no danger of going out, Myranda stood to inspect the strange place she'd wandered into. She found the bundle she'd stepped on and could now clearly see that it was indeed a full suit of plate armor. It appeared to be badly damaged and fairly frozen to the ground.

"Why would an empty suit of armor be in the middle of a field?" she wondered aloud. The answer came quickly and brought a chill to her spine that the iciest of wind never could. It was not empty.

She backed slowly away, dropping the piece she held. Myranda hated death above all else, a fact that had made her life a good deal more miserable than those of the war-hardened villagers who shunned her. They saw death not only as a necessary part of life, but a positive one, a source of glory, respect, and honor. They heaped more praise upon a fallen soldier than the poor man or woman could ever have hoped for in life, a fact that bothered Myranda all the more.

As she moved away from the body, her eyes darted all over. Something caught her panicked gaze and froze her in her tracks. Peeking out from beneath the frost-covered shield was a patch of coarse brown cloth. A pack! One could not live in a time of war and not know what such soldier's packs contained. Money, water--and, best of all, food. The body could not be more than a few days old. In this cold, the rations in his pack would still be edible.

Myranda may have hated death, but if being near to a corpse for a few minutes could save her life, she would not hesitate. She grasped what little of the cloth was visible and pulled with all of her might, but it was no use. The pack was frozen to the ground and pinned beneath the heavy shield. If she wanted to free the pack and its precious contents, she would need something to pry the metal sheet off of it.

Myranda's eyes swept across the cluttered campsite. Surely there must be something she could use, but what? The chest plate from the corpse? It had been partially torn free, but the thought of tearing the piece of armor from the fallen soldier's ice-cold body turned her stomach. Not nearly enough, though, to make her forget how starved she really was. Reluctantly, she locked her cold-numbed fingers around the frost-covered metal and threw her weight against it. After three failed attempts, she kicked the plate in frustration, her other foot slipping on a patch of loose snow. She lost her balance and tumbled to the ground, her head striking something far harder than ice.

The impact dizzied her. As she rolled to her knees, she punched the ground. The food that could keep her alive for another day was mere inches away and she could not get it. It was maddening. Myranda rubbed her sore head and looked up with her blurred vision to see what had delivered the painful blow. The light of the fire danced on a highly polished, almost mirrored surface. Even before her eyes had regained their focus, she knew that this was the object that had led her here.

Standing out of the frozen earth was a sword that was beyond elegant. The hilt was covered with a myriad of different jewels. The blade itself, at first seeming to be a flawless surface, revealed itself to be engraved with an exquisite design, composed of countless lines as thin and delicate as a spider's web. It was a weapon unlike any she'd seen before. The price of a single jewel from the hilt could keep food in the bellies and clothes on the backs of an entire family for a year. The sword as a whole could easily provide her with a lifetime of luxury and leisure far greater than she could ever imagine.

The value of the sword did not concern her--at least, not at this moment. Regardless of the price it might fetch in the future, at the moment it represented a far greater find. It was the means to extract the only thing that mattered to her right now, the food that would give her the strength to leave this frozen wasteland. It represented life itself. When her senses at last returned to her in full, she reached out to the lifesaving tool.

The very instant she touched her skin to the ornate handle of the exceptional blade, she felt a crisp, sharp burning. It originated in her palm and shot straight down her arm. She hit the ground hard, agonized and trying desperately to pull her hand from the torturous burning. Her fingers, though, would not obey her. Instead they locked tightly about the source of the torment and would not release. The pain grew to the point that Myranda was certain it would force her into unconsciousness. She was a heartbeat from blacking out when the pain relented, her fingers loosened and her hand came free.

Myranda gasped for breath, cradling the afflicted hand. What was it that had just happened to her? Had she triggered a booby trap? She turned her watering eyes to her left hand, fearful of the state she might find it in. Her survival was unlikely enough without a wound to deal with. Slowly she opened her fingers. To her great relief, the palm was merely red and tender, as though she'd scalded it in hot water. A simple bandage would suffice. Myranda pulled herself back to the fireside to recover.

"This is why I hate weapons. I find a sword and it manages to injure me twice without once being held by its owner," she said, eying the offending tool angrily.

Myranda touched the tender hand to the lump that had already formed on her head from the first encounter with the blasted weapon. She cursed the blade over and over again in her mind, never once thinking about the fact that if her head had found one of the weapon's cutting edges when she'd fallen, she would not have lived to suffer. When she was through letting her anger pour out at the sword, she stared broodingly into the fire and tore a bit of her inadequate blanket to treat her hand. As she did, light from the flame danced on the ground around her. Slowly her hungry eyes drifted to the sword, then to the pack, then back to the sword . . .

"No! It would take a fool to try to grab that blade again. I have lasted for days without food. One more day will not kill me. Besides, that food is probably rancid. It has been out in the open for at least a number of days.

Why risk burning the other hand to free some spoiled food?" she reasoned aloud.

Her stomach growled loudly.

"Of course, the touch to the sword wasn't that bad. It did not kill me. After all, it was probably a booby trap, and how likely is it that it would be set to trigger more than once? It is cold out, so the food has probably been preserved fairly well," she reasoned again, this time the hunger getting the better of her.

She moved carefully toward the weapon and, extending her bandaged hand to the handle, while keeping the rest of her body as far from the blade as possible, touched her fingers to it. She cringed at the expected onslaught, but when none came she knew it would be safe to use the hand that still had some strength in it. She wrapped her right fingers around the grip and pulled, but the icy ground held tightly to the sword, allowing only the slightest movement. Myranda put her left hand around the grip as well and pulled as best she could. On a normal day the sword would have come free quite easily, but hunger had robbed her of more strength than she knew. Had she not taken the chance tonight to free the food, the morning would have found her without the strength to stand.

Finally, the weapon came free. She dragged the sword across the icy earth and slid its tip beneath the edge of the huge shield.

"I am very sorry about this, sir," she grunted to her fallen benefactor. "I do realize how disrespectful this is." Grunt. "But I am left with very little choice."

Several minutes of prying and apologizing later, she'd cracked the icy buildup and freed the pack. Eagerly, she pulled it open. Savior! Salted meat and hard biscuit. By no means a banquet, but it was more than enough to save her. The food was well past its prime, but so long as it was still edible, it would serve its purpose. Aside from the food, she found a small bag of copper coins and a rock-hard frozen flask of water. There was also a pan for cooking and something that roused her spirits even higher. There were two loops of fabric across the top of the pack that could be only one thing.

"Tent straps! You had a tent, stranger! And if you had a tent, then I *have* a tent. I just have yet to find it," Myranda said.

Grabbing the unlit portion of the largest stick in the fire, Myranda held the makeshift torch, swept it about near to the ground. Before long, she found what was left of the tent. It was flat against the ground and crusted with ice, one of the supports shattered. Myranda set what was left of the tiny tent near the smoldering fire. The heat slowly filled the half-collapsed cloth shelter and gave her the first comfort she had felt in days.

She had only just fastened the tent flap when a heavy, wet snow began to fall. Myranda put the pan on the coals and heated some of the food she'd found, smiling to herself about her accuracy in detecting the coming snow. It was a skill to be able to read the clouds. The northern lands were shrouded in thick, gray clouds for most of the year. One could not simply see clouds on the horizon and predict rain. It was more a feeling, a nearly imperceptible change in the color of the gray, a new quality to the wind. Even she wasn't quite sure how she knew, but whether it was to be rain or snow, hail or sleet, she always knew. It was a gift.

She nearly burned herself as she snatched the meat eagerly from the pan. She had stood the hunger this long, but the smell of the cooking food made the pain a thousand times worse. Myranda took her first bite of food in days, the first full meal in more than a week. Her eyes rolled and her jaw tingled at the first taste of food. When she'd eaten the ration for the day, she slipped into a sleep few would ever know. If there was one thing she'd learned in her years of endless travel, it was that starving made any meal a feast, and exhaustion made any bed fit for a king. She was warm, full, and happy now, and that was all that mattered.

In a flash, she found herself in the middle of a sun-drenched field. She was bewildered and disoriented. The ground was warm against her bare feet. As her eyes adjusted to the light, they saw the beauty of the field. It was the finest sight she had ever seen, a vast meadow of lush green grass as far as the eye could see. She breathed in the freshness of the air and let out a triumphant sigh of joy. Myranda closed her eyes and began laughing, sheer happiness spilling out of her.

When she opened her eyes to take in more of the splendor, they came to rest on a tiny speck of black. It was the smallest fleck of darkness, but in such a place nothing could have been more foreign. It floated near to her, then off and way, almost out of sight. Slowly, it drifted down and touched the ground. Gradually, almost imperceptibly, the ground began to darken. The life-giving soil turned a charred black color, spreading outward like a stain across the countryside. The green grass faded slowly, so slowly that it was barely noticeable. She stood, helpless, as her paradise blackened. It was as though the world was being consumed by night from the ground up.

When all of the life had been drawn from the grass it spread skyward. Night flooded the field in spite of the sun above. In a grim finale, that too was blocked out by a curtain of black clouds. Only darkness remained, a darkness stirred by a frigid wind. Myranda strained her eyes, searching desperately for some wisp of what had been before. She saw faint, flickering lights far off in the distance. She rushed toward them, but one by one, the embers of light winked out, swallowed into the darkness as all else had.

"No!" Myranda screamed, opening her eyes. A sliver of light peeked through the flaps of her tent.

It was not real. The horror she had *seen* was false, a dream. The horror she had *felt,* though, was real. She took several minutes to catch her breath and steady her pounding heart. Never before had a dream been so vivid. She shook herself in a vain attempt to chase the tormenting images from her mind. The only comforting thought came in the words her mother had spoken to her long ago. Even with the eternity that had passed since she lost her mother, the voice still echoed in her ears. Now memories were all she had left.

"A nightmare is the best kind of dream. The only one that brings happiness when it ends," she repeated.

The fright had brought her to full wakefulness instantly, with no hope of returning to sleep. She smiled as she wiped a drop of sweat from her brow. How long had it been since she had been too warm? The feeling of sweat trickling down her back was one she'd not felt in weeks--months, even. Of course, once the cold hit her when she left the tent, the novelty would wear thin rather quickly. Carefully, she pulled the flap of the tent aside. A cascade of snow from the previous night's fall assured her that it was at least not dangerously cold, or else the wetness of the snow would have frozen it into a shell of ice. She crawled out of the dilapidated tent, favoring her stricken left hand.

With the light of the morning filling the field where she'd slept, she could finally see the scene she had stumbled through in darkness the night before. It had all been blanketed with several inches of dense snow that elsewhere might have been a terrible storm, but amounted to little more than a light flurry to the people of the Northern Alliance. She waded into the ankle-deep snow and surveyed the campsite.

Where she had thought there was a great mound of rocks the night before could now be seen for what it really was. Even buried beneath the snow, the mound clearly had the shape of a beast. The form indicated a dragon, but it was a bit bulkier than she'd imagined a dragon to be. Of course, she had no interest in finding out if she was correct, particularly because she would have to step into the pool of blackish liquid that stained the snow around the fallen creature. A liquid that was too thin to be pitch, and too black to be blood.

"Well, you killed it and it killed you," Myranda said, looking at the fallen soldier, its form barely discernible through the snow. She looked to the dragon. "That goes for you too. But why were the two of you here, I wonder? The dragon can come and go as it pleases, but this is awfully far from the front to find a soldier from either side."

She knelt and brushed the snow from the shield. It was standing nearly straight up after the prying she had done to free the meal the night before. She expected to find the crest of the Northern Alliance, or perhaps that of the southern land of Tressor. Instead she found the same simple crest she'd seen among other marks on the sword and armor. It resembled a smooth, curving letter V, with a rounded bottom and downturned ends, or perhaps a pair of smooth waves with a trough between them. Centered above them was a single point.

"So, you were not of the north or the south. That must be why you were in this forsaken place. You fall into the same lonesome caste as I. Non-supporter of the Perpetual War. You refused to join either side. You should consider it something of a triumph that you had managed to be killed by something other than an angry mob. I know it is no consolation, but the end you came to here prevented my own. I sincerely thank you for it, and I hope that whatever powers pass judgment on you in the great beyond will take that into account. I thank you for the food, the shelter . . . and the sword."

It had not been her intention to take the sword, but even she could not resist such a treasure. Even the most treacherous buyer would be forced to dole out a sizable price for such a weapon, and it was unlikely she'd find a buyer of any other kind. Myranda never even entertained the possibility of being paid a fair price for the piece. These days the shopkeepers were nearly as cutthroat as the soldiers, with barely enough wares to go around. Still, something of such value was sure to at least provide her with the funds to buy a horse, a tent, some food, and perhaps some clothes more befitting of the season.

She rolled the sword in her blanket and took some of the softened biscuit for breakfast. She then transferred the food, as well as the water and the heavy blanket, from the soldier's pack to her own lighter one. If only it had been smaller or she had been stronger, she could have taken the tent with her, but the days of walking would be made difficult enough with her newly-filled pack without a mound of heavy canvas and wooden poles. When all had been prepared, Myranda went on her way.

#

It was surprising how much spring was put into her step by a decent meal and good night's sleep. Her pace was twice that of the weary trudge of the day before. A trained eye and the clouds overhead told her that it was just past noon when she finally saw something on the horizon. A building with a spire. A church. The sight brought a wide smile to Myranda's face. She'd been turned away by every type of shelter, but never a church.

Quickening her pace, she came to the door of the small building and pushed it open. There was not a single occupied pew, nor was a single candle lit. The only light was that which filtered through the clouds to the simple stained glass window.

"Hello?" Myranda called out.

"In the priest's quarters," came the answer.

Myranda walked up the dim aisle and, on the wall left of the pulpit, found a door.

"May I come in?" she asked.

"Of course, all are welcome," the kindly voice replied.

Myranda opened the door. Inside, the warm orange light of a cozy fire danced in an otherwise unlit room. A large, fine chair faced away from the doorway and toward the fire. Aside from the luxurious-looking seat, the room was nearly bare. The walls were empty, not a painting to break the view of plain wooden planks. In the center of the room, a simple table and chair stood awaiting the next meal to be served. The corner held an immaculately made bed with a coarse gray blanket and single pillow. The only other furniture in the room was a suitably humble chest of drawers and a cupboard.

"What brings you here?" asked the unseen priest.

"I thought I might warm up a bit before I went off on my way again," Myranda said.

"Well, I am always glad to share what the heavens have provided for me," he said without rising.

"I am quite grateful. If you don't mind me asking, why do you keep it so dark?" Myranda asked as she walked into the room of her gracious host.

"I've little use for light these days," said the priest.

When she was near enough to spy the face of the priest, the answer to her query became quite clear. He was a kind-looking man, dressed in plain black vestment. Old, but not terribly so, he had sparse white hair on his wise head and a carefully shaved face. Most notably, though, was the blindfold over his eyes. Myranda had a vague feeling that she'd seen him before.

"Oh, I am so sorry!" Myranda said, covering her mouth. "You are blind!"

"Now, now, not to worry. It was none of your doing," he said.

"How did it happen?" she asked.

"It is the place of a holy man not to burden others with his troubles, but to relieve others of their burden," he said.

His voice had a powerful, clear tone, deep and commanding. It radiated wisdom and authority. He sipped something from a clay mug and cleared his throat before speaking again.

"May I offer you some tea, my dear?" he asked, raising his cup.

"Oh, I couldn't bother you for that," she said.

"No bother at all," he said, slowly rising from his chair.

"Oh, please, let me," Myranda offered.

"Nonsense, nonsense, sit down. You are my guest. Besides, if you get in my way I may lose my place and be lost in my own home," he assured her.

Myranda took a seat and watched as the priest paced out a practiced number of steps to the cupboard and ran his fingers over the contents until he found the correct canister. It was astonishing how smoothly he navigated the task without the aid of vision. In no time at all, he had placed her cup on the table and found his way back to his seat. She slid the cup in front of her, warming her near-numb hands on its warm exterior.

"That was amazing," she said.

"Oh, yes. Folks come from all over the kingdom to watch me make tea," he said lightly.

"I only mean that I had thought that losing one's sight would leave one helpless," Myranda said.

"I've still four senses left. A hand without a thumb is still a hand," he said.

"But you cannot count to ten," she said.

"You can if you remember how," he answered swiftly. "My goodness, why are we talking about me? I have been here for years. You are the newcomer, what about you?"

"What would you have me say?" Myranda asked.

"I would not mind a description. My ears can only tell me so much. I know your height from where your voice comes from, and your build by the creak of your chair, but try as I might, I still have not found a way to hear hair color," he said.

"Oh, well, I have got red hair, long, and brown eyes. My clothes are gray," Myranda said, embarrassed.

"And I am sure you are every bit as lovely as your voice," he said.

"Oh . . ." Myranda blushed.

"And your name?" he asked.

"Myranda Celeste," she answered. "And yours?"

"You may call me Father," he said. "So, from where are you headed?"

"North," Myranda said.

"North West or North East?" he asked.

"Just North," came her reply, worried about the line of questions that were sure to follow.

"There is nothing north of here but miles and miles of tundra," he said.

"I know," she said gruffly.

"The only things that would send a person through that waste are very good confidence or very bad directions. Not to offend, but I am inclined to believe that the latter is the case," he said.

"No, no. I just . . . misunderstood; I asked for the shortest way to Renack, and he sent me this way," she explained, hoping that the priest would not pry further. Her story was suspect enough as it was. The truth would reveal the reason she had been shunned, and she would at least like a chance to let her feet stop throbbing before she was thrown out in the cold again.

"Oh, well, that certainly would explain it. It could have used more conflict, though. The best fairytales always have plenty of conflict. The essence of drama, you know," said the priest, clearly aware that Myranda was hiding something.

"What? How did you know I was lying?" she asked, realizing the purpose of the comment.

"Listen hard enough and you begin to hear more of what people say than they had intended. Care to tell the truth--or, at least, a more compelling tale?" he asked.

"I wanted to know the easiest way to get to the next town. That was true, but I was purposely misled," she said.

"Why would someone do that? You could have died out there," he wondered.

"I had made myself . . . unwelcome," she said, carefully dancing about the key bit of information sure to cost her the respect of her host.

"Do I need to ask, or will you save me the trouble?" he asked, clearly in search of the missing piece.

Myranda sighed heavily. There were no two ways about it. She simply could not lie to a holy man.

"I . . . showed sympathy for the soldiers killed in a battle . . . both sides. From that moment on, no one there would help me. When I finally found someone who would speak to me, I asked for directions and he sent me through the field, assuring me it was the surest way," she confessed.

"A sympathizer," he said coldly. "It stands to reason why you would have been sent down such a disadvantageous path."

"I will leave, I don't want to--" Myranda began, rising from her seat.

"No, you may remain. I am a man of heaven and it is my place to show compassion. I will hear your confession and oversee your penance," he said with poorly-suppressed disgust.

"I will take my leave, I have caused you enough trouble," she said, gathering the pack that she had only *just* let slip to the floor, and turning to the door.

"Young lady, for your wrong to be forgiven, you must repent," he demanded.

Myranda froze. She turned back to the priest.

"Forgiven? Wrong?" she said, anger mounting.

When the priest asked her to redeem herself, it stirred thoughts she'd long ago pushed aside. So long as she'd cost herself the comfort of the shelter already, she may as well at least free her mind of its burden.

"I will *not* apologize for what I *know in my heart is right,"* she cried out.

"You have sympathized with the Tressons. These are men who seek only to kill your countrymen. Every soft thought for them is a knife in the back of a brother," he said.

"Don't you understand? Somewhere on the other side of the line that splits our world, another priest is giving this same speech to a person who had shed a tear for the Alliance Army. Any life cut short is a tragedy. I do not care how or why!" she proclaimed, giving voice to feelings long suppressed.

"If we allow our resolve to weaken, we will be overrun! Today *you* waste thoughts on an enemy. Tomorrow you poison the mind of another. Before long, there will be no one left with the will to fight!" the priest said, spouting the same tired ideas that Myranda had heard all of her life.

"At least then the war will be over," she said. "I will take an end to this war regardless of the cost. Enough lives have been lost already."

"Even if it costs you your freedom and the freedom of all of the people of the Northern Kingdoms?" he asked.

"Freedom? What freedom do we have? In the world we live in, there are but two choices to be made: join the army or run from it. If you join, you will pray each day that you will live long enough to pray again on the next. Pray that the impossible happens, that you live to see your children march off to the same fate as you try for the rest of your life to wash the blood from your hands. And if you cannot bear to throw your body into the flames of war, then you can live as I have. A fugitive, a nomad. Known by no one and hated by everyone. What worse fate could the Tressons have in store? What worse fate exists?" she proclaimed.

"It is talk such as that which will cost us victory," the priest said.

"Victory!? There is no victory in war! War takes everything and gives nothing! I only wish my words were as destructive as you would have me believe! If that were true, I would shout myself hoarse, I would not sleep until my words had poisoned the thoughts of everyone who had ears--but the cold truth is that nothing I say or do will have even the slightest effect on this wretched war. I am nothing! A shadow! A whisper! Dismissed and forgotten!" she ranted.

Her heart pounded and tears clouded her eyes. She shakily lowered the tea cup to the table. In the heat of her impassioned speech, she had managed to douse herself and a good deal of the room with the piping hot contents. The bandage on her left hand was dripping with it, rekindling the faded pain of its last scalding.

"I am very sorry for how I have acted, and I am sorry for the trouble I may have caused you, but I am *not* sorry for the thoughts and feelings that you insist are wrong. I will leave you now, before I say or do something *deserving* of regret," Myranda continued, in control of her emotions again.

"Were I you I would turn left at the sign post that you will find outside of my door," the priest said. "The people of Renack are decent, patriotic citizens. Should they discover your sadly misguided beliefs, I doubt they would trust an icy field to do you in. Bydell is to the east. Nothing but scoundrels and deserters. You just may find someone there who shares your blasphemous views."

These last words were heard through the slammed door of his quarters. Myranda moved with swift, motivated strides. She would have no more of this place if she could help it. The cold wind of the outside staggered her like a blow to the face. It had grown even colder than when she had sought shelter just minutes before. The patches of scalding hot tea turned icy at the first exposure to the stinging cold. The fuming girl gritted her teeth and leaned into the wind. It never ceased to amaze her how, seemingly regardless of which way she turned, the wind blew in her face. It was as though someone up above was toying with her, seeing how much torment it would take to break her. She turned her eyes skyward.

"You will have to do better than that!" she assured her unseen tormentor.

Not long after storming out of the church, she found the signpost of which the priest had spoken. Renack to the west and Bydell to the east. Both were ten miles away. A few hours by foot. It was a long hike by any means, but along a road, she could make it to either town well before nightfall. She might even make it to a pub before the tables had filled for supper. But which town to go to? Reluctantly, she headed off to the east.

As she walked, she questioned her choice. The advice of a person who knew how she felt about the war had nearly cost Myranda her life the previous day, and here she was making the same mistake.

Her father would have frowned on this. Her thoughts turned to him. It had been even longer since she'd seen his face than her mother's. She had to struggle to remember his features. He had been a soldier, never home more than a few weeks before he was off to another tour of duty. He still found time to teach her some of the most valued lessons she had ever learned, though. Even though she had not been more than six when she last spoke to him, he had made sure she knew something of the real world. He would tell stories of adventures he'd had, always with a piece of advice at the end. Above all, he'd taught her to pay attention and to learn from her mistakes.

She shook the memories away. Those days were gone now, too painful to remember.

With her reminiscing over, the infuriating words of the priest quickly returned. Again, she physically shook. What she needed now was distraction, anything to distance her mind from the pain and anger.

"So, Bydell and Renack. Each the same distance from the church. What other towns have I been to that shared a church between them? Lucast and Murtock . . . Skell and Marna . . ." she thought aloud.

She grimaced as the distraction proved inadequate to force the words of the priest from her mind.

"Bydell!" she forced herself to consider. "Where did that name come from? I wonder if it is by a dell."

Myranda continued to force her mind onto this and other suitably pointless subjects for the remainder of the cold and lonely trek. She had exhausted nearly every last meaningless avenue of consideration by the time she sloshed into the smoky, dark interior of the Bydell tavern. The sign over the door labeled this place The Lizard's Goblet, a name she wished she'd had to toss about in her mind on the trip. The reasoning behind such a name could have filled at least a few minutes. The smell of roasting meat and the tantalizing sound of wine being poured set her mind firmly on her empty stomach.

The tables of the noisy room were all at least partially filled. As she scanned the establishment for a place to sit, she could feel eyes staring back. Myranda's eyes passed the faces of at least a dozen men far too young and healthy to be anywhere but the front line. They each had found some way, likely underhanded, to avoid their obligation to serve. Now they sat, drinking and laughing in this place, criminals for choosing life. Among the rogue's gallery of faces was a particularly suspicious-looking person in the dark far corner, still shrouded in his gray cloak. Nearly every man in the whole of the room wore a similar cloak, as the King had made them available for free as a favor to the downtrodden masses.

When she finally located a seat she would be comfortable in, she moved quickly to claim it.

The seat she chose was at the counter where the drinks were served. The odd plate and knife scattered about the bar assured her that she would be allowed to take her meal there as well. It was not the most luxurious of chairs, but with a handful of empty seats between herself and the nearest denizen of the bar to ease her nerves in such a rowdy place, it would do well enough. She sat and awaited the tavern keeper's service.

Several minutes passed, punctuated by stomach rumblings reminding her of the fact she had yet to be served. A glance down the bar revealed the keeper to be in a very spirited conversation with a gruff customer he shared more than a casual resemblance to. She decided that they must be brothers, and chose not to interrupt their conversation. Surely he would take her order soon. As this thought passed through her mind, a particularly thick cloud of pipe smoke wafted past her face. It was all she could do to keep from gagging. She turned a watering eye to the source of the offending fumes.

Behind her, an old man with a patch over his right eye let out a long, raking sound somewhere between a cough and a laugh. The outburst lasted for a disturbingly long time, shaking his body as it progressed. The long, thin pipe he gnawed on was lodged securely between two of the only teeth left in his mouth. The half-rotten things had been used to clutch the stalk of the pipe so often they had parted to make room for it. She winced as a second, far more powerful outburst spread his lips far enough to confirm the solitary standing of the pipe-holding teeth. Another man sat at the table with him, staring intently at her. He looked as though he had not slept in days. On his shoulder was a scraggly bird of some kind. He whispered to it dementedly, prompting another long, raking laugh from his companion.

Sneaking another scan of the patrons of the tavern, she realized that most of the other men were staring at her as well, a fact that made her more than a bit uncomfortable. Myranda turned back to the bar. A trio of flies were enjoying the remains of the meal left by the seat's previous occupant. It was seldom warm enough outside for flies to survive, so it was more than likely that these creatures had lived for generations due to the lackluster housekeeping skills of the Lizard's Goblet's staff.

The flies drifted lazily off to their next meal when a particularly tipsy couple bumped into the bar on their way to the stairs that were at Myranda's right side. The collision nearly knocked her from her seat, but the couple merely stumbled up the stairs without so much as an acknowledgment of their rudeness. There were half a dozen similar bumps and jostles before the innkeeper reluctantly headed in her direction.

"Make it fast, missy, I am in the middle of something," said the less-than-hospitable man.

"What have you got over the fire?" she asked.

He sighed heavily as he turned to the kitchen.

"Goat," was his rather unappetizing description of the meal when he turned back.

"I will have some of that and some wine," she said.

"No wine," he said.

"Why not?" Myranda asked.

"Haven't had a drop in weeks. Very expensive stuff, you know," he said.

Myranda turned to a nearby table where a man was pouring himself a tall glass of the very beverage she sought.

"Are you certain?" she asked.

"Wine is very expensive," he repeated. "People who cannot afford wine usually order ale."

Now it was clear. The wine was reserved for the better-off of his customers. He did not think she could afford any. Judging by how this man did business, the price was surely prohibitive.

"Ale will be fine," she said.

He pulled a heavy tankard out from underneath the bar and held it below the tap of one of the numerous kegs that lined the wall between himself and the kitchen. He dropped it down in front of her, sloshing a good deal of it onto the sticky surface of the bar. Myranda wiped the rim and sampled the beverage as she watched the keeper shuffle into the kitchen in no particular hurry. His back was to the girl when the intensely bitter flavor of the ale struck her, sparing him the rather contorted face it brought about.

In truth, it was not particularly a bad brew, as ales went, but she not been fond of the best of them, and this was not nearly as good as that. She briefly entertained the notion of skipping the drink and simply awaiting the meal, but the barrel clearly indicated that this was a home brew, and the owners of taverns tended to take great pride in their creations. It was best not to turn her nose up at it. For the sake of harmony, she took another swallow. At any rate, it was a darn sight better than the leathery rain water she had been living off of from her flask day in and day out, and she did not look forward to the flavor of the contents of the soldier's flask either.

The plate of food was set before her: a slice of rather overcooked goat meat accompanied by a mound of boiled cabbage. A knife clattered to rest beside her plate. She carved a piece of the charred meat, speared it with the knife tip, and tasted it. The morsel required more than its share of chewing to render it fit to swallow. She followed the meat with a mouthful of the typically bland cabbage. Cabbage seemed to be the only vegetable that existed these days, and the flavor was always the same. Absent.

Myranda's jaw ached by the time she had done away with the shoe leather of a main course. It was barely the equal of the disturbingly old provisions that were even now growing older in her pack, but it was thankfully enough to satisfy her appetite. When she pushed the pitted metal plate aside, she was greeted quite swiftly by the innkeeper.

"Will that be all?" he asked insincerely, more interested in her money than her satisfaction.

"Oh, yes. Thank you," she said.

"Five coppers for the food, two for the ale," he said, holding out his hand.

Seven copper coins. That was a bit more than she'd expected. If she recalled correctly, there had been twenty or so coppers in the soldier's bag. Her first thought as Myranda reached for the bag was whether she would have enough for a room that night. That worry was pushed aside by the chilling realization that the bag of coins was not hanging from her belt, where she had left it. She patted desperately about, hoping to hear the jingle of coins somewhere, but the only sound she heard was the impatient drumming of the fingers of the man waiting to be paid. Anxiety burned at the back of her mind as she rustled first one side then the other of her tattered cloak, shaking any pockets she had on her person. She knew she'd had it when she had come in. There had been the distinct clink of coins when she sat down. Her mind raced. Where could they be? As her panic grew, the bartender's patience wore thin.

"Today, Missy. The other customers want service," he said sternly.

"I--I just--" she stuttered, pulling her pack to her lap to search it.

When she pulled the bag in front of her, the sudden shift knocked the heavy bundled sword free. It clanged to the ground. Quickly she bent to retrieve it. She plucked it awkwardly from the floor and sat up, finding she had been joined. It was the tall, cloaked figure she had noticed in the corner earlier. The hood was pulled forward, and in the dim light of the tavern his face was wholly hidden. He stood at least a full head taller than she, but the coarse cloak hid his build. He pushed the fold of the cloak aside to extend a lean, leather-gloved and gray-sleeved arm. As was nearly the requirement in the biting cold of the north, not an inch of skin was uncovered. The stranger opened his hand and a silver coin fell to the bar.

"The young lady's meal is my treat," spoke the stranger in a clear, confident voice. "She and I are old friends. I do hope you will be staying until morning, there is so much to catch up on."

"Oh, yes, well . . . I had planned to if I could afford it," she said.

A second coin fell to the bar.

"Your finest room, good sir," he said.

The keeper pulled a ring of keys from his stained apron. Carefully, he selected the least worn of the keys, placing it on the table and sweeping up the coins. The stranger stopped him.

"Not so swiftly, kind keeper. I think a bottle of wine would make a fine companion on a night such as this," the stranger added.

"I am sorry to say that I have none," the innkeeper said, the silver apparently earning this newcomer the polite treatment.

A third coin clattered to the table.

"Do be sure, I am *quite* thirsty," he said.

"Wish I could oblige, but you see . . ."

A fourth coin dropped.

"Perhaps a glance in the back would not hurt," the innkeeper said.

He walked through the smoky doorway and returned immediately with a bottle.

"As luck would have it, I have a single bottle left from last season. Drink it in good health," the innkeeper said with a wide smile as the equivalent of a large pile of copper coins was swept into his apron.

"Thank you, and thank *you* very much. Good . . . to see you . . . again. I will just get up to my room now," Myranda said as she hurriedly gathered her things, as well as the key and the bottle.

Bouts of luck like these were rare, and tended to turn sour quickly. She wanted to make sure she made it to the room before this one gave out. The warped stairs groaned as she rushed up them to a very poorly-lit hallway at the top. The left wall was lined with windows hung with heavy drapes drawn against the cold. A few of the last amber rays of the sunset found their way between the drapes to cast weak light on a row of thin, flimsy doors. They totaled seven, the last adorned with a fancier, arched top. She approached it, squinting to make out the number of the door and match it to her key. After pulling the drapes aside to shed light on the door, she tried her key.

Though the key clearly matched the lock, it refused to turn. She turned the worn piece of metal every which way, but in the frustratingly dark hall she could not see what the problem was. She glanced at a candle holder on the wall and grumbled. Its candle had burned beyond the point of usefulness long ago without being replaced. Eventually she managed to force the key into the appropriate position, turning it and gaining entrance to the room.

She closed the door behind her, mercifully finding it easier to lock than to unlock. It was a modest room, shrouded in near-complete darkness, but it may as well have been a palace. Sleeping in a half-collapsed tent next to a smoldering fire in the middle of a tundra had a way of improving one's appreciation of the lesser luxuries, such as walls that were thicker than her clothes. Without even lighting a lamp, she dropped her pack on one of the two chairs set at a small table on one side of the room.

She dropped herself onto the second chair and released a sigh of satisfaction. With effort, she pulled her left foot to her right knee and undid the stiff laces of her boot. Slowly, she slid the boot from her aching foot for the first time in days and flexed her toes. The second foot had only just received the same treatment when she heard a knock at the door that startled her.

"Who is there?" she asked, getting back to her feet.

After the all-too-brief rest they had received, the sore extremities were reluctant to go back to work. She hobbled painfully as she stowed her things, particularly the sword, safely behind the bed.

"Your friend from downstairs," answered a familiar voice.

Myranda took two steps toward the door, but stopped. She wanted very much to thank him for all of his help. Unfortunately, it was more than likely that he had come with a particular form the gratitude should take in mind. In times like these, kindness was a rarity, but charity was nonexistent.

"I . . . I am a bit tired just now," she said.

"Tired? Well, I suppose we shall talk tomorrow then. Enjoy your rest," he said--disappointment in his voice, but no anger.

Myranda placed her ear to the door to hear the light retreat of footsteps, followed by the scratch of a key in a similarly misshapen keyhole. His response was not what she had expected. There was not a hint of resentment or malice in his voice after he had been denied entrance to a room for which he had paid. He did not even try to convince her otherwise. It was contrary to every lesson she had learned in her years alone and every piece of advice she had ever received, but Myranda decided that she would let the man in. She would not allow the bitterness and cynicism that had infuriated her so in the past guide her own decisions.

She limped to the door and turned the key, which was still in the lock. The door creaked open and she stuck her head out to see his darkened form still struggling with the temperamental lock. He turned his hooded head in her direction.

"I am very sorry; you are welcome to come inside," she said.

"Nonsense, I would not dare deprive you of a good night of sleep," he said.

"I insist," she said.

"Well, if I must," he said lightly.

When she had allowed the cloaked stranger into the room, she shut the door, but left it unlocked. Just in case his intentions were less than pure, she wanted to be sure that she could usher him out quickly.

"I am very sorry if I had seemed rude a moment ago," she said, pulling the second chair out for him.

"Rude?" he said. "Am I to take it that you are not tired, then?"

"Well, I am, but--" she began.

"Then what is there to warrant apology?" the stranger asked.

"I should have asked you in. The room is yours, in all reality. You paid for it," she said.

"You hold the key, the room is yours," he said, easing himself onto the chair. "Interesting, the fellow sells wine but has no wine glasses. No matter, it is not the glass but the contents, eh?"

He placed two tankards on the table while Myranda found a lamp and managed to light it. She turned to her guest, who still had his heavy hood pulled entirely forward, hiding his face far back in its shadow.

"You know, thanks to your generosity, this room is near enough to the chimney to provide a comfortable temperature. You do not need the cloak," she said.

"I would just as soon keep it," he said.

"Well . . . that is fine, I suppose," Myranda said, removing her own cloak and hanging it on the bed post.

The stranger carefully poured out a third of a tankard of the wine for each of them.

"Here's to you, my dear," he said, bringing the cup beneath the hood and sipping awkwardly.

After getting a taste, he lowered his glass to the table, smacking his lips thoughtfully. Myranda sampled it herself, immediately startled by an intensity closer to brandy than wine. It was quite a bit stronger than she had expected. As it dripped down her throat, she felt the fiery heat spread, finally taking the lingering chill from her insides, just as she hoped it would.

"Intriguing flavor," her guest commented.

Myranda coughed a bit as the powerful drink seemed to hollow out her throat.

"It does the job, though," she managed.

"Admirably," he agreed, lifting the cup to his lips for a second awkward sip.

"Wouldn't it be easier to drink if you pulled the hood back?" Myranda asked.

"Drinking would be easier, I am sure, but things would become . . . uncomfortable," he said, tugging his hood even further forward.

Myranda looked uneasily at her guest. There was something very unsettling about his rigid refusal to reveal his face. She sipped at the wine as the darker reasons for such a desire flooded her head. He might be self-conscious, or perhaps if he were to reveal his face, he would place her in some kind of danger due to some dark past that is haunting him.

"Well, since we are here under the pretense that we are old friends, I think it would be best to learn your name," he said, breaking the uneasy silence and Myranda's train of thought.

"Oh, yes, of course. My name is Myranda. And yours?" she asked.

"Leo. A pleasure to meet you, Myranda," he answered, putting his hand out for her to shake. She did so graciously.

"And a pleasure to meet you as well, Leo. I really cannot thank you enough for helping me. I have yet to meet another who would have done the same," she said.

"I do not doubt it," he said, a bit of anger in his voice. "So tell me, how did you come to be in such a predicament?"

"I had brought a bag of coins with me. It must have been stolen," she said.

"Where you were sitting, you were asking for that to happen," he said.

"I know it," she said. "Had I been thinking I never would have chosen that seat."

A moment of silence passed. Myranda took another glance at the hood.

"Is it because you are cold?" she asked.

"Pardon?" said the stranger.

"The cloak. Are you cold?" she asked again.

"Not particularly," he said. "You do not strike me as a local. Where do you call home?"

"Nowhere, I am sorry to say. I honestly cannot remember the last time I had spent more than a week or so in one place," she replied.

"Really? We have something in common, then!" he said, pleased. "I spend most of my days on the road myself. In my case it is the nature of my career. Is it likewise with you?"

"If only. My nomadic nature is strictly by choice," she said.

"Hmm," he pondered. "You have chosen a life you hate. You will have to elaborate on that."

"Well, suffice to say that those that I encounter tend not to be especially fond of those like myself," she said, immediately worrying that she had said a bit too much.

"Oh? Another common trait," he said.

"Really? Is . . . that why you have got your face hidden?" she asked.

"Alas, I am found out," he said, throwing his hands up in mock despair.

Myranda's imagination seized this new fact and constructed a new set of possibilities. What about his face could make him an outcast? He may be the victim of some terrible disease. Worse, he could be a wanted criminal. There were more than a few outlaws who would find themselves in a cell for life if they ever showed their faces again. She was even more uneasy now. What sort of man had she let into this room? Could the kindness have been nothing but a ruse?

"What sort of man are you?" she said, her worry showing through. "I must know."

"Now, now, Myranda, fair is fair. If you pull back your hood, and I will pull back mine," he said. "What are you *hiding?*"

"Very well," Myranda sighed. It would seem tonight would be spent outside again. "I am . . . what you would call . . . a . . . sympathizer."

She hung her head, awaiting a voice of disdain. She did not have to wait long.

"A sympathizer!?" he said in a harsh whisper. "Oh come now! Is that all!?"

"What?" she said, looking up.

"You are a sympathizer. I would hardly place us in the same boat. Sympathy is nothing!" he said angrily.

"You mean you don't care?" she said, a hint of a grin coming to her face.

"I have got quite enough worries of my own. What do I care what side you root for? It hardly seems fair that I have to show you my face after a measly little confession like that," he complained.

A full smile lit up Myranda's face and she let a bit of joy escape in the form of laughter.

"You, Leo, are too good to be true. Generous, gentlemanly, and understanding," she said.

"Well, let us see if you still think so highly of me in a few moments," he said, lifting his hands to his hood.

"Leo, after all you have said and done tonight, I cannot imagination anything behind that hood that could keep you and I from being friends," she said.

Leo's leather-gloved hands clutched the edge of the hood and quickly drew it back. The smile dropped from Myranda's face. A mixture of fear and revulsion spilled over her. It was no human that looked back at her. Protruding from the neck of the cloak was what appeared to be the head of a fox. It was in proportion to the body, with a deep orange fur covering all but the muzzle, chin and throat, which had a creamy white color. His eyes were larger and more expressive than an animal's, brown and the only remotely human feature. The corner of his mouth was turned up in a slight smirk as he read her expression.

He twitched a pointed, black-tipped ear as he pulled a fiery red pony tail from inside the hood. It fell to nearly his waist, lightening along its length to the same color as his throat. Myranda couldn't keep a gasp from escaping her lips.

"Not what you expected, eh?" he asked. "I told you things would become uncomfortable."

Myranda closed her eyes and reached for the glass she had put on the table. Leo slid it to her searching fingers. Grasping it, she gulped down the contents hoping to settle her churning stomach and rattled nerves. When she lowered the glass, Leo filled it to the brim, then stood and began gathering up his ponytail.

Myranda ventured another peek at her visitor.

"What are you doing?" she asked.

"Unless I have greatly misread your reaction, it would seem you do not much relish my presence," he answered as he tucked the hair inside his cloak and restored the hood.

Now knowing the shape of the face that the hood had concealed before, Myranda wondered how she had not noticed earlier. Though a normal hood might conceal him, it would be perilously close to revealing the tip of his snout, even with the hood pulled comically far forward. Yet his face seemed to vanish into inky shadow the instant the hood was pulled into place. Leo was nearly to the door before she had finished sputtering and coughing from the powerful wine she had forced down.

"Don't go!" she coughed.

He stopped.

"Please--" Cough, cough. "--sit down, I should not have reacted so horribly. I was startled," she said.

"Are you sure you do not want me to go?" he asked, turning to her.

"I insist you stay for a while. Nothing has changed. I still owe you for all of this, and you have still treated me with more kindness than anyone I have met in years," she said.

Leo returned to his seat. "Would you prefer me to keep the hood up?" he asked.

"I want you to be comfortable," she said.

Leo opened his cloak and removed it, tossing it to the bed. Now that it was no longer obscured, Myranda finally got a glimpse of his build. It was lean, bordering on gaunt, but healthy. His clothes were plain and gray, quite simple and very worn. He slipped the leather gloves from his hands, revealing a second pair of black gloves, these composed of his own fur.

"You . . . you are a . . . m--a m--" Myranda stuttered.

"A malthrope? Indeed. To my knowledge half fox and half human," he answered.

"I was not sure if it was alright to call you a m-malthrope," she said, the word sticking in her throat.

"Mmm, I understand. It is not exactly term for mixed company. Certainly one saved for the end of an argument," he said knowingly.

He was right, of course. The term carried the very most negative of connotations. Speaking it as a child was a sure way to a sound scolding. Malthropes were the thieves, murderers, and scoundrels of horror stories told to frighten children into good behavior. Half man and half some manner of beast, they were monsters and fiends. The kindness and consideration Leo had shown could not be farther from what she had been taught to expect from these creatures.

"I thought there were no more m--no more of your kind left," she said.

"You are not far from correct. I've more fingers on my hands than I have memories of others like me. Clearly we are not the most popular race," he said, his demeanor was somehow cheerful despite the loneliness and isolation he described.

"How is it that you have made it for so long in a world so hostile to your kind?" asked Myranda.

"Well, thanks in no small part to that little wonder I threw on the bed. I had to spend every coin I had and more than a year searching for a wizard willing to produce it for me. With it on, no one can see my face," he said.

"But, how did--" she began.

"Now, now. By this time you should know my policy. Money has its value, but information the greatest treasure of all. You must give to receive," Leo said.

Myranda sipped at the wine again. She had consumed quite a bit of the powerful stuff and done so very quickly. Her judgment was a bit impaired. Had she her wits about her, she likely would not have said what she said next.

"A trade then. I will tell you all you care to know about myself and my people, and you return the favor," she offered.

"A fair proposition," he said, extending his now-bare hand.

Myranda grasped it and gave it a firm shake. It was peculiar experience shaking the hirsute appendage, but she was careful to appear as though she didn't notice.

"Now, where to begin? I was born in a large town south of here called Kenvard," she said.

"Kenvard . . . was that the old western capital?" he asked.

"One and the same. My father was Greydon and my mother was Lucia. She was a teacher. *The* teacher, really. Because of that she knew every man woman and child in town by name and so did I. When I was about six years old, though, the front came very near to our walls. Father was away, serving in the army somewhere else as he often--no, *usually* was. I was in the garden with mother. The church bells started ringing, which at that time of day was the signal to meet in the town center during an emergency.

"We had not even made it halfway there when the arrows started to fall. Flaming arrows. They fell like rain. In a heartbeat the whole town was aflame. Panic spread as it became clear that a force had surrounded the town, and siege was not their intention. A siege we were prepared for, but they wished to destroy us. To eliminate the town. My mother gave me to my uncle and sent us away to find safety. She went off to round up the screaming children that had been separated from their parents. Somehow, we found an exit clear of attackers and escaped the town. To this day I have not seen another familiar face from Kenvard," she recounted, tears welling in her eyes.

"I had heard about the Kenvard massacre. Totally pointless. The city of Kenvard had no military value. It was filled with women and children. Perhaps ages ago, when it was the capital of the entire kingdom of Kenvard, such an attack would have made sense, but ever since it was merely made part of the Northern Alliance, there are dozens of cities that would have fallen more easily, and done more damage to the war effort. Needless destruction. Until now I had thought there were no survivors," Leo said.

"There were at least two. My Uncle Edward and I spent a dozen years trying to find a place that would have us. It was not easy. Uncle never forgave the Alliance Army for failing us, and he could not quell his hatred for the men who had attacked either. He became a man consumed with hate. He was not shy about his feelings, either. Before we had been in any community for very long, something would trigger a rant about the uselessness of the Alliance Army. It did not matter to the townsfolk that his hatred for the enemy burned just as brightly--he was a traitor for speaking ill of the beloved army.

"Then, when I was eighteen, we stayed just a bit too long. His words had been heard by a neighbor, and before we could gather our things to escape, an angry mob battered down our door. I do not even remember which village it had been, all I know is that for the second and final time a member of my family met their end due to this wretched war. Not by combat, but by the war itself. Since then, I have been on my own, going from place to place. I am a bit more discreet about my feelings for the war, but I am constantly on the move regardless, either because I misspeak, or I fear I might, or . . ." She trailed off.

"Or what?" Leo asked.

"No, it is just foolish," she said.

"I would still like to hear it," Leo said.

"Well . . . I saw the death of my mother and uncle with my own eyes. My father, he was a soldier, and by this time he would have been one for nearly thirty years. My head tells me that he must have been killed by now. Soldiers who make it past their first few years are few and far between, let alone their first few decades. My brain tells me he cannot be alive. My heart pleads me to believe that he still lives. Whenever I find a nice home, and I have been careful to behave as the other villagers do, it is the hope that my father might be in the next town that tears me from my place," she said.

"Sometimes hope is all we have. Tell me, though, if the Tresson army stripped you of your home and loved ones, why do you feel sympathy for them?" he asked.

"At first I didn't. I shared my uncle's blinding hatred for them. Years passed and slowly my eyes began to open. The men who performed that terrible deed, they were only soldiers. Our men have laid siege to targets to the south time and again. It is not through spite or malice that these men kill, but through tradition. This conflict started more than a century ago. None of us have ever known any other life. They kill because their fathers did, as did theirs before them. The war is to blame, and every man woman or child, regardless of which side, is a victim of it," she answered.

"You are wise beyond your years," he said, and began to ask another question but she stopped him.

"Uh, uh, uh. You know the rules. I give, you give. Time for you to answer one of my questions," she said.

"Right you are, though I must warn you, yours is a difficult tale to follow. Let us see. I am not sure where I was born, but it was somewhere in the deep south. I spent the first ten years of my life in an orphanage for, shall we say, unfortunate children. It housed children of every race and background that were, for whatever reason, left behind. Be it due to injury, illness, deformity, or . . . species, none of us would ever see a home.

"I would wager to say that there were only two things that all of the other children shared. A longing to be a part of a normal family, and a healthy hatred for me. I am frankly shocked that I was allowed to live as long as I did. One of the caretakers was a softhearted old man who, for whatever reason, did not loathe me. I am certain it was only through his intervention that I was not murdered by the other orphans and caretakers.

"By the way, you would think that if a child just so happened to be the spitting image of a story's villain, they would spare the child that tale. Not so. I heard so many stories of my kind performing unspeakable evils so many times that I know them all by heart. The others remembered the lessons taught by those stories as well. Never trust my kind," he said.

"Now, clearly those were not the most ideal years one could hope for, but after I turned ten, things found a way to become remarkably worse. The old man who had protected me for so long died. His body was not even in the ground when the others proved once and for all that he had indeed been my savior for all of those years. They showed me what they thought of my kind in no uncertain terms.

"I was forced to run away and go into hiding. As much as my *differences* had seemed a curse before, they began to show their blessing side when I was faced with life in the forest for months at a time. This nose may not win me any friends, but it can sniff out a rabbit half a forest away, that is for sure. It was years before I set foot in a town again--at least, during the day. I had managed to sneak into farmhouses and such to steal an easy meal on occasion, but I never let anyone see me.

"To this day I wonder what made me decide to return to the world that had chased me away. I suppose the human in me has as much say in what I do as the fox, because one day I wandered into a small town. What was it named? . . . Bero. Well, I looked about as you would expect after years in the woods. I was wearing barely a shred of clothes, absolutely filthy. My hair was about so long," he remarked, indicating shoulder-length with his hand. "and a knotty, matted mess. As a matter of fact, I have yet to cut it since that day, so somewhere among these tresses are the very same locks I wore on that day."

"At any rate, my return to civilization was not warmly greeted. I received what still stands as the worst beating of my life, and was thrown into a shed until the townsfolk could claim a live bounty. In those days you could turn in a live malthrope for one hundred-fifty silver pieces or the tail off of a dead one for seventy-five. Fortunately those fellows got neither, as I was able to escape that shed in time.

"Had I a decent head on my shoulders, I would have learned my lesson, and returned to the forest until some hunter or woodsman killed me in typical fairytale fashion. Then at least my memory would have been passed on from generation to generation to scare children. Instead I let the vengeful instincts of youth guide my actions. I decided that if humans did not want me among them, then among them I would remain. Before long I found that during the winter I could bundle up enough to go unnoticed. The next clear step was to go to the place where such gear was commonplace in all seasons. And so I came to be a denizen of the Nameless Empire," he said.

"Please, not that I mind, but we prefer to call it the Northern Alliance," she said, realizing how evil the alternative sounded.

"I know," Leo said, drawing his vulpine visage into his peculiar little smirk. "I wanted to see how you would react. Besides, now it is my turn to ask you a question."

"Go right ahead," Myranda said.

"If you are so often on the move, how is it you manage to earn money enough to survive?" he asked.

"Well, the money I had intended to buy dinner with was in a satchel I had found on the body of a dead man in the middle of a field north of here," she said smoothly. Now that the second glass of powerful wine was nearly empty, it did not even occur to her how strange and awful that must have sounded.

"I see . . . so do you roam the wastes in search of expired aristocrats, or have you got a more conventional means of support?" he asked, raising an eyebrow.

"Oh, I do whatever I can. Help in a field, clean a house, that sort of thing. Anything anyone with money needs done. If the odd jobs in a town dry up, I move on. Yet another reason I never sit still," she said. "What about you? What do you do?"

"That is a shade more difficult to explain. As you pointed out, the Perpetual War tends to get under the skin of the good people, north and south. It seeps into everything that they do. As such, battle is as much a matter of sport and pleasure as it is a matter of combating the enemy. Here and there, particularly in the north, arenas can be found. People gather there to watch various fighters clash in the name of entertainment," he said.

"I have heard of those places," Myranda said with a sneer.

"Well, it is in those places that I earn a living," he said.

"You earn a wage by beating others to death?" Myranda said, shocked.

"No, no. Not to death. We would run short of fresh talent rather quickly if that was the case, what with the army offering the same opportunities for far greater prestige. No, our matches last until the other fighter, or fighters, either submit or are unable to continue. When I fight, I wear a helmet with a face mask that completely conceals my face. Needless to say, a faceplate with a snout draws a bit of attention, but I have led the crowd to believe I am a man *pretending* to be a beast to gain a psychological edge over my opponents," Leo explained.

"Clever," she said.

"I hate the mask, though. The thing is practically a muzzle. I will wear it every day, though, so long as the prize money continues to flow. I just won a three-week-long tournament a few days ago. Placed a hefty bet on myself. All told, I took away more than two hundred silver pieces. That ought to last for some time. After all, I get most of my food, drink, and even shelter from the forest. Aside from medical and clothing, I have no expenses," he said.

"I wish I could say the same. There are a few rather expensive purchases I need to make, but before I do, I will have to find a wealthier town," she said.

"Why is that?" he asked.

"Well, this town has a rather sparse market. I will need to find a town that has a store that buys and sells weapons or jewels," she said.

"Jewels? Interested in buying jewelry?" he asked, raising the eyebrow again. "You do not strike me as the jewelry type."

"Oh, no, that sort of thing does not appeal to me. I need to buy a tent and a horse," she said.

Leo furrowed his brow and scratched his head. "You *are* aware that those are items not typically found at a gem dealer or a weapon smith," he said.

Myranda laughed, covering her mouth and shaking her head. "I am sorry about that. I did not quite make myself clear, did I? You see, I have got something that I want to sell so that I can afford those things."

"Ah, now I see. What did you have in mind? I thought I heard something clang right before I helped you out," he said.

"Well, um, right you are," she said. She still had enough sense about her to know that she should not show off the sword to someone she barely knew, but he had seen it fall. It would be terribly rude and distrustful to hide it from him now. She would show it and hope for the best.

She stood and quickly stumbled back down. The room was spinning.

"Careful now, I think that the wine had a bit more of a kick than you had realized," Leo said, standing to help her.

"It certainly did," she said. A tinge of fear raced through her as she worried that there might have been more than just wine in that glass. The dizziness and fear faded together after a few moments. "I must have stood too quickly."

Myranda carefully pulled the sword from its hasty hiding place and placed it on the table, pulling the blanket off. Leo's eyes widened.

"That is a fine weapon," he said.

He leaned close and cast a gaze of admiration upon the mirror finish.

"Excellent temper . . . clean edge," he said, scanning the weapon eagerly with his expert eyes. "Would you mind if I lifted it?"

"Go right ahead," she said.

He slipped his gloves on before touching the elegant weapon, apparently fearful of smudging the surface. He then lifted it, carefully considering its weight and looking down the length of the blade, admiring its quality.

"Superb balance, surprisingly light. I do not have much use for the long sword in my work, but I can tell you that this is a remarkable weapon," he said, placing it down and removing the gloves.

"I was most interested in the handle," she said.

"Why? There was nothing specifically remarkable about the grip," he said, puzzled.

"What about the jewels?" she asked.

"Oh, *Oh.* I had not even noticed. Cosmetic touches like that are the last things I look for," he said. "Those *would* raise the price a tad, I would say."

"I should hope so," Myranda said, wrapping the sword and replacing it.

"A word of advice. If you want the best price, see a collector, not a smith. Shop owners always pay less than what they think they can sell something for. Collectors pay what the piece is worth. As much as those jewels are worth, I would wager the workmanship and uniqueness of that piece would fetch a still higher price," he said.

"I am not greedy. So long as this treasure earns me what I need, I will be more than satisfied. If it pays for a want or two, all the better," she said.

"Trust me, you will have quite enough," he said.

Putting the sword down again had disturbed the bandage. She adjusted it, frowning at its appearance. The filthy bar had lent more than its share of filth to the already tea-stained cloth, turning it black and greasy wherever it had touched the table.

"What happened?" Leo asked, indicating the injury.

"Oh. I burnt myself," she said--best not to be specific in this case, particularly considering the fact even she was unsure of exactly what happened.

Leo nodded thoughtfully. "You will want to let the air at that. Burns heal better that way. Just a few hours a day ought to do. Less of a scar," he said.

"Is that so?" she asked.

"Trust me. I spend most of the year recovering from one injury or another," he said, placing his hand on his shoulder and working the joint until a distinct snap could be heard.

"Why not see a healer, or a cleric?" she asked.

"Aside from the fact that they are nearly impossible to find? Believe it or not, when those folks do their job, they tend to want a look at their patient. I would rather not have them find out what I am--and if a healer cannot tell at the first glance I would frankly think twice about allowing them to work on me," he explained.

"Right, foolish of me to ask," she said.

As the hours of the night passed, Myranda made up for an eternity of solitude. She spoke until her voice nearly failed her and drank in Leo's words as deeply as she did the wine. They were equally rare luxuries to her, and she would enjoy them as long as she could. Weariness and wine were a potent mix, though, and finally her eyes were too heavy to ignore. Even so, she fought to stay awake to share more tales with her friend. It was Leo, always the gentleman, who insisted that she get some rest. He stood to leave.

"Before you go, I must ask you something," Myranda said.

"Don't let me stop you," he said, slipping his gloves on.

"You have every reason to be as bitter and angry as my late uncle. How is it that you have come to be so kind?" she asked.

Leo threw his cloak about his shoulders as he answered. "Simple. Would you have let such a grim and angry person through this door?"

"I suppose not," she said.

"Of course not. You reap what you sow in this world. I do not mean to say that I have *never* been as you described. I spent the better half of my years hating your people with all of my heart and soul. Perhaps a part of me still does. The truth is, whether I like it or not, your people rule this world. I can either live a life of hate and solitude, or I can do what I feel is right and hope for the same in return. Until today, though, I'd had little luck. Meeting you serves to remind me that there is some good within everyone, even if you have to dig to find it," he explained.

With that, the unique creature pulled his hood into place, instantly becoming one of the nameless, faceless masses again. He then pulled the door open, wished her a good night's rest, and shut it behind him.

Myranda spent a long moment staring at the door. She had learned much in the past few hours. It shamed her, but she could not deny the fact that had she seen his face before she'd known his nature, she would have treated him with the same disdain and prejudice he had come to expect. All of her life, she had heard the horror stories of what these beast men did. To think that one of these "fiends" would show her the patience, warmth, and understanding that even the priest lacked . . . In short, Leo was everything that Myranda feared had been lost forever in the wake of this horrific war.

Without his lively presence in the room, Myranda realized how tired she really was. She rose from her chair and sat on her bed. Doing so jostled a cloud of dust from the poorly-kept quilt. A glance at the bandage reminded her of Leo's words. Carefully, she removed it. The coarse, grayish material had absorbed only a drop or two of blood. Her palm had been entirely swollen the day before, but now there was only a stripe of redness along her palm and a single welt toward her fingers. She laid back and winced as the tightness in her back slowly eased away.

Finally she shifted herself under the covers and stretched, prompting the odd crack or snap from her weary joints. She smiled as she lowered her head onto the greatest luxury of all, a pillow. Before drifting quickly to sleep, she placed her left arm over her head on the pillow, exposing the afflicted palm to some much-needed fresh air.

The very instant she closed her eyes, she found herself transported to the blackened field that had poisoned her sleep the night before. Fear and desperation filled her as she searched for some remnant of the light she had remembered. In the distance, a handful of faint, flickering lights seemed to beckon to her. She ran toward them--but, one by one, the shining embers flickered out.

The ground became uneven and she stumbled, feeling the cold, dead grass crunch beneath her palms. Unwilling to waste even the time to stand, Myranda crawled toward the lights. There was a feeling within her that if she looked away for even a moment, the last piece of light would be lost to her forever. A sudden coldness beneath her hand started her, and she reflexively closed her fingers around it. Whatever it was that she had found, it was firmly planted in the frigid earth. She wanted to move forward, but at the same time, she could not bring herself to let go of the freezing object she'd found. She pulled and strained, finally looking to the artifact she had stumbled upon.

Even as she could feel the speck of golden light in the distance flit away forever, she saw the item she'd found replace it. It was a lantern, and the second her eyes met the wick, it fizzled to life. In the oppressive blackness, the dim flame seemed blinding. When her eyes painfully adjusted, she rubbed them to find that the world she was accustomed to had returned. The light she blinked at was the handful of rays that made it through the heavy curtains. The dream was over.

Blinking the sleep from her eyes was a matter of moments. Shaking the powerful emotions and painful throbbing from her head was another matter. She looked in vain for a basin or such to at least wash her face, but the room was rather poorly stocked. Dejected, she slowly gathered her things and laced her boots. When she was certain she had everything, particularly the sword, she entered the hallway, locked the door behind her, and sought out her only intact pocket to place the key. On the way to the stairs, she stopped in front of the door she'd seen Leo at the day before. After a long moment she continued on, deciding to let him sleep.

The tavern was a very different place in the wee hours of the morning. Pale light from the cloudy morning sky replaced the warm light of candle and lamp. The only motion was the stirring of flies upon a half-finished plate of food left by an unsatisfied customer the night before. Where had been a room full of rowdy patrons now was only one, a filthy man who'd had a bit too much of the ale and made a pillow of his leftover cabbage.

Behind the bar was a wiry young fellow, likely the owner's son. He'd leaned his chair against the wall and gazed lazily into space through a few greasy locks that hung in front of his half-closed eyes. Myranda approached him, hopeful of procuring a few pieces of the meat from last night. In her experience, if the meat was past its prime, the kitchen would usually part with it free of charge. It might not be tasty, but it would be nourishing, and so long as it filled her stomach, she was satisfied.

"Sir?" she said.

He did not react.

"Um, sir?" she repeated loudly.

She waved her hand before his eyes, only to hear a long, grating snore. She shook her head. It was one thing to sleep on the job, but teaching one's self to do so with open eyes was a trick. He had earned the sleep, she would not rouse him. Her stomach already grumbling, she pushed the door open slightly. A biting wind blew some stray snowflakes into her face. She paused for a moment to pull up her heavy hood and fasten its frayed cord, all the while letting the arctic breeze whisk inside. Once she had finished preparing herself, she opened the door fully.

Despite her precautions against it, the full force of the wind passed right through the cloak. There was a time when it had been as thick and warm as the ones that nine out of ten of her fellow northerners wore, but time and use had rendered it thin and ragged. The sleeping innkeeper shifted uncomfortably as the cold air found its way to him. Myranda glanced back at the motion, suddenly reminded of something she needed to do. She walked up to the counter and dug the room key out of her pocket. The groggy keeper gave a glance of acknowledgment and drifted back to sleep.

Again, she pushed open the door and faced the blast of wind from outside. The vague white light from the clouds reflected off of the barely disturbed snow. Her slowly-adjusting eyes glanced at the mottled gray sky and dark horizon of the nearby Rachis Mountains to the east. The colorless landscape did little for her sour mood, as the chosen beverage of the night gone by made its presence known as a dull, constant ache in her head.

Finally, she could see well enough to take in the more specific sights around her. A scattering of the town's residents were up and about in these first hours of daylight. Five were huddled together against the wind, all but one wearing the ubiquitous drab gray cloak. She began to look away when the inn door swung open to allow yet another cloak-clad, faceless villager into the cold. The newcomer stood briefly beside the others, not even evoking a glance from them. It then turned and waved at Myranda with a familiar black-gloved hand. The figure, indistinguishable from the others, rushed over to her.

"Leo?" asked Myranda as the figure approached.

"Indeed," came his familiar voice. He hunched over a bit, turned his hooded head to and fro slowly, and slouched. "The bed is a devious invention, letting one sleep until after sunup. Some folks need the dawn to catch their breakfast."

"Why are you slouching?" she asked.

"I am still tall enough to draw attention. On a bright day like this, the shadowy face can seem a bit suspicious," he explained quietly.

"So I suppose you are moving on then," she surmised.

"As quickly as possible. It was fine meeting you--" he began.

"Well, now, wait a moment. I am quite through with this town. We could walk a bit together. I would appreciate a friendly ear for a few minutes more," Myranda offered.

"Wonderful, as long as we do so quickly," Leo agreed.

The pair moved swiftly out of town. Fresh snow crunched beneath their feet, and a stiff and constant wind blew in their faces, but they made sure to keep a quick pace until they were well outside the village walls. When Leo was satisfied they were quite alone, he slowly straightened and tugged his hood back enough to break its spell and reveal his face. His return to his full posture was accompanied by a sigh. Myranda shook her head.

"I am so sorry that you have to live like this," she said, nearly sickened by the behavior of her own people.

"Oh, it is not so bad. I only spend time in a city once in a great while," he said.

"It should not be that way. I honestly do not see how you could treat me so kindly when my people have never done the same to you. How can you put the anger aside?" she asked.

"You must remember that at least half of my interactions with other races are in the form of combat. When every alternate memory you have of a human consists of forcibly delivering him into an unwelcome slumber, and getting paid quite well to do so, the anger tends to fade a bit," he said with a grin.

Myranda nodded. She tried to picture this thoughtful, helpful gentleman in battle, but it seemed absurd. As her mind wandered, she casually rubbed her sore palm with her right thumb.

"How is it coming?" Leo asked.

"Pardon? Oh, the burn. Very well. Thanks for the advice. It itches a bit, but not nearly as it had yesterday," she said. In fact, it had recovered so much, she had forgotten to bandage it that morning.

"Let's have a look," he said, stopping to gently take her hand into his gloved hands. He looked it over thoughtfully. Over the night the redness had all but disappeared, leaving a thin, raised area where the red had been.

"There will be a scar. Two of them. Here and here. If you want to keep them small, leave the bandage off and don't scratch at it," Leo advised.

"You are starting to sound like my uncle," she said as he released her hand.

"The man must have given some fine advice," he said.

The pair continued on.

"So, how long can I expect your company?" Myranda asked hopefully.

"Until I find a decent hunting ground to live off of for a few days. A pine forest will do," he said.

"I hope we do not find one. I would hate to have to say goodbye," she said.

"We all say goodbye in time. I always say it is a *good* bye when we choose it and a *bad* one when we are forced. As such, I much prefer *good* byes," he said. "And besides, I am long overdue for a time in the wilderness."

"Don't you ever get lonely?" Myranda asked.

"Now and again. Woodland creatures are a fine lot, but engaging conversation is not among their talents," he said.

"So you can speak with animals?" asked Myranda, intrigued.

"I am speaking with you, aren't I?" he pointed out.

"I mean besides humans. Can you speak with creatures who cannot speak . . . No, that just sounds silly. How can I say this? You speak the language of your human half exceptionally well. Do you have to same talent with other foxes and the like?" she finally asked.

"Yes, I suppose. I can smell the scents and hear the sounds that you cannot, and I can understand them. If pressed I can make myself understood to them, but the need has yet to arise," Leo explained.

"That is amazing. I would love to be able to do that," Myranda said.

"You aren't missing much. Most animals are concerned with little more than where predators are, where prey is, and how to get from one to the other," he said.

"Are there any messages I am missing right now?" she asked.

"I am not sure. Stand still," he said.

The two halted. After a quick glance to assure they were still alone, he pulled back the hood entirely. His ears twitched slightly, and he drew a long, slow breath into his nose.

"Not terribly much. A pair of rabbits passed through here. They have nested a fair way off of the road in that direction. They are both scared half to death that we might find them," he said.

"Astounding . . ." said Myranda.

"If you say so," Leo said, replacing his hood and continuing on.

"Oh, come now. You don't think it is amazing that you can simply perk up your ears and take a whiff and learn all of that?" she asked.

"No more amazing than the fact that you can understand the impenetrable accent that these townsfolk mumble day in and day out," he said. "That was another reason I lent a hand. For once I heard someone speaking properly."

"Well, my mother was a teacher. I had little choice. How is it that you came to speak so well?" she asked.

"To speak a human tongue without the benefit of actually having a human tongue is a supremely difficult task," he said. "I simply decided that

I may as well put all of that effort into speaking *correctly*. That goes for all of the languages I speak."

"Oh, you speak other languages?" she asked, nearly slipping on an icy track beneath the snow. The pair of gray lines left by a trade wagon was the only things as far as the eye could see that interrupted the canvas of white.

Leo's answer came in the languages he described. First was the slow, flowery dialect of the southern empire, Tressor. These words Myranda understood.

"The glorious tongue of my homeland," he said in Tresson.

What followed was an odd grouping of syllables spoken in a very clear and precise manner. Myranda racked her mind, but she could not place the sounds.

"I recognized Tresson, but what about the second?" she asked.

"Just a silly little language I learned from the fellow who taught me to handle a sword properly," he explained. "Your guess is as good as mine as to where that verbiage originates."

"Well, you spoke Tresson wonderfully. Tell me, do you remember much of Tressor?" she asked.

"A bit," Leo answered. He sniffed the air and turned to the eastern horizon briefly before turning his shrouded gaze back to her.

"Well?" she said expectantly.

"Oh . . . descriptions. Warmer. Much warmer. It only snows in the winter, and rarely even then. There tends to be a lot more green and a lot less white. The trees shed their leaves in the colder months. There are pests of all sorts buzzing about your head. I've got many an irritated memory of flies, mosquitoes, and the like flitting in and out of my ears. Mostly in.

"What else? The towns are more spread out. The space between is littered with farms. Very large farms . . . with many, many workers," he reminisced, his last words carrying a tone that betrayed a distant repressed emotion.

"It all sounds so lovely. Like a paradise," she said.

"I, for one, am glad to be rid of it," he said. "I have a natural coat that I cannot remove, and the summer can be downright unbearable. About the only thing I do miss is the hunting. My, but those forests were stocked. I could go for weeks without repeating a meal."

He breathed a sigh of remembrance, but pressed onward. Myranda scanned the stark white countryside and tried to imagine it as he had described. Gentle rolling hills, a brilliant green instead of white. Warm breezes blowing, perhaps a fluttering of butterflies among a patch of wild flowers. She realized that no sight like that had ever truly blessed her eyes. Indeed, the closest she had come was the dream a few nights ago, before the darkness had come. Leo might as well have been describing a dream, though, because it was a place she would never be. It might exist somewhere, but crossing the battlefront to see it was as likely as reaching the stars with a step stool.

"It reminds me of what I imagine when I think about the Chosen," she said.

"The Chosen?" he replied

"The Chosen Five. Surely you heard that old tale when you were a child," she said.

"As I said, most of the tales I was told focused on convincing me just how awful my brethren were," he said.

"Oh, well, you missed something. There is a long story that my parents used to tell. It tells of a time in the future when the war is at its absolute peak, and the world itself is on the brink of destruction. On that day, the gods will look down on the world and proclaim that an end to the fighting must come. And thus there will arise five warriors with the strength to strike down the strongest foe, and the wisdom to set things right again. The tale differs greatly from person to person in terms of just what these warriors will look like. As for me, I picture five noble knights in shining silver armor, astride white horses, riding across a green meadow," she said, thinking back to the bedtime stories of her youth.

"Sounds nice. I would have liked to hear that one," he said.

Pleasant conversation filled an hour or so more of walking before one of Myranda's frequent glances to the east brought her the sight she'd been dreading all day. Melorn Woods, a small forest well known for its hunting. It would certainly suit the purposes Leo had in mind, which meant that her company would soon be leaving her. Carefully, Myranda shifted to the right side of the road, away from the forest. If she could keep his eyes on her, he might not notice the woods for a few minutes more. Leo only smiled when she did so.

"Clever," he said. "I suppose I should be flattered."

"What?" Myranda said, mock innocence on her face.

"You don't want me to see the forest over yonder," Leo replied, pointing squarely at the woods without looking.

"I did not . . . How did you . . ." Myranda stuttered confused by the immediate collapse of her plan.

In answer, Leo pulled his hood back and shifted his finger to the tip of his sensitive nose, tapping it twice before tugging forward the hood to conceal it.

"Oh, yes . . . I had forgotten," Myranda said.

"This is where we part, then. I truly enjoyed your company. If ever you find yourself at an arena, do look into the fighters' listing. I fight under the name 'The Beast,'" he said.

"I never thought I would have anything to do with one of those places, but now I just may," she assured him.

Leo held out his hand for a farewell shake, but Myranda pushed it aside and embraced him warmly. He reluctantly returned the gesture.

"Before I go, I have been meaning to ask. How much money was stolen from you?" Leo said.

"I would say there were at least twenty copper coins in the bag. I had plans for that money." She sighed, shaking her head.

"Well, it just so happens I have got a bit more money than I can carry, so if you will just do me the favor of taking it off my hands. . ." said the friendly creature, digging into the heavy bag in his cloak.

Even before he had finished making his transparent excuse, Myranda was shaking her head.

"I couldn't take your money. You have already done so much for me. It just wouldn't be right," she said.

"Well, if you say so," he said, placing a hand on her shoulder. "Until we meet again."

With that he turned to the woods, quickening into a sprint that no man could match. Myranda watched as her unexpected friend disappeared over the hill and into the forest. Almost immediately, the loneliness closed in around her. She sighed heavily and pulled her hood up into place, the long goodbye leaving her ears badly stinging from the cold.

The sigh turned to a startled gasp as she felt a trio of ice-cold objects creep down her back. After frantically tracking them down with her hands, she retrieved the culprits. Three large silver coins, worth fifty coppers each. Leo must have slipped them into her hood just before he left.

Myranda placed the sneaky gift into the one pocket that had not been worn through by overuse. With no company to occupy her mind, Myranda focused on the unfamiliar jingling of money in her pocket to distract her from the long road ahead. Not unlike the rest of this war-torn land, the coins had a rather troubled past.

There had been a time, long before her own, when the three kingdoms that had become the Northern Alliance were still separate. Each had coins of their own. There were different sizes, designs, and names. Then came the war. The reason for the conflict between the vast southern kingdom of Tressor and the small mining kingdom Vulcrest was lost to the ages, but hostilities soon became such that Vulcrest could not hope to face the mighty foe alone. The sister kingdoms of Kenvard and Ulvard were called upon for aid. Before long, any distinction between the three kingdoms was lost--as with nearly all aspects of life, the money was stripped of its individuality for the sake of unity.

Gone were the colorful, cultural names like Dellics, Glints, and Ouns. Instead there were the four types that remained today: copper pieces, half silvers, silver pieces, and gold pieces. The likeness of kings and queens of the past were hammered away, leaving the coins as plain and faceless as the people who spent them.

The aimless wandering of her mind had done its job at least as well as the wandering of her feet. Before she knew it, she was approaching a shoddy wooden wall around an equally shoddy little town. Both were likely a remnant of the bygone age when the three kingdoms were separate. In those days, forts such as these dotted the landscape along the borders. Now most were left to rot, and some were made into trading posts. Such was the case here.

A weathered and faded sign proclaimed the frosty place to be Fort Wick. A few steps more took her past the decrepit gate that had once held doors heavy enough to turn away a battering ram. Now one was wholly missing, burnt during a particularly harsh winter, no doubt. The other had dropped from its massive hinge and buried its corner in the earth, never to close again. The buildings, what few there were to speak of, were in slightly better condition.

At the town's center was a large building surrounded by a handful of smaller ones. Here and there, the ancient gray wood of the walls gave way to the brown and yellow of new wood where the old had been replaced. Where once had been the cots of dedicated soldiers now stood shelves of poorly-made tools. A former armory held the flimsy wares of a leather smith. Most importantly, in what had been a stable in the years past could be found a market marked by a carving of crossed swords. Perhaps inside she could relieve herself of the burdensome sword and gain the means to reduce her burden further.

Myranda hurried to the door and pulled it open. Inside, a simple, smoky oil lamp cast its sallow light on case after case of weapons of various types. An elderly man sat behind the counter, lazily shaving pieces off of a wooden stake. Judging from the mound of shavings on his shirt and the plank of a counter, it had been his sole activity for some time. The sight of a customer stirred him from his seat. The fellow had a head of wiry gray hair that had grown wildly out of control. He was exceptionally thin, but moved with considerable speed at the prospect of a sale. He glanced past her to the closing door, but when it shut without another customer, his eager look to a step toward confusion.

"Ah, hello, little lady. What can I do for you?" he said, in a voice to match his withered features. "Have you lost your way?"

"Do you sell these weapons?" she asked.

"I do," he assured her.

"Then it would seem I have found my way," she said.

"I see. My apologies, miss. I don't get many young ladies through here. Truth be told, haven't had many people at all through here," he said.

"Then I would think you would be happy to see me," she said.

"Oh, that I am, miss. As a matter of fact, I've got just what you'll be wanting right here," he said.

The feeble old man tottered to one of the cases behind the counter, mumbling all the way.

"Just the thing for dainty hands. Nice and light . . . and small," he muttered.

He hobbled back to the counter with a leather pad with an array of small knives arranged on it. The eager salesman placed it down, beside where Myranda had placed the cloth-wrapped sword while he walked. The hidden prize drew a curious glance from the old man.

"Did I put this here?" he asked, scratching his head.

"No, sir, I did," she assured him.

"Oh . . . why?" he asked, the years having taken their toll on his mind, it would seem.

"I would like to sell it to you," she said.

"Oh, well, we can settle that later," he said, shifting quickly back to his sales pitch. "First, take a look here. A stiletto, and a fine one, you can be sure of that. Nice and thin, but tough. Toughest metal made. Won't bend, not one bit, you can be sure of that. Someone tries to bother you, young lady, you just put this little knife right through their ribs. Won't take hardly any effort, you can be sure of that. Push it in right up to the hilt. Won't have any trouble from that troublemaker any more, you can be sure of that."

"That is very nice, but I would really like to show you this sword," Myranda said.

"Now, now, miss, I am not in the habit of picking up rusted relics from the public, even from those as lovely as yourself," he said with a wink.

Myranda weathered the unwelcome compliment for the sake of the deal she hoped to make.

"I think this sword will pique your interest," she said.

Myranda pulled the ragged cloth from her prize and carefully watched the merchant's face. His eyes widened briefly in astonishment, but dropped quickly back to their cool and sullen state. Now the game would begin. Uncle Edward's advice often echoed in the place of her mother's in

Myranda's head, and when it came to haggling, he had a wealth of advice to give: "The only difference between a ten-copper price and a five is confidence. You can give them the most unreasonable of prices, but if you are confident about it, that price will not move an inch."

For Myranda an additional requirement arose that made her perhaps a bit less of a skilled bargainer. Certainly confidence was essential--but, for Myranda, honesty was required for confidence. She was an excellent liar, but she simply functioned better with the truth on her side. As such, she had become something of an artist at sculpting the truth into something she could use.

"Where does a little lady get such a big sword?" asked the old man.

"It was left to me by a very dear friend," she said. That soldier in the field had saved her by leaving the sword. That made him a dear friend in her book.

"So it is old, then . . ." he said, searching for a reason to drop the price.

"The age has no bearing. This blade is immaculate and in perfect condition," she said, careful not to fall for his trick.

A few words crept up from her memory.

"Note the clean edge and excellent temper," she added, quoting Leo's observations.

The two haggled back and forth for the better part of an hour. In the end, he bargained her down to fifty silver pieces, plus the stiletto and a sheath. Rather, she bargained him up from five. Both knew that the sword was worth ten times what he was paying, but she wasn't greedy. If she was equally skilled in her dealings with the other merchants, she would walk away with all she needed, and even some change in her pocket.

"Now, I don't have all of the money right here. I deal mostly in coppers, so unless you want to carry around a few thousand of those, I will have to get some exchanged with my supplier," he said.

"Of course," she said. "How long?"

"Three days. Nearest inn is Bydell," he said, pointing a shaky finger in the direction from which she came.

She'd had enough of that town, and decided on a second option.

"Is there a church nearby?" she asked.

"A churchgoer, eh? Good to hear it. These days, folks don't pay the reverence to the good word like they ought to. Particularly you young folks. To tell the truth, I haven't found the time to make it up there myself. The spirit is willing, but these old legs won't get me there. Time was I could . . ." he rambled.

The old man attempted to regale her with a painfully long tale of his athletic exploits of youth. After the third off-topic story, Myranda cut in to request directions to the church. He indicated that there was a fork in the road a half-hour south. If she took a left there, she would find the church about an hour down the road. She thanked him, and, after getting the less than generous offer in writing, headed down the road.

The sky had an unfriendly look to it. Myranda quickened her step. Snow came suddenly and severely this time of year, and to be caught in it would be very treacherous indeed. As the minutes wore on, the air became colder, and stinging pieces of ice were hurled into her face by a swiftly stiffening wind. She pulled her tattered hood forward and leaned into the wind, which blew out of the southeast. She had only just reached the fork when the wind began to carry not only snow from the ground, but also fresh flakes from the sky. She took the left turn and exposed her right cheek to the blustery assault that the left had thus far endured. The cold bothered her little, her mind locked instead on the consequences it brought with it.

A snowfall alone would slow her, so long as there was little wind. Likewise, wind alone was more an annoyance than a threat. Together, though, they were deadly. The wind and snow were growing in intensity with equal ferocity. If she did not get a roof over her head soon, all of that bargaining would have been wasted. Periodically, a gust came so strong it stopped her in her tracks. Myranda closed her mouth and breathed through her nose, longing to gasp but knowing that air this frigid could tear at her insides if she didn't warm it first.

The sun was still high in the sky, but the curtain of snow blocked its rays, making early afternoon seem like dusk. The road in front of her was a wall of white. In these conditions, she could pass within an arm's length of shelter without seeing it. Finding what her eyes told her useless, Myranda closed them to spare them the stinging wind. Now she had only the sound of her feet to guide her. Even under layers of snow, the crunch of a road had a different timbre than that of the turf of the field. Before long, she was not so much walking as wading through snow that had already drifted to knee height in some places. With each passing step and each icy flake, the hope of reaching the church seemed to fade.

A streak of ice beneath the snow caused her to slip. She stumbled forward to catch her balance, but instead caught a sharp blow to the shoulder from an unseen obstacle. Sparks swirled against the black of her closed eyes as she reeled from the impact. She opened her eyes a sliver to see what had happened, and nearly cried out in joy at the sight of the frosted over shingles of the church. Feeling along the wall with what little sensation her fingers had left, she came to the door. Eagerly she pushed the gateway to savior, but after only a few inches it stopped and would not budge.

"Hello?" Myranda said, banging desperately at the door. "I need help! Please let me in!"

Even if there had been an answer, she could not have heard it over the howling wind. She shoved the door with all of the strength she could muster. It slid open a bit more. One more valiant push allowed just enough of a gap for her to slip through. She angled herself through the opening, a task greatly complicated by the large pack and long sword she carried. When she finally tumbled inside, she heaved the door shut against the biting wind.

After spending several minutes catching her breath and brushing the caked snow from her clothes, she inspected the clearly unoccupied church. A pale white light filtered through the snow-encrusted windows, dimly illuminating what little there was to see. Aside from the odd broken chair or pew strewn about the floor, there was nothing in the way of furniture. It was clear that this place had been ransacked long ago and stripped of anything of value, leaving a large, empty room with a raised platform at one side and a fireplace.

Myranda slid to the ground with her back against the door. Even with little more than the wind and snow out of her face, she could feel her cheeks redden with warmth. She sat for a time, letting her heart slow to a more normal pace and listening to the wind rattle what few shutters remained on the windows. When she finally recovered from the onslaught, her trembling having subsided somewhat, she rose to inspect the fireplace. The flue was clear, so at least a fire would be safe. She gathered together some wood from a broken pew and carefully arranged it in the hearth.

Eventually, she was able to get a fire started. After basking in the much appreciated warmth, she pulled her provisions from her pack. The last of the purloined food would have to serve as her meal for the day. In truth, it might have been wiser to ration the precious stuff, as this blizzard had the potential to block her way for days, and there was no other food to be had. The meat was old already, though, and only getting older. She would rather have a full stomach today than an upset one tomorrow. She dropped all of the salted meat into the pot and put it over the fire.

The fire was weak and not nearly able to heat the whole of the empty church, but, huddled near it, Myranda finally began to feel like herself again. The smell from the food was not exactly appetizing, and stirred memories of her uncle's hideous attempts at cooking. It seemed that whenever he tried anything more complicated than applying heat to a pot of water, the results were sickening. Myranda's father would kid that if he churned out one more concoction, he would ship him over to the enemy.

That had been one of the last times she'd seen her father. Myranda tried to push the unwelcome memories away, but a tear came to her eye when she pictured the two of them together. It was foolish, but something inside her refused to believe that her father was gone. Somehow, after all of these years, she would still ask after him in each new town, even though every answer thus far had been one of ignorance or doubt.

A draft from one of the several broken windows whisked through the largest hole in Myranda's worn cloak, reminding her once again that it needed to be replaced. Of course, she could never do that. Links to what little past she had were too precious to give up simply because they had lost their usefulness, and this cloak was the last thing she owned that had belonged to her Uncle Edward. She pulled the blanket from her sword and wrapped it around her. As she recalled the history of the cloak, she vaguely remembered relating it to that Leo fellow she had met. Quietly, she wished he were here to keep her company again.

The light of the fire danced on the mirror-like finish of the blade. She stared at the pristine edge. It had likely been used in battle, certainly left to the elements, and yet the edge looked to be as keen as the day it was forged. Her eyes drifted to the grip. The jewels there were like none she had seen before, though, in truth, she had seen very few. Gazing into the deep blue gem at the hilt's center, she swore that she could see on forever, like looking into an endless dark tunnel.

Myranda reached for the magnificent weapon, but stopped. She turned her palm up, the very same one she had risked to touch it with the first time. It had healed quickly. Now all that remained was a thin pink scar running across her palm, with a single red mark just below her middle finger. The longer scar, centered on her palm, was a long, curving line that twisted back and forth on itself. It resembled a pair of smooth waves with a trough between. The red mark was centered above this trough. It was the very same mark that adorned the blade. The blade, not the handle.

Carefully, she touched the scabbard and flipped the sword to its other side. There was no mark anywhere near where her hand had touched the sword. How could such a scar have been formed?

"Magic," she decided aloud. The owner had some sort of spell cast on the sword to brand the would-be thief with the mark of the rightful owner. For such a fine blade as this, a security measure of that type would hardly be out of place.

Satisfied with her own explanation, she looked back to the fire. Using the corner of her blanket to shield herself from another burn, Myranda pulled her pot from the flames. The heat had done little to improve the flavor of the food, but the ration was nonetheless filling. With the meal gone, she realized that so long as the storm raged, she would have nowhere to go. Her weary muscles made it quite clear how they felt she should spend the spare time. She sought out perhaps the only unbroken chair in the church and sat upon it. Sitting on the cold floor was one thing, but sleeping on it was quite another. Once properly situated, she wrapped herself all the more securely in her blanket and drifted quickly off to sleep, regardless of the fact that there were still hours of sun left.

The single night in a proper bed had spoiled her, it would seem. The clattering shutters and sudden drafts pulled her from slumber a handful of times through the afternoon and night. At first, she would jerk awake and look around, but soon she tried simply to ignore them and get back to sleep. In a way, the light sleep was a blessing. It spared her the terrible dreams that she had been suffering. Not once in her life had she had a recurring dream, though she had often hoped for one. Such dreams were said to carry great meaning. The dark and frightening images of her nightly torment did not bode well for the future.

#

After she'd had her fill of fitful slumber, Myranda opened her eyes. The yellow light of the fire flickered on the walls of the otherwise darkened church. This struck her as odd. She had not fed the flames for hours. She tried to turn to the mysteriously lively fire, but something stopped her from shifting. Still groggy, she struggled to gain a glimpse of the tightness about her chest, straining until she could just barely see the cause. There were coils of rope wrapped tightly around her, securing her to the chair. Panic gripped her as tightly as the ropes as she struggled. Both rope and blanket trapped her hands. Despite the maddening effort to free them, there was little progress and even less hope of escape. In her struggle, all she managed to do was to knock her chair to the floor. With much effort, she was able to slide the chair along the floor to where she had left the sword, only to find it had been taken.

Myranda regained her wits. This struggling was getting her nowhere. She had to think. Who would do this? Who *could* do this? All that she had of value was the sword. Why would someone who had the skill to bind her without awakening her even do so when they could have merely taken the sword? She tried to struggle again, hearing the jingle of silver in her pocket. They had not even robbed her.

"It doesn't make any sense! Steal the sword, tie me up, and *feed the fire!?*" she cried in frustration. "Why would you feed the fire? Unless . . ."

Unless whoever did this was still here. She held perfectly still and strained her ears, fearful to even breathe. All that could be heard was the tap of shutters and the crackle of flames. Myranda's rattled mind shaped each of them into a half heard footstep. Finally she gave up listening. What could she do, even if she heard her captor? Nothing while she was tied up. She glanced about in her limited view from the floor for something, anything to free her. The fire! She could burn the ropes! A second thought brought the realization that her blanket and clothes would likely burn to ashes before the binding even lit, let alone what would happen to her skin. There had to be another way.

Irregularly scattered about the room were pieces of broken wood. If she could make her way to one of the piles, free her hand, get a shard, and work its jagged edge at the ropes that held her, she just might be able to free herself. It wasn't much of a plan, but it was at least more than she was doing now.

Tipping over had slid her painfully to the side of the chair. By alternately working her right shoulder and right foot, she was able to inch along the floor. Each tiny slide the chair made produced an earsplitting grinding noise. If the captor was still near, he would most certainly hear it, but that didn't matter. Her best chance was to try to escape. After what seemed like an eternity of awkward sliding, she managed to reach a handful of the wood shards on the church floor.

With her hands tied firmly beneath a blanket, there was no obvious way to get at the shredded wood. An option came to mind. It was foolish, it was desperate, and it likely wouldn't work. It was also her only choice. Taking a deep breath and tensing, she heaved her shoulder down upon the woodpile with all of the force she could muster. The cruelly sharp edge of one of the pieces burst through the blanket and bit into the flesh in her shoulder. Agonizing and damaging as this was, it was the result she had been hoping for. She cried out at the savage pain of it and slowly wriggled her left hand beneath the blanket to the site of the throbbing new injury. The rope permitted nearly no movement, but through sheer effort she managed to bring her fingers to the now-blood-soaked wood. She grasped weakly the shard and worked at pulling it from its new home.

As painful as its appearance had been, the shard's removal was doubly so. With the utmost of care, she pulled the piece of wood through the tear in the blanket, out of her shoulder, and to a point just above the topmost of her bindings. A knife would have freed her with a few slices, but the jagged splinter tore only a few fibers of the rope at a time. After an eternity of patient scraping, the rope held by a tiny strand. Myranda strained at the weakened rope and it snapped. The other coils loosened and she was finally free of the chair.

The injured arm was the first to reach the floor, and she had to roll quickly off of it. All of that time bound in the same position made standing a difficult task. When she was on her feet, she looked around her and strained her ears. She was alone. Whoever had tied her up had left and all of the noise had failed to prompt a return. A sharp throbbing in her arm drew her attention. It was bleeding fairly heavily. Convinced that she was safe from her captor, at least for the moment, she decided to care for the wound. The blanket was ruined; it might as well serve one last purpose. She tore it into strips and used it to bandage the afflicted limb. The blood from the gash had seeped through her shirt and the blanket, pooling on the floor. Looking at it intensified the dizziness that its loss had caused.

With the most pressing of her concerns attended to, Myranda set her mind to the task of escaping. She assessed the situation. Of course, her pack was gone. A pull on the door revealed it to be solidly secured from the outside. The windows were all small and near to the high ceiling. There would be no escape through any of those. The sole window large enough to allow her to escape was the shattered stained glass window behind the pulpit, but it was even further out of her reach. She had to try the door again.

She grasped the heavy wooden handle and tugged it with all of her strength. Slowly a tiny crack opened, one that closed the moment she relented. It wasn't much, but it was hope. Myranda scoured the assorted piles of wood until she found a reasonably sturdy plank. Placing its edge between the doors, she used it as a lever. Even with the added leverage, the doors would only open an inch or two. After carefully wedging the lever in the opening so that all of her hard work would not slip away, she put her eye to the narrow portal to the outside.

It was night, and the perpetual cloud cover kept even the slightest hint of moonlight from reaching the snowy field. In the pitch blackness, she was barely able to make out a few coils of the same rope that had bound her securing the door. There was no way she could sever it in the same way she'd cut her own, and the harder she pulled at the door, the tighter the rope held.

"Of course!" she said, immediately clasping a hand over her mouth.

The rope! She could use it to escape. Hurrying to the severed bonds, she tied the ends, producing a strong rope of considerable length. Choosing a heavy piece of wood, she tied it to the rope. The resourceful young lady ran to the broken stained glass window and hurled the weighted end of the rope. A twinge of pain in her shoulder robbed the throw of some of its strength and the rope fell short. Shifting the rope to her left hand, she tried again, reaching the window but failing to hook onto it. A third throw held.

After testing the strength of the rope, she tried to climb. The injured shoulder again slowed her, but she refused to let it stop her. With supreme effort, she managed to pull her feet from the ground, only to come crashing down again a moment later, preceded by the subdued but unmistakable sound of metal biting into wood. She looked up from the ground to see a single throwing blade protruding from the wall. Myranda traced the path of flight back to its source, a dark form crouched on the rooftop outside one of the smaller windows.

A scraping sound drew her gaze back to the window. With nothing securing it the wooden grapple fell to the ground outside, dragging the precious rope along with it. All that was left behind was a useless length of rope no longer than her arm. By the time she looked back to find person who had thwarted her escape, the window was empty.

"Who are you!? What have I done!? Why are you holding me here!?" Myranda cried out to her captor. Silence was her answer.

Beaten, Myranda stood the fallen chair upright and sat down, no more free now than when the ropes had bound her, and with a rapidly stiffening right arm to remind her of her defeat. She surveyed her prison once more. Tiny windows topped the sloping roof on either side, they themselves topped by a smaller roof. Above the entrance was a small room that once held the church bell. The hole that had been made for the bell pull to hang through now showed a few dry, rotted strands. A plank with some stray rungs dangling from it was all that remained of a maintenance ladder.

She trudged to the door she had wrestled partially open. The inch-wide portal to the outside remained, for whatever reason, undisturbed by the kidnapper. The fiend could have easily pushed her wedge from the door and robbed her of this tiny accomplishment, but instead it remained, whistling with the frigid wind of the outside. Earlier that day she had prayed to find this place and to be allowed inside, but now all she wanted was to leave. She put her eye to the crack.

The sky to the east was beginning to take on the rose hue of dawn, coloring the stark white snow a faint crimson. The only soul to be seen was the captor, dressed in the same blasted cloak as any other northerner. The stranger sat with eyes to the east and back to Myranda. Far off in the distance, a speck of black was moving toward them along the snow-mounded road. As it drew nearer, it revealed itself to be a horse-drawn sleigh. It was not unusual for such vehicles to be seen so soon after such a terrible storm. Blizzards were anything but uncommon, and waiting for the roads to clear was a surefire way to be caught in the next. However, it was clear that no one had been along this road for many months, save for whoever had looted this place. This sleigh's appearance could not be a coincidence.

When the sleigh was near enough, Myranda could see that the horses, the sleigh itself, and the four soldiers who stepped out of it, all bore the unmistakable emblem of the Northern Army. Her heart lifted. She had not been happy to see a soldier of either side for years, but today they represented her only chance for rescue.

"Here! I am in here! Help me!" she cried out, beating on the door with her fists. A sharp pain in the shoulder quickly put the hammering to an end, but she continued to call out.

When she was certain that she had been heard, she put her eye back to the crack in the door. The four soldiers stood silently before the door, each in full combat armor, complete with face masks. The first was speaking calmly with her captor while the others looked on. They made no motion toward the door. She strained her ears to hear what the two were saying. Only the soldier spoke loudly enough to hear.

"The one who touched the sword? We are charged with her return, as well as that of the sword," he said, in response to the kidnapper's unheard comment.

The sinister figure pulled a bundle from inside the cloak and held it out, obviously the sword that had been taken from Myranda. The soldier took the weapon with gauntlet-clad hands and uncovered it. After as close an inspection as he could manage without raising his face guard, he looked to the kidnapper.

"It seems to be the piece we require. We shall take the girl and be on our way," he said, moving toward the door. The captor stopped him with a hand to the shoulder.

"What?" the soldier said, irritated.

The kidnapper held the hand out palm up.

All hope was dashed away as she struggled to comprehend the pieces as they came together. He was waiting to be paid! The Northern Army was in league with the stranger who had captured her! Why? And why did they want her? A thousand thoughts of fear burned across the back of Myranda's mind and her heart fluttered in her chest. The exchange between the conspirators continued.

"The capture and return of the swordbearer is the responsibility of the Alliance Army. Regardless of what orders you may have received, your interference is considered a treasonous action. Owing to the fact that your interference was entirely beneficial, you will not be charged," the soldier said.

Her captor said something too quiet to hear, but the fiend's body language betrayed more than a bit of anger.

"I have received no word of such an agreement, and even if I had, it would have been deemed illegal. You shall receive no payment. I suggest you accept this fact and be grateful we do not kill you where you stand," he said.

Her mind raced. How could anyone want her or the sword? She had only just found it in the field a day or two ago. It had obviously been there for some time. And how could anyone have found her here so quickly? No one knew she would be here, not even she, until the old man had . . . the old man. He must have assumed she had stolen the sword, and he told her where to go. Apparently she had not learned her lesson about who to trust for directions. The cloaked figure must be a bounty hunter. Things were looking grim. If the Alliance Army had come to take her away, she might be witnessing her last sunrise. In criminal matters, only an accusation was needed to be thrown into prison, and if the weapon was valuable enough to hire a bounty hunter *and* alert the army, she would remain locked away for the better part of a decade.

As she worried what the future held for her, the exchange between the bounty hunter and the soldiers became very heated. The other soldiers, who had stood silently until now, began to encircle the blade-for-hire. The leader stepped between the door and his underlings and began working at the ropes, blocking Myranda's view of the spectacle. Despite the overwhelming emotion, she could not help but notice an odd quality about him. It was something in the way he moved. It seemed . . . foreign.

A flash of light reflecting off of something metal shifted her gaze to the action behind the approaching leader. The soldiers began to move back, but never even made it to a second step. One by one the soldiers jerked awkwardly and dropped to the ground. Their ends were brought in a heartbeat by a single strike too fast to see. The clang of falling armored bodies drew the attention of the leader. His head had not yet turned when a blur of steel removed it from his shoulders.

Myranda backed away, but the grim spectacle lingered in her mind. She stumbled back from the door, her head spinning and her stomach churning. The sight had physically sickened her, and she could not keep her feet. She settled dizzily to the ground, coughing and gagging.

Somehow she managed to maintain her composure. When she felt well enough again, her eyes turned to the door. The murderer was still out there, she could feel it. The tides had turned again. Her desire to wrench the doors open and taste freedom was swiftly replaced with a repeated prayer that they remain shut, that monster outside would not come in. She kept her gaze locked on the door for what seemed like an eternity, fearful even to blink.

The light of morning crept across the floor in front of her. Myranda strained her every sense to try to learn what the killer was up to. Only the occasional whinny of horses and the drip of melting snow broke the silence. Slowly, careful to make no sound, she rose to her feet and crept toward the doors, eyes focused intently on the slit of light between. She was only a step or two away when the ribbon of light darkened. She rushed backward, tripping over a piece of wood and hitting the ground hard. There was a blur and a hiss as the fiend's blade split the restraining ropes. The doors swung open, leaving the dark silhouette of the murderer as the light reflecting from the snow fairly blinded Myranda.

Squinting against the sudden brightness, Myranda felt for a piece of wood and brandished it. She'd seen what he could do to trained warriors, but no one would take her life without a fight. If this monster was going to finish her off, she would be sure to make the decision a regrettable one. The form of the bounty hunter had only begun to clear when it leapt from the light. Now it was hidden somewhere in the darkness inside. Myranda's eyes were useless, as the contrast of light and dark kept her from seeing anything. Before she could even react, she felt the board she'd grabbed torn from her grip. Her arm was pushed painfully behind her back and she was forced forward.

Fighting all the way, Myranda was led outside. Each time she resisted, a sharp pain in her already-injured shoulder forced her to continue. The snow was ankle-deep at its shallowest, and as tall as she in drifts. When she was nearly to the horses in front of the sleigh, her arm was released with one final thrust. A second iron grip locked onto the back of her head, keeping her gaze forward. One of the horses had been cut off of the sleigh, every symbol of the army's ownership removed from the equipment.

"Go. *Now!*" came a whisper to her ear, harsh and disguised, but certainly a male. His final word flared with anger, offering some hint of a voice.

Myranda gasped as she felt the cold edge of a knife pressed to her throat.

"If you so much as glance in my direction, I will do to you what I did to them," he said, turning her head to the remains of the soldiers.

Where once had stood a man now lay a mangled mass of metal. The snow around the heap was pitted where flecks of blood melted through, and armor showed smudges of blood far blacker than she had seen anywhere but the field a few days ago. There was no flesh or bone among the spent armor either, only a scattering of bluish-gray dust. There had been more than a blade at work in the murder of these soldiers. Some unholy magic had ravaged their bodies. He had taken more than their lives; he had taken their humanity. Now they could not even be honored for their sacrifice with a funeral. It was horrible.

She climbed with difficulty to the back of the horse. It had never been meant for an individual rider, so it had no saddle. Myranda had ridden bareback before, but she preferred not to. Now, however, was no time to object.

As she snapped the reins and went on her way, she filled her head with the mindboggling facts of the day. This bounty hunter captured her, bound her, and stole her most valuable item. Yet, at the same time, he left her money and made sure to keep the fire going, even though he did not warm himself by it. The fire must have been for her--but why? It was clear that she herself had some value to him, but after killing those who seem to have come for her, he provided a means to escape and demanded that she use it. Why? Was this some sort of cruel game?

Myranda urged the horse forward. Despite the dozens of paces already between them, she could feel the place in her back where a knife might slip in at the first hint of hesitation. She pushed the horse as hard as she could to put as much space between herself and the killer as she possible. Minutes passed--she knew not how many--before she reached the fork in the road and decided she felt safe enough to stop.

The horse breathed great, steaming gasps as she gave it its first rest. It was unaccustomed to speed, being used only to pull a sleigh. She looked to the beast's back and frowned. Her pack had never been returned to her. All that she had left was the three silvers that the friendly fox had given her earlier. It was just yesterday, but it seemed ages ago. She looked to the south. No sense going back to the man who had sent the soldiers and murderer after her. She would head to the next town, replace her lost goods, and decide what could be done.

Now that the desperate fear had released its grip on her, she became aware of three things. First, the cold was absolutely biting. The night she had spent away from it only served to make it feel many times worse. Second was the pain in her shoulder. It had been burning steadily from the cold, but she had only now become aware of it. Last, as the horse began at a gentle trot, she heard a peculiar jingling. It was different from the sound of the various buckles and straps of the horse's equipment. Curious, she looked about for the source of the sound. She soon found it. There was a bag, tied to one of the horse's straps. The removed the satchel and opened it. The sight made her head spin.

It was the bag of coins she'd had stolen from her. There could be little doubt. Everything from the ancient-looking bag to the weathered coins were familiar to her. How? How had it gotten here? The killer must have been there, in that tavern, that very night. How else could he have the bag? And why would he give it to her? Did he want her to know? She shook the bag and discovered the sheathed stiletto had been placed inside, along with a note. Eagerly she snatched it out, sure that the message had not been there when she had last had it.

It was on a coarse paper, written in a precise hand. The words read:

Your life ended the day you touched that sword. By nightfall, every gossip and snitch will know your name. By sunrise, every guard and soldier will know your face. When night comes again, you will find no safety among your own people. Use your last few hours of anonymity to get as far from society as possible.

She shivered, but this time it was not the cold that shook her. She was a part of something that she did not understand. The sword was gone, but she still was not safe. What possible reason could they want her for? Why would touching a sword make such a criminal of her? And why would the killer give her this advice? The questions came in droves, the answers not at all.

She tried to focus on the positive, if any could be found. Her first thought was that she had been lucky enough to escape with her life. The soldiers had not had that good fortune. Also, she now had a horse. It was the very thing that she'd hoped to gain by selling the sword. In a way, she had gotten from the vile weapon what she had intended. Now she was freed from the burden of walking--not that she could enjoy it. It gave her more time to think at the one point in her life when it was the last thing she wanted to do.

In all that had happened so far, there was only one thing that was certain. It was not over. The words on the note were true. In days the stories of her deeds, whatever they might be, would reach the ends of the continent. She did not even know what she had done wrong, but in just a few hours everyone else would, and they would have already marked her guilty for it. It did not matter that the only people who knew the truth were dead or outlaws themselves--a tale such as this had a mind of its own. It could move unaided across the land, whispering itself into people's ears, all the while gaining speed at the expense of accuracy. Gossip had a way of defying the laws of nature sometimes. People would know.

The more she thought about the day that had passed, the more troubled she became. Try as she might, she couldn't shake the images of death and the chilling sense of fear from her mind. Her distraction from the trip, unpleasant though it may have been, coupled with the speed of traveling on horseback, brought her to her destination in what seemed like no time at all.

#

Afternoon was approaching as she entered the village. Unlike the other places she'd been to, this town was alive with activity. Cloaked people busily cleared mounds of snow from the streets. Smoke rose from chimney after chimney. A well cared-for sign heralded the bustling hamlet as Nidel. The eyes of the people hard at work stayed, for the most part, on the task at hand. This gave Myranda some comfort. They did not know yet. Indeed, how could they? Even if they had been told every detail of what had happened, there were only two people who knew what she had done *and* what she looked like. As long as she didn't behave strangely, she would be just another visitor . . . for now.

Even with the rock-hard proof she had offered herself of her current safety, she could not help but feel stares, as though she had been changed by what she had been through, and every man, woman, and child could look upon her and know. As though the smear of blood staining her cloak spelled out the tale of its creation. Her rumbling stomach broke through the thoughts swirling in her head. Down the street, a gaily-painted sign with a picture of a roast turkey beckoned her to its door. After seeing that her horse had been attended to, she stepped inside. It was a far cry from the establishments she'd been to recently. For one, the windows and lamps kept the place quite well-lit. Also, it was spotless. Nowhere were the flies and vermin that had called the Lizard's Goblet home. Finally, there was barely a soul in the place. Only the lone waitress, a plump and energetic young woman who sprung eagerly to her feet to greet and serve the new arrival, and a single patron, accompanied by a pile of bags and packs, could be seen.

"Good morning, miss!" she said, overjoyed to have a customer to serve. "Just have a seat anywhere you like and tell me what I can get you."

The entire left wall had a long wooden bench attached to it, with tables dispersed regularly along its length. It was there that she took a seat, sliding behind a table. She glanced at the other customer, a young man with white hair, who sat at the other end of the bench. He was intent on reading a thick, leather-bound book and took no notice of her. The smell from the kitchen was heavenly, a mix of baking bread and roasting meat. Myranda pulled back her worn hood and took in the tantalizing aroma. The waitress interrupted her quiet appreciation with the simple phrase.

"Miss?" she said.

Myranda shifted her gaze to the young lady.

"What would you like to start with?" the eager server asked.

Myranda's stomach rumbled a plea for haste.

"What do you have that is fast?" she asked.

"Well, the roast beef has just finished, and we have some biscuits still from breakfast," she recalled.

"Gravy?" Myranda asked hopefully.

"What sort of a place would we be if we served biscuits without gravy?" the waitress said with a smile.

"Biscuits and gravy, then. And a glass of something besides wine," she said, remembering the throbbing head after her last indulgence.

"Cider?" the waitress asked.

"Perfect," Myranda said.

"Won't be a minute," came her cheerful reply.

The waitress scurried off with the order. Myranda leaned her aching back against the seat. She noticed movement to her left and saw the young man gathering up his things. He hoisted what looked to be a very heavy pack to his shoulders effortlessly in a well-practiced motion. When he had collected all of his goods, he headed off toward the door--but rather than leaving, he dropped the packs on the floor beside Myranda and sat at the table adjacent to hers. He opened his book and took to reading again.

"It is very good here," he said without looking.

"What is?" she asked. Ordinarily she would be pleased to have company, but in light of recent events, the attention made her nervous.

"The gravy. I'm not one for sauces, but this place is an exception. I make sure to eat here each time I come through town just to get it," he said. "You just wait, you'll agree."

Myranda nodded. She looked at him. He was a shade taller than she, white hair out of place, framing a young face. His clothes were a refreshing--and practically unique--departure from the ubiquitous gray cloak. It was a lighter, almost white coat, with a bit of fur peeking out of the sleeve and attached hood. Had he been outside, it would have been simple to pick him out from a crowd. As she looked at him, she realized that he was likely the last person she would be able to talk to, possibly for the rest of her days, without pleading for her freedom or her life. It would be best to take advantage.

"What do you do?" she asked.

"This and that. Yourself?" he replied.

"I seem to be limited to 'that,'" she said.

"It's just as well. 'This' can get boring after a while," he said.

The stranger turned a page.

"What is your name?" she asked.

"Desmeres Lumineblade," he said.

"That is a unique name," she said.

"Not particularly. My grandfather had it, as did his. My guess is that they liked the name Desmeres and hated the name junior," he said.

A moment passed.

"Don't you want to know my name?" she asked.

"No need. There is only the two of us here. After lunch we go our separate ways, probably never to meet again. Until then, you talk to me, I talk to you. No cause for confusion, no need for names. That's why people always do introductions when they meet up with a third person," he said.

"Well, it is Myranda," she said. "Just in case we meet a third person."

"Myranda. Lyrical," he said, his eyes still trained on the book.

The food was set before Myranda and she eagerly partook. He was right, it was delicious. When the edge had been taken from her hunger, she decided to give the thought swirling in her head a voice.

"What is that you've got there?" she asked, indicating the book.

"One of the unfortunate consequences of 'this.' Notes on dealers," he said.

"Dealers?" she inquired.

"Weapons dealers," he said.

Myranda frowned.

"You sell weapons," she said flatly.

Desmeres tipped his head and squinted an eye. "Not sell--design . . . and collect."

"Really?" she asked.

"I detest people who lie to strangers," he said.

"It was only a few days ago that I had even heard that such a thing as a weapon collector existed, and now I have met one," she explained.

"There happens to be another one just two doors over. Waste of time though. The only thing of note in this town is the gravy," he said.

"Why collect?" she asked.

"Why?" he repeated, closing his book. "Why not? A good weapon is a tool. A great one is a masterpiece. Art, plain and simple. Crafted with care, every detail lovingly shaped, balanced, polished. If sculptures were crafted with such care, the sculpture and the model who posed would be indistinguishable. Have you got a knife?"

"No . . . well, yes, right here," she said, remembering the stiletto that had been returned to her.

"There, you see. Straight, sturdy, sharp. A tool. Here, have a look at this one," he said.

Desmeres pulled a sleek, curving blade from his belt.

"Now, this? This is a blade! Look at the curve. Look at the edge. Simple. Elegant. Organic. This could have come from an animal. Based on the shape of a dragon's claw. And watch this," he said.

He closed his fingers around the handle, then opened all but the index finger. The weapon balanced on one finger.

"The creator worked for months on this. It would be at home in a gallery or in a foe's back. I challenge you to find another work of art with that flexibility. Of course, this particular blade has more than good breeding--it has a history," he said. "They say it was used by none other than the Red Shadow."

Myranda respected his passion for the subject, even though she didn't share it. It was rare to see such interest in anything, save the news of the most recent battle. The weapons he collected were the heart of the war, and so she despised them, but here was a man who admired the form above the purpose. It was a refreshing step aside from the prevailing obsession of her country folk. She could see his point, as well. What he held was truly a thing of beauty. As she looked at the piece, her thoughts turned to the sword. It was every bit as lovely as the dagger, and likely as well-crafted. She wondered how much this patron of the arts would have paid for such a piece.

His mention of the Red Shadow bothered her, though. Everyone had heard of the notorious killer, but Myranda had always tried to convince herself that the tales of his assassinations were fiction. The reality that the blade brought to the subject chilled her. Stories told of a man who killed a wolf with his bare hands and wore the bloodied skull as a helmet. Whenever a man of high breeding was found dead, rumors of the Red Shadow would flow anew. A tiny, nagging thought that there might be a connection to her own life was quickly silenced in the back of her mind. That thought was too much for her to consider right now.

"A realization dawns. You know what brought me here. I am now at a disadvantage," he said, interrupting her thoughts.

"Pardon?" Myranda said, confused by the odd phrasing.

"What are you up to on this fine day?" he asked.

"Trying to decide what is next," she said.

"Fair enough. Try not to strain yourself, though. It will happen just the same," he said, putting his book away and gathering his various bags together. "I've got to get to Fort Wick by sundown."

"I've . . . never mind," she said, choosing against mentioning her meeting with the old man who may or may not have sent the soldiers her way.

"Right . . . well, until next time," he said.

The young man pulled his shallow hood up and stepped out the door. His form through the window in the unique garb was comically different from the otherwise uniform clothing of the others. A wave of sadness swept over her at the sight of a dozen or so people outside in the ever-present gray cloaks. She had always felt bothered by the fact that she could travel for days, see a hundred or more people, and not be able to tell one from the other. She suddenly felt pride in the tattered, bloodstained cloak she wore. It may not be glamorous, but it was different. She, at least, would be remembered for more than a moment.

The sadness turned to fear, though, at a single thought. The murderer wore the very same cloak as everyone else. Any one of the people on the street could be the man who had captured her. She turned from the window. Worse! She was a fugitive. The unique cloak she had prided herself on would be more than enough of a description to seal her fate and assure her capture. Best not to think about it. She would buy a new cloak, but there was very little she could do. If the Alliance Army wanted her, she would be found.

With great effort, she finished her meal without succumbing to the anxiety eating at her mind. No sooner had the last crumb been finished than the waitress reappeared, eager to sell more.

"Anything else for you today?" she asked.

"No, thank you very much," Myranda said.

"Five coppers," she said.

Myranda dug into the satchel she had found on the horse's reins and gave the waitress five of the coins. The waitress lingered, jingling the coins in her apron. Myranda took the less than subtle hint and fished out two more coppers and dropped them on the table. The waitress widened her smile.

"Thank you, miss, and you have a perfectly lovely day," she said.

"And to you," Myranda said.

Myranda remained in her seat for a time. What was next? She was unsure who knew who she was, or what they thought she did. Did they still think that she had the sword? If it had belonged to a high-ranking military official, the penalty for its theft would be equal to that of treason. The sentence was worse than simple execution. An example would be made of her. Torture, humiliation, and shame would fill her days until she was finally put to death in as gruesome and public a manner as could be managed.

She swallowed hard and looked to the darkening scar on her left palm. That blasted sword had marked her in more ways than one. Her life had been far from pleasant, but it had gotten worse with each passing moment since the instant she had touched the cursed blade. Perhaps the spell that had branded her hand carried with it a hex that would plague her with such misfortune for the rest of her days. Her heart sunk further. Magic had always intrigued her, but she'd seen it at work only a handful of times. Now it seemed that magic was at work, making her wretched life into a positively abysmal one. She closed her hand.

"Pardon me?" she asked the waitress.

"Yes?" came her chipper reply.

"Do you have rooms to rent?" she asked.

"Not here. Look for Milin's Inn. Right across the way." She pointed.

"Thank you," Myranda said.

She left the restaurant in search of a better place to wash up and keep her horse until she had bought the supplies she would need. She found the inn quite easily, and found facilities for the horse alongside of it. She gave a few coppers to the stable hand and directed him to see to it the horse was taken care of. Inside the building, she found a well-lit, tidy lobby. A man with an eye patch stood behind the counter, with a young boy slouching in front of the door. Her entry provided the same degree of excitement that it had in the restaurant earlier.

"Welcome to Milin's Inn. What can I do for you today?" the owner asked.

"I need a room for the next few hours," she said.

"I am very sorry, but we require that our customers pay for at least one night. I assure you that once you've seen our room, you will not want to leave," he said.

"That will be fine. Any room. Cheap, if possible," she said.

"Our rooms start at twenty coppers a night," he said.

"That is a bit steep," she said.

"The best price in town for the best rooms in town. You pay for quality," he said, in a well-rehearsed manner.

Myranda reluctantly parted with one of the silvers. The keeper gave her back a half silver and five coppers. Two of the coppers found their way into the boy's pocket for showing her to the room and giving her the key. The room was cozy and clean, far more so than the one at the Lizard's Goblet.

Myranda locked the door behind her. As the day had progressed, the afflicted shoulder had begun to throb and stiffen.

She threw the stained cloak on the bed. Rolling back her sleeve, which proved to be a particularly painful experience, she found the bandage utterly saturated with blood. Myranda clenched her teeth and winced in pain as she pulled it away. The simple gash was swollen and red, crusted with the crimson remains of the blood. It was not improving. She knew from experience that wounds that took on this appearance seldom healed on their own and never healed completely.

A testament to the quality of the inn, there was a pitcher of clean water provided for her, along with a basin and a stack of clean towels. She filled the basin and cleansed the wound. Each time she wrung out the cloth the red tint of the water deepened. When she was through, the water in the bowl had the look of some terrible wine. The cloth was pink, stained for good. Since she knew that the cloth would never come clean, she used it to replace the bandage. The cool, moist cloth soothed the pain slightly, but if she ever wanted full use of her right arm again, she would need a healer.

After doing her best to clean the bloody stain from the cloak, she left the room, locking the door behind her.

The innkeeper gave her a smile, as did the porter, as she left the inn. It was refreshing to be looked upon so graciously, though she knew that the silver in her pocket was the only thing that had earned her such treatment.

In a way, she preferred the disdainful stares she received when people found she was a sympathizer. Those reactions, even though they were rooted in ignorance, were at least rooted in honesty. These people would treat her like a queen so long as she could pay her bill.

The cold air hit the moistened shoulder and stung, stirring her to get through her errands quickly. She moved from business to business, being served by elderly men and women, children, the disabled, and anyone else unfit for the role of soldier. These were the people who had populated the towns for as long as she could remember. It wasn't long after childhood that she herself had begun to feel the questioning stares of the townsfolk, wondering why this healthy young lady was not on the front, putting her life on the line for the war effort.

She had heard that women had not always been obliged to go to war. They were to stay behind and tend to the affairs of the home. Those years were long gone. Now the towns were growing more and more sparsely populated as the generations of people were being killed in battle before they could even spawn the next crop of warriors. The faded bloodstain on her cloak was likely the only thing keeping the people from questioning her presence in this town, earning her the assumed status of injured soldier on leave. Such were not uncommon in the larger towns until a few months ago, when they stopped showing up.

\#

After a day of spending, Myranda headed back to the inn with a handful of essential items for the days to come. A small, one-person tent was tucked under her one good arm, and a sturdy new pack filled with provisions was slung onto her back. Only a few pieces of copper remained in her pocket, but she had all she needed. Her last errand was to seek someone to give attention to the afflicted shoulder.

Healers had been a scarcity ever since enemy pressure required all available clerics to report to duty immediately. That was several years ago. Still, until recently here and there one could find an apprentice cleric or an alchemist deemed unfit for duty. Now even *that* was becoming rarer, as each year more laws were passed to prevent medical practitioners from treating anyone who had not served in the Alliance Army. It was just another way to prevent the people from avoiding service.

Myranda had just given up looking for one when she noticed a very urgent message arriving. A horse was galloping as quickly as its legs would carry it through the half-cleared street. When it reached the center of town, the rider jumped off. He seemed to be as winded as the horse, and drew an eager crowd around him.

"The old church is on fire!" he exclaimed.

The eyes of the crowd turned to the north horizon. A wisp of black smoke in the distance confirmed his story. Myranda felt a pang of fear burn in the back of her mind.

"That old place was bound to come down one of these days. It had been rundown for years," a grizzled old man said.

"That isn't all. There were men, some of ours, dead. I went to see the fire, I saw them on the ground, four of them. It wasn't anything normal that took these men, though. There was nothing left but dust, like some black magic struck them down or something. No sign of the culprit. I've just come from Fort Wick. No one had been in or out since yesterday, except one girl. She must have done this, and she came this way!" cried out the winded man.

Myranda walked as calmly as she could back to the inn as people flooded out of every door to hear the new tale. It would not be long before one of them put the pieces together and came after her. She dropped off the key to her room with the stable attendant and loaded her things onto the horse. She then led it slowly and calmly into the narrow backstreet behind the stable. When she was sure that she would be unseen, she climbed to the horse's back and rode out of town.

"Please," she whispered, "just let me escape notice for a minute more. If I can make it over the hill without any eyes falling upon me, I have a chance."

The horse stepped briskly though the knee-deep snow of the uncleared road out of town. Several nervous glances over her shoulder assured her that the chaos brought by the news had yet to subside enough to organize a search for her, but it was only a matter of time. When she had reached the foot of the hill, she knew that she was out of sight of the townsfolk. Only one idea came to mind. She pulled her things from the horse's back. Stuffing anything she didn't need into the new cloak she had just bought, she strapped it to the horse's back.

"Well, it was nice having you around while it lasted. I hope things turn out better for you than they did for me," she said to the horse.

With that she gave it a slap that sent the animal galloping down the road. Already she could hear the angry cries of a posse leaving the town. Myranda scraped at the heavy mound of ice and snow left by the side of the road by the blizzard. The dense drift was well-packed enough to allow a hollow to be dug. A few moments of frantic digging produced an alcove in the snow drift facing the field. She threw her pack into the hollow and followed it. The first lynch mob had just reached the top of the hill when she covered herself over as best she could. The horse, running wildly, was too far away from the mob to be clearly seen. The angry people of the town followed it as though she was still on its back. The sound of their furious voices would surely keep it running, and the lack of a rider would keep it well ahead. With any luck, her decoy would keep the mob on the move for the better part of the day.

Myranda held her breath as half of the town poured out onto the snowy road on every available horse. It was not until the thunder of hoofbeats had receded into the distance entirely that she pulled herself from her frigid hiding place. Ice clung to her cloak and chilled her to the bone, but at least the terrible throbbing in her shoulder had numbed.

Shivering, she reached into the snowy alcove and pulled out her things. All that was left was the sturdy pack, loaded with some food and water, and the travel tent. She set her body to the daunting task of hoisting the essential apparatus to her back and her mind to the still more taxing task of escaping the area, as well as the near impossible task of clearing her name.

In a perfect world, she would merely have to explain the truth to be freed of blame. In the here and now, though, she was a stranger and the victims were the beloved soldiers. She was as good as dead. There was a task at hand, though, so the task at mind could wait. The pack was across her back, the tent tied to the top. She was anything but a small target and could barely walk under the weight of her things. If she was to escape this place with her freedom, it would be through nothing short of a miracle.

Myranda scanned the horizon. Rolling white fields turned quickly to rocky, impassible mountains in the east, the Rachis Mountains. Crossing them would be difficult. They formed a chain that traced a crooked line across the Northern Alliance, beginning at the hilly plains just beyond the capital in the far north, and running nearly to the Tresson border. Crossings were scattered and tended to be well regulated. Best to avoid them.

South was where her pursuers had been led and north was the way she'd come. Neither was a viable route of escape. Westward was a snowy field that sloped smoothly downward, likely ending in a stream or river. Streams meant bridges--which, in turn, meant roads. There would be plenty of fresh water and means to find a road when the time came. Her pack had food enough for a few days, and by that time, there was hope that the tale would have been twisted enough as it was passed from ear to ear that she could escape immediate suspicion.

At the very least, the time would dull their memory enough to offer a chance of escaping recognition.

It was as good an idea as any. At least it meant walking downhill. She set off to the west as the cloud-shrouded sky reddened with the coming evening. To say her progress was slow would be a monumental understatement. By the time the last few rays of sun were fading, the light they cast was enough to reveal angry villagers streaming back to the town.

Myranda was still near enough to see them, which meant that they were near enough to see her.

She kept low, confident that she would not be spotted, though fearful that her trail might. That would continue to be a concern for her until a fresh snow had wiped away the footprints. Fortunately, in the north, a snow storm was seldom far away.

After nearly an hour of patient watching, the last of the lynch mob that had ridden off in search of her finally returned to the town and dusk had turned to a typical moonless night that made only their torches visible. Perhaps a few more steps south would serve as a fair campsite, provided she could wake early enough to take down her tent and move on before the road got busy. Myranda turned her back to the town, now completely shrouded in the blackness of night. It was this darkness she'd been waiting for. No one would see her now. All she had to do now was erect the tent against the biting cold of the northern night, and she would be safe until morning.

Unfortunately, the very night she had awaited for safety had been awaited by others--others who wished their activities to go unseen as well. They'd seen her leave. They'd followed her. Now she was far enough from prying eyes to allow action to be taken.

Myranda had just finished wrestling the thick canvas of the tent into place. It was with no small amount of difficulty, as the cold had taken most of the feeling from her hands. She forced the last wooden stake into place and attempted to massage some feeling into her icy fingers. Blowing into them and rubbing them vigorously had managed to restore some tingling when she heard a peculiar rustling. Her first thought was that a rabbit had found its way into the mass of fabric of the tent and was trying to free itself. She turned to the tent only to hear the sound again, from behind her. Myranda turned quickly, her heart nearly skipping a beat.

Five figures stood before her. They wore cloaks, just as everyone else did, but these were different. They were nearly black, as opposed to the lighter gray of the others. They stood, silent and moved only by the breeze, staring at Myranda with unseen eyes from within cavernous hoods.

"Who are you?" she stammered.

The figures remained silent. Myranda backed toward the pack she'd left just inside the tent.

"What do you want?" she asked, fear mounting.

Slowly, and with an eerie smoothness, the figures began to approach her. Myranda fell to the ground and reached into the tent. Keeping her eyes on the silent ones, she fumbled with her good arm inside the pack. Inside she found the handle of the stiletto protruding from the coin bag. She pulled it free.

"Stay back! I did nothing wrong! I do not want to hurt anyone! Just leave me alone! Please!" she warned, praying that they would listen.

Still they advanced. She brandished the knife as her uncle had taught her. As a member of one of the more successful military families, she was no stranger to the use of a knife, but she loathed to do so.

She struggled to her feet, thoughts swirling in her head. Where did they come from? How had they come upon her unseen and unheard? She tried to keep her distance, but the snow gripped her feet while her pursuers seemed unaffected. One of them circled in behind her. She reeled around and caught it with the tip of the blade.

The razor-sharp knife sliced easily though the fabric. Though she could not feel the blade meet flesh, her attack prompted a shrill and ear-piercing shriek that was far too spine-tingling to have been made by a creature of nature. Startled by the horrid cry, she released the knife. It disappeared through the slice and fell to the ground. The wounded attacker pulled away violently, briefly allowing the cloak to open. The few rays of cloud weakened moonlight must have been playing tricks, for what they illuminated could not be. Nothing. The cloak was empty.

Myranda froze as she tried to comprehend what her eyes were telling her. Inside of the garment was nothing more than air, yet it swept about as though it were worn by someone agonized by the attack. Her distraction was long enough to allow the creature behind her to act. Her hood was pulled back, and something clutched her head. Instantly her mind became clouded. She could not hold onto a single thought as the world seemed to spin around her. Myranda tried to fight it, but against her will she slipped into unconsciousness.

#

Far to the north, in a dimly-lit room, a pair of individuals waited. The first, a tall, graceful elf woman in ornate armor, stood facing a wall of maps. Beneath her arm was her helmet, and on her face was a look of concern, impatience--and, most of all, anger. Seated at a large desk behind her was a nobleman. His face was a mask of deliberate composure, and his clothing was of the finest variety. In appearance and demeanor, he seemed as though he should be sitting in a royal court at the right hand of the king. In front of him were scattered countless sealed documents, military dispatches, coded messages, and royal declarations. His fingers were steepled in front of his face, and his eyes were locked on the door.

"Does he normally take this long?" the woman asked petulantly.

"Patience, General Teloran," replied the man.

The elf sighed and turned back to the map. It showed the whole of the continent, though there was no reason. The top third of the map, representing the Northern Alliance, was cluttered with figures and military patterns representing every aspect of the year's battles. Below that, a thin line representing the front was obscured almost completely by carefully recorded combat figures. The rest of the map, showing the enormous kingdom of Tressor, was virtually untouched. General Trigorah Teloran, formerly a key field commander, ran a finger over the map, tracing a faint line near the front. It had been ages since she'd seen the enemy, since she'd seen real combat.

"Have you retaken Orin Ridge?" she asked.

"That is not the matter at hand," the man wearily commented.

"With all due respect, sir, until it is won, the war is always the matter at hand," Trigorah replied. "We are too far from the front here. Even with Demont's methods, the information is cold when it reaches us. We never should have left Terital, General Bagu. We need--"

She was interrupted as the door flew open. Through it marched a rather slight man. He was dressed similarly to Bagu, through the exquisite garments seemed out of place on him. His were not the features of a nobleman. In place of implacable composure was a look of sharp determination, tempered with annoyance, as though he was perpetually being kept from far more fruitful endeavors. A gem-tipped staff of some kind was strapped to his back. The harness that held it was coarse, and clearly worn in complete dismissal of the regal bearing the vestments had been intended to represent. As for the staff, it had silvery metallic sheen to it, and the jewels of the tip gave any who observed them the nagging feeling of being watched. In his hands were a stack of papers.

"General Bagu . . ." he began, turning slowly to acknowledge the elf. "Teloran . . ."

There was no attempt to disguise the distaste with which he spoke the latter name.

"General Demont," she acknowledged.

"What have you to report, General?" Bagu asked levelly.

"There are some things which may be stated with certainty. The sword had been found, and it has been handled. The girl who found it has been apprehended, and is even now in route to General Epidime's . . . facility," Demont explained.

"And the sword? Is it in hand?" asked Bagu.

"It . . . is not. We've reason to believe that it is still in the hands of the assassin. The girl was not delivered by him either. She had to be gathered," Demont responded.

"It was to be expected. Assassins are not to be trusted," Trigorah stated, fury smoldering under her voice.

"Well then. General Teloran, gather half of your Elites. Your assignment is to find precisely where the sword was found and trace its path and that of the girl. Locate and identify *any* who might have come into contact with it. When you are certain that this task has been thoroughly and completely performed, find your way to the sword and bring it to Northern Capital," Bagu ordered.

"As you wish, sir," General Teloran replied.

"Then go. Demont, remain here," he said.

After collecting the pages containing the details of Demont's findings, Trigorah set off, purpose in her stride. She stepped through the door and into the massive entry hall of this, Verril Castle. At one end of the long, vaulted room was the throne, currently vacant as the King attended to the affairs of state. Opposite it were the massive doors that lead to the castle courtyard.

The General donned her helmet and marched toward them, drawing the images on Bagu's map to her mind. Slowly, meticulously, she envisioned what moves should be made. Foot soldiers here. Cavalry there. Siege weapons at the ready here and here. Yes. When these distractions were dealt with, when the Alliance proper was cleansed, then she would be at the front once more. And she would be ready.

#

Consciousness slowly returned to Myranda. All around her was darkness. She was unsure if she had even awoken. The ground heaved with sudden, regular jolts. The air was heavy with an oppressive heat and an indescribably horrid smell. It was a gruesome combination of stale blood, perspiration, and half a dozen other odors that she'd never known before and hoped never to know again. She tried to feel along the floor, but a jingle followed by a resistance revealed that she was shackled to the floor.

Her sleep-addled mind turned over the possibilities. The answer was not a pleasant one. She remembered seeing them here and there all of her life. The black carriages. Where one could be found, something terrible had always happened. And now she was inside. Caught. Condemned.

She struggled against the chains periodically for hours. It was useless, but anything was better than allowing her mind to dwell on the situation. No one who had been thrown into one of these carriages had ever been seen again. The crack beneath the doors let in little air and no light. The lack of air made it difficult to stay awake, but the dark was a blessing. It spared her what was sure to be a horrific sight left by the last unfortunate soul to occupy this place. Tears welled in her eyes as she began to realize that this is how it would end for her.

Sleep had come and gone a dozen times or more since she had first awoken. There was no telling how long it had been. The only thing she could be sure of was that her captors were moving recklessly fast, stopping only occasionally, seemingly to change horses from the sound of it. She was jarred awake when the lurching of the carriage came to an abrupt end as it had with each such stop, but it was different this time. Outside, muffled by the thick carriage walls, a struggle could be heard. Myranda cringed at the screech of steel against steel and the terrified cry of horses.

All at once, the tumult became silent once more. She could hear the latch that held the heavy wooden doors shut being worked. The door dropped open with a thunderous crash. Outside it was night still--or, more likely, again. The crimson light of a torch illuminated the interior of the prison carriage, revealing Myranda's chained form, along with walls scarred by the frantic clawing of untold hundreds of tortured souls over the years. A blast of chill from the air shook Myranda's perspiration-soaked body.

The man who held the torch was enormous. More than a head taller than Myranda and easily three times her weight, he had a build that betrayed a mass of muscle beneath a layer of bulk. The light of the torch fell upon half of his face. Scars old and new told the tales of battles gone badly. He wore no cloak. In its place was an overused suit of leather armor and a crude iron helmet.

"We will free you," spoke the man in a voice to match his features.

He was joined by a second figure. This time a woman. She was about Myranda's height, and perhaps a few years older. One look at her face, though, showed a pair of eyes with the fierceness and resolve of a person twice her age. She wore similarly decrepit armor, as well as a sword at her side dripping with the evidence of its most recent use. The woman held her torch high and smiled as its light fell upon Myranda's bloodstained shoulder.

"It is she," she said, relief and accomplishment in her voice.

The pair of rescuers climbed inside. The woman investigated the grim reminders of past passengers by torchlight. She shook her head in anger and pity. The man revealed a pry bar, with which he made short work of the chains. When Myranda was free, he helped her to her feet, but the untold time she'd spent immobile had robbed her of the strength to walk. He carried her outside and onto one of two horses that were waiting at the ready.

The bracing cold chilled her to the bone almost immediately. She watched through heavy eyes as the rescuers stripped the fallen soldiers of their weapons and armor with ruthless efficiency. When all that could be claimed from the carriage had been similarly pillaged, the woman threw the torch inside. The black carriage took quickly to flame and the three watched with satisfaction. The woman soon put her feelings to words.

"You'll have no more of our lives, you wretched devil," the mysterious woman whispered.

The trio rode swiftly through the night, Myranda riding behind the woman who had rescued her. They had taken the four horses from the carriage, but the time inside had taken far too heavy a toll for Myranda to ride for herself. Aside from the obvious draw on her body, she began to feel that her mind was failing her as well, as the countryside whisking by her was unfamiliar. They were headed though a sparsely-treed field toward a dense forest that seemed to go as far as the eye could see. Behind them, far in the distance, a mountain range rose up from the horizon, a mottled green stripe at its base.

"Where are we?" she called out over the pounding of the hooves.

"The Low Lands," the woman answered.

The Low Lands! If her memory served her correctly, that meant that in her time in chains she had been taken to the other side of the mountains she'd decided not to attempt just before she was caught. She must have been asleep for some time. As tales of the Low Lands slowly came to her mind, she began to wonder if she was any better off now than she had been in the carriage. All through her life, if a tale of murder, crime, or disappearance met her ears, the setting was the Low Lands.

Judging by the size of it, the forest they were heading into was Ravenwood. It was a place that had come to be called the Endless Forest. Now at the fringe of the awe-inspiring sight, Myranda could not think of a more appropriate name.

There was a small break in the clouds, but the light was short-lived. The near-full moon overhead was soon filtered through the increasingly thick foliage of the forest once said to have consumed half of a division of Northern soldiers who had entered, but never left. She swallowed hard and hoped that she would not share their fate. Her fingers were completely numb, and her shoulder had worsened to the point that she could scarcely move the whole of her right arm.

#

After hours of riding at as great a speed as they could manage, the trio was still within the forest, and had not used a single road. They finally came upon a large log hut. When they reached it, the others helped her from the horse and inside. A fire that had been left unattended for some time barely smoldered in the hearth. Myranda was led to a crude wooden chair, a blanket thrown about her shoulders. The large man left to tend to the horses, while the woman took a seat in another chair, a restrained look of satisfaction showing on her face.

"I am Caya," she said, extending her hand.

Myranda extended her right hand painfully in an attempt the return the gesture. She managed to weakly touch the fingers of her rescuer before she couldn't stand the pain anymore.

"Myranda," she said.

"We all heard what you did. Inspiring," Caya said.

"What are you talking about?" Myranda asked. "Who are you? Where am I?"

"You are at the headquarters of the Undermine. I am the regional commander. You've done more for our cause in just a few days than years of subtle operations," she explained.

"What have I done?" Myranda asked, her mind still too clouded to put the pieces together.

She knew of the Undermine well. Most people blindly supported the war. Some people, like herself, quietly loathed it. The Undermine was a group so steadfast against the continued conflict that they had come to actively oppose it. There were supposedly pockets of the Undermine in every major town. It was said that they commonly would carry out strikes on military targets with the intent of forcing a withdrawal from active combat. When the military or government spoke of them, the messages tended to be equal parts denial and propaganda against.

"No need for modesty. Everyone knows. You stole an item prized by the scoundrels in the military and slew four soldiers sent to reclaim it," She said.

"You know about it? Here! Already?" Myranda said in disbelief.

"Please. Nothing travels faster than bad news or a good rumor. This was both," Caya said. "We've been looking for something that could shake up the men in charge this much for years. Word has it that they got you, but not that which you stole. Is this so?"

"Well, I suppose, but you don't understand," Myranda tried to explain.

The large man entered. Caya turned excitedly to him.

"Tus! They still haven't found it!" Caya shouted.

The stalwart fellow nodded. She would soon learn that, from him, this was the height of emotion.

"What is it you have taken? Where did you find it? How did you hide it? I must know!" she urged.

"What weapon did you use to kill the men?" Tus added.

"I will tell you all that I know and all that I have done, but when I am through, I fear you will not think so highly of me," Myranda said.

And so she told the tale of the last few days. She spoke of the frozen body, the sword, and the merchant. She told of her imprisonment and release from the church. As she spoke, the faces of her rescuers shifted from joy to disillusionment. In the space of a few minutes, she shattered the image that the tales of a dozen gossips had painted of her.

"Well, Myranda. I am truly sorry to hear the truth. I had hoped to find a powerful ally in you. Instead I find an unfortunate victim of circumstance," Caya said.

"I, too, am sorry. I hate this war with all of my heart. If I could help you, I would," Myranda said.

"I doubt anything you could do now could match that which you have done by accident. You see, our operatives have reported motion at the very highest levels due to your actions. Whatever that sword is, it means an awful lot to some very important people. You are a marked woman. The minds that twist and shape the entire kingdom are turned to you and what you've done. The ripples are still spreading throughout the ranks," Caya explained.

"All of my men tell your story. They would beat the door down to meet you," Tus said. "Their spirits are strong now. The men are ready to fight."

Caya's look had slowly changed from one of sorrow to one of thought.

"All may not be lost. Myranda, are you willing to join our cause?" she asked.

"Of course," she said, "though I cannot imagine what help I could give you."

"You've done enough already. More importantly, my people believe you have done much more. What they think of you is all that matters. You may not be able to fight beside them, as I'd hoped, but tales of your deeds will stir them to greatness nonetheless. So long as they do not learn the truth, merely having you in our ranks will give them the heart to fight double. In return for your membership, we will keep you safe from the clutches of the army.

"If what you say is true, only one man aside from Tus and myself still lives with the knowledge of precisely what has transpired, and he is a murderer. It is unlikely that such a man will turn to the people he has been killing to offer a description. Yes, yes. You must be kept from the light of day for a while. Perhaps a few months. The descriptions that the soldiers are passing around will fade from memory. Before long, so long as you offer a bit of disguise, you'll be able to walk the streets without prompting a second glance," Caya said.

"You will be trained. Another hand on another hilt," Tus added.

"Yes, good thinking, Tus. In time, you will become what the men believe you to be. This may yet be a great day for our cause," Caya agreed.

Tus remained stern as ever, but Caya showed enough joy for the two of them. Myranda mustered a smile for their sake. Things were spinning out of control. Days ago, she lived a simple life, albeit a restless one. Then she seemed to be at the center of something she knew nothing about, but was apparently of monumental importance. Now she would be the figurehead of a group of renegades who were working toward an end to the war, but through a means that was nearly a match for the atrocity of the battlefield. Her simple life had been tied in knots.

"Enough. There are plans to be made. Our man in the field said that the description the soldiers have been given lists you as a young girl of average height, average build, and an injured right shoulder. Not terribly specific, but we should still try to change as much of it as possible," Caya said.

"Of all of the things on list, might I request we begin with the shoulder?" Myranda said.

"One would assume that time would solve that problem for us," Caya said.

"I am not sure that such will be the case," Myranda said.

She pulled aside her sweat and filth-soaked cloak. The sleeve of her tunic was stained again, and when it was pulled back, the two warriors nodded knowingly.

"You did this two days ago?" Tus asked.

"Yes," Myranda said. "Plus whatever time I spent in that carriage."

"Mmm. Only a few days and the arm is ruined. Nasty. It heals badly. You will lose the arm," Tus said.

The wound *had* worsened. The whole shoulder was swollen, and red streaks of blighted tissue ran outward from the gash.

"But it was only a piece of wood," she said.

"Worse than a blade. Dirty. Causes . . . well . . . things like this. Not often, but sometimes. Not the lucky sort, are you?" Caya said.

"I've led a less than blessed life," she said with a feeble grin.

"Well, Tus . . . we'll get some food in her and set her up in one of the cots. At sun up we'll send her down to Zeb. We can't have our new mascot crippled," Caya decreed. "I'll draw up the writ and stow the new weapons and armor."

"No," Tus said, not as a refusal, but as a statement.

"What now? No food, no cot?" she asked.

"No Zeb. I put a knife in him," Tus said.

"Not another one, Tus," Caya said with frustration.

"He was speaking to the Blues," Tus said, referring to the Alliance Army.

The blue-tinted armor had been around since the beginning of the war, more than a century ago. Each of the three Northern Kingdoms used a different shade, but all were blue. Before the Kingdoms merged, the only thing that all three forces had in common was the color. Hence the name.

"I had a feeling. Six months of training . . . wasted on a traitor. People join us as spies to try to get themselves some favor with the officers in the army. Death is too good for them. With Zeb down and Rankin a runner, we've got no field healers," Caya lamented.

"Rankin went runner? Scum," Tus declared.

"Runner?" Myranda questioned.

"We pay a local white wizard a hefty price to train healers for us. Every so often one of the apprentices is given the money to pay him and never shows. Runs off with the silver. I tell you, I am beginning to wonder if there are any decent people left in this world. Send out the word. We need a new healer. I doubt we'll get any volunteers. The men and women who join us all want to be the one to draw the blade across the throat of the next general. There is no glory in healing," Caya explained.

"Wait!" Myranda said.

There was the solution, right in front of her. It would keep her off of the battlefield, provide her with a hiding place, and even give her six months of hot meals and soft beds.

"I'll be the new healer! Send me to the wizard!" she eagerly offered.

"You? I . . . I think that just might work," Caya considered. "Right, Tus, food and bed for her. I'll give her the letter of intention to give to Wolloff in the morning. Myranda, you had best get your rest. You have a long walk ahead of you."

"Wonderful! I . . . a long walk?" Myranda asked. "What about the four new horses?"

"Horses are for those who require speed. A sore shoulder can wait, but targets of opportunity open and close like the blink of an eye. Two steps too late and a chance is gone forever. Wolloff's tower is just on the north side of Ravenwood. On this terrain, on foot, I cannot imagine it taking you more than five days. So, eat, rest, and leave. We've much to do," Caya stated.

In a few moments, a clay bowl filled with perhaps the worst porridge Myranda had ever eaten was set before her. When she'd managed to swallow the horrid stuff, a cot and blanket were placed mercifully near to the rekindled fire. She settled stiffly onto the bed, such as it was, and basked in the warmth of the fire. Her body had dealt with such extremes of heat and cold, it was fairly screaming. Cramps twisted her muscles through the whole night. She closed her eyes and an instant later she was awakened by a rough prodding from Tus. The sun had yet to peek over the mountains.

"Food. Eat it slow. It will last," Tus said, tossing her a pack.

She managed to catch it, much to the detriment of the injured shoulder.

"Flint," he said, holding up a second pack. "And tinder. One night, one fire. It will last. Walk close to the mountains. Too close to the roads, the patrols will kill you. Too close to the mountains, other things will kill you."

With that ominous warning, she was sent on her way.

#

The cottage was not even out of sight when she began to regret not asking for a new cloak. Fortunately, though, it was not nearly so difficult to walk in the forest as it had been in the field. The dense needles of the evergreens held much of the snow, keeping the ground at a manageable depth. Closer to the mountain, the trees were a bit thinner, but a strong and constant wind kept the ground still more manageable. The iciness of the breeze tore at her, but the greater ease of movement made it worth the discomfort. She had been in danger of freezing to death often enough in the past to know that she was in no such danger now--at least, not if she kept moving.

As she walked, she marveled at how much more alive the woods were than the field. The whistling of the wind carried with it the calls of a dozen different animals. She recognized the call of an eagle overhead and the distant howl of a wolf. Tracks speckled the ground here and there. Some were from moose, others from elk. A long line of impressions in the snow gave her the feel of tracks, but were far too large. More likely they were the places where great lumps of wind-blown snow had fallen from the trees.

When the sun was beginning to slip from the sky, she collected some of the fallen tree boughs and moved to the far side of a stand of stout old pines. Carefully she lit the fire where it would not cause the tree-borne snow to melt and rain down over her. She pulled open the pack of food, relieved to find salted meat rather than the coarse and heavy biscuit that, when soaked for a great deal of time in warm water, became the hideous porridge she had choked down the night before. After eating what she judged to be the day's ration, she marveled at the fact that a bedroll had been included with the other things in the pack. The attitude of those that had sent her off gave her the feeling she would be expected to do without.

The night was actually a bit more pleasant than the previous one. The bedroll was a bit softer than the cot and the fire kept her reasonably warm, at least on the side facing it. Wind whipped down off of the mountain constantly, but the trees served as a decent wind break. The morning found her better rested, and she moved even more quickly than the previous day. By sundown of that rather uneventful day, she'd covered easily twice the ground. Night was spent in a similar manner, and just as she drifted off to sleep, she wondered if, perhaps, her luck was changing.

The very instant her eyes opened the following morning, she regretted her thought. The sky was wrong, too dark. Worse yet, the air had the unmistakable feel of coming snow. Her bedroll and tree system would do no good against a blizzard. Myranda thought hard. If she recalled correctly, telltale hollows were scattered along the mountainside. They could only be the mouths of caves. That meant shelter. She quickened her pace and trained her eyes on the mountain. Whole sections of the slope had been swept clean by the wind, and in one such section there was a large, hollow opening. It extended far enough back that its end was shrouded in darkness.

Ice crystals were beginning to sting her face when she reached the mouth of the cave. To escape the powerful wind, she had to make her way much deeper than she had expected. The darkness was complete, save for the bit of light that found its way back from the mouth. She leaned her pack-covered back against the cave wall and slid to a seat. A bit winded from the rush to shelter, each breath burned her lungs with sheer cold. As she slowly recovered, she realized how much warmer the cave was than the outside. She brushed some of the more tenacious ice crystals from her cloak and took a deep breath through her nose. It was not the dank, moldy smell she expected, though there was a hint of it. Instead there was a rich, earthy smell, with a hint of smoke behind it.

"I suppose I am not the first person to shelter in this cave," she said aloud. Only her echoes came as a reply.

Perhaps the cave was so warm because someone had a fire going further inside. For a moment, she considered trying to find whosoever shared the cave, but she decided against it. Partially, she was afraid she might not be welcome, but mostly she was too tired to rouse herself. If the cave had a current resident, her call a moment earlier would summon it. When she heard the sounds movement echoing from beyond her sight, then silence, she decided she was welcome enough to wait out the storm.

She glanced at the mouth of the cave. The wind sounded fairly weak, and the snow had not even whited out the horizon. It wouldn't be long before she could safely continue on her way. Her eyes were just about to turn back to the darkness of the cave when she saw the area just outside the cave mouth darken. She squinted at the odd sight, confused. A strange sound accompanied it, something akin to the rustling of leather. As it grew louder, it was joined by a scratching and thumping noise from within the cave.

The noises were growing at both ends, so much so that she could feel the ground shake with each thump. Confusion turned to fear as the answer became painfully clear. This cave had a resident--but it was not a who, it was a what, and it had a visitor that concerned it more than a simple human. She rose to her feet and broke into a sprint for the mouth of the cave. The uneven floor of the cave slowed her, and before she had gotten halfway to freedom, the first of the beasts appeared.

It was the first she had ever seen of a dragon, and if she hadn't been so terrified, Myranda would have been fascinated. The creature was enormous--from tail to snout it was easily ten paces. At the end of a stout, curving neck was a reptilian head that could effortlessly consume Myranda in little more than a bite. It folded its wings neatly onto its back after touching down thunderously. Wide plates of amber scales armored the underside of the creature from the tip of its chin to the end of its serpentine tail. The rest of the beast was covered with red scales larger than her hands. It crouched on all fours to stalk inside. The forelegs, ending in claws that looked like a bestial mockery of human hands, flexed and moved effortlessly along the rocky floor. The powerful hind legs thrust the massive creature along with a terrible smoothness and grace that seemed out of place for something so large.

Myranda spun around to race back into the depths of the cave, perhaps to find an alcove to hide in. She was met with an equally spine-tingling sight. Emerging from the darkness was a second dragon. It was slightly smaller than the first, with sleeker, more delicate features that led her to believe that this was a female. It was also red with a yellow belly, and stalked fiercely at the intruder. A few steps more and they would clash.

Panicked and cornered, Myranda backed toward the wall, afraid to take her eyes off of the spectacle for even a moment. The hammering of massive footfalls rose to near deafening levels and even the breathing of the creatures added to the thundering din. Perhaps it was the shaking of the floor, its unevenness, or her fear, but somehow at the very moment that the dragons collided she lost her footing. A sharp pain in the back of her head dizzied her, and she fell to the ground. She managed to keep the awesome clash in her vision for the last few moments of consciousness.

#

Hours passed before her wits slowly returned to her. She became aware of a throbbing in her head and a heaviness on her chest. It must have been well into the afternoon, as the mouth of the cave was shrouded in shadow, leaving Myranda in near blackness. She tried to raise her left arm, but found it pinned down somehow. A brief attempt to use her right arm reminded her quite forcefully of its malady. She managed to wrestle her arm out from beneath whatever had held it down. Her first act was to feel the back of her throbbing head.

Satisfied when she felt no blood, only a nasty lump, she turned her one useful arm to the task of identifying the cause of the heaviness on her chest. Whatever it was, it was smooth and hard, like a stone or piece of wood. It was also large. As large as her thigh, and roughly the same shape.

Had a piece of the roof fallen? No, it was not as heavy as a like-sized piece of stone. The surface of the object was covered with small, overlapping areas. As she ran her fingers over it, giving special attention to a raised, rougher area, she felt the entire object shift. It pressed toward her fingers, then dropped back down heavily. The movement concluded with a soft puff of warm air across her face.

Myranda held her breath as her heart raced. Now she remembered where she was. She was in a dragon's cave, and that left very little doubt as to what had laid its head upon her chest. Despite her best efforts, she began to tremble in fear. The creature seemed not to mind, the deep, rhythmic breaths on her face leading her to believe it had drifted back to sleep.

With her one healthy arm, Myranda set about the task of escaping her predicament. She slid her hand underneath the head, finding it mercifully light enough to lift. Slowly and smoothly as she could manage, she tried to lower the beast's head to the cave floor beside her. After an interminable sequence of awkward movements, she succeeded in doing so without waking it. She rolled off of the packs, still affixed to her back, and slammed down hard on the injured shoulder. The pain was intense, but she managed to remain silent. Another few tricky movements brought her to her feet, heart still pounding in her chest.

Myranda cast a glance at the spot next to where she'd been lying, only to find that the weak rays of sun that made it this far into the cave were falling on an empty floor. Her panicked search for the creature was ended when she felt something rub against her right hand. She was startled, pulling her hand away and looking desperately for the culprit. There beside her, sitting on its haunches, was a small dragon, staring back at her. Myranda froze. This creature was barely a fifth the size of the ones she'd seen earlier, perhaps the size of a large dog--but if it chose to, it could certainly reduce her to a bloody meal in seconds.

A long moment passed before one of the two moved again. The beast took the initiative. It walked to her left side and reared onto its hind legs briefly, brushing its head across her hand. Not knowing what else to do, and eager to prevent the creature from rearing up again, she dropped her hand to her side. The dragon swiftly thrust its head into her palm. The feeling of the ridges above its eyes brushing against her fingers for the third time made her realize what the animal was after. She stroked the dragon's brow. It sat beside her, pushing back with every stroke.

So, you like that? Myranda thought.

With little else to do, Myranda stroked the beast and thought. It had the feminine features of the smaller dragon. All in all it was a near perfect miniature of the beast that must have been its mother. Its head was more or less waist-level for Myranda, and from tail to nose it might be as long as she was tall. It had wings delicately folded on its back, still moist from hatching. The eyes were reptilian slits in a beautiful gold iris. A larger, thick scale swept back from the creature's forehead, clearly distinguishing where the head began with an almost crown-like flourish.

The forelegs, now that she could get a fair look at them, were indeed very much like her own arms. The paws in particular were like hands, though each toe was stouter, and tapered into a nasty-looking claw. Despite this, the creature's flexing and scratching at the ground betrayed a near-human level dexterity. As the creature enjoyed its stroking more and more, it scratched harder and harder at the stone floor, scoring lines into it with ease. The contentment was further evidenced, it would seem, by the curling of the tail. It writhed about with snake-like motion.

In her fascination, Myranda forgot that the natural masterpiece beside her was still an enormous danger. If she tried to run it would certainly chase her and easily catch her. She carried no weapon with which to fight it, though she doubted she could bring herself to harm the beautiful creature even if she had. Worse yet, either of the two larger dragons could return at any moment. Something had to be done.

In an act of pure optimism, Myranda tried to simply walk away, hoping to escape without rousing any of the creature's more predatory instincts. The dragon merely followed, stopping when she stopped and continuing when she did. This would not do. With all other options exhausted, she turned to reason.

"Listen," she said, turning to address the dragon directly. It was startled at first by the sound of Myranda's voice, so she lowered to a whisper. "I am very glad you like me. I like you, too, but you can't follow me. You see, I am afraid you might not be so kind when your stomach starts to rumble. At that point, I fear I will be little more than a wounded animal to you, which I am sure you will find quite tasty."

The little dragon stared back. She took another step, and the beast followed. Myranda sighed and looked around the cave. The evidence of the clash between the two dragons earlier was in no short supply. Deep gashes in the rock were littered about the walls and floor. Pools and spatters of thick, dark blood painted whole sections of the poorly-lit cave. She could not help but wonder how she had managed to escape injury. The whole of the cave had been their battleground, and she had been helpless in the center. Regardless, her luck could not afford to be pushed any further.

"I know you just hatched, and you might not know this yet, but you have a mother. She is very large, clearly very protective, and I do not want her to get the wrong idea about me. Just stay here and let me leave. That way you and I can both continue living. Please?" she begged.

The dragon stared back innocently, but followed again when Myranda tried to leave. She turned back.

"Please, you need to stay here. If you don't, someone will come looking for you and find me. You must have brothers and sisters. Don't you want to stay with them? Why don't I just take you back to where you hatched? Then you can see your family again and you will forget all about me. If I am lucky they will still be asleep and I won't be torn to shreds," she said.

Myranda took a deep breath and turned her back to the cave's mouth. Darkness became more and more complete. Before long, she found herself feeling along the wall, muttering about how insane she was for doing this. A few minutes had passed and she had traveled far into the cave when she kicked something. Feeling for it, she found a piece of wood with oily cloth on the end. A torch! Without questioning why such a thing could be found in a dragon's cave, she blindly retrieved the flint and lit it.

The light of the torch revealed a grizzly scene. The contents of a pack identical to her own were scattered about the floor. Against one wall, the pulverized remains of a human skeleton lay on the floor, scorched black. Myranda shuddered at the sight of it. A twinkle drew her gaze to a bag against the opposite wall. It had been torn, leaving its contents strewn about the floor. Silver coins.

"This does not bode well," she said, her heart beating so hard she could fairly hear it echo. "At least we know what happened to Rankin. He didn't run after all."

A minute or so more walking brought her to what she had been both dreading and searching for, but it was not what she expected. The floor was stained with blood, and a pile of gold objects lay before her. The smashed shells of half a dozen dragon eggs lay nestled among the gold pitchers, scepters, and coins. Their contents were never given a chance at life. Only one egg was empty, the one egg that had been spared. Tears welled in her eyes as she cast light upon the faithful mother. It lay, battered and torn, curled up around the egg that the young dragon beside her had hatched from just hours ago. It moved no more, succumbed to its wounds after driving the attacker away.

The tears ran down Myranda's face. Hours ago, it had seemed a monster, but it was now a fallen hero. Her home had been invaded, her family had been destroyed, and her life had been given, all for the precious gift that now looked over the tragedy with the innocent eyes of a newborn. The hatchling was too young to understand the sight before it, yet somehow Myranda sensed some sorrow in the creature, as though it knew what had occurred. She turned to the young dragon, tears still in her eyes.

"You are an orphan, just like me," Myranda said, kneeling to come eye to eye with the beast. "If you and I are to share the same plight, we may as well share it together. I know how empty the world can be when you are alone."

She dropped the torch and hugged the little dragon about the neck. It seemed pleased at the attention, regardless of the cause. Myranda then retrieved the torch, wiped away her tears, and headed back toward the cave's mouth, dragon in tow. It never occurred to her to take even a coin from the fortune that made up the nest. To her it was now a monument to the sacrifice that had been made, and she would not disturb it. Besides, plundering a resting place had been the cause of this whole mess in the first place.

When she reached the mouth of the cave it was nearly sundown. From the looks of it, the storm that had chased her into the cave had run its course rather quickly. There was little new snow on the ground, and the wind was no more than the constant breeze that came down off of the mountains. Already the colder temperatures of night were closing in. She hurried to the nearest cluster of trees that would spare them the icy breeze and gathered some wood for the fire.

This was the first time the dragon had left the cave. It stared with wonder and excitement at the world opening up before it. The creature pranced through the snow, rushing to trees, bushes and plants, drawing in the scent and moving on. It discovered a set of tracks made by a moose and scampered in the direction of the smell, turning back after a few dozen paces to return to Myranda's side. It watched her with fascination as she readied the fire, having trouble getting the frosty wood to light.

"You know, you could lend a hand here," she said with a grin. "You could huff out a little fire and I could have a seat and relax."

The creature looked at Myranda, then at the wood, and then in the direction of some noise only she could hear.

"No? I didn't think so," Myranda said.

When the fire was finally lit, Myranda laid out her bed roll and sat upon it. She pulled her pack in front of her and pulled out some of the salted meat. It had been cooked once, and could be eaten cold if she wished, but if was not the most appetizing of foods warm, let alone cold. She put her piece on the end of a stick and held it over the fire. Instantly she had the undivided attention of the little dragon. Most creatures would have been frightened to go near the fire, but this one stood among the flames to get a better whiff of the tantalizing fare.

"No, no, no," Myranda said.

The dragon turned to her. Myranda pulled the meat away and continued to admonish the animal.

"I know you must be hungry, but that food is mine. Hot food is mine," she said. "Here, you can have this. I wish I had something better for your first meal."

Myranda pulled out a second piece of meat. The dragon sniffed the meat, then opened its mouth for the first time since Myranda had first seen it. It was a tad unnerving seeing the rows of needle sharp teeth in the front, and smaller gripping teeth in the back. She had nearly forgotten the nature of the beast that was her new companion. It snatched the meat from her fingers greedily, a tooth grazing her skin. The hungry dragon gulped the food down without chewing, flicking its tongue between teeth here and there to catch stray drops. A second and third piece of meat met the same fate for the sake of distracting the ravenous creature from Myranda's own meal. The dragon sniffed at the pack while Myranda was eating, pawing at it. After being scolded several times for doing so, the little creature stopped. Instead, it sat, impatiently watching Myranda finish her meal. The very instant Myranda's hands were empty, the dragon stood, rigidly awaiting another piece of meat.

"I'm sorry, but that is all for today. You've already eaten half of my share for today and all of it for tomorrow. I hope that one of us becomes an exceptional hunter exceptionally fast, or there are several hungry days ahead of us," Myranda said.

Myranda took out her canteen and took a long swig. The dragon smacked its tongue several times, making it clear that it too needed to wash down the excessively salty meal.

"I know, it makes you thirsty eating that stuff. Particularly if you eat twice your share. I've got water here, but . . . I don't know how to give it to you. Well . . . here," she said, pouring a bit of it into her cupped hand.

With the limited mobility of her injured shoulder, she had a hard time of it, but the effort did not go unappreciated. In a flash, the tongue was out, writhing about as though it had a life of its own. It had a very slight rough feel to its top side, and a smooth bottom. The feeling was bizarre as it curled in her palm and between her fingers. She found the tongue sweeping with special interest over the slight abrasion the tooth had caused. As she refilled her palm once more, she found the dragon's interest lingering on the drops of blood that seeped from the cut here and there. It was time to put an end to this.

"We need to find a better way. Partially because my hand is freezing, but mostly because I am afraid you are getting to like the taste of me. Not that I don't trust you. It's just that the food will be running thin soon, and it is clear you have a healthy appetite. I do not want to give you any ideas about an alternate menu," she said, as though the dragon could understand.

She looked for some vessel to pour the water into. Failing to find one, she decided that the dragon could drink in the same way she did.

"Open up," she said.

The dragon looked back, confused.

"Look, see? Like this," Myranda said, pointed to her mouth and opening and closing it a few exaggerated times. "Can you do that?"

Eventually the dragon imitated long enough for Myranda to spray some water from the canteen into the gaping maw. The dragon quickly learned what to do now, and continued to hold its mouth open until its thirst had been slaked, at the cost of the rest of the contents of the canteen.

"Now I have to melt snow down to replace it. If this keeps up, you are going to be the world's most spoiled dragon," she said.

Unslighted by the remark, the dragon padded over to the bedroll and lay down.

"Tired already? You just woke up!" Myranda remarked.

It paid her no mind, curling its tail around its legs and settling its head comfortably onto its folded over neck. Myranda smiled. It was good to have a companion, though a baby dragon would hardly have been her first choice. As she stared at the creature, it shifted to rest its head on her lap. Myranda began to pet dragon in the way it had come to crave. As she did, both sighed in contentment.

"You know, you need a name," Myranda said. "Would you like that?"

The dragon made itself more comfortable and puffed out a breath.

"When I was a little girl, I used to lay like this, with my head on my mother's lap. That was a long time ago, but I remember it like it was yesterday. It was back in a place called Kenvard. You know, down there it isn't always snow that comes down. We actually would get rain for most of the year. Not just rain, but thunder and lightning, too. I was afraid, and when I couldn't sleep, I would come out and lay like this, and she would tell me that it was all going to be all right.

"You know what she called me? Myn. I misspelled my name that way the first time I tried to write it, and she called me that ever after. I think it suits you. After all, I was a lot like you back then. Young, naïve . . . I was not covered with scales, though. I suppose we weren't so alike, but still. I think that is what I will call you. How do you like it?" she asked.

The beast yawned and stretched.

"I suppose I ought to take that as a yes," she said, wedging herself into the bedroll beneath her freshly-named companion, and drifting off into a purposeful sleep.

#

Morning came with a sharper than average chill. The dragon had slept the whole night through on top of Myranda. When she awoke, the creature seemed deathly cold. The night had taken quite a toll. Myranda scolded herself for not realizing the danger Myn would have been in, exposed to the elements all night.

"Myn? Are you all right?" she asked desperately, nudging at the frighteningly cold neck of the dragon.

It slowly opened its eyes and yawned sluggishly. The little dragon stood and stretched stiffly. She seemed weak, her tail dragging the ground and her head sagging. Myranda was well and truly fearful for the dragon's health when, suddenly, it puffed out its chest. A moment later a surge of brilliant orange flame erupted from the creature's mouth. Instantly she seemed to perk up. Myranda was more than a bit startled, but the improvement in Myn relieved her.

"So, you *can* breathe fire," she said, standing and placing a hand on the neck of the dragon. Myn was a good deal warmer, which reminded Myranda just how cold the air was. "I wish I could."

When the bedroll had been packed away they set off. The events of yesterday had set Myranda behind. The food would run out today, leaving them both hungry--with at least another day of travel ahead of them, *if* they hurried. Myn had no trouble keeping up with the brisk pace that Myranda set, often running ahead to inspect the odd flutter or rustle, disappearing from sight periodically. Sundown brought her much nearer to her goal than she'd expected. Having a friend to talk to, even one that did not understand a word she said, helped the miles pass quickly. They set up camp at a clearing that Tus had described before she had left the headquarters. At the center was a larger tree with an arrow carved into it. The arrow pointed off into the thick of the forest.

"You see that?" Myranda asked Myn. "Tus said his partner carved it. It points in the wrong direction, so that people will not find their trainer. Clever, in a terrible, cruel way. Imagine if we were lost. That arrow would send us off to our end. Isn't that nice of them? It must take a heart of stone to do what they do. And I have joined them! What a lovely turn my life has taken! The good news is that this arrow means that, so long as we wake bright and early, we can make it to Wolloff's by midday tomorrow. It seems a life of restless wandering has made me quite the hiker. That will teach Caya to underestimate me!"

Myn seemed unaffected by the sarcasm that flowed. Myranda tossed the last piece of meat to the dragon, who snatched easily out of the air. A fire was started, again without the help of the dragon, and Myranda cooked her woefully inadequate share. The whole of the day had been spent at a near run, leaving her exhausted and famished. She had barely finished her food before she nodded off.

The dragon joined her on the bedroll and the two slept blissfully until morning. The next day afforded a much slower pace, as the destination was so near. Hunger burned in her stomach, making Myranda wish she had saved her food for breakfast. Myn, on the other hand, seemed more energetic than ever.

"What has gotten into you?" she asked.

Myn merely stopped to look at Myranda, then continued her excited prancing about. A squirrel appeared between two trees ahead and Myn launched herself after it. Despite the tremendous distance between the predator and its prey, Myn was nearly upon the creature in moments. The hapless animal shot up a tree, only to be followed with equal speed by the hungry dragon. Snow rattled from the branches as the chase continued unseen. Just as Myranda reached the base of the tree, the squirrel reappeared, launching itself from one of the upper branches. Myn leapt with all of her might after the morsel, her jaws agape. She snapped them shut just a hair away from the rodent's tail. The lucky squirrel continued on into the next tree. The far heavier dragon did not fare so well. She plunged earthward, colliding with the trunk of the tree and sinking into a pile of snow below. More snow rained down from the shaken branches, thoroughly burying the downed dragon.

Myranda rushed to the landing site, concerned for the little dragon. Myn emerged from the drift, shaking off the snow. All that seemed to be injured by the horrid-looking fall was her pride, as her face bore as near to a look of embarrassment as the reptilian features would allow. After a glance at the tree, the dragon knew her prey was gone. She trudged sheepishly to Myranda's side.

"That was a nasty fall," Myranda said, patting her on the side. "Is this what you've been doing on your little jaunts out of sight? You made a very nice attempt though. If you keep that up, I'll be the only hungry one."

Myranda shook her head.

"You are two days old, and already you've come closer to catching your own meal than I did in my first ten years! Why do I feel as though we humans were not treated fairly in nature's balance?" Myranda wondered.

Before long, a rather precarious-looking structure peeked out above the lower tree tops. As it grew nearer, it became more and more apparent that the tower was standing out of sheer habit. Large sections of the wall had fallen away, planks of wood hastily put in place to patch them. The roof showed the faintest hint of having been painted blue, but time and the elements had wiped it away ages ago. Finally, they reached an equally faded red door with a barred slot at eye level. Myranda gave a knock. After a particularly long wait, the slot slid open and a pair of ancient eyes peered out.

"Aye," came a thickly accented voice.

"I was sent here by Caya," Myranda said.

"I know no one by that name," he said.

"I have this," Myranda said, producing the writ.

"Give it here," came the voice, a pair of withered fingers appearing at the slot.

Myranda offered up the paper Caya had given her. It was snatched away and, after a few moments of irritated muttering, the voice rose again.

"The money?" he asked, or rather, demanded.

"I was not given any. Caya needed time to get the silver together," she said.

"NO! NEVER AGAIN! WE HAD AN AGREEMENT, I AM TO RECEIVE TWO--YE GODS, WHAT IS THAT!?" he ranted.

Myn, intrigued by the new scent and new voice, stood on her hind legs and leaned her front feet against the door. That had just managed to bring her eyes to the slot, and she peered eagerly inside, startling the ranting old man.

"Myn, get down from there! I'm very sorry, Mr. Wolloff. That is just Myn. She is a dragon," Myranda explained.

"I can see that! I have eyes, haven't I! What is it doing here?" he demanded.

"I . . . It is difficult to explain," she said.

"Never mind. Get inside, but the dragon stays outside," he said.

"I don't know if I can keep the dragon from--" she began.

"The dragon stays outside!" he screamed.

Myn jumped back, startled by the man. The door flew open to reveal a white-haired man. He was precisely as one might imagine a wizard, rendered frail by the mass of years gone by. His clothes were simple, and immaculately white. A brass amulet with a clear crystal hung about his neck. He grasped it and spat out a trio of arcane words. A sharp, brief pulse of light came from the stone within to signify the casting of the spell. Myn dropped to the ground as though struck. She was no longer moving.

"What did you do?" Myranda insisted.

"Relax, lass. I put the little demon down for a rest. Now get inside before I wake it and sic it on ye!" he said.

Myranda reluctantly moved inside, keeping her gaze locked on the motionless dragon until the door slammed shut.

"Are you certain she will be all right?" Myranda asked.

"Aye, *she* will be just fine. As for you, I'll expect a bit more speed and obedience from a pupil. That *is* what you have come for, I trust," he said.

"Yes," she assured him.

"Right, then you will be needing food, I suppose," he said.

"I would appreciate it," she said.

"You will find the kitchen there," he said, pointing a crooked finger at one of the three remaining doors.

Myranda turned to the door. The room she stood in was, to say the least, well used. Books with faded writing lay open upon every surface. Half-empty vessels of strong-smelling powders and liquids were scattered about, making the air stale with the smell of potions. A rickety table with a single chair made up the dining area, it would seem, while the parlor consisted of an overstuffed chair strategically placed between the crackling fireplace and the table. She walked to the flimsy wooden door her host had indicated.

"I shall take my meal in here. When you are finished you may bring it out to me," he called after her.

She stopped in her tracks.

"You want me to prepare food for you?" she said in disbelief.

"Aye. You know how to cook, I assume," he said without looking up.

"Well, I do, but I have just spent days out in the cold, most of them on my feet," she said. He quickly cut her off.

"Then I would imagine you would jump at the chance to spend some time in front of a warm fire," he said with an infuriating cheerfulness.

"I--" began her retort.

"I do not want to hear it. Until that woman sends me my silver, you are not a guest, not a student, not a customer. You are an unwanted tenant! AND RENT IS PAST DUE! You will do what I say, when I say it! That goes double when we are in training! NOW GET TO WORK!" he commanded.

Myranda backed into the kitchen, taken aback by what he had said. As she gathered the meager selection of ingredients, the girl wondered two things. First, why was this man so ill-tempered? Second, how could someone who seemed so fragile be so forceful and commanding? When he spoke one could not help but act. Perhaps learning magic taught such a trait. She half desired and half feared gaining that quality in her time here.

The meal, a simple vegetable stew, was finished and set before Wolloff in one of the plain clay bowls she managed to find in the kitchen. He shoveled the food into his mouth as Myranda cleared the uncushioned chair of books and other debris so that she could join him at the table. By the time she was able to sit, the wizard had nearly finished. When the last of his share was finished, he pushed the bowl across the table, turned back to the fire, and returned to his reading.

Myranda finished her meal and carried the bowls to the kitchen to wash them. By now, she knew better than to expect gratitude from her host. She returned to her seat, sitting quietly and thinking of the dragon sleeping in the cold just outside the door.

"You know, the dragon . . ." Myranda began.

"The dragon stays outside. It breathes fire and my home is filled with sensitive, irreplaceable, *flammable* objects. The blasted creature lives outside. It does not need to come in!" Wolloff said.

"Well, when will she wake?" she asked.

"In a few hours. Listen, lass, I cannot be answering questions all day. You'll be occupying my time for months, so I'd like to get a wee bit of my own work done tonight. You'll be spending most of your time in the tower. That is where I teach, and that is where you will sleep. Why don't you head up there and make yourself at home? Anything to get you out of my hair!" he said.

Myranda rose and headed quickly to the door, eager to be away from the irritating man. The stairs inside the tower were quite a match for its exterior. Less than a handful of the entire spiraling flight were fully intact. The rest had corners or centers crumbled away or cracked. It was only with great care that she managed to reach the top. There she found a room, perhaps half the size of the room downstairs. It was round, with curved bookcases lining the sections of wall between windows, of which there were three. One faced south, one north, and one west.

The windward side of the tower bore no window, keeping the stiff breeze mercifully outside. As a result, the meager heat from the fire below, which ran up a column of chimney that marked the center of the tower, was quite enough to heat the room. There was an old bench, a table scattered with various mystical apparatus and books, and a trio of chairs, one of which was broken. The entire room was covered with a layer of dust. It was clear that no one had put this room to use in some time. There were shutters over the windows, though like everything else here, they were in various states of disrepair. The southern one did not even close tightly, instead knocking erratically in the breeze.

Myranda dropped her packs onto the bed, coughing at the plume of dust it stirred. She sat down on the bed's edge and wrestled the nearly worn-through boots from her feet. With only the use of her left arm, it proved to be quite a task, as cooking had been. She contemplated asking Wolloff to heal her shoulder immediately, but the thought of having to deal with him again bothered her more than the wound, the ever-present pain of which had come to be bearable simply through familiarity. In truth, with any luck, the temperament of Wolloff would lose its edge in the same way.

The tired traveler rubbed her feet. They'd not felt fresh air in a week. Her knees and hips were sore, as was her back from the packs she'd had to carry. All things considered, she had been through an ordeal, and she could tell it would take some time to recover. A smile came her face as she fell back onto the bed. She realized that, at least for the time being, she had a home. Her travels were over. For a time she rested, but it was not long before her thoughts turned to Myn.

She hoisted herself to her ailing feet and hobbled to the clattering shutter, pushing it wide open and holding it. Two stories down, she saw the prone form of the dragon, still asleep. She seemed to be comfortable enough, perhaps because of the hint of sun that had broken through the clouds to lend her its warmth. Even so, the shadow of the mountain was creeping closer as the sun descended. She resolved to be sure that if the little dragon had not woken by the time the sun had disappeared entirely, she would see to it that Myn was brought inside, regardless of what Wolloff had to say. Until then, she actually had some time with nothing to fill it.

Myranda took a seat at the table, looking over the contents of one of the dusty books. The pages were filled with intricate symbols that she could not understand. Though their meaning was hidden to her, there was an aura of power about them that was undeniable. She ran her fingers across the page, feeling the hair on the back of her neck stand on end. She put down the book and turned her attention to the half-dozen jewel shards that were scattered here and there. They were similar to the one that adorned Wolloff's amulet, but varied in color. Most were a dark blue, though some of the smaller pieces were a murky red. In stark contrast to the other gems was a single, perfectly clear, colorless crystal in a cloth-lined case.

Toward the center of the table was a sophisticated apparatus of glass tubes and vials. Some had blackness staining them, as though they had spent time over a flame. Next she looked to the other books. The aged tomes could be found not only lining the walls, but in mounds on the floor, piled high in chests, and even under the bed. She approached one of the bookcases. Hundreds of leather-bound books, the gold leaf or hand-inked names long since flaked away, stood awaiting the trained eye of a wizard to unlock their secrets. Finally, she found a book, apparently a newer one, which had a name that was not only intact, but also in her native tongue.

She pulled the thin book from its place and opened it. The title read *The White Magics of the Northern Alliance.* Inside, the pages displayed the very same runes that had populated the pages of the other books, though these were drawn with less care, or perhaps less skill. Above the dense blocks of runes were names accrediting the spell crafters, like *Talia's Poison Guard* or *Merick's Touch of Soothing.* Each spell was further accompanied by lengthy descriptions of the effects, as well as recommendations of when they were to be used. Her untrained eye could make no sense of the spells themselves, but she eagerly read over the descriptions of the wondrous incantations. With each sentence she became more excited about the months to come. She would be able to produce such effects in time!

Just when she thought she was as thrilled as she could be, she came upon a page that seized her attention. It was labeled *Celeste Spell of Cure Affliction*. Celeste! In all of her travels, she had never encountered another person who shared her family name. That meant that this spell had been crafted by her own flesh and blood! Some forgotten ancestor or distant cousin. She read over the description, hungry for more information. Alas, nothing more was said of the author. However, the indication of the spell was identical to her shoulder's malady. It told of wounds twice as bad as hers healed fully in minutes, usefulness restored to limbs rendered immobile.

Myranda riffled through the pages of the book in search of other spells bearing her name. Finding none, she carefully placed the precious book down, opened to the page of interest. She then rushed to the bookshelf again and pulled the first book down. Supporting it painfully with her injured arm, she pored through the pages hoping to find her name again. Failing to find it, she searched another, and then another. Over the course of hours, she managed to exhaust the contents of one whole bookshelf. Most books bore labels in Tresson. It was a language she knew well enough, but one that would not likely hold information about her clan, as they had resided in and around Kenvard for countless generations.

Only when the light from the window had faded past the point of usefulness did she stop her search. She dejectedly replaced the book that had stirred her hopes so, turning to the window. The dim glow of a cloud-shrouded moon made her realize that she had completely forgotten her dear little Myn! She ran to the window. The dragon's impromptu bed was empty, a set of tracks leading off into the woods. The panicked shriek of a pursued woodland creature, followed by a tree in the distance shaking free of its blanket of snow assured Myranda that her little dragon was well occupied and quite healthy. She would be just fine.

Satisfied with Myn's wellbeing, the time had come to tend to her own. She looked to the bed. If she was to sleep in the dusty old relic, it would need some preparation. The blanket had to be shaken out, the mattress checked for unwanted residents, and the pillow treated similarly. This would be her home for a while, such as it was, and she would have to make it livable. She set about her task, and was just dusting off her hands and contemplating sleep when there came a bellow from Wolloff.

"Dinner!" he cried in more of a demand than an alert.

As she made her way down the treacherously darkened staircase, she reconsidered her situation. She would be eating a second warm meal in the same day, a rare occurrence in her nomadic lifestyle. Better yet, she had a soft bed in a room away from the cold waiting for her. In comparison to what she'd become accustomed to, this was utter luxury. If she had only to cook a meal or two to afford such a paradise, it was a bargain. This thought was still in her mind when she encountered Wolloff at the bottom of the staircase, candle in hand and a scowl on his face.

"Oh, by all means, take your time! I would hate for you to break a sweat! It would be a bloody travesty!" he said with a practiced tone of false concern.

"I am sorry. It is just that I have a rather serious shoulder injury," she explained, as she felt a few exertion-fueled throbs.

"The last I checked, climbing the stairs was more in the realm of the leg's operation," he said.

"I know, I know," she said, not eager to prompt another biting comment. One followed regardless.

"That's fine. What's say we get some meat in this meal, shall we? I do not take the trouble to keep the cupboard stocked with rabbits so that I can eat like one!" he said.

In the kitchen, she found he had left out a smoked rabbit for her to cook. She roasted it and brought him a plate, lacking the strength in her right arm to carry her own plate at the same time. When she finally set down her own serving and took her first bite, she noticed her host casting a glance or two at the afflicted shoulder. Apparently it was clear that cutting the meat required more of her arm than it was willing to give. When both were through eating, he pushed his plate aside and gave her a stern look.

"Right, let's see it then," he said.

"See what?" she asked.

"See what?" he said, rolling his eyes. "A song and dance. Your shoulder, you dullard! What do you think I mean!?"

Myranda rolled up her sleeve, cringing at the pain. Wolloff began to unfasten the blood-soaked bandage.

"This looks to be a week old," he said.

"It is. How did you know?" she asked.

"I have been at this for some time, lass. Has it looked this way from the start?" he asked.

"The morning after," she said, cringing again as he prodded at the wound with a small metal hook he had produced.

"Hold still, this will be over soon," he said as his probing became more vigorous.

"What are you--ow--OW!" she cried.

He showed her the end of the hook. There was a small piece of blood-soaked wood clinging to the end.

"That was in my arm?" she said.

"Aye," he said. "Were I you, I would have removed that. Clean the wound in the kitchen and we will get a fresh bandage on it. First thing in the morning, we will get you started on that arm."

"Get *me* started on it? You mean that *I* will be the one healing it?" she said.

"Aye. To a layman, that injury is a curse, but to a budding white wizard, it is motivation. The sooner you learn the art, the sooner you end your suffering," he said, turning back to the book he had been reading.

Myranda's head was spinning. It was only now striking her how near she was to achieving what had been a lifelong dream. Ever since that terrible day when she lost her family to the siege of Kenvard, she had longed to find some way to undo some of the damage the war had done.

After carefully rinsing the injury clean, she returned to the main room where Wolloff stopped his reading just long enough to apply the first real bandage the gash had seen. The difference between the proper dressing and the coarse makeshift counterparts she'd been using was quite clear. Aside from doing a far better job of protecting the wound, it was worlds more comfortable, as it did its job without needing to be tied so tight that it numbed her fingers.

"Right, first light we begin with your training. Get rest," Wolloff said.

Myranda fairly ran up the stairs. Tomorrow! Tomorrow she would take the first steps toward a new life! Imagine! In a few short months she would be able to save lives! Her mere touch would soon restore the stricken! She slid into bed with these thoughts and more rendering sleep all but impossible. The clouds outside hid the moon, casting her room into utter blackness. Eyes closed or open, images of a war-torn landscape hung in the air, with herself, dressed in white, one by one bringing the fallen back to health.

The aspiring wizard was suddenly torn from her reverie by the loud clatter of one of the shutters. She turned her head to the source of the sound. In the darkness, she could only just make out the open window to the south. Myranda stumbled to the shutter and inspected it. She could swear she'd wedged it closed earlier. Pulling it shut, she took more care to see to it that the window would not come open again. After making her way blindly to the bed, she slipped under the covers once more and tried to get to sleep. In a few moments, though, she felt a familiar weight drop on top of her.

"Oof. Myn! You know you aren't supposed to be here! Get out of here now!" Myranda reprimanded.

In response, the dragon simply made herself a bit more comfortable.

"No?" Myranda said with a sigh. "Well, I tried."

Now reunited with her constant companion, she tried valiantly to get some rest. The thoughts of the wonders to come kept her mind racing long after sleep should have come.

#

After what felt like mere moments of true slumber, Myranda was jarred from her rest by a gentle prodding on her uninjured shoulder. She opened her eyes, expecting to see Myn standing over her, wanting breakfast or some such. Instead she saw Wolloff.

"Good morning," he said with forced gentility.

"Good morning," she said, yawning and stretching.

"Oh, please, don't get up. Are you aware that you've a dragon on your lap?" he asked.

"Oh, my, I am sorry. She must have climbed in the window last night. I tried to get her to leave, but--" she hurriedly explained.

"Never mind that. No harm done," he said quietly.

"I thought you would have been angrier," Myranda said, slightly concerned by the rare and excessive showing of civility she was experiencing.

"Oh, aye. I am *particularly* perturbed, but it is my considered opinion that when dealing with a wild beast, it is best not to provoke it with harsh words," he said.

"So, you will not yell until Myn leaves?" she asked, sliding herself into a sitting position and waking the dragon.

"Aye, but as soon as the wee creature is out of earshot, you will hear what I am at this moment only barely able to contain," he said, twitching with suppressed anger.

"Why am I tempted to keep her around?" she said meekly.

"Because you have forgotten that, as a wizard, I've a host of more powerful and *far* more permanent methods of disposing of the creature than a *blasted sleep spell!*" Wolloff said, the final words carrying a hint of the rage he was feeling.

The awakened dragon looked sleepily at Myranda, and then at the wizard. When she noticed the second human, her eyes shot open and she leapt to the floor. Situating herself between Myranda and the perceived threat, she shot Wolloff a steely stare and adopted a fierce stance. She opened her wings and bared her teeth. When the wizard refused to back down, Myn lashed her tail back and forth, knocking down a pile of books. Instantly, Wolloff grabbed his medallion. Myranda placed a reassuring hand on Myn's side.

"Myn, don't worry. Wolloff here is a friend! He won't do anything . . ." she began, before glancing at the furious wizard just in time to see another twitch. " . . . terrible to me."

She continued to pat the dragon on the neck and soothe her until she was willing to relinquish her defensive stance.

"That is right. You must be tired of being cramped into this tiny room. Why don't you just go play outside in the warm sun, and catch something to eat?" she said.

As Myranda gestured repeatedly to the window, Myn shifted her gaze to the broken shutter, which had once again come undone. A bird fluttered by. Myn locked onto the creature and darted out the window and down the wall in a twinkling. Myranda ran to the window and watched as the little dragon rushed toward the same stand of trees she had terrorized the day before.

Wolloff joined her at the window, concerned solely with the distance between himself and the dragon. As he watched he spoke, his voice rising as the overprotective creature moved further away.

"These books around you represent three lifetimes of tireless search. My grandfather, my father, and I have spent our youth scouring this embattled land for any scrap of knowledge that it could muster. Every hint of mystic knowledge available in the realm of healing has been assembled here. I will *not* allow all of that to go up in a puff of smoke because an uneducated *apprentice* could not follow orders and let her blasted dragon let fly a spark! *Understood!?"* he cried with growing anger.

"Yes" Myranda said, sheepishly.

"Right . . . then let us begin," he said, quickly composing himself. "First, you will need to learn how to pronounce each rune. As a whole, they compose a complex written and spoken language, but for our purposes, you will need to learn only a small part of it. However, if you learn anything of the mystic language, learn it well. A misspoken arcane word can be dangerous."

"Dangerous?" she asked.

"Aye. At best, the spell will not work. Equally likely is the mistake changing the behavior of the spell in unpredictable ways. I cannot stress this enough. Ignoring all else, you must only speak a spell with an effect that you are absolutely sure of. Years ago, a colleague of mine attempted a spell intended to light a fire. He mistakenly substituted the target rune for the self rune. Needless to say, it was an unpleasant thing to witness. Even more unpleasant to clean up. It was, though, a fine reminder to speak with care," he said.

Aside from two breaks for meals, the day was utterly filled with study. Learning to pronounce these words was far more difficult than any other she had learned. This was because each word carried power, and if too many were spoken together, a spell would be cast. So each attempt was separated by a long and purposeful silence. Whenever Myranda was not as careful as Wolloff would like, she would be treated to a variation on the same long lecture about the "undesirable" results that such behavior could bring. Despite the difficulty, she did manage to learn a handful of words. During dinner, she decided to ask some questions that had been bothering her.

"Wolloff?" she asked.

"Aye," he said, as usual without looking up from the ever-present book.

"Why do we have to learn a different language to cast spells?" she asked.

"Strictly to save effort. The language that these spells are scribed in is one that the spirits are attuned to. When you speak an incantation, you entreat the forces around us for help. I've seen similar effects brought about in nearly any spoken language, but in those cases the mind of the caster must attune itself to the spirits. The process tends to be longer and slower. Sometimes chanting is involved. I personally cannot see the benefit, but to each his own. Nothing you will be doing will require much more than you'll learn of the runes," he said, as though he'd answered the question countless times before.

"What if---" she began.

"Listen, all that needs to be answered shall be. Any question that you have that does not find an answer in the months ahead is not one worth asking. Please keep your magic-related inquiries to yourself," he said.

From that point forward, he rigidly refused to answer any more of her questions, rather forcefully suggesting that she retire to her room and practice what she had learned thus far. She climbed the increasingly familiar staircase to her room. The fading light of the setting sun illuminated the page that she had left open on the table. After finding and reminding herself of the runes she knew, she carefully located the book she had found earlier and analyzed the spell that bore her name. Not surprisingly, most runes that she had learned were present in the spell. She grinned at the thought that Wolloff was preparing her for this very incantation. A few days more of study such as this and she would know all of the runes on the page. She could be casting it by week's end. With this thought in her mind, she felt the wound on her arm. The sliver Wolloff had removed was enough to take from it the constant pain. Soon she would be rid of the wound, once and for all.

Her thoughts were interrupted by the violent swinging of the shutter, and she knew without looking that it was not the wind that had dislodged it. Sure enough, the little dragon was at her side again. She stroked the loyal creature's head and continued her review. Myn delighted in the sound of Myranda's voice as she muttered this word or that from the symbols scribed on the page. Soon the sun was behind the mountains, leaving her with no light to learn by. This was Myranda's cue to retire, with Myn taking her usual position on top of her.

"So, how did your day go? Keeping busy?" she asked her silent companion. "New words. You know, I haven't learned a new language since I was a little girl. It wasn't particularly easy back then, but now there is the distinct possibility that if I mispronounce a word I could wind up as a jackrabbit or invisible. That has added a whole new dimension to the learning process, I can tell you. I'll tell you something else, too. He may know this magic backward and forward, but he could stand to learn a thing or two about manners. I was afraid that when my time here was up I couldn't bear to leave it, but if he remains as he is today, after six months I shall be glad to be rid of it."

Morning came quickly, and Myranda was sure to be up with the sun so that she would have time to coax Myn to leave before Wolloff arrived, lest she receive yet another of his long-winded lectures. She managed to do so with little time to spare. Wolloff's slow, plodding footsteps could be heard approaching just as she closed the shutter.

The day passed almost precisely as the previous one had, as did one after, and the one after that. Daylight was spent studying, night spent with Myn to keep her company. It might not have been the most luxurious life, but it was just exactly what she needed: stability, safety, and even education and companionship. For the first time in ages, she could feel her tightly-bound mind decompressing, her perpetually tangled nerves unraveling. She was living, not merely surviving. After so long, it was a state she was unaccustomed to, and brought with it the nagging fear that it would be fleeting.

#

Several days of travel had brought Trigorah and her men from their headquarters in Northern Capital to the southern edge of an icy field. She had most of the other Elites combing it for some sign of where the sword had been found. If the reports were correct, then the girl had passed through the nearby towns heading south. Of the three nearest towns, only the people of the village due north had any memory of the girl described in Demont's report. They spat when they spoke of her, decrying her as a sympathizer and traitor. One man recounted with pride sending her directly through this field.

The general considered the facts. An unprepared, unequipped individual as the townsfolk had described would not likely have survived the journey to the next city, even if she'd known to head there directly. She must have found some manner of shelter before then. The only conceivable source, barring something within the tundra itself, was a small, poorly-kept place of worship. Trigorah approached it. There were horses and riders in front of it. As she drew nearer, she realized that she recognized the uniforms of the men assembled before the church as not merely Alliance Army, but her own Elite. Anger and confusion welling up in her, she spurred her horse forward.

"General Teloran!" piped one of the soldiers, offering a salute.

"At ease, what is the meaning of this? I left no orders for you. Why are you here?" Trigorah snapped.

"We've been assigned a temporary commander, General. Commander Arden," he replied.

"Arden? Stand aside, soldier," the general hissed.

Fury in her eyes, the general stalked inside. In the darkened interior of the church, near a door at the far end of the room, a massive man was clutching a frail, blindfolded old priest in one hand and an oddly elegant halberd in the other. The old man was fairly dangling from the aggressor's ham-sized fist.

"You seen 'im. I know you did!" he barked.

"Put him down!" Trigorah ordered.

The hulking man's head jerked in her direction.

"Don't in'erupt, Gen'ral. I know dis old man saw somfin," Arden growled.

"He hasn't seen anything, you imbecile! He is clearly blind!" Trigorah cried, yanking the helpless old man from his grip.

Arden considered this for a moment.

"That don't mean nothin," he decided.

"Father, if you will just take a seat in the other room, I will have a word with my . . . *associate* . . . and then I require a few words with you myself," Trigorah said diplomatically.

The priest gratefully felt his way to the door to his chamber and closed the door behind him.

"What the *hell* do you think you are doing with *my* men, *Arden?"* Trigorah fumed, pronouncing the thug's name in an almost mocking tone.

"You ain't doin yer job no more, they said, so they decided I oughta. Said somebody's gotta find the 'sassin, since you couldn't," he replied.

"I *found* the assassin's accomplice! *Someone* saw fit to *hire* him rather than imprison him," Trigorah replied.

"Uh-huh. And he did his job. Probably I wouldn't of had to get involved if he'da just been paid, but what do I care 'bout 'scuses?" Arden shrugged, adding. "Yer men follow orders good. I think I'll keep 'em."

Trigorah shuddered with anger.

"Huh-huh. Tell you what. You gotta find that sword, right? And I gotta find that 'sassin. What's say we make a wager? You find yer bounty first and I refuse to take yer men, even if they're offered," Arden suggested.

"And if you win?" she asked.

"You know what I want if I win," Arden replied.

The general's eyes narrowed.

"Don't flatter yerself, elf. I want what's in here," he said, attempting to poke Trigorah on the helmet only to have his hand knocked away. "I got a lot of questions, and I wanna be able to ask 'em in *my* way. And, naturally, I'll be hanging onto yer men."

After a moment, Trigorah offered her hand. Arden shuffled the halberd to under his arm, its blade swiping dangerously near to Trigorah's head, and shook her hand.

"Right. I'm off then. Have fun with yer priest," Arden said, plodding out toward the door and barking an order to the men outside.

Trigorah entered the priest's chambers. He was sitting in a large chair, strangely composed despite his recent ordeal.

"I apologize for the actions of Arden. They were inexcusable," Trigorah began.

"Mmm. And yet you work with him," the priest replied.

"Through no choice of my own, I assure you," General Trigorah said.

"Everything is a choice, my child. Some choices are made poorly. They can have terrible consequences," he replied coldly. "Tell me. Is that the sort that our glorious army sees fit to employ?"

"These are hard times . . . regardless, I again apologize. I shall endeavor to make my time here brief and leave you in peace," Trigorah replied.

"As you wish, though it is not often I am graced by the presence of a general. May I offer any hospitality?" he said, the realization of his current guest finally taking hold.

"Only answers, Father. Were you visited, perhaps two weeks ago, by anyone? Anyone out of the ordinary?" she asked.

"Mmm. You'd be after the girl, then, I suppose. What was her name now? Myranda. Myranda Celeste. A sympathizer," he recalled.

Trigorah hesitated for a moment when she heard the name.

"You are certain about that?" she asked.

"Quite sure. Up to some mischief, is she? Stirring things up?" he asked.

"So it would seem," Trigorah replied quietly.

"Mmm. I feared as much." He nodded.

"I don't suppose you were able to determine if she was carrying anything," Trigorah pressed.

"I imagine she had a pack. I heard the odd clink or thunk when she sat down. At least I think I did. It was quite a few days ago," he answered.

"Thank you. That is all. I appreciate your time," Trigorah said, turning to leave.

"Anything to lend a hand to the Alliance Army," the priest said as she closed the door and hurried out.

Trigorah's rigid, analytic mind clashed against these new developments, churning though them. Some she set aside for further study, others she tried push to the back of her mind. Not every fact had been a welcome one. One thing was for certain, though. The task at hand was now no longer simply a matter of duty. It was a matter of honor.

#

The first disruption to Myranda's comfortable routine came at the end of the first week. Just as she was heading up the stairs, a visitor came to the door. Three rounds of eager knocks had passed before Wolloff made it from his chair to the door.

"Finally," he said, pulling the door open to the familiar visitor. "I was beginning to think I was doing this for my health."

He took a pair of bags from the young boy at the door. As Wolloff hefted the bags and peered inside, the boy lingered, casting excited glances around the wizard.

"What's got you so antsy, boy?" he asked.

"Is she here? Myranda?" he asked.

"These bags seem a bit light, lad. Turn out your pockets," he said.

The boy heaved a sigh and did so. Wolloff inspected them, then grumbled about him finding a better hiding spot.

"Now what are you on about? Marna?" he asked.

"Myranda! She came here for training," he said.

"Oh, Aye. The girl. She has retired for the evening. Why?" he asked.

"I was hoping I could meet her. All of the other men are talking about her. She singlehandedly put the voice of the Undermine in everyone's ears and our name on everyone's tongues. She killed four so--" he gushed.

"Fine, fine. Spray your blasted hero worship in the girl's direction. DOWNSTAIRS NOW!" he bellowed.

Myranda came down quickly, having already learned that keeping Wolloff waiting was far from pleasant.

"This little urchin wants a word with you. Watch yourself. The brat has sticky fingers," he said.

She looked at the youngster at the door. There was something familiar about him. He was wearing a set of sparring pads, such as those worn by squires and apprentices in mock battle. Dirt had found its way, in large patches, to every piece of exposed skin. He couldn't be more than half of her age, and was overflowing with the misguided enthusiasm that such youth afforded. He offered his hand, and when she returned the gesture, he grasped it in a vigorous and continuous shake.

"Oof. Easy. The shoulder is still a bit sore," she said.

"Oh, right, the arm. From the fight. She told me! I can't believe I am meeting you! I'm Henry. And you . . . You are the one! You did it!" he blurted.

"Calm down. I am only a person" she assured him.

"Only a person!? Caya said, she's my sister, she said that it is your fault that all of these orders are flowing down from the top and, and messages are coming out so fast and so often that there isn't even time to use codes, and, and, we are learning where the higher up people are and what their names are and what they are doing and where troops are coming from, and, and that means that there are openings and that means that we can hit them and cause real damage! Not like we've been doing! We can really hurt them and that means we need all the people we can get, and she gave me a knife and this great armor and it is all thanks to you!" the young boy spouted, almost without breathing.

"Right, that will be enough, lad. Just run off and tell your sister that if any more of this silver finds its way into your grubby little mitts, I'll be asking for three bags next time," he said, ushering the boy out the door and slamming it shut.

"Saints alive! The mouth on that boy. His parents should have just dressed up a monkey and cut off its tail. At least then they would get some peace and quiet now and then. What on earth was that yammering about, anyway? Have I got a celebrity as a pupil?" he asked.

"I . . . seem to have become something of a rally call for the Undermine. The popular belief is that I stole an artifact from the army and eliminated the four soldiers sent to retrieve it. Now the highest levels are up in arms, which I suppose creates no end of openings for Caya and her people to attack," she said.

"Am I to take from your tone that you do not fit the role in which you have been cast?" he asked.

She shook her head slowly.

"I never killed those men. I only witnessed it, and even that was too much for me. I didn't steal any artifact. I found it on the body of a dead man and thought I could sell it. I never wanted any of this," she said.

"And how many people know that?" Wolloff asked.

"Only Caya, Tus, you, and whoever really did it," she said.

"Right, you keep it that way. If what you say is true, you've stumbled onto something that has finally gotten this group on its feet. It is therefore in all of our best interest that those who you have inspired continue to believe what they have been told," he said, nothing but earnestness in his voice.

"Do you really believe in this cause?" she asked.

"Not in the least. It is my honest belief that Caya and all of her high-minded dealings will be crushed underfoot at the earliest convenience of any detachment of the army. Nevertheless, this engagement with the Tressons must come to an end, and the sad truth is this: the pointless, flawed actions that the Undermine has taken are the only steps toward anything resembling peace in years," he said.

"There are movements toward peace. I am always hearing about missions of peace that are shunned by the south," she said, confused.

"Aye, you are always *hearing* about those things because that is what the propaganda mill is churning out. Don't be fooled, lass. They've got about as much truth to them as the yarn Caya is spinning about you. I spent many years in the direct service of many of the officials who are at this very minute wringing their hands over what to do about you. Not once in all of those years did I see, or even hear mention of, a single peace mission. Yet one step into the public and the tale of the latest diplomat slain at the peace table is on everyone's lips.

"The truth is this is a war without diplomats. A war without negotiation. And such a war can only end in annihilation. Worse, the decisions of the men and women who guide the fate of this alliance seem solely aimed at stalemate. I was released from my position when it was decided that it was simpler to replace a fallen soldier than restore a faltered one. Egad, do you realize that they've actually made it illegal to practice white magic in the service of anyone but the Alliance Army? Even Clerics and those wretched potion-making Alchemists are being shut down. They say it is to make certain that those most in need are treated first, but I cannot name *one* of my brother healers who has spent even a single tour alongside a front line soldier. And now even schools of magic are being pressured into dropping what little white magic they taught!" he raved.

"But why?" Myranda gasped.

"Your guess is as good as mine. Near as I can tell, they are trying to make sure people like the Undermine can't get treatment. Whatever the reason, the proclamations have been made. Since then, the healer's art has all but disappeared from our land. The only end that our leaders seem dedicated to is ruin, and indeed that may well be the only one that is possible for us. With that truth revealed, I made it my goal to bring us to that end swiftly, that from the ashes of our land there may arise something better," he said.

"I can't believe this . . . all of things I've heard about--the conferences . . . the meetings . . . the betrayals . . ." Myranda said numbly.

"Fiction. The only northerners the Tressons have met in decades are the ones they are clashing swords with," he said.

"But how? Why?" she managed through her struggling grasp of the latest revelation.

"Pride, stubbornness, honor, stupidity? Take your pick; it doesn't matter, the result is the same," he said.

His tone and composure were that of a man who had come to terms with these truths long ago. For the first time, Myranda began to understand the bitter, cruel exterior he had shown thus far. How could anyone who had learned what he'd learned in the way he'd learned it behave any differently? Wolloff grinned as he saw the look of pained realization come to her face as it had to his long ago.

"Sorry to burst your bubble, lass, but the truth is important. Unfortunately, wisdom and happiness are old enemies, and where one can be found, the other seldom lingers. You'd best get yourself upstairs. You've learned a bit more than I'd intended to teach today," he said.

She trudged upstairs, the lessons of the day washed away in a flood of pain and sorrow. As much as she had loathed this war, she'd always assumed that the one common desire of the world was to bring it to an end. Wolloff was right. There was no reason that could justify abandoning any hope of peace in favor of destruction. And what of the people of Tressor? Had they made pleas for peace that fell upon the unwilling ears of the North? So many questions, and no answers.

So troubled was she by the new knowledge, Myranda did not even notice Myn creeping in for her nightly visit. The little dragon had no way of knowing why Myranda was so dejected, but it was quite clear to her that this was so. She climbed onto the bed beside Myranda and stared into her eyes. A tear of anger and sorrow rolled down her cheek. Myn sniffed it, deciding immediately that she did not like it. She laid her head on Myranda's shoulder. The two did not stir until long after day finished its slip to night. Sleep came, but it was shallow and fitful, offering little in the way of rest and naught in the way of dreams. That, at least, was a blessing, as the images of darkness and desolation that invariably filled her dreams might just have been more than the disillusioned girl could bear.

It was not until the approaching footsteps of Wolloff stirred Myn to leave that the trance-like sorrow was broken.

"Morning, lass. Today we learn the last few runes for your cure, and the techniques to cast it," he said.

She pulled herself from the bed and eagerly set her mind to the task of learning--anything to push the poisonous thoughts from her mind. Myranda threw herself headlong into the process, and managed to memorize all that needed to be learned before midday.

"You are a person of many faults, lass, but slow to learn is not one of them," said the old wizard, in as near to a compliment as he had yet uttered. "Now it is time to learn how to cast your first spell."

"Learn to cast it? What have I spent the whole of this week doing?" she asked.

"Learning the spell," he said.

"But not how to cast it?" she wondered.

"No. Where is that spell book?" he said, looking over the cluttered table. He spotted the book Myranda had set aside--the one that contained the spell that bore her name. He flipped it open to that very spell. "There. It is a bit sloppier, but a passable spell. Read it. Only substitute this rune for this one to cast it on yourself."

She looked over the spell, but there was no need. With the exception of the last few runes, she had memorized it. The last pieces of the puzzle let her finally speak it aloud. Slowly, carefully, she pronounced every last word of the arcane phrase. As she spoke she felt a soothing warmth grow beneath the dull pain of her wound, but the moment she finished casting the spell, the warmth quickly faded, leaving the swollen wound as it had been.

"Not terribly effective, was it?" the wizard said with a knowing grin.

"No, it didn't last," she said.

"Didn't last?" he asked with the tiniest hint of surprise in his voice. "I'll wager you feel a bit tired now. Don't you."

"Well, more so," she said. The sleepless night had left her quite weary, but there was a different feeling, a deeper one, that came when she finished speaking the words. It lingered in the back of her head, like a yawn that wouldn't come.

"Exactly," he said. "It is because you lack focus. With the exception of the very best written of spells, the forces and spirits around us will take little notice of what you say. The words must be spoken, but past that, the spectral realm cares little if it is a whisper or a cry. It is the state of the mind that speaks the word that interests them. It is only when your mind is tightly gathered to the task that you are likely to be granted your whims in any meaningful way.

"Furthermore, magic is not free. Regardless of how you bring about the desired effect, you give a little of yourself. If you entreat a spirit, it will draw its payment from your own spirit. A focused mind satisfies their appetite far more swiftly and thus spares you much of the fatigue that would normally come. More importantly, not all of the forces of this world are benevolent. Many will attempt to take a far greater toll than is their right--or, worse, may take a more substantial payment that you are not willing or able to give. Focus protects you from such treachery."

"How do I focus?" she asked.

"Ah, therein lies the crux of the art of wizardry," he said.

He rummaged about on the cluttered table, gathering up all of the crystals before selecting a slightly cloudy, pale yellow gem.

"Give me your hand," he said.

She offered her left hand. Wolloff furrowed his brow at the odd scar before placing the gem in her hand and closing her fingers around it.

"Now, close your eyes and concentrate on the crystal. All that exists is my voice and the crystal. All other thoughts must be silenced. That crystal is very impure. It will grow warmer and glow as you devote more and more of your mind to it," he said.

It was no simple task to do as he said. The temperature of the crystal did change as she drew more of her mind toward it, but even the merest distraction dropped the piece to cold. There was no telling how long it had been before she was finally interrupted, but it must have been some time, because the shadows were casting differently than they had when she began. Her concentration had been broken when Wolloff snatched the gem from her hand. He had a stern look on his face.

"You wouldn't be trying to make a fool of old Wolloff, would you?" he asked, angrily.

"What do you mean?" she asked.

The wizard's face twisted briefly with concentration, the crystal taking on the same glow as a candle.

"You managed this degree of concentration," he said, the light wavering slightly as he spoke.

"I don't understand," she said.

"I've been at this since I was nearly your age. When I was learning what I have just taught you, I had to practice it for just shy of two months to achieve this degree of consistent concentration. In all of my years, I have met but a handful of colleagues that had done so more quickly than I. The fastest was my mentor, who managed it in two weeks. You've done it upon your first day of trial, and in *less than two hours!*" He growled.

"What have I done wrong? Why are you yelling?" she asked.

"Done wrong? You've wasted my time and your own by allowing me to teach you things you must already know!" he said.

"I didn't know anything, I swear! The only knowledge I have of magic is what you have taught me!" she assured him.

"We shall know for sure in a moment," he fumed, grasping his amulet.

Myranda quickly stood, knocking the chair down as she tried to back away. The wizard had a menacing look in his eye that chilled her to her spine. He spoke a string of mystic words, only a few of which were familiar. The spell was a mystery to her, save that the last few words targeted it upon her, and bound the effects to her flesh. Just as soon as the final word had left his lips, she felt the muscles in her arm clench tightly. All feeling left her fingers, and the numbness began to spread quickly up her arm. In a few moments, the arm hung loosely at her side. She tried to move it, but it would not obey, not even a twitch.

"What did you do?" she asked desperately, clutching at the lifeless arm.

"As if you don't know," he said.

Myranda's numbness spread, her panic spreading with it. Her right leg was quickly claimed and she was left unable to stand. Soon the whole of her right side was lifeless, and what little feeling she had left in the left side was draining away. By the end of a minute she was collapsed on the floor like a rag doll, utterly numb and scarcely breathing. Wolloff walked over to her, but she lacked even the control to focus her eyes on him. He leaned down to inspect her breathing, then slowly left the room.

She heard the door slip shut. He had left her. Hours passed with only her thoughts to keep her company. Her eyes offered only blurred blobs of color and light. She could hear clearly, but there was nothing for her to listen to aside from the passing breeze. All other senses were gone. The feeling of complete helplessness was maddening. She devoted every ounce of her apparently considerable concentration to moving even a single finger, but failed. The light blurs turned to dark ones before the footsteps could be heard returning.

"Right. I am quite convinced. Had you received the education I'd accused you of, you would certainly have learned to defend against a little hex like that," he said.

He swept his hand through the air and spoke a few words. Myranda instantly regained the feeling she was robbed of.

"And no one would allow such a spell to take effect if they could avoid it," he said.

"You could have just believed me," she said, pulling herself from the floor with much difficulty. Unbeknownst to her, the time on the floor had caused her muscles to cramp.

"I have a personal rule that has served me quite well in the past: never take at face value that which can be proved," he said, taking a clear, rose-colored gem from the table.

"Well?" she asked, hoping for an apology.

"Well take this. This gem has been fairly well-refined. It will aid your concentration. Take a few moments to pull your mind together, focus on the gem, then cast the spell again, as I told you to before," he said, as though the hours of paralysis he had caused had simply never occurred.

Myranda clutched the new gem. She ought to have known better than to expect him to make amends for his distrust. That didn't matter, though. She had a very important task at hand. Not only did she have the opportunity to rid herself of the crippling injury, but she was about to take the first real step toward becoming a healer. Without the warmth of the gem to guide her, it was difficult to know when she had reached the appropriate level of concentration. When she felt that her mind was similar to the way it had been that morning, she spoke the words.

Even the simple task of pronouncing the words was difficult to do without causing her mind to lose focus. Just as before, she felt a soothing warmth in her wound that served to distract her further. As the last few words were spoken, the warmth increased greatly.

"Right. You may relax now. Let the spell do its work," Wolloff said.

She let the outside world flow back in. Instantly, the strange weariness that she had felt before was back, and far stronger. She felt dizzy, and nearly fell off of her chair. Her arm, though, felt wonderful. The terrible pain she'd come to live with was replaced with a gentle tingle. She pulled up the sleeve and loosened the bandage. Before her eyes the redness and swelling subsided. In moments, the debilitating injury was returned to the state it had been in when she received it. A simple, albeit severe, gash. Much to her chagrin, though, it was there that the spell seemed to stop its work.

"Fine. That will be all for today," he said.

"Wait! What happened?" she asked, trying to stand. The dizziness that swirled in her mind forced her back into the chair.

"You cast the spell, the spell worked," he said, irritated by the need to explain the obvious.

"But my arm. It isn't healed," she said.

"No. The spell you cast was simply to remove the affliction that had been worsening the wound. The actual healing spell is quite different. We will begin learning that one tomorrow. It is significantly longer, and it contains a few runes that you have yet to learn. If you get your wits about you by the time I've made supper, we will work a bit after."

"Supper . . . you mean you don't expect me to prepare it?" she said.

"As entertaining as it would be to see you run in a screaming conflagration from my kitchen after falling face-first into the fire, I am in no mood to clean it up. Rest for a bit. When you've coordinated yourself enough to risk the stairs, you will find some of yesterday's dinner waiting for you," he said, taking his leave.

The young woman took his advice, though she'd hardly needed to be told. It was late afternoon, but it may as well have been midnight. As soon as he'd left, Myranda dragged herself to the bed and collapsed. This was the most bizarre weariness she had ever felt. Her body felt fine. It was neither sore nor weak. In truth, it was the first time in weeks that she could say she felt virtually no pain whatsoever. And yet she could barely move. It was as though she lacked the will to command her muscles.

Perhaps because of this, the sleep she yearned for simply would not come. Her mind badly needed it, but her body would not oblige. Instead, she remained in a daze for several hours, fully awake, but mentally drained. Finally, more out of boredom than refreshment, she opened her eyes to a darkened room. It must have become night only recently, as there was a bit of rosiness to the sky at the tip of the mountains. She wondered, as she gazed out, where her little dragon was. It was not like her to be gone much past sundown.

"Where could she be?" she asked to no one in particular.

The answer came in a swift and sudden manner. Myn's head appeared, peering down through the window from above. Myranda, startled by the unexpected appearance of her friend, stumbled backward. The dragon darted behind her, using her head to prop up the faltering girl.

"Thank you, Myn. I suppose I've not quite recovered yet. I feel quite a bit better, though," she said, feeling her way to the bed. She sat, the dragon leaping up to the bed beside her.

"So what have you been up to? Not only hunting, I hope. If you spend so much time hunting each day, the forest will be emptied by the time we leave," she said.

The dragon, enthralled by the sound of her voice, moved to Myranda's right side. When she had finished talking, Myn glanced at her right arm, sniffing at the injury. A look of confusion or curiosity came to her face as she took another smell and gave Myranda a questioning look.

"Oh, my arm. Yes. I learned to cast a spell, and now it is healing properly. Thank you for noticing," she said.

Myn seemed pleased, as though the smell of the tainted injury had been a source for concern for her, and its disappearance was a great relief. She gave her little reptilian version of a smile and lowered her head for the standard reward for a job well done. Myranda gave her the pat on the head she was hoping for with her vastly improved arm.

"I'll be right back. You've eaten your meal, but I've yet to have mine," she said.

Myn coiled herself up on the bed, watching Myranda open the door and carefully descend the stairs. If the stairs had been tricky before, navigating them in near darkness and while lightheaded was an entirely new experience. She made it to the base, thankfully in one piece, and found Wolloff reading by the firelight. On the table was a plate featuring the last of the roast and a few boiled vegetables. She sat down and ate quietly.

"It held up well," Wolloff said.

Myranda nodded in agreement.

"Perhaps you would like to take some up to your dragon," he said.

Myranda nodded again before realizing what had been said.

"What?" she said.

"That is who you were talking to, was it not?" he asked.

"You heard that?" she said.

"No, but now I know that I was right," he said.

Myranda sighed and swallowed hard. "How long did you know?" she asked.

"If you recall, I was there the first morning she showed up. Did you really think I wouldn't check to see if it had happened again?" he said. "You will find it very difficult to fool a wizard, lass."

"I am very sorry, but we have been together every day since she was born. I cannot keep her away. I assure you, she is very well-behaved. She has only breathed fire once and it was only because she was cold. If she--" Myranda hurriedly explained.

"Relax, lass, I would not be so foolish as to put the fate of my collection in the hands of an apprentice. You couldn't ignite a single page if you tried. The moment I saw that beast, I put a series of spells into effect. You can't even light a lamp up there without a word or two from me," he said.

"Why didn't you say something earlier?" she asked.

"It is just my way," he said, getting up and placing his book on the table. "So, do you feel up to learning a bit more tonight?"

"Not quite," she said.

"What a shame, because that is precisely what we are going to do," he said.

#

The following weeks brought much knowledge and little rest. Wolloff felt that, since she was gifted with a unique strength of mind, she ought to be pushed harder than his other students. In weeks she learned spells that had taken the other apprentices months to perfect. She could soon heal everything from a bruise to a broken limb to any number of diseases. He would see to it that she practiced nonstop until the spell was casting just as it should be.

Surprisingly, Wolloff more often than not provided the meals. He seemed to believe that her education was of the highest priority. Each morning would see a new spell taught and rest would not come until it had been cast. Each day followed the same routine--until one morning more than a month later. On that morning, Myn was acting strangely.

The dragon had continued to leave with the approach of morning, usually waking Myranda in the process. Something was different, though.

When Myn jumped to the floor, she sniffed at the air, clearly worried. She then climbed to the north window to gain a better sample of whatever scent it was that bothered her so. The little dragon was so distracted she did not even leave her station at the window when Wolloff entered.

"Oh, I see, we do not even do the old man the courtesy of pretending to follow the rules anymore, eh?" he said.

"Something is wrong. I think she smells something," she said, growing more and more concerned at the dragon's strange behavior.

"Do you have any idea how strong that snout of hers is? She *always* smells something," he assured her.

"Even so," Myranda said, straining her eyes on the horizon.

A sound, silent to the others, visibly shook Myn. She launched herself out of the window and ran to the north with a speed Myranda had never seen the little creature muster. There was something more than hunger driving her as she streaked through the snow. Myranda called out to her, but the dragon did not even turn.

"It is about time . . ." Wolloff said.

"This is not normal. Something is definitely wrong," she said.

"Oh, aye, but keeping a pet dragon in your bed with you every night is the very picture of normality," Wolloff said.

Soon Myn disappeared between the trees. Myranda turned to the wizard, who was about to begin the day's studies.

"I am serious. Something out there has got her attention like nothing else I've seen before. We've got to see where she's gone, and what she's gone after," she insisted.

"I do not see why--" he began.

"Please! You are a wizard. Surely you can do something to find out," she begged.

Wolloff looked at the desperate apprentice. Normally, he would be infuriated by the gall of a student interrupting her teacher, but looking into her eyes he saw naught but fear and worry. He heaved a frustrated sigh.

"I can see we are not likely to get anything done while this mystery stands," he said.

He gripped the amulet and spoke some arcane words. The crystal within began to glow.

"There is someone . . . a human . . ." he said, mumbling a few more words. "Aye, quite a few."

"Who are they? What do they look like?" she pleaded.

"I cannot actually see them. That would require a distance-seeing spell, and I have not cast such a spell in years. I am merely detecting their minds," he said, his next few comments scattered among lengthy pauses. "I can tell you that they are quite strong-willed. Not on the level of a wizard, or even you for that matter, though . . . I sense that they are looking for something. No, no they have found it. There is anger. Perhaps a . . . yes, a battle . . . There are fewer of them now . . . fewer still. Whatever they found is putting up quite a struggle."

"It could be Myn!" she said.

"Aye, it could be." He nodded. "I've focused the spell on the discovery of human minds. Whatever they have found, it is not human."

"Well, search for her! Search for Myn!" she demanded.

Wolloff clenched his eyes tighter to maintain concentration.

"This may come as a surprise to you, but seeking out a dragon's mind has not been of tremendous usefulness to me over the years. I would have to do a bit of research to discover that particular inflection," he said. "At any rate, it does not matter. The ill-intentioned invaders--or, at least, those that remain--are leaving. Right, back to work then."

Myranda reluctantly turned her mind to the task of learning again. She tried to imagine that Myn had just gone off for the day as she had for weeks before. It was no use, though. She could not pull her mind from the worry she felt. Her spells fizzled and failed. Even spells she had mastered in her first days of learning were beyond her ability. Finally, Wolloff grew frustrated.

"Right. That is all for today then," he said.

"I am sorry. I am just . . . I can't stop thinking about Myn. She could be in trouble," she said.

"Aye, could be, and probably is. She is probably flayed open on the side of a road, but that is of little consequence. You are to be a white wizard. The tragedies of the world must cease matter to you," he said.

"How dare you! My friend could be hurt. That will always matter to me. A healer should have compassion," she said.

"Caya sent you so that you could learn to heal the injured. To that end, you've shown tremendous potential, but mere potential means nothing. What matters is performance. Life would be wonderful if we were only asked to perform in the most pleasant of conditions, but the truth is that it in those places a healer is useless. If you are to be helpful at all, you will need to be treating men and women torn apart at the seams. Soldiers screaming in pain. Faces you may recognize shrouded in a crimson mask of blood--or, worse, faded white as a ghost with death's claws about them. At times you will not have the opportunity or resources to give help to all who need it. You will have to decide who must die and who can live. What good will you be if the imagined fate of a blasted meaningless creature renders you helpless? You are useless!" he proclaimed.

Wolloff rose from his seat and opened the door to leave. He slammed it angrily behind him as Myranda turned back to the window. She was shaken by his words. Their truth had struck her to the core. Casting the spell with nothing on the line was difficult enough, but to attain the necessary state of mind while a life hangs in the balance? Impossible. The emotions could not be pushed aside.

Perhaps the true test of a wizard was the art of detachment. Whenever tales of a wizard were told to her, they were cold and unfeeling, minds set solely to task. A part of her yearned to be free of the burden of her emotion--but in her heart, she recoiled at the thought. The image of herself showing anger and disdain in place of compassion and concern turned her stomach. Such a fate was worse than death. To deny her heart now would be to turn a deaf ear to it forever, and right now it was telling her that her friend needed help.

She marched down the stairs, her course of action clear.

"And what are you up to?" Wolloff asked mockingly.

"I am going to help Myn," she declared.

"And how do you suppose you will find her?" he asked.

"I don't know," she said, donning her worn cloak and tattered boots.

"Well, off with you, then. I have taught you the basics, and it was that which I was paid to do. My conscience is clear. You, however, ought to bear one thing in mind. Caya has invested a tidy sum and she is expecting a healer in return. How will she feel when I tell her that her new mascot and only healer has frozen to death seeking to rescue a beast from a danger that is not even certain?" he said.

Myranda gave him a long, hard stare, considering his words. Finally, she opened the door and set off into the cold. A single look at the sky and whiff of the air assured her that she could not have chosen a worse time to venture into the woods alone. As was the curse of the north, snow had come at least once a week for the whole of her time in Wolloff's tower. Most were light flurries, but some brought with them wind and cold sufficient to endanger any creature that could not find shelter. Today would be such a day. A stiff breeze foreshadowed the harsh winds that would be tearing at her face within the hour.

The sharp slicing of Myn's claws into the snow left a clear path to follow, but the rising wind was quickly wiping them away. Racing against time, Myranda trudged through the snow, knee-deep at times, as quickly as her legs could manage. She ignored the savage burning of the wind in her eyes, knowing that if she lost sight of the trail for even a moment, she might never find it again. All the while, she kept her left hand clenched angrily about the front of her cloak, holding it closed and squeezing at the mark that had brought her such misfortune, as though if she punished it enough it would release her from its accursed grasp.

The shadows lengthened as she trudged onward. Long ago, the prints had been wiped away. She moved now on hope alone. For once, luck did not fail her. Ahead, she found a patch of snow stained red by the blood beneath it. The patch stood out against the stark white that surrounded it. The snow, blown about by the savage wind, had faded but not erased the remains of the battle that Wolloff had described. It must have been a terrible one. Though she could not be certain, the half-hidden footfalls scattered about the clearing seemed to have belonged to a half-dozen or so men.

Four did not live to see the end of the battle. The bodies must have been taken; in their places, helmets had been left, hung atop swords stuck into the earth in the center of the bloody spill that marked their end. The helms were elaborate, iron with dark blue enamel covering the whole surface, save a few areas that bore gold detailing. Rising from the peak was a white plume that looked to be horse hair.

"So they were soldiers," she said through wind-burned lips.

She searched the ground with her eyes, but there was no sign of Myn having even been there. The telltale dimples in the snow left by the soldiers' horses all led almost directly to the north. Myranda, with nowhere else to go, followed them. If Myn had not reached them before the battle had ended, then she might have met them further on.

It was not long before she found the site of a different battle. More blood spilled, and a single helmet, left seemingly out of carelessness rather than memorial. Beside the blood-spattered helmet was a deep furrow left by the spirited movements of a creature's claws. Further on, there was a deep pit in the snow, almost to the ground, that bore its own stain, though this blood was of a thicker, darker variety. Precisely the kind that was left in the wake of the elder dragon's rampage. There was no doubt. It was Myn's.

"No!" Myranda cried out.

She threw herself into the snow, digging her fingers into the windblown flakes just as the first crystals of the long impending storm began to fall. Myranda stood. The pit was empty. Squinting, she made out a tiny speck of red, followed by another, and another. She followed the trail of drops to its end. There she found the prone, motionless form of the little dragon. She was cold to the touch, nearly as cold as the snow that half buried her. Two vicious injuries marred her hide, clearly the cause of her collapse. Myranda dropped to her knees and placed her ear to the dragon's chest. There was the weakest thump of a struggling heart to be heard. The tiniest whisper of life, the smallest glimmer of hope.

Myranda analyzed the wounds. There was a horrid gash running along her neck and down her side, cleaving whole scales and clotted with sticky, near-black blood. The second injury was smaller, a notch cut into her crown scale. The thick protective piece of armor had done its work. Only a trickle of blood escaped the wound left by a blow that would have killed a lesser creature.

The novice healer prepared to make use of her fresh knowledge. Suddenly her heart dropped as she realized her carelessness. A crystal! She'd forgotten to take one! She had never been able to cast a spell without one. There was no time to lose though. If she delayed for even a moment, she could lose her friend forever. She placed her hands on the dragon's neck. The creature's unique blood burned at her fingers, but she ignored it. Her mind needed silence for the spell to work. Every thought had to be washed away to provide a trance deep enough to allow her words to reach the ears of those forces that could put them to reality. The lack of a crystal made it difficult, but the high emotions made it near impossible.

She tried, and tried, but she couldn't manage to ignore the fear and sorrow she felt for the only creature that cared for her. Tears flowed from her eyes and stung her cheeks as the flood of powerful emotions fought back. The harder she tried to focus, the more she thought of the danger her friend was in. Her mind swirled, but she could not relent. The feelings intensified until she could not bear it. Finally, she spoke the arcane words. If she could not draw the strength from calm focus, then she had no choice to try to draw it from the maelstrom in her mind.

The words began to do their work, though weakly. Slowly she felt the gash begin to close beneath her fingers, but not completely. She spoke the words again, and again. Each speaking brought the wound closer to disappearing, and brought Myranda closer to collapse. The last trickle of the blood escaped the wound as the apprentice wizard finally passed the breaking point, falling forward. Large, icy flakes of snow began to fall with all of the force of a blizzard as the world faded from her view.

#

In the city of Nidel, General Trigorah pored over her notes of the weeks gone by. Progress had been slow, painfully slow. Her duties had required her to track the path of the sword and those who may have contacted it. To that end, she'd been quite successful. Indeed, in front of her was a description of the very weapon she sought, provided by an elderly weapon shop owner who had agreed to buy it. The last of the prospective witnesses had been identified, and their current whereabouts noted.

Every last story that there was to hear had been heard, and the last of the truth was being gleaned from them. There was the strong indication, though not the certainty, that Myranda . . . that the *target* had been in possession of the weapon when she left the weapon shop, but not when she had arrived in the town of Nidel, and certainly not when she had been captured.

It was here that things had ceased to fit together. There was the church. Trigorah knew her target to visit places of worship when seeking shelter. There had been a church, burned, and four soldiers killed. That didn't make sense. Why burn the church? To hide evidence? Perhaps, but the remains of the soldiers, some of Demont's men, were left for all to find, when they could easily have been thrown among the flames. If evidence *was* being destroyed, it was evidence of some other crime.

From the descriptions of her target, it seemed highly unlikely that she would have been capable of defeating four soldiers. And then there was the fact of her escape. The carriage was burned. More fire . . . but this time well-used. Aside from requiring that the girl be captured as well as the sword, the escape made it clear that she could not have been working alone. No, there was another hand at work here.

As she stared at the totality of the information, a solution stared back at her. All of this had a familiar ring to it. A color . . . a texture to the events that she'd become sensitive to. She knew that the assassin had been sent for the sword, and that he likely still held it. That much was not a mystery. The mystery was where he could be found, and it was one of which she'd spent decades frequently in the pursuit of a solution.

She didn't have the time for that. She needed progress quickly. Some sort of step forward. The reports of the escape held clues. The horses were missing. The armor was missing. There had been looting. Not unheard of, save for the destruction of the black carriage. That was an act of vengeance. Only one group sought weapons, armor, and revenge. The Undermine. Trigorah stood and stalked out to her waiting Elites.

"Saddle up, men. We are heading east," she ordered.

#

The first rays of the sun stirred the two travelers. They were both near-frozen, spared a complete blanket of snow only by their proximity to a thickly-needled pine tree. Great mounds of the white stuff surrounded the tree and buried the lower third of their bodies. Myranda managed to get her numbed limbs beneath her and roll off of Myn. Even after being healed, Myn had lost too much blood to last the long, cold night alone. She would have surely died if not for the impromptu blanket in the form of the unconscious body of Myranda. The dragon hoisted herself to her feet and released a mighty blast of fire. Instantly, the warm blood surged through her body, bringing new life to cold muscles. A second blast brought her strength and comfort back to normal.

The brief blasts of warmth that Myn had created did little to restore feeling to Myranda's icy fingers. She gathered together the only wood available, green boughs broken free by the powerful wind. Some of the snow was pushed aside to provide an appropriate place to start the fire, but she knew that she had little chance of sparking a flame. She had no tools to do so, and the fresh wood would be slow to light. The cold had robbed her of nearly all dexterity, and she knew that if she didn't get feeling back into her legs soon, she never would. She looked pleadingly to Myn.

"Fire. Please understand me, Myn. Just this once I need fire," she said.

The dragon looked back innocently.

"Here, feel. Heat does not return so easily to me as it does to you," Myranda said, placing a hand on Myn's neck.

The little creature pulled away from her icy touch and glared at the offending limb. She traced the arm back to Myranda's face, then back at the hand. When she looked to her face again, there was understanding dawning in the young creature's eyes.

"Yes, yes. I am very cold, I need fire," she begged again.

Myn's chest puffed up as she made ready to blast a third column of flame directly at Myranda. She pulled quickly away.

"No, no! Not me! There! The wood!" she said, gesturing desperately.

Myn furrowed her brow as she looked doubtfully at the wood. When she looked to Myranda again, she saw the face reserved for when she has done something right, so she knew what to do. A blast of fiery breath directed at the wood did in a moment what would have taken ages for Myranda to do. She held her hands over the fire as Myn sat next to her in the warm glow.

"Well, Myn. I suppose this makes us even. I have saved your life, and you've saved mine. Once I get a bit more feeling in these frost-nipped digits, I will give you the reward I know you are waiting for. I am going to give you the best scratching you've ever had," she assured her friend.

After a few minutes a strong tingling came to her nearly frostbitten fingers. Though it was painful, she welcomed it, as it meant her hands had not been damaged by the cold. As soon as the painful sensation subsided enough, she gave Myn what she wanted. The dragon drank in the joy as her companion stroked lovingly at her head. In truth, through the thick scales, she could barely feel it, but she loved it just the same.

Myranda continued to indulge her friend until her hand was exhausted. Even so, the dragon looked at her as though she was a criminal for stopping. Her offense was short-lived, as a sound and a scent drew her attentions to the woods. She was off in a flash. Myranda had managed to take most of the chill from her body by the time Myn came back with what had been a moderately sized wild turkey.

"That is quite a catch! What are you going to do with all of that . . . oh . . . oh my . . ." she said, turning away from the gruesome answer to her question.

The powerful jaws of the dragon, who just minutes before had been as gentle and loving as a kitten, now made short work of the prey, tearing great pieces of meat away and eating them in greedy gulps without chewing. A few more swallows and the bird, bones and all, had all but disappeared. It was this seldom-seen side of her friend that disturbed her. She often forgot that the dragon was a wild animal. When the snapping and crunching had ended, Myranda ventured a peek at the very satisfied creature. The dragon licked the stray drips of blood from her maw with a few deft swipes with her long tongue.

"You've something to learn in the way of table manners," Myranda said.

She looked at the odd scattering of leftovers from the primal meal. As disgusted as Myranda was at the spectacle of the creature eating, it had not been enough to make her forget that she hadn't eaten the day before. She smirked. In the past it was not at all uncommon for her to skip a day or two between meals. The opportunities to eat were often few and far between. Her time in this rather austere place of learning had managed to spoil her nonetheless, as she had become accustomed to the luxury of a daily meal.

The smile faded from her face as she turned her eyes to the south. It had taken the hours from noon to nightfall to find this place, and that was on a good night's sleep and with fear speeding her stride. The return trip would take twice as long, even ignoring the thick blanket of fresh snow.

The hungry girl's gaze turned to the leftovers beside Myn once more. Among the mangled feathers and other debris was a shred of meat. Myranda plucked it from the snow and, in a decision motivated more by hunger than good sense, deemed the sorry morsel edible. By the time she had stripped away the feathers and other less than appetizing parts from the meat, it was barely enough to fill her palm. She skewered it on a pine bough and held it over the fire. Myn watched her friend with her usual curiosity before disappearing into the woods once more.

"Don't stray too far," she said more to herself than the dragon. "After this mouthful is savored we need to head back to Wolloff's."

With a bit of time to spare while the meat heated, she let her mind wander. The spell she'd managed to cast had muddied her thoughts more than a night collapsed in freezing cold could repair. The lingering cobwebs led her mind in slow, meandering circles around a fleeting concern. Something about the battleground she'd passed through to reach this place. It didn't seem like Myn was involved in that first clash . . . but someone must have been. Someone who could take four well equipped soldiers before . . . before what? And why were there soldiers in Ravenwood to begin with?

The smell of burning food brought her thoughts back to reality. It seemed she had daydreamed just long enough for her food to leap from one side of edibility to the other. The meager chunk of meat was now a charred piece of sinew dangling from the end of the stick. Left with little recourse she took the piece into her hand and surveyed it with a frown before trying her best to gnaw off a bite to choke down. It was like chewing on leather. The crunching footsteps of Myn's return made her decide that it was better to go without than to risk whatever damage she might do to her stomach by swallowing the shriveled wreck. As if to add insult to injury, Myn carried with her another fresh kill.

"Another one?" Myranda said with a frown, spitting the taste from her mouth and tossing the glorified piece of charcoal aside. "Aren't you full yet?"

The dragon marched up and dropped her prize in front of Myranda.

"What are you doing? If you are going to eat it take it over there. I don't want to see that sight again," she requested.

The dragon just nudged the meal a bit closer with her snout and plopped down, staring expectantly at Myranda.

"Is . . . Is this for me? You little angel!" she proclaimed, throwing her arms about the Myn's neck and hugging her warmly.

The little dragon reveled in the attention, even after the hug had ended, as Myranda rained loving praise down on her while she prepared the meat. Just the sound of Myranda's voice brought joy to her heart. It was, after all, the first sound she had heard in life, and to hear it lifted by happiness and gratefulness was more than enough payment for services rendered.

Getting the turkey ready to eat without the aid of a knife proved to be quite a task, one further complicated by arms and legs still clumsy from a night in the freezing cold. Soon enough, though, she was savoring the tantalizingly fresh meat. She pulled whatever parts seemed warm enough to eat away and eagerly devoured them while the rest of the bird cooked. Before long, she had taken the edge from her hunger and then some. She was shocked by how good it was. Even the meals she ate at Wolloff's were generally composed of meat that was far from its prime. This was a meal fresher than even a king could enjoy. A final bite convinced her that the age-old phrase was wrong. Eat like a king? Ha! Eat like a dragon! She threw the leftover meat to Myn, who snapped it up quickly.

"Well, now. We have slept. We have eaten. Let us be on our way!" she said.

Her legs were the things most affected by the long cold night and did not serve her quite as well as she would have liked. She nearly fell to the ground twice while kicking snow onto the fire to extinguish it. As a result, she had to stick to traveling where the snow was thinnest, taking wide circles around the now-towering drifts that the blizzard had dumped into her return path. Luckily, the snow was thick and heavy, with only the top few inches thin enough to sink into. Otherwise, even the shallow valleys between drifts would swallow her up to her waist. After a few minutes of walking, her legs finally seemed to remember how to handle the snow, and walking became less of a conscious affair. It only then that she noticed how Myn was acting.

The usually jovial beast seemed more and more spiritless with each passing moment. Her tail, normally alive with twisting and curling, hung down behind her, dragging a faint line in the snow. Every few steps she would draw in a long, slow breath through her nose and look about longingly. Myranda grew concerned. Myn had never acted this way before. For all appearances, she seemed to miss someone. But who?

"What is it, little one? Who do you miss? Was it the one the soldiers were fighting?" Myranda asked.

The duo was passing through the site of the first battle. The snow was much deeper, with only the very tops of the grave markers visible. Myranda lifted a helmet from one of the improvised memorials and showed it to the dragon.

"Did these men take it from you, the thing you miss so much?" she asked, showing Myn.

The beast's eyes locked onto the armor piece, fury burning behind them. She clamped onto the helmet with her teeth and shook it viciously. Her teeth scraped at the intricate enamel and the pressure of her jaws dented and bent the thick metal plates. She continued to thrash it about while walking until she came to a seemingly random patch of snow. She dropped the helmet and pawed at the fresh white powder madly.

"What are you doing?" Myranda asked, further confused by her companion's strange behavior.

More than two feet of digging later, the snow took on a pink tint. She buried her snout in it and inhaled deeply. After a second sniff she raised her head again, sorrow behind her eyes. She offered a long, soulful call, halfway between a howl and a moan. It was the first sound that Myranda had heard the dragon make, aside from a few hisses and grumbles. This was different. There was a voice behind it, pouring out sorrow. This was not just a mindless creature. This was a thinking, feeling being.

After a pause, with her head hung low, she locked her gaze on the helmet again. Puffing out her chest, she unleashed a burst of flame longer and hotter than Myranda had ever seen her muster. She then snatched the blackened and sizzling piece of armor out of the wet pit of melted snow and continued to gnaw and shake it, as though she was punishing it for her sorrow. Even when they began walking again, she continued her catharsis.

#

The sky was rosy with sunset when the two found their way to the door of the tower. No doubt due to some mystic meddling, the building and the area around it seemed wholly unaffected by the night of snowfall. Myn was fairly exhausted from her wrestling with the helmet, but refused to release it from her mouth. When Myranda pushed the door wearily open, she was greeted by a slow, deliberate clapping from Wolloff.

"Congratulations, lass. You risked your life, passed out, and nearly starved and froze, but you managed to bring back a meaningless animal safely," he said.

Myranda came inside, stomping the snow from her boots.

"And what is this?" he asked, shocked at what he saw.

"What?" Myranda asked, looking down.

Myn had followed her inside and positioned herself between Myranda and Wolloff. She dropped the helmet heavily to the floor and bared her teeth in a fearsome snarl.

"I draw the line at letting the beast use the front door," he said angrily.

"Well, tell her so," she said, in no mood to apologize.

"I am not the one that trained her," he said.

"Neither did I," came her reply. "She was only a few days old when I came to you and if I had been training her since then, I think you might have noticed."

"Then how did you get her to bring that food back for you? Don't tell me you just asked," he said.

"No, I didn't even ask her. She did it on her own . . . How did you know about that? Did you follow me?" she asked.

"No. Distance-seeing. While you were off on your fool's errand, I looked up the appropriate spell so that I could keep an eye on you. You were only a day or so away, so it was child's play. You say that the dragon decided to bring you food of its own accord?" he said, eying the creature curiously.

"She did," Myranda said.

Wolloff rubbed his chin as he looked at the dragon, who looked as though she would tear him to pieces if he took a step closer. He reluctantly allowed Myn to stay inside, with the stipulation that she behave herself. Myranda assured him that she would so long as he did the same. When Myn was satisfied that Wolloff was of no real concern, she fetched the mangled helmet, brought it to Myranda's feet, and commenced the destruction.

"You brought that from the battleground, as I recall," he said.

"Yes," she said.

"It--what's left of it, that is--looks like an Alliance helmet. A fancy one at that. I must remember to inform Caya. Troop action this far north is rare, and this deep in the forest is rarer still. I don't like it," he said.

There was very little instruction that night, with Myranda retiring gratefully to her bed soon after he prepared a meal for her. Evidently Wolloff felt that her experiences in rescuing the beast were lesson enough.

#

The weeks that followed passed much as those before had--with one notable exception. Myn, who was protective before, was now overprotective and always by her side. For the first two weeks, she didn't leave Myranda for even a moment, not even to hunt. She was worried for her health, but Wolloff dubiously assured her that after a big meal, a dragon could go months before eating again. In time, the dragon did leave, but only long enough to satisfy her hunger. At all other times, she was with Myranda, chewing and clawing at the helmet and watching Wolloff like a hawk.

The first order of business in terms of instruction was the addition of a spell that could be of greater use to her than any she had learned to date. It was more difficult to cast and was not always appropriate, but given enough time to do its work, the spell could heal even the direst of wounds. Wolloff called it the healing sleep, a spell that put the recipient into a deep slumber and drew upon their own spiritual strength to continuously cure whatever damage or disease was ailing the body. Myranda had difficulty testing such a spell. She could not use it on herself, and Wolloff would certainly not allow her to test it on him. She did cast it on Myn once, with great success. Unfortunately, the creature, upon waking, made it quite clear she did not like being forced into sleep, likely remembering when Wolloff had done it when they first met.

It was just past the end of the third month of training, the midpoint, before they were interrupted again. Spring should have come, but this far north, and in the Low Lands in particular, the only indication of this was a sprinkle of rain mixing with the snow occasionally. Such a storm was passing through toward the end of the daily training session in the tower when a commotion could be heard in the main room down stairs. The sound alone was enough to put Myn on guard.

"Wait here. I will see what has happened," Wolloff instructed.

The wizard clutched the amulet and cautiously descended the stairs. Myranda waited anxiously at the top of the flight, Myn standing rigidly in front of her, still clutching the chewed-up helm in her teeth. After an eternity of silence, Wolloff's voice rang out from below. It was filled with desperation and concern.

"Come quickly!" he yelled.

She rushed down the stairs. When she reached the bottom, she was met with a terrible sight. It was Caya. The once proud warrior was at death's door. Blood was dried over a dozen wounds, and still ran from a half-dozen more. She looked as though she had ridden the whole night through without rest, soaked to the skin from the freezing rain and muttering, as though she had something important to say, but no words would come.

Myn looked over the battered woman. Normally she would view any human as a threat to her precious friend, but somehow she seemed to know that this was different. This was serious.

"I will tend to the more serious wounds. You put her into the healing sleep," Wolloff ordered.

Caya put her hand on the wizard's shoulder.

"No sleep!" she commanded. "No time."

The two healers did their best to close the wounds and undo the damage that had been done. As her strength began to return, Caya spoke.

"They came, they came from the south. Elites. We didn't have time! We were unprepared! How could we be prepared? The Elites are after the Red Shadow, not the Undermine! They haven't been in the Low Lands for over a year! It must be a second squad. It must be! And they are coming. They are coming for you, Myranda," Caya said, almost in a daze.

Myranda let the words enter her ears, but paid them no mind. There was a job to do. Everything else had to wait. She focused her mind around the crystal and chose the appropriate spells, casting them with equal care. The dutiful healer kept at it, making sure that every last wound was closed before she let the things that had been said enter her mind.

"What is going on? Who are the Elite?" she asked.

Caya rubbed her restored legs.

"The Elites. They are the very best of the old guard. A soldier who survives a dozen battles is a veteran. Two dozen is a legend. When a man passes into the realm of myth, he is made a member of the Elite. To form a second squad to find you, you must be worth more to them than even I had thought," Caya explained.

Myranda's head was spinning. Some of it was due to the effort of casting the spells. Mostly it was the harsh reality that was crashing down around her. She had only vaguely heard of the Elites, but she shuddered to think of the man they sought. The Red Shadow. The assassin. How could she have done something to become as highly sought as he without knowing it? The man had killed colonels, barons, ambassadors! All she had done was find a sword!

"They dismantled the headquarters. Barely escaped with my life. Lost three good men. They will be here in hours. We need to evacuate," Caya said.

"Evacuate! We cannot evacuate! What of my books!?" Wolloff said.

"Leave them!" she demanded.

"I will not!" she said.

"You must choose between your books and your life," she said.

"My books *are* my life!" he proclaimed, no hint of humor in his voice.

"I cannot afford to lose you, Wolloff. Move now! Time is wasting!" she commanded.

"The books are irreplaceable. They are one of a kind. If I lose them now, the knowledge within them will be lost forever. You say that you cannot afford to lose me, but it is my knowledge of these books that you need. *I will not leave them!"* Wolloff said.

The two strong-willed individuals launched into a simultaneous debate, both unwilling to wait for the other to finish talking. Myn became agitated, baring her teeth and scratching at the floor, ready to take action if the argument became anything more. The sound of the helmet dropping to the floor drew Caya's attention.

"Where did this beast come from?" Caya demanded.

"She belongs to Myranda. Keep your hands away from her mouth," Wolloff said.

"And the helmet? Where did she find it?" she asked.

"Some time ago, there were some soldiers to the north of here. The beast had a run-in. What does it matter?" he said.

"That is certainly an Elite helmet! They came so near to you and I was not *alerted!"* she cried out.

Immediately the two started yelling again. As the endless arguing raged, Myranda's mind was working quickly. There had to be some sort of solution. Slowly an idea revealed itself. It was not a perfect one, but time allowed for little else.

"Wait!" Myranda yelled.

The two turned to her.

"If we ran. All of us. Right now. What would we do?" Myranda asked.

"There is a safe house to the northeast. We would head for that. Then I would contact some of our field agents to gather enough intelligence to make a decision where to go next," Caya said.

"And how would we get there?" Myranda asked.

"With a lot of legwork and all of the luck in the world, we just might make it there with our lives," she said.

"Then we stand to gain little by running, at least together," Myranda said.

"What are you suggesting?" Wolloff said.

"They want *me,* right? In fact, you just might have been left alive simply to lead them to me," Myranda said.

"I had considered that," Caya said.

"Then if they find me, they will look no further," she said.

"No!" Caya said. "We need you. I won't let you turn yourself in to save us. If you do that, you seal our fate more surely than their swords ever could."

"I am not suggesting that I give myself to them. I just want them to find me. We have one horse. Yours. These men are in full armor and are likely well-equipped, am I correct?" she offered.

"Very well-equipped. It might be weeks before they need to resupply," Caya said.

"Then they are weighed down. If I go with no supplies and no armor, then I can certainly outrun them. All I need to do is let them see me, and then lead them away," she said.

"But where will you go? The safe house? Myranda, the Undermine is in chaos after this attack. If you hope to find any sanctuary, I must be with you, or you will never be trusted," Caya said.

"No safe house. If I take refuge with your people, then this will only happen again. Maybe in weeks, maybe months, but it will happen. I refuse to have my life be a burden upon you. Do you have a map?" she asked.

"Of course," Wolloff said, revealing one and spreading it on the table, knocking the contents to the floor.

"We are here, correct?" Myranda asked.

The two others nodded in unison.

"Then it can't be more than two days at full gallop to the eastern forest, Locke's Forest," she said.

"No horse, not even mine, could spend two hours, let alone two *days* at full gallop. The poor thing is dead on her feet as it is," the Undermine leader warned.

"I've learned a few spells that should keep her moving," Myranda said.

"Mmm. Full gallop . . . day and night . . . with no equipment . . . Perhaps you could make it in two days," Caya conceded.

"Do the soldiers patrol Locke's Forest well?" Myranda asked.

"They patrol it constantly," she answered.

"But do they patrol it *well?"* Myranda asked again.

"That forest is a quarter the size and has at least as many trees as this one. I would wager to say there aren't enough soldiers in the world to patrol something that dense *well,"* she said.

"Then that is where I will go," she said. "I have Myn. She can hunt and start fires. I need no supplies to live. The forest is dense. If I stay alert, I *know* I can stay away from them."

"Are you certain you want to do this? These are Elites. They will not give up. They *will* find you," Caya warned.

"There can be no other way," she said.

"Very well, then. I will tend to the horse. Wolloff, give her anything she needs," Caya ordered.

"I have precious little for myself, you know," Wolloff said.

"Now is not the time for selfishness, Wolloff. You will be reimbursed when the Undermine gets back on its feet," she said.

"The Undermine has never *been* on its feet," he said. He turned his head and looked unhappily at Myranda. "Come, time is wasting."

He led Myranda through the door that had not opened since she had arrived. Unlike the other rooms, this one was meticulously clean. One side was much like a closet, hung with white robes like the one he wore. The other had numerous exquisite amulets and scepters. He carefully pulled a robe from the many and smoothed the wrinkles. He then selected a small, delicate locket. Finally he uncovered a small, sturdy chest that bore a lock, but no means to open it. He whispered a word or two and the works of the lock clicked open. Inside of the chest was a handful of gems far clearer and much larger than any to be found upstairs. A few more words and the locket unfolded like a flower blooming. He placed the gem inside. It clicked shut of its own accord.

"Put this on," he said, holding out the robe.

She slid her arms through and pulled it shut. He then draped the locket about her neck.

"There. I bestow upon you the white robe of the healer. You know all that you need to undo the work of all but the most monstrous of plights. This locket will aid your focus. You hold the distinction of being the only student I have ever had to reach this level in less than five months--you've done it in three. Congratulations, you've set the bar quite high," he said.

Caya returned, slamming the door.

"Wolloff, you are low on oats, barely enough for Wind Runner. Myranda, to the map. You need to plot out a course of action. This will be no normal chase. You need alternatives for every step of the way," she decreed.

Myranda joined her by the table. They proceeded to trace out the course. It would be more or less a straight ride from forest to forest. There was a scattering of towns that would have to be avoided. Caya spoke in an endless string of orders and dictation. She was clearly a strong leader and knew just how to get things done. It was difficult to believe that minutes ago she was near death. Her devotion was admirable.

"What of the beast?" Caya said.

"Pardon?" Myranda replied.

"The dragon. We've yet to enter her into the equations. The success of your escape depends upon a minimally encumbered mount. The creature could add enough weight to give the Elites a chance to close the gap when my horse begins to tire," Caya said.

"I have seen the beast run. She will keep up on her own," Wolloff said.

"Fine. But I want to make this absolutely clear. If she falls behind you *will* leave her. Sentiment is death on the battlefield," she said.

Myranda assured her that she would, but in her heart she knew she couldn't. She prayed that she would not have to make that decision.

#

Within the hour the freshly anointed healer was astride the horse and headed toward the Elite, Caya's voice still in her ears. She was to turn east with all of the speed that the steed could muster at the very instant she noticed even a hint of the plume atop the helmet of an Elite. Until then there was nothing to fill her time but a tense wait, and a few simple spells to restore her horse for the run. When she'd whispered the final spell, admiring the relative ease that new amulet provided, she turned to her companion. Myn sat on the ground beside her, still bearing the helmet in her teeth.

"Are you going to carry that with you for the entire trip? We will have to move very quickly. I hope you can keep up," she said, eager to break the silence.

As an answer, Myn's head shot up. She smelled the air and stood, dancing about anxiously. Myranda saw nothing, and heard only the tapping of icy rain on the needles of the trees. She climbed down from the horse and put her ear to the cold ground. Faintly, almost silently, she could hear-- or, more accurately, feel--the steady beat of dozens of hooves. Myn scampered up a tree and trained her eyes on the south. Her keen sight must have caught something between the trees. Something she hated. The dragon leapt to the ground and streaked southward.

"Myn, *no!*" Myranda called out.

Her faithful friend skidded to a stop, and looked to her pleadingly, her eyes fairly begging to be allowed to do what her heart demanded of her, to get revenge on those that had taken something dear from her. Myranda looked her in the eyes.

"Myn, we cannot. Not now. Follow," she said.

Reluctantly the dragon returned to her side, clamping her jaws onto the helmet as a replacement target. Myranda watched the trees in the distance.

Soon the sound of hooves was booming in her ears. She wanted to run, but she had to be sure that they followed her, and did not continue on to Wolloff's tower. A minute more. A second more. A heartbeat more. Now!

One horse and rider came into view. It was a woman, it seemed, though her height and grace, even in the split-second that Myranda had seen her, betrayed her to be an elf. Myranda spurred her horse to the east. Myn ran beside her. She could match the speed of the horse with little effort, though carrying the helmet and glancing back at her pursuers regularly gave the dragon some difficulty.

The wind tore by them with twice the bite it would have had if they were standing still, and the rain and snow saturated them in minutes, but those were the least of her worries. Myranda turned every few moments, remembering more of the words of Caya.

If you have a chance to escape, you may not know immediately. Those men are riding war horses, bred for strength. Wind Runner is a messenger horse, bred for endurance. It will seem that they are keeping pace with you, and they may well be, but the sprint will wear down their horses quickly. The gap between you should start to widen quickly and suddenly. If it doesn't, then you are done for.

Every few strides, Myranda judged the distance. Her heart pounded harder with each glance that didn't show any headway. Finally, just when her own steed seemed at the brink of collapse, the followers seemed to stop entirely. Their horses broke stride and faltered. Even with Wind Runner slowing considerably, the Elites were out of sight within minutes.

Some relief came to Myranda, but not much. She knew that now the soldiers had seen her. They had followed her trail this far on descriptions alone. If she did not take every advantage she had at her disposal to keep her distance, they would be upon her. And so she continued to spur on her horse. The animal was exhausted and had not had a proper rest in days, but it had to continue, or they would both be caught.

When Wind Runner had run for the better part of three hours, it became clear that, despite her spells, the creature needed to rest. There was no sense destroying the beast now, or she would be stranded, and Myranda was little more than a novice in the ways of magic. Her own strength would need to be conserved as well. The Elites must have fallen an hour or more behind by now; perhaps she could risk some rest. A small stream, surrounded by the very most persistent of weeds, presented itself as the logical place for the group to catch their breath. The horse and dragon gulped at the water. She stood, stretching her legs and trying to keep the rain and ice from her eyes. Myn managed to snatch up a rabbit that foolishly wandered near while Wind Runner ate the weeds most greedily.

Myranda had no food of her own, but the constant fear had left her without an appetite. She could not take her eyes off of the western horizon.

Myn had just begun to gnaw upon her precious toy again when Myranda's eyes locked onto something that she could not identify. The sun had long ago set, making it difficult to make out anything more than shapes. In the distance, far off, there was what looked to be a faint, twinkling star ... but it was on the ground. For a moment she stood in awe of the bizarre sight. She knew, though, that regardless of what it was that was growing nearer to her with each passing instant, with her luck it could not be anything but bad news. She looked to the horse, still weak from the run. Her eyes turned back to the odd sight. It was white with a dash of blue, a single point of light with a barely visible trail behind it. She was reminded of the crystal that Wolloff used. The same light would glimmer briefly in it when he would cast a spell.

"We have to leave now," she said.

She climbed to the back of the steed, with Myn wearily gathering up the helmet in her teeth. She gave the beast a kick, but the mare would not budge. It could not go on. The breaking point had been reached. Myranda turned an anxious eye to the west again. The light was closer, there was no question, but what was it? For once, fate conspired in her favor. A single, powerful bolt of lightning jumped silently from cloud to cloud, brilliantly illuminating the field for an instant. In the heartbeat that the truth was visible, the answer was burned into her eyes. The elf, the leader of the Elites, was riding toward her, a bare crystal held over her head, summoning an unnatural speed that pushed her horse forward at easily twice the rate that Myranda's own could ever hope to muster.

Myranda froze in terror at the sight. There was nothing she could do. Their leader would be upon her in no time. A monumental crack of thunder shook her from her stupor and frightened the horse into motion. Myn quickly bolted. Somehow despite the long run, the young dragon was still able to match the speed she'd managed before. Myranda clutched her pendant.

There was no choice now. The time for magic had come. Enhancements such as the one the Elites must be using were not included in her education, but spells of healing and recovery could bring a strength and energy to her mount greater than many days rest could provide.

She locked her mind into the purest state of calm that circumstances would permit and began to speak her spells. One to eliminate the weariness, another to ease the pain. After a handful more, Wind Runner was running as fast as she ever had, but Myranda was much the worse for wear. She nearly lacked the will to remain on the steed's back. Slowly, she turned to see how close the enemy had become. Not more than a hundred paces separated them now, and the gap was closing with each stride. Myranda closed her eyes and prayed. There was nothing more she could do. It was in the hands of fate now. Or perhaps not.

Myn turned to face the elf. Her teeth still clenched about the helm, she sprayed forth a stream of flame from her nostrils. The enemy horse panicked, and at the unnatural speed, could not maintain control. The pursuing horse and rider tumbled to the ground. Myn dropped the chewed helm and locked her eyes on the new prize. With one powerful bite, she clamped onto the elf's helmet and tore it from her head. The horse, mad with fear, galloped wildly away. Myranda called and the dragon hurried to catch up, a fresh trophy in her teeth and a dazed and angry soldier in her wake. The elf looked after the escaping pair, but was helpless to follow. Safety, at least for the moment, was theirs.

The night passed with Myranda slowly regaining enough strength to recast her spells. In time, even Myn could not keep up with the mystically-aided horse. She leapt onto Wind Runner's back, but it did not slow the beast as Caya had feared. To the contrary, the clutch of the dragon's claws urged the horse forward faster than any spur could.

By first light, the forest that should have been more than a day away was in sight. Such was the ability of a tireless steed. Of course, the toll that was spared the mount was taken on the rider. Myranda was barely awake, each stride threatening to knock her from the beast's back. As she fought for each moment of consciousness, she also wrestled with what she had seen. That soldier, the elf woman. Sometime, somewhere, she had seen her before. The image of her face burned in Myranda's mind. Something from long ago.

The dappled shadows cast from the branches passing overhead prompted Myranda to wrestle her eyes open again. They had arrived. Wind shook the clinging remnants of the night's rain from the trees. The horse, sensing that this was indeed their destination, had slowed to a trot, then to a walk. Myranda stopped the steed entirely. She didn't so much dismount the creature as fall from it.

From the looks of things, they had made it quite far into the woods before she had become aware of it. The weary girl pulled herself to her feet. She had to move away from the trail that they had made thus far, and, alas, abandon the horse. As long as it seemed that she had remained on the steed, the pursuers would follow the hoofprints. All that needed to be done was to move a fair distance without leaving tracks.

This was no simple task, though. The rain had muddied the ground. Tracks would be easy to find. She led the horse to a stream, the bed of which was composed of smooth stones. As it took a well-deserved drink, she stepped ankle-deep into the icy water. Myn looked with curiosity. It took a bit of coaxing for the dragon to join in the unpleasant but unfortunately necessary activity. After more than enough time to thoroughly numb her feet to the knees once again, she left the stream in an area too covered with pine needles to permit tracks to be left behind. A thick, full tree served as shelter as she collapsed on the driest patch of ground she could find. Myn fell on top of her and almost instantly dropped into a sleep of utter exhaustion.

#

Slowly, hazily, a dream came. It was like the stark, bleak field that had haunted her in nights gone by, but somehow different. She was lost, on her feet and wandering. Somewhere nearby, a faint, almost imperceptible light loomed. Stumbling and shuffling, she moved closer to this weak and quickly fading glow. A deep sense of desperation grew in her heart as the light slipped away from her. In this colorless field it seemed to be the last bastion of light against the overpowering dark. She had to find it, she had to touch it and know light once more before it was gone forever. It was near. So near.

#

When her eyes opened, the memory of the dream was gone, but the feelings she had felt lingered. There was something within reach that she had to find before it slipped away. She turned her eyes to some indistinct spot in the distance. Something was calling to her. Myn was still asleep, as hers was a more physical exhaustion. The girl sat and waited. Once again, a days-old hunger was burning at her, but she could not bring herself to wake her friend. The cold, wet day of rest had seized her muscles and joints with a terrible stiffness. She stood and tried to stretch it away.

It was night again and the woods were silent. The ever-present cloud cover and impenetrable canopy made it difficult to see more than a few paces in front of her, but she managed to spot something that made her smile. There was a cluster of arrowroot. It was very rare in this area. She pulled out her knife, one of the few things she'd had the presence of mind to bring with her, and dug them up. They wouldn't be enough to fill her, but at least they would take the edge off of her hunger.

As she chewed the roots, she remembered when she was a little girl and she would hunt for them any chance she could. It was a more peaceful time, and having a little slice of it at a time like this made it all the more disturbing to her that things had changed so much. In those days, the only things she had to worry about were her assignments and when her father would get home. Now she was freezing cold with no hope for shelter, digging for roots for sustenance instead of for fun, and constantly looking over her shoulder for a team of soldiers with specific orders to find her.

Myranda shook the thoughts from her head and dug the knife into the earth to pull out another root. When she did, she noticed something that the scarce light had hidden from her before. There was an impression in the ground--almost undetectable, but undeniable. It was a footprint. The rain had nearly washed it away, so it must have been left before the sleet and rain had started. From the shape, it could only be a boot print. Nearby there were a few more accompanied by hoofprints as well. They could have been left by anyone. Perhaps hunters or woodsmen who had moved through the area a few days earlier. Deep inside, though, Myranda knew that there was something sinister behind these prints.

While she pondered the worst, Myn stirred, padding over to Myranda and flopping down again, offering her head for the usual stroking while she gnawed at her new toy. This helm was different from the one she had left behind. It was more carefully detailed with gold, with a nose guard in the shape of a dragon's head. The dragon had focused her attentions on this piece in particular and managed to snap it off in short order. Before long Myn's hunger got the better of her and she trotted off to seek out a meal. Myranda called after her.

"Don't forget your old friend! I'm hungry, too!" she called, immediately scolding herself for making so much noise.

Before worry could rush back into her mind, Myranda busied herself with the preparation of the fire. She gathered the driest tinder and kindling she could manage, as well as a few thicker branches to feed the fire later. After clearing a place and laying out the wood properly, Myn had not yet returned. With nothing else to do, she picked up the dragon-head piece that had been left behind. Most of the details were intact. It had a gold-bronze color and, like the rest of the helm, was exquisite. There were even eyes carved of amber mounted in the head that were uncannily alike in hue to Myn's own eyes. The piece of armor must have cost a small fortune. One of the dragon's teeth had managed to punch a hole just below where the piece had broken from the rest of the helmet. Myranda pulled a thick thread from her uncle's old cloak, now rolled up as a keepsake in one of the new white robe's pockets, and pulled it through the hole. Instantly, she had a new pendant.

Myn marched proudly back a few minutes later. The dragon must have heeded Myranda's words, because with her she brought two freshly killed rabbits. The dragon lit the fire quickly before gulping her meal down. Myranda cooked her own meal as quickly as possible, and extinguished her fire before eating. The wet wood created copious amounts of smoke and she feared that she would be found if she let the telltale flames burn for too long. As she ate, Myranda felt the vague feeling of uneasiness return. She glanced to the south, then to the footprints. She couldn't explain it, but the tiny yearning, like an itch she could not scratch, soon consumed her. It pushed all other thoughts aside. Before long, she found herself manufacturing rationales for moving southward.

"We really ought to keep moving," she said aloud to Myn. "If we remain here, they are likely to find us soon. After all, we slept here. Days could have passed for all we know. The Elites could be just out of sight. South is as good a direction as any. What do you say?"

Myn's interest rested solely on the leftovers of Myranda's meal. Once she had snapped them up, she could care less what she did, so long as she did it with Myranda. As the creature happily munched, Myranda presented her with the pendant. Myn had earned it, after all. The string was tied about her neck tightly enough that it would not fall or become tangled. She seemed pleased, shaking her neck a bit to feel the weight of it before snatching up the rest of the helm and making it clear she was eager for whatever was next.

With that they were off. The routine of the next few days was a strenuous one. Sleep would come during the comparatively warm daylight hours. Upon waking, Myn would fetch food for Myranda and herself if she so desired. Then the remains of the fire would be eliminated or hidden and they would move at a brisk pace southward. The sheer density of the forest assured that, even if the Elites were to search nonstop, they would not stumble upon any evidence of Myranda or her dragon for days. Although once they found what they were searching for, they would easily be able to follow her, Myranda convinced herself that so long as she was careful and continued her southward trek, she could remain out of their reach.

One curse and blessing of their chosen direction was the fact that the wind was always at their backs. This was helpful in that it did not burn at their faces or make walking more difficult. Myn, however, was near madness from the scent of the Elites that was carried by the constant breeze. The little dragon's uneasiness became a gauge of how near the soldiers were. When her restlessness turned to defensiveness, it was time to quicken the pace. In this way, the soldiers were always kept at least out of sight. Though they were a constant threat, Myranda soon found that she had a more pressing concern.

The footprints that she had found before had only become more numerous, and slightly fresher. Whatever group had been here before, it had followed the same path. Had she been in her right mind, she might have changed direction to avoid trouble. Such a choice would not be made. The intuition that had led her this far had only become more insistent. Whatever was out there, she had to find it or be driven mad by doubt.

As if the uneasiness wasn't enough to addle her mind, the nights on the cold and often wet ground were affecting her health. The stiffness that came to her muscles during rest lingered longer each day, and her breathing was reduced to wheezing at times. She knew what it meant. At least once a year she began to feel this way. It generally signaled the beginning of a long illness.

Myranda smirked. Not this time. She knew the words that could cure her, but she had been warned not to cure an illness before it had become a burden. If a body was cured of disease too quickly, too often, it would weaken, and eventually cease to fight disease on its own, Wolloff had warned. Indeed, many a wizard, kept alive well past the time that nature had intended, had died for precisely this reason, he claimed. Myranda decided that once the wracking cough that invariably came appeared, she would cure it. That should give her natural defenses the practice they needed.

Perhaps five days of constant travel had passed. She had not traveled due south, or the Elites would have surely found her. Instead, she zigzagged along rocky ground and thatch, anything that could obscure her tracks. She was walking the bank of another pebble-bottomed stream when she noticed something in the distance. Myn noticed it as well, and rushed to chase after it. When the creature was flushed out into the open, Myranda caught a clear glimpse of it before it galloped away. It was a horse. A horse just like the one the Elites who pursued her were riding. The image had burned itself into her mind--there could be no doubt.

But how? How could one of their steeds have gotten past her without either of them noticing? And why did it have no rider? Perhaps it was the horse that had run away from the leader of the Elites when Myn had scared it during the rush to the Locke's Woods.

Her mind turned to the footprints and hoofprints. If there was an Elite horse here, then perhaps the Elites had been in this place, days before, leaving behind those traces. But how? They had to be behind her! Myn proved that! Unless they had split up, but then they could have confronted her days ago! None of this made sense! Myn trotted back, pleased that she had frightened away the assumed threat.

"Myn," Myranda whispered, "this is very important. How near are they? The bad ones."

Myn did not understand. Myranda took a series of sniffs to illustrate what she meant. The dragon imitated, but seemed no more disturbed by the scent than usual.

"Again! You need to be sure!" Myranda demanded as a change in the wind brought a blast from the south.

Myn caught a whiff of this new wind. Instantly, her eyes shot open. She turned to the south and took off like a bolt, sprinting across the ground like a creature possessed.

"Myn! No! Not now!" Myranda called out uselessly. She hurried after her friend, following the deep claw marks left by her sprint. This could not have happened at a worse time.

Minutes of running as fast as her legs could carry her had aggravated her ailing lungs severely. She stopped briefly to catch her breath, leaning against a tree. When she took her hand away, she felt something sticky. She looked to the culprit and found her hand reddened with blood. Fresh blood. She rushed on, determined to not to stop until she found her dragon and the thing that had stirred her so. There was danger afoot.

Myranda stumbled into a clearing. She could barely breathe. Her eyes scanned the surroundings. It was a gruesome sight. Soldiers, Elites, a dozen or more, were scattered about the ground. They had been slaughtered, armor pierced and torn. It was as though a wild animal had been let loose upon them. The sight brought painful memories of the battleground she had stumbled through when Myn had run last time, though now the injuries seemed somehow more savage. These were not the clean slices of a sword, but the horrid punctures and tears of a spear or a lance.

The bodies, like the blood she had stumbled upon earlier, were fresh. They had likely been killed just as the sun was setting earlier that day. At the opposite edge of the clearing was Myn. She was nosing a figure that was hunched against a tree. It was difficult to tell just what it was that she was looking at when she finally approached it, so covered was it in all manner of injuries. Perhaps it was some sort of monster. It had arms and legs like a man, and some shreds of clothing, but the numerous tears showed a horrid red fur. Myn was blocking the head, but from what Myranda could see, this creature was as dead as the soldiers that littered the area.

"Myn, get away from there! We need to leave this place--now!" Myranda ordered.

Myn looked up pleadingly. Slowly, the fallen creature weakly raised a hand and placed it on the neck of the dragon. It was alive! Myranda dropped to her knees and more closely inspected the stricken creature. As she did so, it managed to raise its head.

"L-Leo?" Myranda cried out, as the battered face of the malthrope she had met so many months ago stared vaguely back.

"Leo, what happened? Did the soldiers do this to you?"

The near-dead malthrope tried to focus on the hazy form in front of him. His free hand grasped painfully at a cruel-looking rusty spike, nearly as long as his arm and clearly the weapon that had taken the lives of the other soldiers.

"You? Myranda . . ." he said, before drifting into a weak, delirious laugh that ended in a series of coughs. "Irony . . ."

His head dropped back into unconsciousness. Myranda clutched her gem and surveyed his wounds. Many deep slashes striped his arms and chest. The fresh injuries were joined by recent scars, as well as every stage of healing in between. He must have been under constant attack for weeks, or longer. Aside from the lacerations, his legs appeared to have been broken and poorly healed. One eye was swollen shut, a crust of dried blood showing between the lids. An ear had been slit all the way through. In truth, there was not a part of his body that did not suffer from some malady or another. Even the long hair that he'd displayed when she first met him had been rendered a scraggly mess, as though it had been cut away with a dull blade. This, coupled with the scrawny, malnourished appearance of his muscles and the patches of blackened, almost charred fur, told the undeniable tale of torture.

Myranda set her mind carefully to the task of healing the most grievous of injuries first. After forcing him into a deep healing sleep, she spoke the words to close the wounds that still leaked blood. When they had been tended to, she relieved the smaller cuts and swelling. Each spell robbed her of more of her own strength, but the months of training had brought her enough stamina to perform the task at hand. By the time she had cast the last spell she could manage, Leo was far from healthy, but he was most assuredly out of danger. She leaned dizzily to the tree he was slumped against and slid to the ground. Myn, who had watched the whole spectacle with nothing short of angst-ridden worry, curled up between the girl and her patient.

"I may not be able to stay awake, Myn. I need you to be vigilant," Myranda said.

The dragon did not fully understand, but she scarcely needed to be told to protect her companion, perpetually in a defensive position whenever the slightest threat emerged. For Myranda, the world faded in and out for some time while her mind recovered. It was a strange near-sleep that she found to be quite unsettling. She was utterly helpless, not enough of her mind left to form a cogent thought. No less than three hours of such a state passed before she was shaken from her trance by the movement of Leo. He was painfully struggling to his feet. Myn, joyful to see him rise, managed to knock him back to the ground in her enthusiasm.

"Easy, little one," he said, as the elated beast rubbed her head on the weakened warrior.

"Sit, Leo. You shouldn't be awake. Not yet," she said, trying to shake the cobwebs from her head.

"I shouldn't be alive. Those wounds were dire. I should know. I have delivered more than a few myself," he said.

"I healed you," she said.

"Healed me? I don't seem to remember you speaking of such a talent when last we met," he said.

"There was no such talent to speak of at the time," she replied.

"And the remarkably affectionate dragon?" he asked.

"That's Myn. I found her a few months ago. As for the affectionate part, you are the first person she has ever been anything short of hostile toward," Myranda said, as Myn rapidly scampered from her lap to his and back again before running off toward where she had dropped her chewed-up helm to retrieve it.

"Well, I have a way with animals," he said, slowly scanning the battleground.

"Is something wrong?" she asked.

"My mind is not what it should be. I count twelve bodies. Am I correct?" he asked.

"I am not thinking very clearly either, but I believe so," she said.

He released a sigh and slumped against the tree.

"Finally . . . that is all of them. After all of this time, I don't have to look over my shoulder anymore," he said. He tried to raise his hand to his forehead, but winced in pain and let it fall again.

"You must have a broken bone that I missed," Myranda said, reaching for her crystal. A surge of dizziness assured her that it would be foolish to attempt to speak a spell right now.

"You seem unwell. Can I help?" he offered, noticing her wavering posture.

"Don't mind me. You are the one who needs help. Can you move your fingers?" she asked.

"Somewhat," he answered. "And it only hurts when I move it. It is not broken; I have broken it often enough to know the difference."

"You should have a sling for it until I can heal it for you," she said.

Myranda pulled the worn old cloak from inside the new one. Carefully she tore a strip from it.

"Isn't that your uncle's cloak?" he asked.

"It was," she said.

"I thought it meant a lot to you," he said.

"It did, and does, but it is the only material I have that would make for a decent sling. He would have wanted it to be useful. I can't think of a better use," she said, tying a few knots to fashion a sling.

Myranda fitted the sling over the injured arm.

"There," she said.

"It is a fine sling," he said.

Myn returned with the helmet and curled up between them. Leo spied her toy. He scanned the remains of the battle once more.

"That helm. It didn't come from one of these soldiers," he remarked, his voice tense.

"No, no it came from a--" Myranda began.

"An elf woman," he finished.

"Yes, how did you---" she asked.

"She is the leader of the Elites. She was not with the squad that followed me here. Where did you get this?" he demanded.

"We had a run-in with her on the way here," she said, his desperation beginning to affect her.

"Then she is following you! But I . . . Never mind, no time. How long ago did you get here?" he asked, his tone now that of a professional.

"Perhaps a week. They couldn't have made it here until at least a half-day after I did," she said.

He drew in a deep breath.

"They are close, and getting closer. South, now!" he said.

Myn was on her feet and in motion as soon as he mentioned a direction. Myranda helped him to his feet and the trio moved on as quickly as their various impairments would allow. Leo snatched up the metal spike. It was stained with a dozen different shades of blood. Carrying it was a labor for his still-weary body, but he refused to put it down.

"What is going on?" she asked.

"They must think that you are a bit more dangerous than you really are. They are treating you like they treated me. Otherwise they would have found you and killed you hours after they arrived. Instead, they must think you are leading them into an ambush. Once they see the two of us in this condition and the bodies that I left behind, they will put a quick and very unpleasant end to our freedom, and likely our lives," he said.

"How can you be so sure?" she asked. "Why are they after you?"

"Suffice to say a few weeks after I met you this group took time out of their busy schedule of hunting down an assassin to hunt down me!" he said. "I couldn't avoid them for long and very shortly I was subjected to their hospitality in abundance. You learn much about the way people work when you are subjected to their techniques nonstop for a number of months."

"What are we going to do?" Myranda asked.

For a while, Leo was silent. His face was plastered with a look of deep contemplation as he walked. Finally, he spoke.

"There is a place in this forest, not far from here, that can offer safety for as long as it is required. I came here seeking it. The entrance can be reached by sunrise, even at this pace. Unfortunately the Elites will reach us far before first light. It will be a miracle if they do not reach the battleground before five minutes have passed. We cannot fight them. That would be suicide.

"You have to reach the sanctuary. The entrance is a cave with a stream running from it. Go inside and follow the stream. You won't need light. Just follow the water to its source, no matter how long it takes. When you can feel it bubbling from the rocks, I want you to climb the wall directly above it and find the smallest opening. Crawl inside and follow it to its end. From there, feel the walls at every branch and take the path that is smoothest. When the walls are smooth as glass, the path should be clear," he said purposefully, without stopping.

"But how are we going to make it there?" she asked.

"You are going to ride a horse that I am going to liberate from its rider," he said.

"What about you?" she asked.

"I will hold them off long enough for you to get out of sight," he said.

"But you said it was suicide to fight them!" she said.

"It is. I don't care. I am determined to get you out of this alive. You saved my life. No one else in this forsaken world would have given me a second thought. A person like you deserves to make it through this. If they get you, they will lock you away until they know what they need to know, and then they will kill you. It is the fate that someone like me has been headed for since birth, but you don't deserve it. You are so unique, so pure. You *must* go on! Honestly, you should have left me to die. You are better off without me. But you saved my life, and now at least I can have a chance to do the same. Perhaps it will earn me a high place in the afterlife," he said.

"No--I didn't save your life to have you throw it away. We are all making it out of this somehow. The three of us," she demanded.

#

Not far away, the soldiers drew nearer. There were sixteen of them, riding on fifteen horses. A fire burned inside them as they came upon the bodies of their fallen brethren. There were tracks leading into the woods. A trio of them, one human and two beasts. At full gallop, the Elites followed them into the thick, dark woods. With a few brief words, seven of the soldiers dropped back, holding their position while the remaining eight horses continued. Another command from the lips of the leader brought the second group to a halt. There was no one in sight, but the tracks had ended. Trigorah spoke.

"Myranda Celeste," she commanded. Hers was a clear and confident voice that carried every ounce of authority that her rank did. She bore a steely, impenetrable look of duty on her face.

After receiving no answer, the warrior drew her sword in one slow, deliberate motion. The blade sang against the sheath, gradually revealing five radiant blue points along its length, the tips of crystals like the one she had wielded during the pursuit. She then dropped from the back of the horse, signaling that the soldier who had been sharing a horse to take her place. The elf brandished the short sword in one hand and drew a mystic gem from a pouch at her belt. A few more words from her lips and the gem obeyed her just as the soldiers had. She tossed the crystal into the dwindling piles of snow just past the trees where the tracks had ended.

"If you value your life, you will reveal yourself before that crystal's spell is cast," she warned.

The light from the gem grew, illuminating the snow bank with its eerie blue glow. The air seemed alive with energy. Hair stood on end as glowing tendrils flicked out from the blinding gem. On the orders of the leader, blinders were quickly dropped over the horses eyes and all soldiers looked away. Myranda and Leo dove from behind the trees just as fractures on the crystal's surface gave way. The whole of the stand of trees, and perhaps the whole of the forest, was bathed in an utterly silent burst of the same white-blue light that Myranda had come to fear.

When the darkness came rushing back in, those things nearest to the center of the blast were smoldering. Bark was stripped from trees and the snow was reduced to a sizzling pool amid blackened ground. Myranda and Leo climbed to their feet and readied their weapons. Leo held his spike at the ready in his one healthy arm. Myranda held her knife as her father had taught long ago. The elf coolly surveyed her prey.

"You are Myranda Celeste," the general stated.

"I am," Myranda replied. Her mind was not much clearer than it had been when she had first seen the elf's face, but this time, the answer became clear. "And you are Trigorah Teloran."

The soldiers stirred, some drawing their weapons. A motion from the general quieted them.

"I am pleased that you remember me. I have been sent by the highest of authorities to bring you to justice. If you cooperate, no harm will come to you. If you resist you will be taken by force," Trigorah said.

"I didn't do anything, Trigorah," Myranda said. "I did not kill those men."

The soldiers were again rattled, requiring a spoken reprimand from their leader to settle.

"It is not my place to question your guilt or innocence, and it is not your place to do me the dishonor of speaking my given name. Perhaps you were worthy of that long ago, but you lost the right when you ran afoul of the Alliance Army. You will address me as General Teloran or not at all," she demanded, her tone wavering slightly with the anger she felt.

Leo grinned.

"So, Trigorah, how do you like my handiwork? A fitting retribution, I feel, for the torture," he said, attempting to push the anger further.

The soldiers stirred again. One raised a spear and made ready to heave it at the offender. No word came to stop him.

"Take care, malthrope. At the moment, my orders do not include your capture. If you submit, you too will be brought to justice without harm--but another word out of your wretched maw and my men will deliver you to the shallow grave you have earned," the general warned.

"Look at the horrors he has been through. How do I know you do not have the same in store for me? What is to stop me from standing my ground and losing my life rather than face the same fate as he?" Myranda demanded.

"That capture and subsequent treatment of the beast was at the hands of my associate. His methods are quite different from my own--wait . . . you are stalling. *Where is the dragon!?"*

The cries of terrified horses came as an answer as Myn did as she was told. While the tense exchange was taking place, the dragon had taken a wide berth around the immediate threat and sought out those soldiers Leo had predicted would be left as backup. Bursts of flame and slashes of claws sent the fear-crazed horses in all directions. As the dragon continued to stir up unseen chaos, Leo made his move. He swiftly moved in on the nearest soldier and, with a few deft strikes with his unconventional weapon, unseated him from his steed. He then hurled the heavy spike, burying it in the chest of a soldier moving to seize Myranda. The girl rushed to the horse that Leo was mounting, the weapon of a fallen soldier already in his hand.

Suddenly, an increasingly familiar feeling came to her, as a cold blade was pressed to her neck. It was Trigorah.

"Everyone hold still!" the leader demanded.

The soldiers quickly obeyed, as did Leo.

"You could have run, but you didn't. This girl means something to you," she said, addressing the malthrope.

"You won't kill her. Your orders were to take her alive," he said.

"Death is not as permanent as you think," she said. "Now drop your weapon, or would you like to experience the other side firsthand?"

Leo obeyed.

"I thought one more word would mean my death," he said.

"I've changed my mind. I am sure that my superiors are quite displeased with my associate and his failure to prevent your escape. Now I will show them never to doubt me again. I will bring both prizes," she said. "It is a shame. You are a peerless warrior, and Myranda had such potential. I pray that you see the light and join us. It would be an honor to fight beside you. The men you killed were like brothers to me, but they knew the risks. These were the deaths that they had chosen. Their souls will rest peacefully so long they are replaced by those of worth."

Myranda struggled briefly, but it was clear that with the blade of the sword held to her throat, escape was impossible. Her mind raced. The sights and sounds of the conflict flashed through her mind again and again. There had to be something . . . Yes! That would work! If only she could remember. What were the words? Finally the answer came. She worked her hand slowly to the pouch that hung at the general's belt. In one quick move, she shoved her hand inside and spoke the words that the general had used to bring the first gem to life.

The response was immediate. A shaft of light burst skyward, sending the leader reeling back. Myranda rushed to the horse and was scooped onto its back by Leo's one good arm. Chaos erupted as General Teloran tore the bag from her waist and threw it down. Her orders were swift and clear.

"*Retreat!*" she cried, loading fallen men to the back of horses before sharing one herself.

Like a blur, Myn launched herself after Leo and Myranda. As quickly as the horse would carry them, the trio fled south. A monumental burst of light shook the forest from end to end with a force that tore leaves from trees. A white heat burned behind them, bringing the hiss of wind and sizzle of trees to an otherwise silent burst.

Leo leaned low to the horse's ear. Instantly, the same fear that had caused the other horses to abandon their riders subsided from the animal, and they rode on, steadily and purposefully, eyes constantly on the woods behind them.

After a few tense minutes the massive mouth of the cave came into view.

"Are you certain that this is the one?" Myranda asked, as a dozen ancient signs swept by too quickly to read. "There is no stream."

"Not now, but there has been. Look at the ground," he said.

They leapt from the horse's back and rushed inside. The dim light of the night sky revealed signs in every language plastered on the walls. Age had made them all but unreadable. Those few words that survived were far from encouraging. There were a dozen or so racks on the walls holding ancient unlit torches for any adventurers brave enough to venture on. Leo grabbed as many as he could carry and instructed Myranda to do the same. Between the two of them, they managed to take all of the torches.

"Do you think we will need all of these?" Myranda asked.

"No, but *they* will. Don't light one until I say. I want to be sure that they cannot follow us," he said.

In total blackness, the trio shuffled along. Leo led the way, with Myranda cautiously following his echoing footsteps. Myn was completely at home in the cave. Now and then she would spark a burst of flame, casting a fleeting glimpse of the gray, craggy walls. After squeezing through an endless array of narrow passages led only by the water-smoothed floor, Leo seemed satisfied.

"That is quite enough. It will be days before they stumble upon the path we have taken. Light a torch," he said.

Myranda fumbled with her flint, brought out of fear that she would not be able to coax Myn into lighting her fires, and struck out a few sparks. The oil-soaked rags caught, and soon the claustrophobic little alcove was bathed in a flickering yellow light. The walls were a stark gray with a sparkle here and there. Around them was the constant echo of trickling water. Stalactites hung like teeth above the uneven floor. It was warm, with a thin layer of water coating every surface. Myn curled up between the two travelers and resumed her gnawing on the helmet. Despite the madness that she had been through, she refused to drop it.

"Well. That was quite an ordeal," Leo said.

Myranda stared into the light of the torch she had laid on the ground. There was a serious look on her face.

"You seem quiet," Leo said.

"Do you . . . Did I . . . kill someone?" Myranda asked

"With any luck, you killed all of them," Leo said with a laugh. A moment later he regretted his choice of words. "That is not the answer you were looking for, I take."

Myranda was silent.

"She would have killed you. She would have killed us both," he assured her.

"I don't believe that. She . . . she could have killed you time and again. And she could have killed me. She didn't. I really believe that she meant what she said. About fighting beside us. You saw how she remained long enough to collect the injured," Myranda said.

"I know how difficult it is to take your first life. I won't try to soften the blow. There isn't enough sugar in the world to take the bitterness from the act, but perhaps your sorrow is not necessary. My way of life leads me to the wrong side of the law often enough to hear tales of Trigorah. She is as capable a warrior as any that has lived. If anyone could have escaped that blast, it would be her," he said.

Myranda sighed.

"I know . . . she is my godmother," she said.

"What!?" Leo shouted, his voice echoing.

"I remember her from when my father used to visit. Back when I was very young. She seemed so kind then. My father worked with her, and he trusted her with his life. When mother was killed, she was supposed to help raise me," Myranda said.

"Well, she broke that vow," Leo said.

"She couldn't have known I survived the massacre. And my uncle told me she was dead . . . I should have known he would lie about that. He hated the Alliance Army with a passion by then. He would rather die than have me live in her care. Now she is the closest thing I have to family, and I may have killed her," Myranda said, a tear running down her cheek.

"Dwelling on it only makes it worse. You shouldn't sleep with those thoughts in your head. You won't enjoy your dreams. Are you up to any more healing?" he asked.

"I . . . perhaps," she said.

"My shoulder is not particularly pleased with the way I have been treating it," he said, trying to distract her from the subject.

"Remove the sling," she said.

He did so with great difficulty. The injury had swollen considerably. It reminded her of her own affliction, but in this case the problem was within. She pulled a few tatters of cloth aside to see how far the swelling had spread. It was severe, no doubt aggravated by the battle. As she surveyed the swelling, she noticed something odd on the left side of his chest. It was distorted, smudged with blood and charred, but there was no question. There, against the cream-colored chest, was the all too familiar curve and point.

"What . . . what is this?" she asked.

"What? Ouch! I can't see," he said.

"Here, on your chest. There is a mark," she said.

"Oh, that. That has been there since I was a child. I suppose it's a birthmark," he said.

"Look. Here! On my hand. I have the same mark! Remember the burn from the sword?" she said, holding out her hand.

He took her hand and looked over it.

"What in the world?" he said, sitting forward and taking real interest.

"It was all over the sword," she said. "I showed you. Don't you remember?"

"I remember how much it weighed, how well it was balanced, but I couldn't care less about how it looked. That is the least important thing to me," he said.

"What does it mean?" she asked.

"How should I know?" he said, perplexed.

"I got the mark from the dead soldier's sword, so that explains that, but what are you and a fallen swordsman doing sharing a mark?" she wondered.

"I haven't a clue," he said, bewildered.

"Well, maybe he was a relative. Maybe he had the same mark, or knew you in some way," she offered.

"I honestly cannot think of a single other person who has even seen my mark since I left the orphanage," he said.

"Then perhaps it was one of them," she said.

"Perhaps, but I cannot see how anything I did might have left an impression on one of the other orphans. Certainly not an impression big enough to have one of my blemishes adorn a sword that must have cost a fortune to make," he said. "Unless it isn't a blemish. The caretakers branded me with a pair of marks, this could just be a third that I didn't remember. If that is so, then the others could have had it as well."

"Do you suppose that one of your fellow orphans might have been proud enough of his orphanage to advertise it on his equipment?" Myranda asked.

"I have heard of stranger things. Well, with your godmother and our matching marks, this has been a very revealing night," Leo said.

"Indeed, the hand of fate has--" she began, but the smoke of the torch was burning at her already tortured lungs. She launched into a long, painful fit of coughing.

"That doesn't sound good at all. I *thought* you looked a bit off," he said, concerned.

"It is nothing," she managed. "It happens every year."

"Well, do you know how to cure it?" he asked.

"Of course," she said.

"Then what are you waiting for?" he wondered.

"Well, I haven't the strength to care for my cough and your shoulder. I will tend to myself tomorrow," she explained.

"Nonsense. I won't hear of it! You say whatever words you need to make yourself well and worry about me another day," he demanded.

"But the pain must be terrible," Myranda said.

"Please. I have had a dozen more serious injuries a dozen times each, and all I've had to heal them was time. A night more won't kill me," he said. She began to object again, but he cut her off. "You saved my life. I wanted to give mine for yours just a few hours ago, but you denied me. The least you can do is stay healthy long enough for me to repay my debt."

Myranda sighed, stifling another cough. Reluctantly she spoke the variant of the spell of healing sleep that would do its work upon the caster.

As the spell of healing took effect, Myranda's surroundings retreated and a soothing darkness poured over her and into her mind. A moment later a light flickered before her. She briefly thought that she had reawakened, but soon the truth became clear. The cold, thatched ground was not that of the cave, and the white, wavering light was not that of the torch. She had slipped into a dream. The light seemed to come from no source at all, merely a ball of brilliance floating before her. It formed a circle on the ground and a tight sphere of visibility. She strained her eyes desperately into the darkness. Slowly, a figure formed, somehow a still-darker silhouette against the pitch of her surroundings.

"So I have found you," came a voice from the form. It seemed to be her own voice. Hearing it whispered from the unseen lips of another was profoundly disorienting.

"Who are you?" Myranda asked.

"We need you," came the answer.

"Need me for what? I don't understand," she said.

"Do not resist me. I come to guide you, and in turn you may guide me," the voice said.

"How?" Myranda asked as the cold wind began to gust more forcefully.

"You are strong, and the path you follow is closed to me. You are nearly out of my reach. You must choose. Take my hand and the way will be made clear," the voice whispered.

The figure's hand seemed to reach out. Myranda reached for it, but something inside of her resisted. She turned to the light and grasped at it, as though it were a lantern. It remained, but a part of the eerie light trailed along with her hand. She moved her glowing fist to the figure, but it recoiled.

"Reject it. Light is sorrow. To tremble in the light is to be extinguished with it. The brightest candle burns only briefly. Darkness remains eternally. Accept the darkness and endure," the voice demanded, somewhat twisted.

The cold became intense and the darkness pressed in about her. The light fought valiantly, but the walls of oppressive blackness moved closer and closer. This was wrong. She backed toward the light, but it was withering. In a matter of moments, it was no more. The earth beneath her seemed to drop away, and she was afloat in an abyss of darkness. It felt as though the blackness itself was tearing at her.

In a last effort to fight against that which consumed her, Myranda held up her arms defensively. When she opened her hand, a burning ember of light was revealed. As the remnant of the light she had scooped up smoldered in her palm, she could barely make out the form bearing down on her. With a scream, the terrified girl lashed out with the illuminated hand. Her fingers raked the featureless face and a second, piercing, spine-tingling mockery of her cry mingled with the original.

She felt hands clasp her about the shoulders and shake her as the light rushed back. Myranda screamed again, the second scream joined by a third and fourth as her voice echoed off of the cave walls. The light was from the torch, and the hands shaking her were those of Leo. The dream was over.

#

"Easy, now. Come back to me," Leo said, steadying the terrified girl as the nightmare slowly lost its grip.

Myranda caught her breath.

"I warned about those dreams," he said.

"It was awful. I don't think I'll be able to get back to sleep," Myranda said.

"I should hope not. You have been asleep for ages," he said. "I think your dragon was beginning to get worried."

Myn was already on her lap, sniffing and licking at her face.

"How long have I been asleep?" she asked.

"Well, it is difficult to tell without the sun or stars to go by, but these torches usually last about a half a day, and I had to light a new one after I awoke about an hour ago," he said.

"It only felt like a few moments," she said. "That is a very potent spell."

"So it would seem. Well, we had best move on. You will be pleased to hear that I can hear our friends scratching about on the other side of the wall. You must have missed a few," he said.

"Are we in any danger?" she asked, getting to her feet, free of stiffness and pain for the first time in weeks.

"Not yet. I would say that it will be at least a day before they can even find their way back to the wrong turn they must have taken, and then another few hours to reach us. So unless you decide to sing your lullaby twice more, we should have no trouble staying ahead. However, if you have any words that can relieve me of this little malady without a lengthy nap, I would appreciate it," he said, indicating his shoulder.

"Of course," she said.

After a clutch at her locket and a few choice words, injury was healed and the swelling eliminated.

"Ah. Remarkable. You do fine work!" Leo commended, as he gathered up the unlit torches. Now that he was healthy, he could carry them all. The spent torch was stripped of the charred rags and used as a walking stick as the trio marched on.

"If there was something wrong with your legs, you should have told me," she said.

"There is nothing you can do. They are healed already. Not quite the way they ought to have. A handful of fighters I've known had the same problem. Nothing they could do either, healers or no," he said in a disarmingly cheerful tone.

"How terrible," she said.

"Shed no tears for me, my dear. Where we are headed, no ailment will endure," he said.

"That sounds familiar," she said, the flowery prose stirring her memory.

"A play, *One Final March,* spoken right before our hero heads to a battle he cannot hope to win bearing a wound he cannot hope to survive," Leo said.

"That does not speak very well of our destination," she said.

"Don't worry. Some of my fondest memories are in the land that lies ahead of us. But enough about that. It must be seen to be believed. Frankly, if you don't mind, I would dearly love to hear what your life has been like since our last meeting," he said.

"At the usual rate, though. I'll trade you my story for yours," she said.

"Naturally," he said.

As they made their way along the slick, uneven path, Myranda spoke of the events of the last few months. She told the tale of her capture in the church, and her clash with the mysterious creatures in the field, and her escape with the aid of the Undermine. Leo nodded, chiming in at times with insightful comments. He really seemed to care what happened to her, a quality that she found wholly absent in society at large.

By the time Myn's appearance and the time spent under Wolloff's training had been described, she felt as though she was talking to her oldest friend. In a way, she was.

"Good heavens," he said. "That is quite a tale. You lead an eventful life."

"It hasn't always been that way," she said. "But enough about me. You have a story of your own to tell."

"So I do. Fair is fair. Let me see," he began. "I saw you off and headed into Melorn. The hunting was a bit thin, but adequate. Before a week had passed, I decided to find my next tournament, so I nosed around a bit further north. Things were quiet, but eventually I caught word of a small submission tourney nearby. It was informal, a handful of Alliance veterans and soldiers on leave trying to see just who was best at the art of battle. Admittedly an outsider, they were reluctant to allow me entry, particularly with my unwillingness to meet face to face. Luck would have it that one of the soldiers was called back to duty, and I filled the vacancy. One of the organizers caught sight of me. He pulled me aside as I was placing a bet on myself.

"I was in my fighting gear, so he couldn't tell what I was, but he told me that he had seen me fight before, and that he knew I could win this easily. I thanked him for the compliment. He went on to explain that one of the other combatants, a big fellow, was something of local hero. He'd been a part of more winning battles than any other soldier in years and had even earned his way into this 'Elite' squad. In all likelihood, I would be facing him in the final round. Even more likely was my victory. He dangled a sack of silver under my nose and mentioned that a spirited victory would be a tremendous boost to the morale of the people.

"I stood to earn a good deal more by taking the fall than collecting on my own bet, so I agreed. It wasn't the first time. The fighting started and the first few rounds were laughable. There was an old man who wanted to see if he still had what it took. He didn't. Then was a green newcomer who was fresh from his first tour and somehow hadn't seen a battle yet. He went down fairly easily. Finally I found myself face to face with this Elite character.

"I won't lie, he was a formidable fellow. A mountain of a man. He outclassed me in size and strength by a fair amount. Slow, though. If I wanted to, I could land a half-dozen blows in the time it took him to miss one. That and he was, if you can believe it, too well-trained. It was as though I was fighting a textbook. I've read the manual they use to teach these men, so his technique couldn't have been more obvious. I found myself ten moves ahead of him, watching him play into every attack. I would let him get in a glancing blow here or there to keep it interesting, but before long, he started to tire, so I knew it was time to act.

"I dropped a shoulder into a shot that went low and fell to the ground. That, coupled with the serious-looking blows I'd seemingly suffered, should have been more than enough to convince the crowd. He stood over me and I made ready to submit, but there was something wrong. He raised his sword up in what was clear to be a kill blow. I reacted instinctively with a counter. Unfortunately, a warrior that size fully committed to a swing is not easily stopped, even if he wishes it. As a result a sword point to the chest meant as a warning became a blade through the heart."

"In the midst of a rather severe outburst of unbridled hatred, I managed to make good my escape. The mob was easy enough to lose, but time would show the fallen Elite's brothers in arms were another matter. They took time out of their busy schedule of hunting down an assassin or some such and turned their sights to me. I think I was able to stay ahead of them for a few weeks before they cornered me. Learning of my race did little to cool their tempers.

"I . . . Well, I learned what sort of treatment the highest criminals of the nation can expect. It is not pleasant. All the while they grilled me as to whether I was sent, or who I worked for. They tried and tried to find something more in the fellow's death than a simple accident. When they became bored of my repeated assurance of the truth, they left me to rot. I managed to escape and, well, that is that."

Myranda shook her head in disbelief.

"It sounds so awful," she said. "Did they torture you?"

"I prefer not to think back to that particular period of my life," he said.

"I understand. Leo, I know that I don't have anything else I can tell you in return, but do you mind if I ask you a few more questions?" she asked.

"Go right ahead," he said.

"Myn knows you. I am sure of it. The way she rushed to you in the forest that day. She'd run like that before, and all I found was a few pools of blood and the grave markers of Elites. That was long before the Elites came looking for me. That, coupled with the way she is so comfortable around you and the way she listens to you . . . I can get her to light a fire or stop when she is doing something wrong. You gave her very specific directions back there. We would not have escaped those soldiers if she hadn't kept out of sight and hunted down the backup soldiers to scare away their horses," Myranda said.

"Ah, yes. Well, the fact of the matter is, prior to my capture, I did meet this fine young lady. I tried to lose the pursuers in the mountains, so I cut across, eventually finding myself somewhere in the northern end of Ravenwood. I thought I smelled you on the wind, but I dismissed it. Then Myn and I stumbled upon the same hunting ground. There was a bit of tension at first, but we were getting along soon enough.

"I have a way with animals, as I said. She was a fine hunter already, but I helped her to hone her craft, as it were. I could smell you all over her, which puzzled me. At first I thought she might have killed you. Luckily, I was wrong. Once or twice, I caught sight of that wizard's tower you were staying in. By then, I had grown quite certain that you were alive and well inside," he explained.

"Why didn't you come in and visit?" she scolded.

"I was less than optimistic as to the quality of hospitality I might receive from the master of the house. Not to mention, I was afraid I might involve you in my troubles with the Elites. Fat lot of good that did," he said.

"Then why didn't you at least tell me about it with the rest of the recollection?" Myranda asked.

"I was afraid you would scold me for not visiting you," he answered with a grin.

"You know me like a book," Myranda said with a shake of her head.

Leo quickened his pace, and the group moved on.

#

The path had twisted and turned, branching constantly into a honey comb of different passages. Leo expertly led the way. As they progressed, Myranda noticed that the three things that had surprised her about the cave were becoming more and more prevalent. First, it was getting warmer. She found herself carrying her robe under her arm to avoid being smothered by it. Second, water was becoming more and more abundant. It now dripped and streamed from the roof in an echoing cacophony, gathering in pools and making the floor perilously slick. Finally, the faint glitter of the walls increased with each passing step. There were tiny flecks of some kind of crystal embedded all around, catching the light and bending it into a breathtaking array of colors.

As the trio progressed, the torch burned down. When another one had to be lit, the weariness of the constant walking and climbing was taking its toll. After half a day without stopping to rest, Myn was as energetic as ever, and Leo showed no signs of slowing. Myranda, alas, was not so fortunate.

"Stop," she said.

Leo turned.

"Is something wrong?" he asked.

"How deep is this cave? When will we stop?" she asked.

"If memory serves correctly, this is perhaps a third of the way there," he said.

"We have got three more days of this ahead?" she gasped.

"If we keep this pace. The path becomes more difficult further on, so we may take a bit longer, though the last bit might make up some time," he explained.

"I don't know if I can make it. I . . . I haven't eaten since just before I found you," she said.

"That is, oh, a day and a half ago. I seem to remember that you've gone far longer than that without food," he said.

"I have, but there are at least three more days of this. Unless there is food to be found, I don't think I will be leaving this cave," she said. "And what about Myn, and you?"

"Did Myn eat when you did?" he asked.

"Yes. As usual, she ate about three times as much as I did," Myranda said.

"Then she will be just fine. As for me? Well, never mind me," he said. "Regardless, there is something coming up that will either fill your stomach or turn it. Either way, you won't have to worry about your appetite."

"I hope you are right," she said.

They continued on, the path steepening to the point that they spent as much time climbing as they did walking. Leo and Myranda did so with quite a bit of difficulty, but Myn scampered up and down the walls as though she were on the ground. She was truly in her element. In this dank, dreary environment, she was in a state of bliss. Just as the path began to level and the ceiling rose out of sight, Myranda noticed a powerful, gagging odor.

"What is that?" she coughed.

"Oh, so you can finally smell it. That, my dear, is dinner," he said.

"You are kidding," she ventured.

Leo shook his head. Shortly, they came upon a chalky, foul-smelling substance littering the ground. The echoing of their footsteps was joined by a distorted, unidentifiable sound.

"You don't intend to use your robe anytime soon, do you?" Leo asked.

"Unless this cave gets much colder soon, then I don't imagine I would. Why?" she asked.

"Give it to me. I'll need it soon. If you don't mind, I am going to need both hands. Would you take the spare torches?" he asked.

"Of course," she said, exchanging the now-heavily soiled robe for the torches.

"All right. Now, this is going to be a bit confusing. There will be a lot of noise, but don't worry. You should be safe," Leo said as he wiped his fingers on his shirt.

"Wait, what is--" Myranda desperately tried to interject before the chaos began, failing miserably.

Leo placed two fingers in his mouth and unleashed a piercing whistle. The echoes of the ear splitting sound were joined with a myriad of animal screeches. A blur of flapping wings filled the air. As Myranda struggled against the urge to drop to the ground and cover her head, her robe-wielding companion cast it into the air and pulled it tight like a net.

"All right, move! That way!" he said, motioning.

He and Myranda rushed in the direction he'd indicated. They quickly came upon a small tunnel that they had to crawl to enter. Myn lingered just outside, snapping at the frenzied bats. When the bulk of the animals had funneled out of an unseen hole in the roof of the cave, she entered the tunnel and joined her friends, making sure to retrieve her chewing helmet before doing so. Leo snapped one of the wooden handles of the spent torches into kindling and lit it. He then uncovered the quarry of questionable nourishment. The creatures were just about the size of a fist, a grotesque assemblage of skin and bone.

"You can eat these things?" Myranda said, picking one of the creatures up by a wing and grimacing.

"*I* can, at least, when there are no alternatives," he said, popping one of the bats, whole and raw, into his mouth and crunching away.

Myranda managed to retrieve one of the longer splinters and skewer a small specimen to hold over the fire. When it began to sizzle, she, out of necessity rather than desire, managed to pick some of the meat off of it and consume it. Leo ate two or three more as he watched her in quiet amusement. Finally he spoke.

"If you wanted meat, you should have taken a larger one. With the smaller ones, you are better off just eating them whole. The bones are thin, you don't have to worry about them," he said.

Myranda laughed, until she realized that he was serious. In an experience that she would try to forget for years to come, she did as he suggested. It took the better part of an hour to choke down enough to convince her she would not starve. Leo, on the other hand, was quite happy eating until he was full. Myn snapped up the rest.

"Well, after that rather unique experience, I trust we will retire for the night--or day, or whatever it may be?" she fairly pleaded.

"I suppose, but we must move quickly tomorrow. The increasing flow of water is making me nervous. I have a feeling our timing could have been a bit better in this little endeavor," he said.

"Why?" she said.

"Well. This cave has two distinct states: wet and dry. I was expecting to get here during the transition from the former to the latter. I fear that I may have been held a bit longer than I had realized, in which case we may be experiencing the opposite transition. No cause for worry, though. So long as we reach the end in a timely manner," he said.

His words *did* worry her, but his tone was nothing if not relaxed and confident. Everything about the way he expressed himself made Myranda trust Leo more. Myn must have felt the same way, because she had resumed her constant trek from one lap to the other, unable to decide where she wanted to sleep. Eventually, Myranda slid to beside Leo so that the dragon could stretch across both laps while they dozed with their backs against the wall. Sleep came swiftly and was refreshingly free of any disturbing images.

The sound of a fresh torch being lit by her helpful dragon roused Myranda from sleep. Leo was using some of the leather that affixed the fuel rags to one of the spent torches to bind the remaining ones. Once again, he was awake before her, and she'd fallen asleep before him. Though she'd not known him long, she had never seen him sleeping naturally. There was no room to stand, but he assured her that the roof would be tall enough to stand shortly. The trio moved on.

"How is it that you remember this place so well?" Myranda said.

"Well, I spent a bit more time here than was required," he explained.

"How long?" she asked.

"Seven months," he said nonchalantly.

"Seven! Seven months! How did you survive so long?" she wondered.

"I ate quite a few bats, drank quite a bit of stagnant water, and learned to love the dark," he said.

"Why didn't you leave the cave?" she asked.

"Hadn't found what I was looking for," he said. "Well, here we are, the halfway point. After a rough bit, things get much easier from here on."

The dancing light of the torch fell upon a cleft in the stony wall with a fair amount of water trickling from it. The path continued into the darkness.

"We have to climb this?" Myranda asked.

"Yes indeed! Let's get at it," Leo said, as he threw the bundle of torches over his shoulder to be held in place by the former sling.

Once again, Myn shot up the wall effortlessly and Leo managed to climb easily enough despite his ailing legs. Myranda, left holding the torch, had more of a struggle. Leo noticed when the light fell too far behind for him to see.

"Do you need a hand?" he called from above.

"I could use one!" she said.

"There is a ledge up here. When you reach it, we will work something out," he said.

She made her way to the ledge. After some thought, they came upon a compromise. Myranda took the helmet that Myn carried, rolled it in her robe, and tied it to her back with the robe's waist cord. Myn, in turn, clutched the torch, sans a good portion of the handle to make it easier to carry, in her teeth. With her ease of climbing the wall, the dragon was able to put the light wherever it was needed. With both of her hands free, Myranda managed to keep up with Leo with little effort. For nearly an hour, the three climbed, concentration requiring that conversation cease. All that could be seen was what the light of the torch revealed.

An opening came into view.

"Is this the tunnel?" Myranda asked.

"Too big, but the correct one is nearby," he said.

When they did find it, Myranda was not pleased. It was a rough stone tube just a bit wider than Leo's shoulders.

"This is it?" Myranda said, praying for the answer no.

"I am afraid so. A few words before we enter. The walls are far from smooth. Move quickly--but carefully, or you will tear yourself up badly. Push that bundle ahead of you, or you will get it snagged. If it feels that the walls are closing in, just close your eyes. The feeling will pass. Above all, keep moving. You don't want the fatigue to hit you while you are inside," he said.

"How long before the tunnel widens?" she asked.

"It doesn't. We are going to spend, oh, two hours crawling through that, and then there will be a hole that we will drop through," he said.

"Two hours!" she cried.

"Roughly. It will seem much longer, though, so stay focused," he said.

Myn scampered inside. Myranda waited for Leo, but he assured her that she would rather go second. The one bringing up the rear would be working in near pitch-blackness. She hurriedly seized the opportunity to at least see where she was going. The walls scratched and scraped at her hands and arms badly, and rolling the bundled robe ahead of her made her wish she'd left it behind. Her friend's words rang true. Each second seemed to take ages.

"Isn't there another way?" she called back to Leo.

"There are a handful of other paths that lead to roughly the same place, but they aren't nearly as pleasant," he answered.

"What could be worse than this?" she asked.

"Well, one involved sidling along a water-slicked ledge above a *very* deep chasm for roughly twice this distance. Another is a smoother tunnel a bit wider than this," he said.

"What was wrong with that one?" she asked.

"Spiders," he said.

"I see," Myranda replied with a shudder.

More time passed. More than once, she had to take his advice and close her eyes rather than be driven mad by the walls of a tunnel that seemed to be getting narrower by the minute. As if it wasn't difficult enough, her muscles were beginning to cramp up from the awkward movements of following the tight twists and turns of the tunnel. It reminded her a bit too much of moving across the floor while bound the chair in the deserted church. Finally, she couldn't take any more.

"We need to stop for a while. I can't take this," she said.

"As you wish," he said, pausing for a moment before speaking again. "You know, I was thinking."

"What?" she asked.

"That cloth was a bit dry. On the torch, I mean," he said.

"So?" she said.

"So it might go out soon," he said.

"You're joking," she said.

"Am I?" he said ominously.

Myranda continued crawling with renewed vigor. She knew that he had only said that to get her moving, but the thought of having to feel her way through this tube in pitch black, regardless of how remote the possibility, was enough to get her think twice about stopping. After an eternity of crawling, Leo's threat seemed to come true as the light of the dragon-borne torch vanished.

"What happened!?" she called out, panic closing in.

"I think Myn found the hole," he said. "Feel for it. It should be just in front of you."

Sure enough the bundle dropped through a wide hole in the bottom of the shaft. With a bit of difficulty she flipped down to a slippery, sloping floor a fair distance below. The bundle was sliding and rolling quickly away. Myn dropped the torch and fetched it, and Myranda tied it securely to her waist. Leo dropped down. The light revealed the walls and ceiling to be as smooth as the floor, and far smoother than even the base of the former stream they had been following.

"There, that wasn't so bad, was it?" he asked.

"No, it was much worse," she answered, taking a seat.

"No, no, no. Up, up, up!" he said.

"You cannot be serious," she pleaded.

"Oh, come now. We are ahead of schedule. If we keep moving, we could be sleeping with a sky above us. Isn't that worth working for?" he said.

Myranda reluctantly moved on. Leo was setting a rather brisk pace now. Perhaps he was especially eager to be out of this dank hole in the ground. She couldn't blame him. If she had spent as much time here as he'd said he had, then she would be running as fast as she could to escape. As it was, she'd only been underground for a day or two and it was more than enough.

What *did* concern her was his silence. In the times she managed to catch a look at his face, he wore a stern look of purpose. Hours passed in much the same way. The torch burned out and was replaced. Myranda made some attempts to start a conversation, but beyond the answers to her questions, the dialogue died quickly.

\#

Trigorah's heavy boots echoed along the floor of the cave as she made her way to its mouth once more. Her quick action had spared her men from the girl's desperate attack. Now those who had survived the battle were combing the seemingly endless number of passages. They had been prepared with their own torches, but they hadn't lasted for long.

The general cast a quick gaze at the signs and their warnings. A dozen languages described vague dangers. The word "beast" tended to figure prominently in them. This was a cave with a reputation that gave even her Elites pause, but she had a job to do, and she would see it done.

The brief warm snap had ended, and vast fringes of icicles lined every edge and every branch. As Trigorah scanned the twinkling landscape, her eyes came to rest on an approaching form. It was a large man, bearing overused armor, an intricate halberd, and an infuriating smile. He was seated on a steed that seemed dead on its feet. The beast's head hung low and pained breaths came in vast, steamy clouds. When Arden finally reached the cave's mouth, the horse trudged to the nearest piece of greenery and ate of it greedily.

"Have you ever given a moment's consideration to your mount?" Trigorah scolded.

"Horses are cheap," Arden said.

Trigorah looked at him with disgust.

"I figger you know why I'm here," he said.

"The circumstances of the wager," the general said.

"Uh-huh," Arden said, grinning with half-rotten teeth.

"You still seek to collect? You couldn't hold on to your target!" Trigorah hissed.

"I caught the 'sassin before you caught the girl or found the sword. Hangin to monsters don't enter into it," he growled. "You ain't lookin to weasel out, are ya?"

"I still have a task at hand. I will not abandon it," she remarked.

"She went in *that* cave, and you still hope to bring her back? What part, the head?" Arden chuckled. "Quit tryin to wriggle out of this. What're you, a coward?"

"Coward? *Coward!?* You, of anyone, call me a coward? There is a *war!* There is a hated enemy to the south. Has your blade ever tasted anything but the blood of your fellow Alliance?" Trigorah raged.

She smoldered for a moment, then turned to the cave.

"Soldier!" she called.

One of the men under her command stepped from the shadows.

"I want regular sweeps of the cave. Systematic. I shall send a supply team here. In the meantime, my colleague and I have a briefing that cannot be postponed," she said, stalking off to the clearing that sheltered her horse. "I dare say he has *much* to learn from me."

#

With no conversation to occupy her, Myranda's mind wandered. Just as he had instructed her to do, at each branch, she carefully felt the walls, turning in the direction that was smoothest. Soon the tunnel was glass-smooth, and almost perfectly straight. The grade grew gradually steeper, making it difficult to keep footing. Strangely, the sound of echoing drips of water was absent. Hours passed as Myranda gave Leo his quiet time. The second torch since they had awakened had to be replaced, signifying a full day of walking, climbing, and crawling. Myranda made ready to sit and rest, but this time she was not even scolded or encouraged. Her friend merely gave her a stern look that prompted her to proceed.

"How much further?" she asked.

"I can't be sure," he said. "We are close."

Silence followed.

"What is wrong? You were so talkative before," she said.

"Nothing is wrong. I just want to get to the end of this tunnel as quickly as possible. You can't hear it, but I can. This mountain is groaning. It has something up its sleeve. When it makes its move, I want to be ready for it. That means I need to listen," he said, agitated.

Myranda milled over his words before answering.

"It's just that . . . I can't stand the silence. It cuts through me. I've been alone for so long. Talking to myself, talking to Myn. I just need to hear a voice. I need proof that there is someone else out there. It seems like every time I try to get close, the world runs away," she said.

"The world runs away from you!" he said incredulously. "That is not how I remember it. When we first met, what were you doing? You came into an inn and sat as far as possible from anyone else. You closed yourself to your surroundings, so much so that you failed to notice your money being stolen. When I helped you out, you scurried upstairs and locked the door behind you. You were the one running. That is the trouble with your kind. Everything is always about you until the time comes to find fault. Sickening," he said.

His words were tinged with anger. It added a new quality to his voice, something vaguely familiar. Myranda was struck to the core by his words. Partially because they were so harsh. Partly because they were so true. She did protect herself from those around her. She had ever since she was a child. The only way to be sure no one learned of her feelings on the war was to keep them at arm's length. A part of her isolation was choice.

"I am sorry if my words hurt you, but . . . I just need silence right now," Leo said, less an apology and more a warning. He seemed not to be in control of his emotions, as though something had a hold over him.

A few moments passed. Leo stopped suddenly and shuffled to a wall, putting an ear to it.

"Leo," she said.

He clenched his fists and whipped his head around, sudden fury seizing him.

"What *now!?*" he raged.

The final word echoed off of the walls relentlessly. The echoes drove into Myranda's mind, stirring her thoughts. That word. That voice. She knew them. The echoes continued. A dark, painful memory emerged. It couldn't be.

"You . . . you were there . . . at the church . . ." she said, detached.

"What are you saying?" he demanded.

She remembered the voice behind her. The voice of the one holding a blade to her throat as she was sent away from the church all of those months ago.

"The church! Where I was kidnapped! You stole the sword*! You killed those soldiers!* Who are you really!?" she realized.

As if as an answer, the mountain began to rumble and roar. It was deafening. A rush of icy air swept past them.

"Not now! *Not now!*" he cried, launching himself into a run.

Myn looked anxiously to Myranda. Between the roar of the mountain and the flaring tempers, she was beside herself. Myranda sprinted off after the fleeing malthrope. For once she would not be distracted, no matter the madness that raged about her. The steep, slippery tunnel soon betrayed her as she lost her footing and began to slide. Myn's claws clacked at the floor as she struggled to keep pace with the now helpless human. After a few moments, Myranda splashed down into a numbingly cold pool of thrashing water. The dragon joined her in the pool, unable to stop quickly enough to avoid it. The beast managed to keep the torch she had taken to carrying dry, and leapt out of the water. Leo was waist deep in the icy stuff.

"Answer me! I want to know the truth!" Myranda demanded.

"You want the truth? Fine! This torrent of frigid water is rushing in through our only means of escape. We spent the better part of three days getting through this cave, and the water will fill half of it within the hour. If we stay or flee, we die. If we swim, we *may* survive," he said.

The reality of the situation swept over Myranda as powerfully as the water threatened to.

"How do I know I can trust you?" she asked.

"You don't. I've kept you alive this far. Now you have to decide," he said, diving into the churning pool.

Myranda cast a nervous glance at the very anxious Myn.

"He is not getting away that easily," she decided.

She dove into the water after him, with Myn reluctantly following. The dragon hated the cold, but was determined not to leave her friend's side.

Myranda wrestled her eyes open. The water was so cold, it stung her unmercifully, and the sound of the rushing water filled her head. Leo was disappearing into the eerie light of the submerged tunnel. She fought the astounding current, clinging to the slick as ice walls with fingers that had lost their feeling after just a few heartbeats in the water. Wavelike swishing motions of Myn's tail surged her forward until she was able to grip the roof with her claws. Neither girl nor dragon could make any headway. Every ounce of effort went to maintaining their position. A slight ripple in the rocky tunnel was enough to keep Myranda from sliding back, but Myn was not so lucky.

The dragon scratched desperately at the wall of the tunnel. She was losing the fight, flailing and slipping backward. Myranda took one hand away from its grip to guide the beast to the hand hold. Now with a firm grip, the two began to slowly pull themselves forward. Leo's form was barely visible ahead, pulling himself along in much the same way. Just ahead of him was the edge. Beyond that there was only light. Daylight.

As the girl and the dragon neared the opening, the current intensified. Myranda's chest heaved as her lungs begged for air. She reached out, managing to grasp the rounded edge of the opening with one hand. With the other, she grabbed the claw of her friend. In a final flurry of effort, she pulled the two of them into the light. The current split at the opening, half flowing into the tunnel, the rest fanning out along the wall the tunnel emerged from.

The latter current caught them, sweeping the pair forcefully along the wall just as Myranda's breath gave out. Spent air burst from her lips and a desperate, raking breath pulled in a lungful of frigid water. She convulsed as she smashed into the rocky edge of the pool. Darkness was closing in about her as she felt a pair of hands grip her arm and drag her from the pool.

A series of painful coughs spewed the water from her lungs and she gulped gratefully at the fresh air. Her vision was a swirl of indistinct forms as she was helped to her feet.

"Myn!" she managed. "Myn!"

She could feel the shivering beast brush weakly against her before dropping to the dry ground. Myranda was vaguely aware of being led along. Somehow she was on her feet, shuffling with a strong arm supporting her. She was barely cognizant of her own movement. Her helper lowered her to a seat and a blanket was thrown about her shoulders. The shapes that swept before her eyes were clearing. Before long she recognized a hand. She raised her eyes and struggled to focus on the face. Her hearing was nearly as poor as her sight, the roaring water still ringing in her ears. Mingled with the sound of water was a periodic sound she couldn't identify.

As she tried to steady herself, she realized that the sharp, grating noise she was hearing was her own coughing. When she finally calmed herself and her senses returned to her, she looked to her anonymous helper. He was a young man, about her age, with brown hair and a gray tunic. A sturdy messenger bag hung over his shoulder. He was checking her eyes and spouting phrases in a variety of languages. Eventually he struck the correct one.

"Are you warm enough?" he asked.

Myranda nodded.

"Where are the others?" she asked.

"Ah, so you have a tongue, and a northern one at that. Excellent, one of my favorites. The dragon that came with you is sleeping over yonder, and the malthrope has requested to be cared for in one of our cleric huts," he said.

"What happened?" she asked.

"You made it through the cave. You also made it through the waterfall, which may be unprecedented. I will look into it," he said.

"What is this place?" she asked, looking around. Her eyes had not recovered enough to make out her surroundings.

"My, so full of questions," he said. "Though after the ordeal you've been through, I suppose you've earned a few. This is Entwell Num Garastra. In the northern tongue, that translates to . . . the stomach--no, the belly of the beast," he said.

"What!?" she gasped.

"Oh, my heavens, I am sorry. It's just a name. No cause for fear. I'll explain later. Suffice to say you have discovered our village. It is a place of learning. We exist to acquire, improve, and impart knowledge," he explained.

"I'm not sure I understand," she said.

"You will. All in time," he said. "My name is Deacon. And you are?"

"Myranda," she said.

He held out his hand. She shook it, but he pulled away quickly and began riffling through a bag that hung at his side.

"You are cold as death. Excellent! Hold out your hand," he said, revealing a perfectly smooth, palm-sized, egg-shaped crystal.

"What? Why? What is going on?" she asked.

"Open your hand. I am merely going to temporarily manipulate certain physical attributes of your body tissues so as to facilitate the timelier introduction of appropriate heat levels than nature would generally allow," he said in a bewildering flurry of logic.

While Myranda was still trying to sort through his words, he placed the crystal in her hand. He then closed her hand around it and clasped his hands over hers. A flash of light shined through her fingers and a mild glow spread up her arms and through her body. It was accompanied by a curious sensation, or more accurately, a lack thereof. Everywhere the light touched was restored to normal. Cold became comfortable, numb became normal, and nowhere in between. There was no feeling of warmth, no tingling, simply an instantaneous return to normal. A second streak of light swept over her clothes, drying them.

"There," Deacon said. "How do you feel?"

As she began to answer, he scrambled to draw a thick, leather-bound book from his bag and began marking down all that she said with a stylus he had perched behind his ear.

"I feel fine," she said.

"No excessive heat? And tactile sensation--normal? Excellent, excellent," he said.

"What did you do?" she asked.

"The procedure is quite simple. It has escaped common use because the techniques it entails are not generally associated with white magic," he said. "You seem tired. Are you?"

"Very," she said.

"That is not a side effect I had anticipated. Perhaps . . ." he began.

"I don't think your spell is to blame. I haven't slept in more than a day," she said.

"Oh, well, yes. That would explain it," he said. "I can find you a soft bed and some fresh clothes if you like."

"You can?" Myranda said.

"Oh, yes. All of the amenities," he said with a chuckle. "Follow me."

She stood, but woozily stumbled. Deacon was quick to lend his arm to steady her. As the pair moved away from the deafening falls, Myranda gained her first clear look at the place she had been striving to reach for the past few days. Stretching out before her, nestled in the shadow of the cliffs towering behind, was a small village. The houses were simple huts with thatched roofs. The perfect little buildings with the rosy sky behind them looked more like a painting than someplace that might actually exist. There was no snow on the ground. Much to her surprise, the gravelly ground surrounding the falls gave way to emerald green grass.

As if this did not distinguish this village enough, the hamlet was alive with activity. Here was a young man sitting under a tree, there a trio of older men and women in a heated discussion. Birds, butterflies, and even what she swore was a tiny, winged person fluttered by. There were representatives from a myriad of races. Elves, dwarfs, humans--all in the open and interacting. It was a surreal sight, and Myranda was entranced. It was as though she was seeing life as it should be for the first time. Her trance was broken when Deacon was knocked forcefully to the ground. She turned to see Myn standing atop the fallen helper.

"Myn! No, he is helping me!" she scolded.

The dragon was reluctant to release Deacon, her teeth bared and dripping.

"I am sorry, little lady. I did not realize you were awake. I would have asked your permission, I assure you," Deacon said, chuckling as he got to his feet.

He drew his crystal and healed several places where the little dragon's claws met their mark.

"Are you all right?" Myranda asked.

"Fine, fine. It was my fault. I know how attached dragons get. Had I been thinking, I would have made my intentions clear," he said, casting another spell to mend holes torn in the fabric of his tunic.

"How do you know so much about dragons?" she asked.

"Solomon taught me," he said, carefully allowing the still agitated dragon to wedge herself between himself and Myranda.

"He knows about dragons?" she asked.

"He *is* a dragon," he said. "When you feel up to it, I'll introduce you. He is a very enlightening fellow."

Before long, they came upon a hut on the edge of the village. It was just like any of the others, and appeared as though it had never been used. He opened the door and led her inside. There were two rooms. One had a bed, the other a few chairs, a table, and a number of shelves.

"This will be your hut. Equip it as you will," he said.

"You mean, I may live here? This hut will be mine? Just like that?" she said.

"Of course. You made it through the cave. You are one of us. We always keep one hut empty to house the next adventurer to make the trek. We hadn't anticipated three at once. Work on the other huts will begin first thing tomorrow," he said.

"Where will Leo sleep?" she asked.

"Leo is your vulpine friend, I presume. He will be spending a day or two in the cleric's hut. What happened to him? I heard a bit of the chatter when they were hauling him out of the water and it seems he has been mangled physically and spiritually. It is going to take some of our best healers to untie the knots," he said. "As for Myn here, I am sure we can make some arrangements for her, too . . ."

"Oh, she sleeps beside me," Myranda said.

"Are you certain?" he asked.

"Since she was hatched," Myranda assured him.

"Oh, all right then," he said, eyebrow raised.

"Why?" she asked.

"Well, you see, the act of breathing fire is not always a strictly voluntary one. Occasionally, they let loose a puff or two in their sleep. Not enough to kill, mind you, but more than enough to set the bed aflame. Thus, sleeping in a bed with a dragon is generally inadvisable. However, if you have been doing so for this long then it is clearly not an issue," he said. "In a wardrobe in your bedroom, you will find a number of blue robes and tunics. They should fit well enough until we can make some specifically for you. I will make the necessary arrangements for you. You just have a well-earned rest. When you wake, find the nearest person and they will set you on your way."

"But where will you be?" she asked.

"Likely I will be scribing. It consumes most of my time. Anyone in the village will be more than willing to help you, you needn't come to me. However, if you need me, just say my name and someone will point you in my direction," he said.

He took his leave and closed the door. Myranda quickly changed into the fresh clothes. They were a bit too large for her, but as the first change of clothes she'd had in weeks, they were heavenly. She fell into the bed and was asleep before Myn joined her a moment later.

As was too often the case, Myranda's dreams were tortured. This time, though, they twisted at her mind in a new way. Now she was taunted with images of Leo. Memories of all of the good he had done for her intermingled with imagined instances of lies and treachery. She was forced to relive her time captured in the church with the role of her captor now recast with the face of her former friend. The man she had trusted, who had given her the help she needed, was now tying her up. The kind, thoughtful friend was now striking down men and putting a blade to her throat. It was agony.

She was jarred from her sleep by the departure of Myn, who leapt from the bed and pushed the door open. The golden light of sunrise and the sounds of morning filtered through the doors. Myranda drifted in and out of sleep for a time. Finally she heard a voice and opened her eyes. Standing before her was Deacon. He had an amused and slightly apologetic look on his face.

"I am sorry to wake you, but we have something of a situation that you may be able to help with," he said.

"Of course," she said, pulling herself groggily to her feet.

Deacon again offered his arm, but she didn't need the help anymore.

"Leo is undergoing a rather unpleasant procedure. You see, his legs had been broken multiple times in the past. They were left to heal naturally, and many did so poorly. We have found that the best way to deal with such an ailment is to allow the legs to heal correctly," he explained as the pair moved toward the cluster of huts that had been painted white.

"Heal correctly? But you said they had already healed," she said.

"Therein lies the issue. The legs must be re-broken. Generally the patient would be put to sleep or at least deprived of feeling for such a procedure, but Leo apparently asked to have the work done free of aid. Two successful breaks had been made when your other little friend made her appearance. She has taken a stance atop Leo and will not allow any of our healers near. We've tried to take care of the situation with magic, but it appears our spells are not having an effect. A number of the clerics were eager to put the more powerful spells to work, but I thought perhaps you could handle it more easily," he said.

Myranda was led inside one of the huts. Five white-robed healers were in a circle around the table upon which Leo was lying. Standing over Leo was Myn, her jaws snapping at anyone who approached from in front and her tail lashing anyone who approached from behind. As soon as Myranda was in sight, Myn fairly began to dance in place, anxiously shifting from foot to foot. Leo whispered something in a language Myranda could not identify and the healers filed out of the hut. Deacon lingered in the doorway before leaving and shutting the door behind him.

"They tell me you have a problem," Myranda said. "Deacon thought I could help."

"Myn will not let them do what needs to be done," Leo said. "I have spoken to her, but she will not listen. I doubt that there is anything that you can do that hasn't been tried."

"Maybe she just doesn't believe you. You've given *me* very little reason to do so," she said angrily. "If you want me to help you, you owe me the truth."

"I do not owe you anything," he said.

"I saved your life. You yourself said that the favor needs to be returned," Myranda said.

"I led you to safety. If I had not shown you the way into and out of the cave, you would be in the hands of the Elites right now," he said. "No one will be able to enter or leave this place until the falls relent, and months will pass before that happens. The debt is repaid."

"I want the truth," she demanded.

"You wouldn't know the truth if you had it. For all you know, I could simply replace one lie with another. If you want the truth, find it for yourself. There is as much of me here as there is anywhere else. If there is truth to be found, it is here," he said.

"Then why should I help you?" she asked.

"You shouldn't, but you will. I know you better than you know yourself. I know that you would like nothing more than to see me suffer for this supposed injustice, but your heart won't let you. That is your main weakness--your heart. You care too much for those around you. One day it will cost you your life," he said.

Myranda's eyes wandered to Leo's legs. They were twisted and bent. She tried to be strong. She tried to think of the wrongs he had done. The lies he had told. Alas, among all of the half-truths and outright lies, there was one undeniable fact. He was right about her. As angry as she was, she found herself searching for some way to help him. It didn't take long for her to realize that if there was something keeping their spells from affecting Myn, there could be only one cause. There, on the little dragon's neck, the cord that held her souvenir still held firm. The trip through the water had twisted the trinket around, where it came to be nestled between her folded wings.

With a bit of difficulty, Myranda managed to untangle the charm and remove it. The dragon seemed upset, and became more so when the door was opened to allow the healers back in. Without the charm to protect her, Myn was quickly put into a deep, harmless sleep. After a final, stern exchange of looks, Myranda lifted the little dragon and took her leave. Outside, Deacon gave her a hand with the sleeping creature.

"Might I ask what the problem was?" Deacon wondered.

"A few days ago, Myn managed to chew this little ornament off of a helmet she separated from its owner. I gave it to her as a necklace, but apparently it had some sort of enchantment," Myranda explained as the trio moved back to her hut.

The dragon was set on Myranda's bed.

"Would you mind if I had a look at that charm? If it was able to ward off our spells, it must be quite powerful," he said.

She shrugged and handed it to him. Even before it dropped into his hand, he assured her that it was the work of an Entwellian. Looking it over only confirmed it.

"Yes. Yes. I know the man who invented this technique. I believe he is still about if you would like to meet him. Well, in time you will meet everyone," he said, before returning it to Myranda, who affixed it to the sleeping beast's neck.

"What do you do for food here?" Myranda asked. Right now she was a mass of hunger and anger, and she had to do something before one or the other overcame her.

"Oh, of course, you must be famished. This way. I'll join you. I haven't eaten yet," he said.

Myranda was lead out of the hut and along a well-worn path. Around the hut she had been given were a dozen others just like it, simple structures of wood with a thatched roof. Young people of every race lingered in the area, each wearing a similar blue tunic. As they continued, Myranda came to realize that the whole of the village, and a sizable one at that, was arranged in small clusters around courtyards with a larger hut at their center. Different groups of dwellings seemed to be populated by different groups of similarly dressed residents. There were people dressed in white, others in black. There were tunics of red, brown, aqua, and yellow. Scattered among them were older figures, some in deep conversation with one another, others trailing groups of younger villagers. If this was a place of learning, as Deacon had said, then these must be the teachers.

The pair came to a wide, stone-paved road that divided the village down the middle. It ran from the now-raging waterfall to a vast courtyard ringed with short walls. At its center was a majestic-looking structure, the only place she'd seen thus far that seemed to have been built as anything more than a shelter. It had tall, glass windows, a shingled roof, and painted patterns on its walls.

Myranda was led across the central path and around the rim of the courtyard. The huts around her now were somewhat different to those on the other side of the road. Targets and training dummies could be found in the center of the gatherings of huts. The students in this area wore sturdier clothing than the simple tunics she'd seen thus far, each adorned with various intricate badges and patches.

Finally she came to a long, curving hut with smoke rising from a pair of chimneys at one side. The walls were covered with windows, and a scattering of the village's people sat at tables within. Once inside, a simple earthenware bowl for each of them was filled with a thin vegetable stew and a coarse loaf of wheat bread was split between them. Myranda made short work of the stew, abandoning a spoon in favor of the bread, dipping and eating. She had messily dispatched half of the bowl in this manner when she realized the attention she was attracting. She smiled meekly when Deacon handed her a spoon.

"I am sorry," she said.

"No need to apologize. I am always happy to see a new technique," he said.

"The last thing I ate was a half-cooked bat and a few raw ones, and I would hardly call them a meal," she said with her mouth full.

"Ah, yes. Bat. Some of us here see it as a rite of passage to have to resort to bat to survive. There is only a handful who have managed to avoid it. I, alas, have never had the pleasure. Already you fit in better than I," he said.

She merely smiled between bites.

"Correct me if I am wrong, but I believe I heard a few harsh words tossed about behind the closed door. How did things go in there?" he asked.

"He . . . I . . . That scoundrel has been lying to me since I met him, and now he refuses to set things straight! He tells me if I want it, I ought to find it myself!" she raged.

"Well, that should be simple enough. It hasn't been long since the three of you appeared, and already some of the elder members have been telling tales of the last time he was here," he said.

"What do they say?" she asked, taken aback by the sudden source of new information.

"I am afraid I did not linger long enough to hear the tale. It was Keller doing the recollection. He is a rather narrow-minded member of the warrior school, and all of that hand to hand miscellany just cannot hold my interest. I believe he called him Lain more than once," Deacon recalled.

"Lain? Then Leo isn't even his real name?" she fumed.

"Oh, it is . . . well, I don't know that it is, but it certainly could be. You see, Lain is less a name and more a title. The stealth masters tend to attach it to the most prized of their pupils," Deacon explained. "If your friend is rightly called Lain, then he would be the only living one. They are a rare breed."

"I wish I knew more," she said.

"I will show you to the library one of these days. You should be able to find something in his records," he said.

"You keep records?" she said.

"Of course. Otherwise it would be very difficult to assign credit where it is due," he said.

The promise of information about the infuriating malthrope was enough to calm Myranda's anger for the time being, and the first bowl of stew took the desperation from her hunger. As she refilled her bowl, she became curious about her newest friend. He was equally curious about her, and the two decided to start what would turn out to be a lengthy question and answer session.

"When I first came here, you called this place Entwell . . . Entwell Num . . ." She struggled to remember.

"Entwell Num Garastra," he said. "The Belly of the Beast."

"That is it. Why do you call it that? And what is this place?" she asked.

"Oh, well. You see . . . Are you sure you do not know this story? What I am about to tell you is generally the reason people find this place," he said.

"I came here because I was being followed and Leo promised me safety," she said.

"Ah, well, then I will enlighten you. You see, long, long ago, people began entering the cave and not returning. Before long, people began to believe there was a creature within that was taking their lives. Periodically, a hideous roar would serve to support that theory. So it became a test of skill. The king of . . . Ulvard at the time, called upon the strongest warriors and mages to rid the kingdom of this foul beast," he said.

"I do know this tale! The cave we just went through . . . that was the cave of the beast!? I never would have let him take me in if I had known that!" she said, flustered.

"I am told it is clearly marked," he said.

"We rode by a number of signs on a horse. I didn't have time to read them, and the rest were worn and faded," she said.

"Well, the finest warriors, wizards, and adventurers the world had to offer began to file one by one into the cave. The first to return with the head of the beast would be hailed for all of time as the greatest warrior that ever lived. Now, it became clear to each individual adventurer that it was the cave itself, and not some beast, that had taken all that had come before, but that epiphany usually came moments before they joined the fallen.

"Eventually, a remarkable wizard by the name of Azriel found this paradise. She felt that if there was a beast in that cave, then this must be its belly. She was going to turn around and return to the outside world to tell the others, but she needed time to recover. As the days turned to weeks, she fell in love with this place. In time, a second warrior made it through, and then another, and then another. This place became a village populated by the best of the best. With each new arrival, the knowledge pool increased. Now we live to teach, and we live to learn. Unfortunately, in the last few decades the flow of fresh blood has slowed to a trickle," he said.

"Yes, well, these days we have found a much more efficient way to rid ourselves of our finest men and women," she said.

"I assume you speak of the war. So the war is still on? Good heavens, the last new arrival was over thirty years ago and he assured us that the north was on its last legs," he said.

"It has been for some time. Somehow we still manage," Myranda said with a sigh.

"I wonder how the army has managed to . . . one moment, we have a visitor," he said.

Myranda turned to see a dragon, mostly gray with a slightly lighter shade on his belly, push the door open. To her surprise, the creature was only a bit larger than Myn, perhaps as large as a mastiff.

"Solomon, this is Myranda. Myranda, this is Solomon--I was telling you about him," he said.

Myranda crouched down and began to scratch the dragon on the head the way she knew Myn liked.

"You didn't tell me he was just a little baby," she cooed.

Rather than the joyous look that Myn tended to give, Solomon wore a very stern look on his face. Deacon wore a look of concern.

"Myranda . . . Solomon is among our eldest and most sage wizards," he said.

"Oh. I . . . I am sorry. It's just that, oh my, he is so small. I didn't know," Myranda said, mortified.

The dragon turned to Deacon and began what must have been a conversation. Solomon spoke in a near inaudible series of low hisses, guttural growls, and slight movements. Deacon did the courtesy of answering in northern dialect, so that at least she could follow half of the conversation.

"Yes, she did bring the other dragon in. . . Well, we had to do some reconstruction on the legs of the other newcomer and she was protecting him from the healers. . . I would have, but Myranda here was closer, so I asked for her help first. . . Yes, she did," he said, turning to Myranda. "Unprecedented, by the way--I've checked. You and your friends are the first to ever enter this place after the falls had given way."

He turned back to the dragon and continued.

"Yes. . . As a matter of fact, I was able to test my temperature restoration spell on her. . . Well, clearly she is. . . Oh, it is not that dangerous." He turned to her. "You feel well, correct?"

"Yes," she said, made a bit nervous by the direction the conversation was taking.

"There, see? . . . I do not know." He turned to her one last time. "Do you speak any languages besides the northern one?"

"I am rather well-versed in Tresson," she said.

Solomon's reptilian eyes rolled. He let a harsh, grating hiss loose that startled Myranda. His mouth then yawned wide and cracked and snapped as he tested its movement.

"Of the two . . ." he said in a very harsh but understandable voice. Another hiss, twice the intensity of the first, was released before he finished the statement. "I prefer Northern."

After clearing his throat, the dragon's voice was smoother. It was deep, but not outlandishly so, and resonated with power. There was an unquestionable sense of authority in his words. His tone was steady, and there was a slow deliberate cadence to his speech.

"Where did you discover your dragon?" he asked.

"I was in Ravenwood. It was beginning to snow, and there was a cave nearby. I ventured inside for shelter. I didn't know that there was a dragon inside. Then a second one arrived and they began to fight. I blacked out, and when I awoke, Myn was on top of me," she explained.

"Then she is wild-caught. Have you trained her?" he asked.

"Whatever she has learned, she has learned on her own. And I did not catch her. She followed me. I tried to get her to stay, but when I found that her mother and siblings were killed, I couldn't bear to leave her," Myranda explained.

Solomon gave her a long, calculating stare. Finally he spoke.

"Send her to me first. I want her before any others," he said. "And I want to meet the dragon when she awakes."

With that he turned and marched out of the eatery. Deacon leaned close to Myranda.

"This is a great honor. Solomon has chosen you as a pupil. I myself had to endure more than three years of training by lesser teachers before he would see me," Deacon said. "I see great things in your future. Which reminds me. Now that I know that you did not come here as a test of skill, I wonder, what skills have you to test?"

"What do you mean?" she asked.

"Are you a warrior of any sort?" he asked, quickly pulling out the book from his bag.

"No. I can use a short sword and a dagger, but I don't like to," she said.

"Well, that is going to change. Now, magic. Anything?" he asked.

"I just got through learning a bit of healing magic. What do you mean 'that is going to change'?" she asked.

"A healer? Excellent! We do not get many new healers, and even fewer that are native to the north," he said.

"What were you saying about the warrior part changing?" she asked again.

"You are required to pass a few basic weapon-handling and combat trials, aside from whatever magic you may wish to learn. We like to be complete. The northern side of the village is what we call the Wizard's Side. As a healer, I assume you will be spending most of your time there. Here in the south side of the village, Warrior's Side, you will be learning a bit of combat theory and master three types of weapons at the very least. It is the minimum required physical instruction," he said.

"I don't want to learn that. I hate weapons. I hate the war! If I learn how to kill people, I become a tool of the war like the men and women who have been forced to squander their lives in the pursuit of ending other lives," she said.

"I don't think you will need to worry about that. You see, we won't be letting you kill any of us, and you are not likely to encounter anyone else. It is entirely academic," he said. "So, what sort of healing have you learned? Our healers tend to specialize in--"

"You are talking as though I am never going to leave this place," she interrupted.

"Very few of us ever do leave," he explained matter-of-factly.

"Am I a prisoner here?" she asked.

"In a way, but not because of us. That waterfall is blocking the only semi-safe means of egress, and it stops its flow for only a few days every few months. When the falls have relented, escape is possible, but . . . well, for most of us there is nothing for us outside. Here there is comfort, safety, and enough knowledge to live a long, full life learning and perfecting it. I, for one, have never even become curious about the outside," he said.

"You have never been outside of this place?" she said.

"As I mentioned, we have not had a newcomer in more than thirty years, and I am only twenty-five. I was born here," he explained. "Frankly, being outside would be unbearable to me. There is so much to do here. So much that needs to be done. If I had to worry about things like the war or where my next meal was coming from, I would never get anything done."

"That seems sad to me," Myranda said.

"There is no need to pity me. If you are through eating, I would like to show you around this prison you are so sympathetic about," he said.

She agreed and the two were off.

Out of habit, Myranda braced herself as they left the dining hut, ready for a blast of cold, but none came. Anywhere else that Myranda had ever been would still have patches of snow at this time of year, but here it was heavenly. The air was cool, the breeze was mild.

There was something majestic about the waterfall to the west as it fell from ledge to ledge along a sheer cliff, finally reaching the ground to bathe a corner of the valley in its fine mist. The whole of the village was in a vast, half-moon-shaped valley. The curved side was composed of the cliffs of the mountain. On the other side, the ground dropped off sharply. Beyond that was ocean. The end result was a sparse village spread out over a piece of land the size of a large city, nestled in a notch cut into the endless forbidding seaward-face of the mountains. They were far too high to be seen by a passing ship, and Myranda had heard tales of the rough seas that plagued the east coast of the continent. It was no surprise that none had ever seen this place.

None, of course, but the people who now lived here. In a way, the people made the place all the more wonderful. In the north, there was naught but a mass of gray-cloaked forms. No faces, no conversation, just a cloak marching along, stopping here or there to spread the latest word of the war. Here, there was more than the scraps left by a war that had picked the populace clean. There were men, women, and children of all ages. More incredible, there were examples of virtually every race. Peoples she'd seen only a few examples of in her life were plentiful. Stocky dwarfs, graceful elves, and many she'd never seen before. Each spoke their own tongue, filling the air with a symphony of different languages. When approached, some were too busy, but most would offer a hello. Deacon would translate as pleasantries were exchanged, and they would be off.

Their wanderings took them to the Wizard's Side once more, and Deacon began to explain the different areas. There were the yellow-clad novices studying wind magic as a specialty. The people wearing aqua, most lingering near a small lake on the eastern edge of the village, were water wizards and their students. Those dressed in brown were focused on earth magic. Fire apprentices and instructors wore red. The white tunics belonged to healers, and those in black were the war wizards, black magic users.

When someone recognized Myranda as a newcomer, they would sometimes approach her and make a few remarks in their respective language, and Deacon would explain the circumstances of her arrival.

They were engaged in just such a conversation when they were rudely interrupted. Deacon had begun to brag about the spell he had cast on Myranda again, prompting more than a bit of concern from the white-robed elf he was talking to, when a pixie of some sort flitted up and positioned herself directly between them. She began to speak in an agitated manner. Her voice was musical, and the language was bizarre. It rose and fell in tone like the work of a talented flutist.

"All right, all right. Calm down. Yes, this is Myranda . . . Myranda, did you ask to be placed under Solomon's tutelage, or did he ask you?" Deacon asked.

"He asked me," she said.

"There, you see . . . Well, I don't know. Let me ask her . . . She cannot answer directly because she speaks Northern . . . Oh, it is not a vulgar language," he said.

"It is. Listen to me. I sound like an animal," the tiny creature said, shifting languages abruptly.

"You sound just fine. Myranda, this is Ayna. She recently earned the position of Highest Master of Wind Magic," he said.

As he spoke, Ayna was darting around Myranda, inspecting her from all angles. Myranda tried to turn to face her, but the fairy just flitted in another direction in a blur.

"You don't seem to be anything special," she said.

"I never claimed to be," Myranda replied.

"Still, Solomon has been at this for quite a while. He ought to know a prime pupil. It is just like him to snatch up the first good one in years. I want her first," Ayna declared.

"I'm afraid Solomon made it quite clear. He was to have her before all others," Deacon said.

"So I'll challenge him," she said. "Why should he get to influence the newcomers with his element and prejudice them against mine?"

"He holds seniority over you. He can take his pick of any student," Deacon said.

"Fine. I want her next. Immediately. I mean it, as soon as she passes his trial, *that day* I want her in my grove for her first lesson," Ayna said.

"I'll mark it down," Deacon said.

"See that you do. And you, Myranda. Don't let all of that fire nonsense cloud your mind. Air is the true essence of this world. Oh, and do ask Deacon here to teach you a decent language. It must be awful to be confined to this wretched little dialect," she said.

In a flash she was gone.

"What just happened?" Myranda asked.

"It would seem you are caught in a little power struggle. That makes two of the Highest Masters who have demanded you be passed right to them. This is a huge opportunity for you. If you pick things up quickly, you can trim *years* off of the path to mastery! Outstanding!" he said.

"Air magic, fire magic. I never said I wanted to learn anything like that. All I ever wanted was to heal people," Myranda said.

"Don't worry, you'll have your white magic training. It is actually the smallest of our areas of study. Not many white wizards found it necessary to experience trial by beast," he said. "But, in addition, we require that you reach at least a basic understanding of all four elemental magics. I believe I mentioned that."

"I am not sure I like her. Ayna, I mean," Myranda said.

"That's all right. By the time you're through with her you will be *quite sure* that you don't like her," he said.

"How comforting," she said flatly. "What are these buildings?"

Deacon looked about.

"Well, this hut is the home of Caloth. He is an apprentice to Twila right now. She is one of our few dedicated white wizards. That is the hut of Milla. She is fresh out of elemental training and working on her first steps into purely black magic," he said.

"Why do you allow black magic here?" she asked.

"Why wouldn't we? It is a vast and highly developed field," he said.

"But it is evil," she said.

"Oh, no. Magic is a tool. It is no more evil than a hammer or a saw. I see you are confused, and understandably. You see, there are as many different interpretations and classifications of magic as there are languages and peoples in this world. This can cause difficulty when there is a clash in the way magics are understood between Master and pupil. As a result, we have chosen one set of classes that we feel is most accurate and made it standard," he said.

"Go on," Myranda said.

"Well, black magic is first. Quoting our founder, 'Any procedure of non-elemental origin that directly manipulates mystic energies with the expressed and sole intention of damaging or destroying a physical or spiritual form shall this day forward be known as black magic.' It is the mystic equivalent of a sword. It is only evil if it is used for evil, though I have been told the more common use of the phrase black magic in the outside world is as a blanket term for acts of evil through magic. Granted, it *is* the area that lends itself most readily to dark intentions," he said.

"Then white magic is the opposite? It heals," she said.

"'Any procedure of non-elemental origin that directly manipulates mystic energies with the expressed and sole intention of healing or enhancing a physical or spiritual form shall this day forward be known as white magic,'" he quoted.

"Then why do you have people who specialize in fire and air?" she asked.

"Well, the pure magics are specifically non-elemental. Thus the four elements, in our system at least, are considered separately. Within each elemental class, spells are said to have white or black alignments if they are most commonly used to help or hurt, respectively. Either that or they are considered neutral, or gray," he said.

"Gray?" she asked.

Deacon tugged at his gray tunic.

"My specialty. In the words of our founder, 'Any procedure of non-elemental origin that directly manipulates mystic energies with no clear intention or ability to purely aid or injure shall this day forward be known as gray magic.' This is simultaneously the largest and most neglected of the classes of magic," he said.

"Why is that?" she asked.

"Well, gray magic is very much the basis, as well as the next logical extension of, all other magics. As a result, it is very intuitive, and all other wizards know at least a bit of it. A person who devotes his life to the study and development of gray magic is something akin to a chef who specializes in boiling water or a poet who specializes in punctuation. No one will deny the importance of the area, but few will call for work to be done to improve it," he said.

"Why did you become interested in it, then?" she wondered.

"It wasn't the subject that interested me, it was the practitioner. We had only one wizard who was at all versed in the complexities of gray. His name was Gilliam, and he seemed to have devoted his life to being as different from the rest of the world as possible. He was something of a scoundrel. You see, illusions are included in my area, and they were his forte. He could make it appear that he had done anything. Cure the sick, summon creatures, even raise the dead. None of it was real, but he made it seem so long enough to make off with the reward for solving the problem at hand.

"He entered the cave in hopes of conjuring up an illusion of the mythic beast so that he could chase it outside to kill in the view of all around, thus stealing the position of the world's finest warrior. He became lost on the return trip and ended in this place. Before long, he began to irritate the other people here. When I was growing up, I found him to be the most entertaining thing in my life. By the time I was old enough to know why he had no respect among us, I was already hopelessly addicted to his brand of magic," Deacon reminisced.

"Have you managed to add any respect to the field?" Myranda asked.

"I am only twenty-five. Gilliam died six years ago--and, unfortunately for me, he never recorded a single page of his methods. He resented the lack of respect that the others showed his work, so he kept his ways secret. Over the eight years that I studied under him, I managed to memorize the majority of what he had to teach, and I have been spending the years since his death scribing everything he taught. I have barely had time to develop a single spell of my own," he said.

"That spell you used on me, to help me after I got out of the water. What about that one?" she asked.

"That *is* one of mine . . . well, a variation on one of\ his. It is a specialized form of transformation," he said.

"Why does everyone seem concerned when they learn you tried it on me?" she said.

"Oh, don't listen to them. They want to chide me about the fact that I have been toying with the idea for so long. Also, transformation was the spell that killed Gilliam. Well, transubstantiation," he said.

"What!?" she gasped.

"Relax, I worked out the fatal flaws. At least, I think I did. You see, he used a full change in his version of transformation, and I use a shift. The difference is that when you cast a change, you must cast a counter spell to change back. When you cast a shift, the transformation ends when the spell ends," he said.

"What happened to him?" Myranda wondered, more than a bit disturbed at the potentially fatal spell she had been used to test.

"I'll show you," he said.

Myranda swallowed hard and followed as he led her to a small hut in the seaward portion of the village. Beside it was a statue, immaculately carved, of an elfin gentleman with his hands out. Hanging from one hand was a gold chain with a rather rough-cut crystal mounted in it.

"Behold, Gilliam," he said.

"A statue was made of him? Or . . ." she questioned, slowly realizing the truth. "Oh my goodness . . ."

"He wanted to show me how a man could change himself to stone and back again. He succeeded at half," he said. "Poor fellow started to change before he finished the spell. He foolishly cast it in the wrong order. As a result, he did not include the ability for his new form to store his consciousness, so when the change occurred, his soul just drifted away. I could change him back--I have discovered the method--but I would merely be bringing back his corpse. I thought this was a more fitting memorial," Deacon said.

"It's so sad," she said.

"Indeed. At any rate, his death left us without a gray Master, so the task fell to me," he said, "and it has consumed me ever since. I have seldom been asked to aid with the research of others, and I have never had a student. This is my life. Please, come inside."

He pushed open the door to the hut and the pair entered.

As soon as Deacon and Myranda crossed the threshold of the hut, a series of crystals mounted in lamps flared to life, filling the interior with light. Inside, there was a single room that resembled Wolloff's tower, in that it was utterly filled with books. Unlike the tower, though, there was order. All of the books were stored on shelves, the titles clearly inked, though in another language.

Vials and canisters were stored in a separate shelf with the utmost of care. In one corner, there was a bed that looked as though it hadn't been used in a week. At the center of the room was a desk with a crystal for light, an open book, and the only chair in the room. The immaculate room was in stark contrast to its resident. Deacon's dark brown hair was in a constant state of chaos. His clothes were in a terrible state of disrepair, and the side of his left hand was apparently permanently stained with ink.

He walked up to his desk, where a book with blank pages lay open.

"This is your hut?" she asked.

"Indeed it is," he answered as he led her inside. "Oh, no."

"What?" Myranda asked.

"I failed to refill the ink. I have to write at least a dozen pages over again," he said, selecting a canister from one of the shelves.

"What do you mean? How could you fail to notice that you had run out of ink until after you'd written pages?" she asked.

"Oh, I wasn't writing in this book, I was writing in this one," Deacon explained, pulling the ubiquitous tome from his bag and laying it on the table.

Myranda gave a long, confused stare.

"Watch," he said.

First, he refilled the ink. Next, He opened the book from his bag and pulled the stylus from behind his ear. After flipping through his book to see that there were far more than a dozen pages to be recorded, he found the first page and began to trace over the first word. As he did so, the quill on the desk rose up and dipped itself in the ink. It then floated to the blank page and began to duplicate the strokes made by the original. Deacon reached into his pocket with his free hand and withdrew the crystal. Clutching it briefly, he removed his hand from the stylus. Without skipping a beat, the stylus continued tracing over the words on its own. He stood back with a smile as the words from the page were transcribed automatically.

"Had I been bright enough to keep the ink bottle filled, this would have been finished just a few moments after I had stopping writing in my travel book," he grumbled.

"That is incredible!" she said.

"If that is incredible, then you are quite easily impressed. I was able to perform that particular feat when I was twelve years old," he said, putting the crystal away.

"Twelve!? When did you start learning magic?" she asked.

"Shortly after I was born. As a matter of fact, my first words were an incantation. I believe that it was . . . Oh, what did they tell me? Illuminate. I would babble the words over and over and the little crystal that they had given me would start to glow," he said.

"This is a wonderful place," Myranda said, walking about and looking over the books.

"Now *that* I can agree with," Deacon said, turning to make certain that the page automatically turned as it should.

"Did you write all of these?" Myranda asked.

"Well, I wouldn't say that I was the author, but I put ink to my former teacher's ideas," he said.

"And they are all on the same subject?" she wondered.

"Well, different shades, but all gray," he answered.

"Then why are the titles in different languages?" she asked, as she leafed through a book to discover a language that she absolutely could not identify.

"Oh, that. Well, as you have no doubt noticed, very few people here speak the same language. One of the policies of our founder requires each resident of Entwell to learn to understand each and every other language. In this way, everyone may speak whatever language that he or she is most comfortable with without fear of being misunderstood. I, for one, was fascinated with the different tongues. Language became something of a hobby for me, and I am Entwell's unofficial expert on it. To stay sharp, I alternate which language I use with each book," he said.

"But I speak Northern and Tresson. I was unaware that there were different languages to be had," she said.

"Perhaps not now, but our village has existed for six hundred years. Until the war started, there were eleven languages in common use on this continent alone. The language known as Northern was originally called Varden. It was spoken in Kenvard and Ulvard, though the Ulvardians spoke a different dialect. Vulcrest spoke a language called Crich. The eight kingdoms that make up the Tressor region spoke nine different languages prior to joining together.

"Then there are the small continents to the east and their languages. And, of course, the dead languages. There are a handful of non-spoken languages, as well. Finally, there are the beast languages. All told, there are no less than thirty, and I know them all," he said.

"You should be proud," she said.

"I am," he said.

Myranda was mystified by the number of books as she looked around. Wolloff had had his share, to be sure, but these were all hand-written by

Deacon himself. The amount of work it must have taken was mind boggling.

"I have only been to two libraries. One was in a monastery to the west of my former hometown. The other was just recently in the tower of a wizard called Wolloff. This puts Wolloff's collection to shame, and rivals the monastery," she said.

"It is not a contest. This is merely how I have chosen to fill my days," he said. "Now as for--"

There was a knock at the still-open doorway that interrupted him. It was one of the many men that Myranda had seen milling about in the village as they were walking earlier. He delivered some sort of handwritten message to Deacon, who thanked him in what must have been his native language. After reading the note, he folded it and placed it in his pocket.

"Well, the time has come. The Elder wants to see the newcomers now. Let us not keep her waiting," he said.

"We will have to awaken Myn and bring Leo," Deacon explained, leading her out the door. "The Elder will need to see them as well."

"Who is the Elder? Why do we have to see her?" Myranda asked.

Deacon answered as they walked.

"The Elder is the most learned member of our ranks. She represents the very wisest and balanced of the Masters, and is one of only two Archmages. She is essentially our leader, making sure that all relevant decisions are well-made. She will determine what skills you and your friends have, and what training will suit you best. In fact, despite the fact that Solomon and Ayna both chose you to be their student, the Elder must be the one to allow it. If she thinks poorly of the choice, then you will have to work your way through the ranks like everyone else," he said.

The two reached Myranda's hut, where Myn was still sleeping. Deacon focused a brief flash of concentration on her and she was immediately awake. She thanked Deacon by pouncing on him once again for being too close to Myranda. With the dragon keeping the pair carefully separated, Deacon and Myranda sought out the healer's hut, where Leo was just testing out his freshly repaired legs. Myn scampered about him while Myranda gave him a stern look.

Finally, the group entered the large hut at the center of a very large courtyard in the middle of the village. Inside it was solemn as a church. Unlike the crystals that gave light to the other huts, this one was lit entirely with flickering candles. At the back of the room, in a simple wooden chair, was the woman who could only be the Elder that they spoke of. She did not appear very old, but one glimpse of her told of a wisdom that would have taken two lifetimes to gain. She was dressed as simply as the others; only a gold-colored sash draped about her neck made her stand out. Her hair was gray and pulled gracefully back behind her shoulders. She was clearly elfin in nature, with a tall, thin physique and distinctive ears.

The only other occupants of the room were a handful of men and women who were busy at various tasks, mostly involving large leather-bound books.

When the three stood before her, Deacon introduced them in yet another new language. Myranda bowed when she heard her name. Leo stood firm when his was spoken. Myn had locked her gaze on the Elder the moment she had seen her, and refused to look away. The little dragon must have sensed something about her, felt her power, and was entranced by it. The Elder surveyed the trio with a measuring stare. Finally she spoke, her voice clear and confident. The language matched that of Deacon.

"The girl will be a fine wizard. Her mind is strong and her heart is pure. The malthrope may go. I am satisfied with his past accomplishments here. Allow him whatever he requires to further himself. The dragon is still young. Her potential is great. See that she is brought before Solomon. And prepare them. I want each ready with the coming of the blue moon. They must witness the ceremony," she decreed in her complex language.

Leo, clearly understanding her words, took his leave, while Myranda stood confused.

"Just one moment! I will not stand for this!" came a gruff voice from the door, shattering the solemn environment. He, too, spoke the strange language.

Barging into the hut was a dwarf. He wore a look of anger on his bearded face. Every inch of him seemed to be covered in a thin layer of dirt, as though he had spent the day rolling around on the ground. His clothes were brown, though a few shades darker than the tailor had intended, and he was brandishing staff that appeared to be nothing more than a tree root with an unrefined crystal tangled at one end. Myn quickly positioned herself between the intruder and Myranda as the dwarf launched into a rant.

"I will not let this stand! Ayna has just come to me grinning that infuriating grin and twittering about this new student of hers, and how after Solomon finishes with her, she will see what real magic is. I had heard of no newcomers, and my underlings had seen neither hide nor hair either. So, I ask you, why would two of our Masters be anticipating a student that had not had even the most rudimentary of earth training? Because I am being passed over!

"None of you have ever given Earth magic the respect it deserves, and now you have gone to ridiculous lengths to hide the new students from me for the duration of their training. *And what is she doing traipsing about with Deacon?* He is not even a part of the curriculum!" he raged, all without Myranda understanding a word.

As Deacon began describing the situation to the angry wizard, the other people in the room began gathering up their things and slowly filing out. Myn was growing increasingly upset and sticking close to Myranda. Ayna flitted into the hut and joined the argument in her melodic language. Her words, whatever they may have been, seemed to compound the dwarf's agitation.

Throughout the outpouring of anger, Deacon continued to do his best to mediate, speaking the language of the Elder. The majestic woman merely sat, calmly surveying the fray. Solomon stalked into the hut to add a final voice to the heated debate. Myranda found herself lost in an angry symphony of different languages. Deacon's expression was one of helpless concern as his words grew more desperate in tone. Finally, he stepped away from the other three, who had been essentially ignoring him since the beginning. Approaching Myranda, he struggled to make himself heard over the din.

"I think you and I had best take our leave," he said, Myn too concerned with the bellowing of the others to object to his presence.

"You'll get no arguments from me!" she replied.

The trio walked briskly out the door, with Myn nearly crashing into the doorway rather than take her eyes off of the fray long enough to see where she was going. Once outside the door, she wedged herself between Myranda and Deacon once more and spread her attentions between him and the noisy hut. When they were just barely midway to the end of the courtyard, Myranda stopped and attempted to question the odd spectacle that they had just witnessed.

"Oh, no. Not here. We will discuss it at the edge of the courtyard," he said, hurrying her along.

"Why so far?" she asked as Deacon urged her to a near sprint.

"Located within that hut are four of the finest wizards to have ever lived. When tempers run high, magic users tend to punctuate their sentences with spells," he said.

"Is it dangerous at--" she began, cut off by sudden and intense shift in the earth beneath her feet, nearly throwing her to the ground.

The trio stumbled to the edge of the courtyard. When they had first approached the open area at the center of the village, Myranda had noticed the succession of short, thick, stone walls that ringed the yard. At the time she found them curious, but now the purpose was clear. The trio took shelter behind one as the shaking earth grew more violent. It was quickly joined by a vicious tearing wind that might have lifted Myn from the ground had she not dug her claws into the earth.

Myranda peeked her head over the wall to see what was happening to the hut. The supports for the walls were creaking and giving way. Shingles from the roof were torn free by the wind and swirled about without touching the ground. They were soon joined by whole sections of wall. Before long, the whole of the hut had been reduced to splinters and was whirling about in the air. At the center of the maelstrom, just barely visible through the thrashing debris, were the wizards.

The dwarf was waving his staff about, causing pillars of stone to burst from the ground like fangs. Solomon had taken to the air, the savage wind more than enough to keep him aloft without the need to flap his wings. As he struggled to remain relatively stationary and dodge the flying shards of wood, he seemed to be spraying flames at an indistinct and fleeting target that could only be Ayna. The flames twisted and turned unnaturally in the wind, following their target like a serpent. The Elder was still seated in her chair, utterly unaffected by the chaos surrounding her. Though the ground was heaving like an angry ocean, she remained motionless, and the gales of wind failed to cause the slightest flutter in her clothing.

Slowly, she rose from her seat. She raised a hand and instantly order was restored. The wind ceased, causing a rain of debris. The waves of earth froze in place, reducing the once-flat yard to a cluster of rolling hills. Solomon dropped to the ground.

The Elder spoke. After a few sentences, the other wizards departed; Solomon approached Myranda and the others, while Ayna and the dwarf returned to their respective places of study. As the dragon traversed the courtyard, the hills and stone spires receded into the ground. The scattered debris rose silently into the air and gathered again in the form of the destroyed hut. The cracks and breaks took on a bright glow before rejoining into the walls and posts that they had been minutes before. In seconds, it was as though nothing had occurred. The hut was whole and solid, the courtyard was pristine and undisturbed, and the men and women were returning with their books.

#

The speed at which the madness in the Elder's hut began and ended seemed to come as a surprise to Myranda alone. Solomon, none the worse for the experience, stood before them as though nothing had happened at all. As he did so, Myn stretched and strained her neck to gain a better sniff at the creature that seemed so familiar. She refused to give up her faithful position at Myranda's side, but was more than eager to learn more about the gray dragon. Solomon obliged her by stepping near enough for the young dragon to inspect him more thoroughly. For a moment, Myn's curiosity overcame her over protectiveness, as she did not treat this new creature as a threat.

"How did it go?" Deacon asked.

"Reasonably well. Myranda will still be allowed to come under my instruction, provided that each of the others has the same opportunity," he answered, choosing Myranda's language for her benefit.

"Reasonably well!? What about the quaking ground and the whirlwind? That was chaos," Myranda replied, dumbfounded.

"No more so than our last debate," Solomon said.

"This has happened before?" Myranda said, mystified.

"It is not an altogether uncommon occurrence," he answered.

"I would say that anytime Ayna and Cresh--he would be the malignant dwarf who began the hostilities--get together, the result is fairly similar to that little display. I must say that you were more active than usual. What managed to raise your ire?" Deacon asked.

"Ayna was particularly condescending on the subject of those races best suited to magic. I decided to illustrate my effectiveness," he said.

"Did it do any good?" Deacon asked slyly.

"I singed her a bit. The message ought to be clear," Solomon said.

With that, the dragon turned his attention to Myn. The pair of beasts engaged in a rather unique conversation. There was much movement by each, but no sounds to speak of. Deacon later explained that the language that dragons are born with is generally exchanged in tones far too low for humans to hear, and precious few of those. The bulk of the information was being transmitted by the movements and postures each assumed. As Myn became bolder, the two began to exchange contact, butting heads and flicking a tongue here or there. Finally, the conversation ended and Myn sat on her haunches, lashing a tail at Deacon, who had apparently ventured a bit too close to Myranda.

"She is healthy enough. You have treated her well. Bring her to me at sundown. The food that you humans eat is less than appropriate for a dragon. Particularly a young one. I am quite sure that she will appreciate the alternative that I have found," Solomon said.

"If you like. I am not certain that she will remain if I do not stay with her, though. It seems she only leaves my side to hunt and to protect Leo," Myranda said.

"If you must remain, then you will. Starting tonight, you are my pupil. You will do as I say," Solomon said. Though his words were ominous, his tone was as steady as it had ever been. He did not speak as a warning or a threat. It was merely a statement of fact. When he had finished speaking, he departed.

Myranda turned to Deacon.

"Tonight!?" she exclaimed.

"Solomon does not sleep in the same way that you or I do. He tends to most of his affairs at sunrise and sunset, with sleep coming during the day as often as night, or sometimes not at all for a week," he said.

"But why so soon?" she asked.

"I suppose he has a special interest in you. In very short order, the whole of the village will share that interest. No one has been assigned directly to a Master since we made the distinction between the different levels of expertise centuries ago, and now you will be apprenticing to four!" he said.

"I am not sure that I am ready," she said.

"By rights, you should be years from ready. That is of no concern of yours, though. Whatever difficulties you may experience rest squarely upon the shoulders of Solomon now . . . Are you all right?" Deacon said.

Myranda's head was reeling, and she appeared unsteady.

"This is all moving so quickly," she said. "I barely know where I am, and now I am going to be a student to a Master wizard. People are fighting over me. I just . . ."

"Calm yourself. You have time. There is no pressure. The pace is yours to set. It may seem overwhelming now, but it will all be routine. In time, you will be quite comfortable with it. I wish that I could sympathize with how you are feeling, but this is the only world I have ever known. Tell me, how can I help you?" he asked.

"I just don't know. This place . . . how can I do what you want me to do?" she said.

"Myranda," he said, placing a hand on her shoulder. "It will be all right, I--*oof!*"

Myn gave Deacon a sharp butt in the stomach with her head as a punishment for his physical contact, sending him stumbling backward to the ground.

"Myn, no!" Myranda scolded.

"It is all right. It is all right," Deacon groaned. "My mistake. Solomon was right, though. She is quite healthy."

He struggled back to his feet and led her back in the direction of his hut. When they had reached it, he led her inside and had her take a seat.

"You are nervous because you do not know what to expect. I can understand that. I, however, *do* know what to expect. I have done it all before. Just relax and I will try to put your mind at ease," he said as he sat upon the desk before her.

"What is Solomon like?" Myranda asked.

"Oh, Solomon is a fine teacher. I feel he is one of the best that we have. He is very knowledgeable. Northern is not his best language. Here and there, you may find him struggling for words, but it simply is not feasible for him to expect you to learn to understand one of his preferred languages. I would not worry about him. Sol has got the patience of a saint. He is very forceful, though," Deacon said.

"Forceful?" Myranda asked.

"Yes. He is far stronger of body and mind than he may appear. As a result, when demonstrating something, he may do it far more roughly or powerfully than is necessary. Solomon teaches very seldom, so he has difficulty familiarizing himself with the fragility of his student. You may think that he is angry with you, but I assure you, you will not see him angry. He is merely subjecting you to something that, from his point of view, is quite mild," Deacon said.

"I must say, I do not find that very comforting," she said.

"I assure you, there is no cause for concern. He has never killed or injured anyone. I have known him all of my life and count him among my closest friends. He is like a father to me," he said.

"What will be expected of me?" she asked.

"I am not certain. You are technically a beginner, so you should be expected only to perform concentration drills. However, since you are being skipped to the expert level, you may be given the instruction intended for the more experienced. In that case, you would be tested for endurance, and given more complex spells. At any rate, you can be certain that he will teach you to conjure flame, control its size, and dictate its behavior," Deacon explained. "I am quite eager to see how he will handle the process, however."

"I thought you said you have been through all of this before!" she exclaimed.

"I have, but I had to work my way up. Usually a student is already well-versed in a magic by the time they come under the tutelage of the Masters. As a result, all that remains for the Masters to do is survey the skills of the student and administer some sort of test to see that some minimum level of mastery has been met. Then, when the other Masters have done likewise, the student may return to specialize his or her training. Most of us spend only a few days with each Master," he said.

"Is fire magic difficult?" she asked.

"It is one of the more taxing disciplines. Generally, the training is saved until a student has built up more substantial reserves by practicing less energy-intensive magics, like wind," he said.

"So wind magic is easier than fire?" Myranda surmised.

"Officially, all of the elemental magics are equal. Frankly, though, one may come to a rather respectable level of mastery in the art of wind in half of the time it would take to do so in the others," Deacon said, glancing nervously about. "But do not tell Ayna I said that."

"What about her? Is she a good teacher?" Myranda asked.

"Highest Master," he said.

"Excuse me?" Myranda said, unsure of the reason she had been corrected.

"She will require you to refer to her as Master at least, but almost certainly Highest Master. Never teacher. After the years she spent climbing the ladder, she wants to be sure no one forgets it. As for her teaching skill . . . it has been adequate for the lower levels. At least, as long as you behave yourself," Deacon said.

"Behave myself?" Myranda questioned.

"She is quite the opposite of Solomon. Extraordinarily impatient and enormously temperamental. Dare I say that her only redeeming value is her utterly comprehensive knowledge of her chosen art? She has attained a level of intensity and dexterity that previously existed only in theory. I have seen her untie and retie a knot with the force of air alone. Astounding. And the utter power! The woman can bore a hole through an arm's length of stone with wind!" he said.

"That sort of power in the hands of someone with a short temper is not the most comforting thought either," Myranda said.

"Well, the first thing you are supposed to learn as a wizard is self-control. It is perhaps the only lesson Ayna did not excel at. Not to worry, she hasn't caused anyone any grievous harm in years," Deacon said.

"But she *has* hurt someone," Myranda said.

"Not exactly. She was learning some of her more advanced lessons alongside a gentleman by the name of Henrik. It was clear that the teacher was fonder of he than she. That teacher, a woman by the name of Zeln, later said that she found him to be more respectful, and that was why she favored him. Regardless, Ayna challenged him to a duel. They are rare, but not unheard of, and we have procedures regarding them.

"In a wind duel, the purpose is to stay planted on the ground while you attempt to raise your opponent by wind alone. As Ayna is a fairy and not typically a creature of the ground, the rules were bent to instead say that the winner is the one who lifted the opponent highest. Ayna won, but apparently wanted there to be no doubt in anyone's mind. She lifted him until he disappeared in the clouds, then released him. He managed to bring himself to the ground safely, but the sheer force of the wind that lifted him had torn his clothes off and . . . plucked away every last hair of his body," he recalled.

Myranda chuckled.

"Excellent. Your spirits are rising," he said.

"What about Cresh?" Myranda asked.

"He is less volatile, but no less infuriating. Whereas Ayna will launch into a tantrum essentially on a whim, Cresh requires a much more specific stimulus. He is passionate in his art to the point of obsession, a trait shared by most of the other wizards here. In his case, he fairly explodes with fury at even a perceived attack on the relevance of his discipline. You may even insult him personally, but if you speak ill of his art, you had best quickly make amends," Deacon said. "And, before you ask, that little display in the village center earlier is about as far as he ever goes outside of idle threat, and he has yet to hurt anyone."

"Well, that is a relief. And what about water, the only Master I have yet to encounter?" she asked.

"Oh, yes. Calypso. No worries there. Cally is as easygoing as you please. Lighthearted, clever, funny. You'll love her. Her only fault may be that she can be a bit too playful sometimes. She lives down at the lake," he said.

"She sounds nice. I wish I was taking her bit first," Myranda said.

"They are all a treat when you get to know them. I expect that you will be great friends," Deacon said.

"I notice that you don't seem to be on the list of teachers," Myranda said.

"Well, as Cresh was kind enough to point out, I am not a required portion of the curriculum. White and black magics are, but the elementals have seen to it that they come first, and you can reach a fairly high level of mastery on their teachings alone. If I am to be included, it must be by your choice, and I am quite sure your plate is full," he said.

"There may be room for a bit more," Myranda said.

"What do you mean? You wish to learn the gray arts?" he said, cautiously optimistic.

"Since I arrived, I have only met a handful of people willing to speak Northern, and only you have done so without expecting anything from me," she said.

"I don't want you to do this for me," he said.

"Believe me, I have only the most selfish of reasons at heart," she said with a grin.

"This is wonderful. This is exceptional! My first student. There is so much to do! I have to prepare a lesson plan, I have to create trials," he said, rising quickly from his seat. "It is such a wide area, I . . . I don't know where to begin!"

He fumbled through his bag with one hand and felt at his ear with the other.

"Where is my book? Where is my stylus? What a time to lose them!" he said, fairly in a tizzy.

"They are on the desk," she said, amused at the stir she had caused.

"Yes, of course, of course, and at work, too. Blast it, I knew I should have made two of those," he said.

"I think you are the one who needs to calm down now," Myranda said.

"Oh, I can't! Not now, not now! This is momentous! This is important!" he said.

The time passed quickly as Deacon raved about what sort of things he had in store. There was something about his sudden enthusiasm that betrayed similarities between he and she. It was clear that he had been every bit an outsider in his own way as she had been in the outside world. Finally finding someone willing to share time with him seemed to be more than he could handle. The longer they spoke, the clearer it became how deeply involved he was with his studies. As they spoke, they laughed more and more. It was even enough to convince Myn to lower her guard, though she made her presence known whenever he took a step too near to Myranda.

All too soon, the sun disappeared from the sky. It was time. Deacon led Myranda to a hut near the cliffside, Myn in tow. Unlike the others, which were mostly wood, this hut was entirely constructed of stone. Solomon emerged from within. As he did, others began to appear, most notably Ayna. They formed a wide circle around the scorched ground in front of the hut that could only be the training ground.

"Why are these people here?" Myranda asked Deacon.

"To observe," he answered. "As I have said numerous times, this is a first. In Entwell, anything out of the ordinary is of great interest to us."

"Ignore them. Sit, and concentrate," Solomon instructed.

Myranda took a seat on the ground. Myn mistook this for a sign that it was time to praise her, and fairly climbed atop her. A few "words" from Solomon caused her to grudgingly move to the side.

"What are the words?" Myranda asked.

"Words?" Solomon replied.

"I need to know the words of the spell before I can concentrate on it," she said.

A murmur swept through the group of observers. Deacon covered his face with his hand and shook his head quietly. Ayna was less subtle. She laughed an obnoxious, piercing laugh.

"Incantations! The girl only knows incantations!" she said breathlessly.

As calm as always, Solomon explained their reaction.

"Once a student has moved beyond the level of beginner, incantations are rarely used," he said.

"They are the work of children and fools!" Ayna chimed in.

"What else can I do?" she asked.

"Concentrate and I will guide you," the dragon said.

Myranda clutched the locket about her neck. It had mercifully not been lost during her plunge into the icy water. She had only just closed her eyes when Solomon's powerful voice asked her to stop.

"Let me see that," he said.

He had not changed his tone at all, but for some reason the merest request from this creature was like a firm demand from any other. He approached and put two of his finger-like claws behind the crystal, inspecting it closely. Suddenly, he pulled it away. The motion was smooth and steady, but was more than enough to snap the chain that had held it so firmly. Myranda put her hand to her neck and rubbed the welt that the move had caused.

"Terrible," the dragon stated. "Utterly unrefined. You will work without it today. When you are through here, have a new one made."

He tossed the gem away. Before it reached the ground, an unnatural breeze caught it up and carried it to be viewed by the ever critical Ayna.

"Murky as a swamp! Is this what passes for a focus crystal out there these days?" she said, mockingly.

The dragon sat on his haunches raised one hand-like paw. A small flame sparked into existence below it.

"Turn your mind to the flame," he said.

Myranda set her eyes on the flickering form. Slowly, the world pulled away, and the yellow-orange shape filled her mind. She gathered her entire consciousness about the flame, her mind shifting and turning with the slightest motion of the fire. Time was meaningless in such a trance; hours and seconds were interchangeable. Suddenly, the voice of Solomon broke through.

"The fire is like a living thing. Once it is born, it requires only food and breath to grow and multiply. It constantly hungers. Can you feel it?" the powerful voice spoke.

Her instructor's words were far too clear and distinct to have come from the outside world. It was as though he had willed his voice into her mind and mingled it with her thoughts. She poured over the fire with her mind and slowly became aware of a constant and steady draw. The hunger he spoke of.

"Yes," Myranda said, the effort of doing so nearly breaking the concentration.

"Feed it," his voice replied.

At first, Myranda was at a loss. Feed it what? Fire needed wood or oil, something to burn. She had nothing. It mystified her that this flame could even exist, floating in mid-air. What did he mean?

"Feel the heat," the dragon instructed.

Slowly, Myranda became awake of a dull feeling of warmth filtering into her mind from the outside.

"Now feel beyond the heat. Feel it with your mind," he said.

Myranda probed further. After an eternity, she finally found it. The feeling came like a torrent. It was the energy of the fire. Not the temperature or the light, something deeper than that. Something fundamental. The essence of the fire. Feeling it now was like opening her eyes for the first time. It was a new sense, one she would later find was the basis for all of the magic she would be taught.

"Just as the fire has an energy, so does your spirit. Look inside yourself. Feel your energy. Control it," he said.

Myranda turned her focus inward slightly, searching for the same sort of power that she felt in the flame. Gradually, she became aware of an energy within. It wasn't the same feeling as the fire, but it was similar. Controlling the strange power was a challenge. If feeling the essence was like using a new sense for the first time, controlling it was like using a new limb.

Myranda did not know where to begin. Every minor attempt she made to influence it resulted in an almost random shifting and changing of the power. It was like trying to learn to wiggle her ears. She knew what she wanted to do, but she simply could not manage to do it. Repeated failed attempts were only beginning to give her a sense of the nature of her control over this energy when Solomon's voice broke through for a final time.

"That will be all for today," he said.

Myranda brought herself out of the trance. The first rays of dawn were painting the sky orange. Of the crowd that had been watching her, only Deacon remained. He was mid-yawn, book in hand, as always. Myn was sleeping beside her. The night of strong thought had taken its toll. She was feeling the bizarre lack of will that had always followed her practice sessions with Wolloff, but to a far greater degree. Her body was affected by the hours of sitting motionless in the cold of night as well. Both of her legs were asleep and her back was agonizingly sore.

"We will continue tonight. I expect you to be fully rested," Solomon said. "In the meantime, I would like to take Myn to be fed, but she will follow more willingly if you join her."

Myranda tried unsuccessfully to get to her feet, discovering in the process that her left hand was extremely tender for some reason. Deacon approached to help her, but Myn snapped into wakefulness and kept him at bay. Myranda leaned heavily on the dragon to stand. It soon became clear that the dragon would not be able to keep her standing alone, and reluctantly Deacon's aid was accepted.

"I have never been so tired," Myranda said.

"Well, this style of magic is a bit more taxing on the mind. Also, you were not using a crystal. Tomorrow we will give you a training one," he said.

"Why does my hand hurt?" she asked, casting her blurred vision to her hand. It was red and irritated.

"I had warned you about that. When Solomon asked you to feel the fire, he placed your hand a bit closer than he ought to have. Your trance was strong enough to overlook the pain. That is admirable," he said.

"In the three months that I have been at this, I have never felt so--" Myranda began, only to be cut off by an excited Deacon.

"*Three months!*" he interjected.

"Yes, I had told you I had only had a bit of white magic training," she said.

"Around here 'a bit of training' is two years, minimum. You have demonstrated a depth and quality of concentration vastly disproportionate to your level of training," he said, rummaging through his bag to retrieve his book. He hastily scribbled something down in it as he repeated his last words incredulously.

"Have I?" Myranda said. In her current state of mind, the act of forming a sentence was an incredible effort. Comprehension was impossible.

"I will meet you at the arena. Just follow Solomon," he said as he rushed off toward his hut.

With the support of Deacon's arm so suddenly gone, Myranda nearly tumbled to the ground. Thankfully, Myn rushed to the faltering side to shore her up.

The pair made their way unsteadily to a bizarre sight. There was an enormous circle of crystal on the ground, perhaps one hundred paces across. At three points along the edge, there were spires of the same crystal, each elegantly carved from bottom to top with various runes and symbols. The crystal was clear as water, perhaps with a tint of blue. Solomon was waiting at the edge.

In a few inaudible words of his language, he summoned Myn, who would only leave Myranda's side when the wavering girl had taken a seat on the ground. Then the two dragons stepped onto the crystal surface and swiftly vanished. Myranda struggled to decide whether what she had seen had actually happened, or if her ailing mind was playing tricks with her eyes. She was still working at it when Deacon carefully sat beside her, holding a steaming cup in his hands.

"Drink this," he said as he handed her the cup.

Myranda took the cup and carefully put it to her lips. The flavor was powerfully bitter, though after the long, cool night the warmth felt good going down. Almost immediately, she felt her mind clearing. It was as though a fog in her mind was being lifted. A few more sips and she felt almost herself again.

"This is incredible. What is it?" she asked him.

"A special tea made from the leaves of a plant that bears seed only during a full moon," he said as he opened his book and flipped to a blank page.

"I feel as though I could endure another night of training," she said.

"You may feel that way, but the tea only restores your mind, not your mana. Your spirit is still spent. To restore that, you would need the seeds of the plant, or more so its dew," he said, carefully adding a heading to the page that prominently bore Myranda's name.

"Will I be taking this tea after every training session?" she asked.

"I am afraid not. As a rule, it is best to recover naturally," he said.

"Then why have you given this to me now?" she asked.

"Because I am a profoundly impatient man at times," he said.

"Impatient for what?" she asked.

"Knowledge about you," he said.

"Why me?" she asked.

"Simple. Your performance today. I have seen people who have had three years of training and were happy with what you have managed. You have had only three months! Such a natural predisposition toward magic is not unheard of, but it is extremely rare. We can only attest to having three here in our history, and only one that we witnessed. People with your uniqueness are still an enigma to us," he said.

"My performance today was awful. I failed," she said.

"You failed to affect the fire, perhaps, but you learned to sense essence and you began to manipulate your own. Those two skills are the sole benefits of our beginner's training, which normally takes five years! You've nearly completed them on your first day!" he said.

"Then why would . . ." Myranda began as she turned back to the strange sight before her. Suddenly, she remembered what was occupying her mind before he appeared. "What is that? And why did Myn vanish?"

"Oh. That is the crystal arena. To my knowledge, it is absolutely unique in the world. We found the single largest deposit of focus stone in existence when we came here, and in the years that followed, we crafted this. Within it, magic is effortless, concentration is unnecessary, and you will feel no draw on your own mana. Solomon uses it as a hunting ground. Our founder, Azriel, makes her home there. She conjures up a forest and

Solomon hunts down--well, that," he said, indicating three large bags of fish that were being carried to the arena by people in red tunics. Once placed within the arena, they too vanished.

"Azriel transforms the fish into whatever prey Solomon would like and he hunts and eats his fill. I expect now Myn will receive the same treatment," he said. "Now, if you don't mind, Myranda. I have some questions for you."

"Ask," she said, taking another sip from her tea.

As the sun climbed in the sky, Deacon proceeded to ask Myranda to summarize her life, beginning with birth. As she spoke, he faithfully recorded the details. Before long, Myn emerged from the arena, clutching a fish in her mouth. She dropped it to the ground and sniffed it with confusion, as it had not been a fish when she was inside of the arena, but soon decided one meal was as good as another and presented it to Myranda in exchange for the usual reward. Myranda suggested that they take a break to cook the food, lest she seem ungrateful to the dragon, but Deacon merely snapped his fingers and the fish was instantly cooked to a turn.

It was well into the morning before Deacon was satisfied with his answers.

"Excellent, truly excellent. You should head off to bed. I have got to go over your life story and compare it to our notes on prodigies. Also, I will see to it that when you awaken you will have a crystal. Would you like it in an amulet as before, or in a staff? As a beginner, I would recommend the staff. It will give you something to lean on," he said.

"Whatever you think is best," she said.

"Excellent," he repeated, as he walked eagerly off to his work.

"Wait! Don't you ever sleep?" she asked.

"Not if I can avoid it. Tremendous waste of time," he said.

Myranda trudged wearily to the hut she had been provided with, dragon in tow. She pushed open the door and readied herself for bed. When she had climbed in, Myn joined her as always, but she did not go to sleep as she usually did. She had, after all, been sleeping most of the night while Myranda was busy with her training. For several minutes, she fidgeted and shifted restlessly. Finally, she took a long sniff at the air and jumped down from the bed and pushed open the window shutters.

"What is wrong, little one?" Myranda asked.

Myn took another long smell and looked longingly into the distance. It didn't take long for Myranda to figure out what the creature wanted.

"You want to spend some time with *him,*" Myranda said.

Myn seemed to give a quite spirited answer to the affirmative. The little dragon had been quite affectionate to Leo when they were traveling together. It was only natural she would desire his company in this place.

"He cannot be trusted, you know. He lied to me and did terrible things," Myranda warned.

The dragon was unswayed.

"Go," Myranda said.

She had not even finished the syllable before Myn disappeared out the window and scampered off. Myranda pulled herself from the bed and closed the window. When she returned to the bed, she dropped quickly off into a dreamless sleep. Usually she would have been disappointed to be without dreams, but judging from the horrible nightmares she had been having, this was a blessing.

#

Myranda's eyes opened heavily to the fading rays of the sun as they flowed through the open window. Myn had managed to pull the shutters open and let herself in, or she had been helped. At any rate, she had nestled atop Myranda at some time during the day.

The girl rose from bed and dressed. Fresh clothes were a welcome change to the life she had been living of late, though pulling on her worn boots was all too familiar. She briefly considered asking for something better, but so much had been done for her already, she decided against it.

As she stepped outside and felt the cool dusk air, Myn jumped down and followed her. She closed the door and decided to have some breakfast just as soon as she could remember where the food was served. Deacon appeared and walked eagerly up to her as she wandered in what she believed was the correct direction. The young man's face held the telltale signs of a sleepless night, but he seemed none the worse for wear. Indeed, he seemed to be just as excited as he had been the night before, if not more so.

"Good evening, good evening. I trust you slept well," he said.

"Indeed, I did. Did you sleep at all?" she asked.

"Heavens no! Too much to do. Sleep can wait. Come this way. I have something for you to do," he said.

"I was actually looking forward to breakfast," she said.

"Breakfast? Oh, of course. I suppose I had better eat as well, lest I forget again," he said.

The pair took a meal with Myn more than a little distracted by the constant flow of words from Deacon's mouth. He scarcely took a moment to swallow, so eager was he to speak.

"I compared what you told me about yourself to the records we have of the others. The prodigies. It seems clear that there is most certainly a familial influence. Your parents were each uncommonly intelligent. Likely, had they tried their hands at magic, they would have excelled as well. I must say, though, in reviewing your story, I found a few points puzzling. You say just before you entered this place, you discovered that Leo was not what you had thought him to be," he said, taking advantage of her answer to slurp a few hasty spoonfuls of the stew.

"Yes. I recognized his voice as the man who had captured me and killed those men in front of the church. A crime that I was to be blamed for, no less," she said.

"And, yet, immediately afterward, you followed him into the water. You followed him into what must have seemed to be certain death despite the fact he had revealed that all you knew about him was a lie," he said.

"Yes," she said.

"Well, then. You either have incredible intuition or terrible judgment. Not to offend you, of course. Clearly it was the correct decision and you ought to be commended," he said.

"Thank you, I suppose," Myranda said.

"I checked up on him. Asked around. Those that can remember him, and there are precious few, all agree on two points. One is that his name isn't Leo. No one is quite sure what his name is, but it is certainly not what he has told you. Leo, it turns out, was a student that was being trained at the same time. In what I am sure is no coincidence, his disposition was strikingly similar to that of your friend prior to your discovery of his deception. He was a human, and has since passed on," Deacon said.

"I suppose I shouldn't be surprised. All else had been a lie, why not that as well?" she said. A thought came to her mind. "Why are there so few that remember him?"

"That is another thing I was puzzled about. Your friend completed several years of training and left this place seventy years ago, roughly," he said.

"Seventy? No, that is impossible. I cannot tell precisely how old he is, but he does not look old by any means," she said.

"Oh, on this there can be no doubt. It is one of the few things about him that we have recorded," he said.

"But how can you be sure it was his record you found," she asked.

"It was labeled 'Unnamed Lain,' and bore his description. Also, the two wizards and three warriors who remember him all quote that as the approximate time," he said. "He is also the only malthrope we have trained."

Myranda shook her head in amazement.

"Unbelievable. With each passing moment, I realize how much less I know about him than I thought. And now I am fairly trapped in the same town as he, and I cannot even catch a glimpse of him, let alone get him to speak," she said.

"This really means a lot to you," he said.

"I trusted him. I just want to know what manner of person betrayed that trust. I just want to know that there is something about him that is as good and pure as the person he claimed to be," she said.

"I won't lie to you. Between his skills and his seniority here, if he does not wish to see you, he won't," Deacon lamented.

"I've come to realize that," she said.

"He need only answer to the Elder at this point," Deacon said.

Myranda finished her meal as Deacon, having already choked his down as quickly as possible, waited impatiently. The moment she was finished, he led her off in the direction of a cluster of huts on the other side of the village--as always with Myn in tow. Outside of the huts were piles of wood cut to all variety of sizes. The smoke belching out of the chimney of one hut could have only meant that it was the blacksmith's, while another hut, the one that they were to enter, merely had longer, more slender pieces of wood outside to hint at its purpose. Inside was rather well-lit against the now stiff darkness of the night by the array of crystals that not only lined the walls, but lined shelves and display cases as well.

A man and a woman, each so like the other that they could only be spouses or siblings, could be found inside. Each wore an odd pare of lenses mounted on stalks on their heads. The woman was at the back, carving a design onto a staff, while the man was nearer to the front, cutting a notch into a larger piece of wood before roughing the rest out into a staff shape. Both were short and stocky, certainly dwarfs. The man had dark hair and a well-groomed beard. The woman was slightly shorter and looked to be a bit younger.

"This is Myranda. Myranda, this gentleman is Koda and the lady is Gamma. They are our resident staff-makers," Deacon introduced.

Koda put down his chisel to shake her hand and offered what sounded like a cheery greeting in whatever odd language he called his own. Gamma looked up and smiled before continuing her exacting work.

"We will require a training staff and crystal for this young lady," Deacon said.

Myn watched curiously as the stout fellow selected several staffs from the racks that lined the wall and handed them to Myranda one by one. Deacon translated the artisan's questions, which all had roughly to do with how each piece felt, whether she liked the weight, and whether she preferred one thickness or another. Myranda was mostly at a loss for how to answer until Deacon explained that she ought to choose one as though she were choosing a walking stick before hiking.

Once the appropriate staff was chosen, Koda took some measurements of Myranda's height and arm length with a knotted rope, shouting said measurements to his partner, who called them back without looking up.

When Myn decided he had come too close and moved in to back him away, the dwarf apparently found it absolutely hilarious, as he laughingly recounted the event to his partner, who swiftly joined in the laughter.

"What is so funny?" Myranda whispered.

"He had a dog that would do the same thing," Deacon answered.

"Ah," Myranda replied, failing to see the humor in it.

Still laughing, Koda took the chosen staff to a case of gems and selected one, carefully fitting it into the staff. He then handed it to her and informed Myranda by way of Deacon that, based on her preference and the measurements, a custom one would be made over the course of the next few weeks.

Myranda looked down at her weapon. It had a dark brown, slightly red color, and was carved along its length with runes similar to those that had formed the spells Wolloff had taught. The crystal was mostly clear, though there were veins here and there that were a bit milky. It was slightly smaller than her fist. Much larger than the one in the locket that Wolloff had given. From end to end, the tool was a bit taller than shoulder height.

"Excellent choice. Now, if you are ready, it is time for your second day with Solomon," Deacon said.

The trio found their way to the training ground where Solomon was waiting. Deacon took a seat at the edge of the stone circle on the ground where the teaching took place and readied his book. Myn gave a dragonish greeting to her fellow creature before taking her seat faithfully beside Myranda. With the crystal of the staff on the ground in front of her, she awaited the flame to be conjured before her. No sooner had it been done than she slipped swiftly into the trance.

With the aid of the crystal, it took a fraction of the time that it had taken the day before. Everything about it was more vivid. Sensing the essence of the flame and of her own spirit before had been like flailing in the dark in comparison. Now she could sense things about the strange energy she had been oblivious to the night before. It was as though they had a color and a texture that she had missed last time. What's more, they were not alone. Every inch of her surroundings had a power to it. The air, the earth, and particularly the other people. As her gaze strayed from the flame, she marveled at the galaxy of different auras that surrounded the people of the village. When Solomon began prompting her to do so, she tried to manipulate her own power and found its reactions to be a degree more intense.

"Do not manipulate your essence as a whole. Separate a part of it," his voice directed.

Slowly, she willed some small part of the power she felt within her away from the whole.

"Now. Sense the power that the fire feeds on. You must feed the fire," he said.

With her new, clearer view of the energy, Myranda could certainly detect the power being drawn into the flame. Though manipulating her own energy was still new and unpredictable to her, she tried and tried until she found the swirling ball of spirit changing its nature, becoming more like that which the flame yearned for.

"Excellent, now bring it to the flame," he said.

With the merest thought, she guided her mystic concoction to the flame and was nearly startled out of concentration. The fire leapt up, many times its size and many more times its heat. At the same time, she felt an odd draw on her essence. It was a unique feeling, to be losing this strength that only the day before she did not know she had. The draw was steadily growing more intense as the fire shrunk. By the time the burden stabilized, the fire was barely more than an ember floating in the air.

"The flame is yours now. Do not lose it," he ordered.

Myranda pushed herself to provide more. Almost imperceptibly, the flame began to return. In time, it returned to the size the dragon had conjured. Maintaining the size of the fire was unbearable, like carrying some vast weight. Not only her mind and spirit, but all of her body seemed taxed by it. Beads of sweat formed at her temples, her hands began to shake.

The draw quickly became unbearable. It seemed days, weeks, a lifetime since she had begun. When she had no more to give, Myranda relented. The fire, floating in air before her, fizzled and died. As the trance lifted, she saw that it was still night. Though she felt that this lesson had taken a great deal longer than the last, it had in reality been less than half the length.

"That will do for now. Rest if you must, practice if you can, but come here fully refreshed tomorrow," Solomon said before retiring.

Myranda, despite the massive increase in effort, felt far more herself now than she had the day before. The staff really had made quite a difference, at least in the cost of the spell. To be sure, the world still seemed to be shrouded in a haze, and thinking was difficult, but she was able to climb to her feet and walk with the aid of the staff. Deacon approached her, but now that his help was unneeded, Myn judged him unnecessary and forced him to keep his distance.

"That is a respectable endurance for only the second lesson," he said.

Myranda thanked him, shaking her head in an attempt to clear the cobwebs that were hanging about her mind. He continued to talk, but she found it difficult to focus on his words and walk at the same time. In fact, she had taken fifty steps or so before she realized Deacon had repeatedly been asking her where she was headed, and she did not know the answer.

"Where do you suggest?" she asked.

"If I were you, I would head home to meditate until I had a bit more of my wits about me," he suggested.

"Meditate?" she asked.

"Oh, of course, how can I be so foolish? You have not been taught to do so. It is quite useful, I assure you," he said.

Deacon escorted her to her hut and pulled a chair before hers.

"If you can manage it, I need you to gather your focus enough to sense your own essence again," he said.

"I shall try," Myranda offered.

She sat in her chair and focused about the gem. It required a fair amount more effort than last time, but soon enough she was aware of the mystic energies again, both outside and in.

"Do you feel the energies of your surroundings? Good. Now, let them flow through you. Let them become one with you. Simply relax your body, mind, and spirit, and let the outside flow in. Blur the line between yourself and your surroundings," he said.

Myranda tried to comply. Her mind was still struggling--but then something strange happened. As the energy around her began to mingle with her own, she could feel her strength returning. It was slow, very slow, but noticeable. While she recovered, she "looked" at the essences around her.

Before her, she could see the strong pure light of Deacon's spirit. Weaker, but still pure, was Myn, beside her. The spirits of the wizards and warriors of this place speckled her mind in a galaxy of different hues and intensities. In the distance, she sensed one that was different. She focused on it. This new way of detecting the world was different from seeing, though. She "saw" all around her. Above, below, behind, each and every direction was visible to her at once, with distance seeming inconsequential.

As she trained her mind on the peculiar essence in the distance, it seemed to draw nearer and grow more distinct. It was subdued. Intense and yet restrained, as if consciously reigned in and pushed down. On the surface, it appeared no more powerful than the others, but deep beneath there was a fundamental strength that seemed to continue inward eternally. It could only be Lain.

After a time, she decided she had recovered enough, pulling her mind from its focus and lifting herself from the meditation.

When her eyes opened, the change was remarkable. She almost felt normal, as though the training had not occurred. It was difficult to say precisely how long the meditation had taken, but Myn was asleep on the ground beside her, meaning it had been at least a number of minutes. She looked across to Deacon. He sat cross-legged on the chair, his hands folded about his crystal, and his head down. As she stood, now steady enough to forgo the staff for aid, the dragon stirred and gave an angry stare at the still-present intruder. Myranda shook her head and decided to pull Deacon from the meditation as well.

"Deacon. Deacon, I am finished, thank you. It was quite helpful," she said.

The young man did not stir at all.

"Deacon?" she called.

In answer, Deacon released a raking snore and rolled his head slightly to the side. Myranda chuckled. She knew he needed sleep. Myn backed away cautiously at the noise, then moved in close to investigate. As the dragon realized that Deacon was asleep, she decided upon a proper method to wake him. She opened her mouth, ready to deliver a motivating bite on the leg.

"Myn, no!" Myranda reprimanded. "Deacon is my friend. He is not going to hurt me or even try to, so you really should be nicer to him."

The dragon let a short, sharp puff of air out of her nostrils and took on a sulky demeanor. Partly because she was scolded, but mostly because this meant she would have to share Myranda's attentions with another. This was something Myn was becoming very impatient with. Deacon's crystal slipped from his fingers and rolled past Myranda, who turned to pick it up. Myn seized the opportunity and gave Deacon a swift snap with her tail.

"Ouch!" Deacon exclaimed, waking with a start.

"Myn!" Myranda yelled, turning to see the dragon strut away with a decidedly satisfied look on her face.

"Quite a lash on that one. Now I'll have to be careful around both ends," Deacon said, yawning and rubbing the sore area.

"I think you should go get some sleep," Myranda said, handing him his crystal.

"Oh, no, no, no. I couldn't sleep now. That meditation seems to have done you well. Perhaps you would join me? I have someone who I think you will want to talk to," he said, the sleepiness slipping away the instant he remembered what he had in store for her.

"I suppose I am up to it, but are you sure you are?" Myranda asked.

"Of course! Come along. We really ought to see him before dawn," he said, ushering her out the door.

As the trio walked, Myn reluctantly walking beside Myranda rather than between her and Deacon, Deacon's excitement became contagious.

"What is it you have up your sleeve?" she asked, as she was led to a portion of the village that had a small stand of trees. It was deep within the Warrior's Side.

"Well, you have been permitted immediate Master-level training in all of our mystic disciplines, so I got to thinking. If it is agreed you have this remarkable propensity for magic, perhaps you will do equally well in combat. After all, you told me your father was a particularly successful soldier," Deacon offered.

The smile left her face.

"I don't want to fight, Deacon," she warned.

"Now, now. Hear me out. I managed to coax the Elder into granting you the Master-level trainer of your choosing. We have a great many. I intend to introduce you to each and every one until you find the one you feel you might want to spend a little time with," he said.

"I have no interest in learning how to hurt people. I want to help people," she said.

"That is fair enough. I can respect that. It is an important thing to have value for life and the quality thereof for all living things. Still, there is a bit you could stand to learn. Particularly from some of our more senior experts," he said, urging her on.

"No. I don't want to," she said, remaining firm.

"Please. Just talk to one. Just one. I think you will change your mind," he said.

Myranda sighed and continued on, slightly annoyed that the excitement she felt had been for something she found so hideous. As she approached a tall, thickly-leafed tree, Deacon motioned for her to stop. She studied the tree, which seemed awfully healthy for the time of year. If not for the unnaturally pleasant weather in this place, the tree would be a sparse husk.

"I have a student here for you," Deacon called into the near-pitch-black branches.

"No," answered an all-too-familiar voice.

"You know that when you were sworn as a Master, you were to take on at least one apprentice in order to pass on some small part of your knowledge. It is our way," Deacon reminded him.

"Not her," the voice said, startling all but the dragon by coming from behind them. Both humans turned quickly to see the malthrope casting a vicious look at Deacon.

Considering that such a short time ago he was near death, he was in remarkable condition, though from his posture, some injuries were still nagging him. His clothes were the same tunic as most of the others, but his was black. In the darkness of the night, sheltered by the shadows of the trees, he could take two steps back and disappear from sight.

"I am afraid that she is presently our only student not currently engaged with another Master, and you are the only Master not tutoring at least one student," Deacon said.

"And if I refuse?" he said.

"I had a word with the Elder. She informed me that if Myranda chooses to study under your tutelage, you are honor-bound to provide it. You took the oath," Deacon informed.

Now Myranda understood. This was the only way that she would be able to learn the truth from the one she knew as Leo. Deacon was helping her to force him to listen.

"You still owe me an explanation!" Myranda demanded.

"Do not do this, girl," he warned.

"I choose him," she said.

"You have made a terrible mistake," the malthrope fumed.

"I have had enough of the lies. It is worth it to hear the truth," she said.

"Excellent. Superb. I will inform the appropriate people. As a Master with an apprentice, you naturally have access to any resources you find necessary to teach. Myranda, on those days that you are not overly taxed by your lessons in magic, you will report here and take lessons in combat from our skilled expert. I will leave you two to get better acquainted for now and get some much-needed rest," Deacon said, walking away with a grin.

The malthrope and the girl exchanged long, angry stares. Myn was aware of the tension, and confused by it. This was the first time she'd had the two of them to herself since they left the cave, but they were not the same. For a time, there was silence, but it was broken when the warrior turned back to the tree.

"Where do you think you are going?" Myranda demanded.

"I came here to restore my strength. I intend to do so," he said, fists and teeth clenched.

"You owe me the truth, Leo--or whatever your real name is," Myranda said.

"What makes you think I owe you anything?" he fumed.

"I trusted you, and you betrayed that trust," she said.

"That is no fault of mine. If you place your trust too easily, such can be expected," he said.

"You have been lying to me since you met me," she said.

"What does it matter?" he said.

"I saved your life!" she said.

"And I saved yours. You would have been dead if I hadn't brought you here. Those Elites are relentless. If you go where they *can* follow, they *will* follow. They would have captured you, brought you to their superiors, and made an example of you," he retorted. "You saved my life once, but by bringing you here, I have saved you a thousand times over."

"Why then? Why save me if when you first met me it was you that wanted to capture me? And why did you release me?" Myranda asked.

The malthrope turned away.

"You have done nothing to earn what you seek, and you have nothing to offer in exchange. Were I you, I would become accustomed to mystery," he said.

"Don't do this to me, Leo," Myranda said, almost pleading. "My life has been so empty. So uncertain. You know everything about me. The fate of my home town. The fate of my family."

"Seek sympathy elsewhere," he said emotionlessly.

"I don't want your sympathy. I just want answers," she said.

"Why do you want to know? Do you really think that knowing the truth will make you happier? I assure you, it never does," he said.

"I don't care. I must know what you really are. I must know what you wanted with me, why you captured me, why you let me go, why the Elites were after you. What is your name?" she said. "I cannot bear the secrets any longer. If I must earn the right to know, then I shall. I will do anything. Just tell me what," she said. "I am asking you for so little."

"Are you?" he said.

The creature stood silent and cast a judging stare. After some thought, Myranda could see that he had come to a decision. He reached behind him and revealed a dagger. Myranda was a bit unnerved, but held firm. He then tossed it in the air and caught it expertly by the tip, pointing the handle in her direction.

"Take it," he said.

"Why?" she asked.

"Take the weapon," he ordered.

She did so.

"Now use it," he said.

"How?" Myranda asked.

The malthrope pulled up his sleeve and clenched his fist.

"No," she said, dropping it to her side.

"Cut me," he said.

"Absolutely not," she said.

"You said that you would do anything. Draw a single drop of blood and I will tell you every detail," he said.

Myranda froze. This was what she wanted. She approached him, gripping the dagger firmly. It was a simple thing. Just a cut. It needn't be a large one, either. Just enough to show blood. She passed those words through her mind again and again as she tried to muster the strength. She put the blade to his arm and took a deep breath. Just a little pressure. Just a tiny push. Her hand was shaking. Finally, she dropped the weapon to the ground.

"There, you see? It isn't in you to hurt another. Just as it isn't in me to reveal myself. If you truly expect me to betray who I am and tell what you wish, then I expect you to do the same," he said. "That is fair."

"You are cruel," she said.

"I am just. And to prove it, I will offer you a second chance. Show up for training tomorrow. I will be your opponent. For every solid blow that you land, I will answer a single question," he said.

"I don't want to hurt you," she said.

"I doubt that you could, even if you wanted to. But if you do not wish to receive my training, then have that obsequious wizard of yours tell the Elder that you waive your right," he said.

Myranda turned away in disgust and left the creature behind. After a dozen or so steps, the lack of constant clicking footsteps behind her drew her attention. As she looked back to find Myn, in the darkness of the trees, she could just barely make out malthrope crouching, scratching the dragon's head. A moment later, he seemed to vanish from sight and the dragon came prancing to her side. Myranda crouched to scratch her head as well.

"I wish I could see him as you do," she whispered.

The sun was beginning to rise, which, in her new routine, meant soon it would be time for bed. After a swift detour to Deacon's hut to affirm that he indeed was asleep, Myranda found herself with time to herself without her guide. She walked about, trying to clear her head before she retired for the evening. Here and there, a curious villager would stop to speak with her, sometimes willingly speaking her language, other times lacking the patience to do so.

Those who did speak to her seemed to treat her as a novelty or oddity, except for the handful who were her age, who had feelings ranging from thinly veiled jealousy to outright resentment. Mostly, though, she was ignored. Everyone here was passionately pursuing one interest or another, and they found in that pursuit all that they needed. By the time morning had come in earnest, Myranda had gone to bed, drifting off to a troubled sleep.

#

General Trigorah paced across a courtyard. There were soldiers here, standing at attention, but they were Demont's men, not her own. Cold eyes stared at her through slits in face-concealing helmets. She long ago had come to the conclusion that these men obeyed her not because they respected her or because of any chain of command, but because Demont had instructed them to do so. The fact made her uneasy in their presence.

The doors of the low, stone building before her creaked open. A pair of individuals stepped out. The first was Arden. There was a dash of confusion and impatience mixed with his usual expression of mindless cruelty. Beside him was a young woman, one who Trigorah was unfamiliar with, clutching the halberd. She nodded at the general as she dropped a bag into Arden's hand with the telltale jingle of coins.

"Excellent work as always, my good sir. I do so enjoy our associations. Keep your schedule open. I expect we shall need your services again quite soon," the woman remarked.

"What're *you* lookin at, elf?" Arden barked at Trigorah as he passed.

"You are wanted inside," the young woman remarked to the general, ignoring the outburst.

General Teloran shrugged off Arden's glare and stepped inside, beginning her long trek downward. This was one of the various "deep forts" that the other generals were so fond of. All but the topmost level was below ground. Staircases were placed at alternating ends of each level, making the journey downward and upward a long and time-consuming endeavor by design. Wall after wall of cells passed by her as she descended deeper. Finally, she came to the final door and opened it.

Inside, she found a tall, pale woman dressed in a black cloak embroidered with sigils of unquestionably mystic origin. In her hand was a silver rod, embossed in a manner similar to the cloak and topped with an expertly-cut gem. At the sight of her visitor, the woman's face lit up with an almost manic look of excitement.

"General Trigorah, so good of you to come quickly," the woman said.

"I try to be prompt, General Teht," Trigorah replied.

Teht was unique among the other generals in that Trigorah did not dread dealing with her. This was partially due to the fact that General Teht, despite having been a general at the time Trigorah was promoted, was not granted the same royal privilege that the other generals enjoyed. As a result, Teht was Trigorah's one fellow general that could not give her orders. Another reason was that she was, in many ways, Trigorah's mystic counterpart, sent to the far corners of the kingdom on tasks not unlike her own.

"Well, on this occasion I am most appreciative, as I've something quite exciting that I need to be off to. After all of these blasted trips south, I've finally been given something important to do," Teht declared enthusiastically.

"South? You've been south? How far?" Trigorah asked.

"Far enough. It seems as though that is the only place they send me. And always for the same reasons. Training. Give these spells to the casters on the front lines. Go have a word with that necromancer we've got down there . . ." Teht wearily complained.

"So they *have* been sending wizards to the front lines. I've been telling Bagu that a few well-placed magic-users could make an enormous difference," Trigorah said. "How have they been fairing?"

"Adequately. Status quo. Regardless, they've got me on a new project now. I'll be helping Demont and Epidime with something. Something *major . . .*" the general rambled.

This was almost certainly why Teht was not given the same level of seniority as the other generals. She had a habit of speaking vaguely about things that were clearly intended to be high-level secrets. It showed a staggering lack of military discipline that often made Trigorah wonder how she could have ascended to such a position.

"So I shall be spending my time in that mountain fort Demont keeps. You know the one. I shall have my own underlings. This is what I have been waiting for!" Teht continued.

"I am pleased to hear it. When you were at the front line, did--" Trigorah pressed, eager for fresh news.

"Never mind that. I've got your new orders here. I'd say they'll be keeping you busy. Epidime will be loaning this fort to you so that you can carry them out. I believe you'll be getting a few of the wagons and your pick of the latest set of draftees to patch up the holes in your Elites," she interjected. She handed Trigorah a thick bundle of pages.

"Elites are drawn from veterans, not--" Trigorah began.

"Yes, yes. Whatever the source, you have your pick. I'm off," she said, raising her staff.

Before Trigorah could object, Teht spoke a sequence of arcane words. Recognizing them, General Teloran hurried through the door and closed it. A moment later there was a thunderous clap. When the door was opened again, Teht was gone and the sparse furniture of the room had been hurled to the corners.

Trigorah had witnessed the spell only once, and fortunately from a safe distance. She could not be certain what it was that she had seen that day, but two things were certain. The spell allowed its caster to travel great distances quickly, and it left the departure point in a terrible state. She'd since made it a point to retreat at the sound of those words. It was a technique that Bagu and the others tended to use only under great duress, but Teht used it at every opportunity.

Such impulsiveness was a sure way to an early grave.

Trigorah righted a chair and the table and set her orders out. They were familiar, and rightly so. She had written them. It was the list of citizens likely to have had an opportunity to make contact with the sword. The only additional information came in a single page added to the end of the report. Just a few simple words:

In addition to current tasks, revise list and detain all identified individuals for questioning, release pending the acquisition of the sword.

"All identified individuals." There were dozens, perhaps hundreds, and since she'd delivered the report, the Undermine had become involved. She scanned the pages again. Shopkeepers. Patrons of taverns and inns. Most of those she'd found were bystanders. Not that it mattered. She stowed the instructions with trembling hands. Orders were orders . . .

#

Back in Entwell, Myranda stirred. Despite her efforts to the contrary, the one who had betrayed her trust infiltrated her dreams. There was so much about him that conflicted. He had taken the lives of the soldiers with grim efficiency, yet he showed naught but tenderness toward the dragon. He knew precisely how to manipulate her. Even before she had told him about herself, he had known exactly what type of person she would have opened up to.

Such thoughts and images taunting her throughout the day shook her from sleep far sooner than she would have liked. The sun was only nearing the horizon, but there was no hope of going back to sleep now. She looked for Myn, who was missing again. She could be in only one place, but Myranda couldn't bear to face him right now. But perhaps there was someone else she could speak to.

Myranda left her hut and headed to the training ground. In the stone home of Solomon, the dragon still lay asleep. The interior of the hut was a very strange sight to behold. The small dragon lay atop a pile of gold just large enough to accommodate him. Here and there, a section of wall was blackened by flame. On a pedestal in the rear of the cave was a large, clear gem that looked to have been pulled directly from the ground without the benefit of a gem-cutter's chisel. The room had the same earthy smell that she had found curious in the cave where Myn was found. Myranda tapped him. The creature's eye pulled slowly open and identified the intruder.

"It is not yet time for your training," he managed without lifting his head.

"This isn't about my training. It is about me. Why did you choose me?" she asked.

"You will have time for questions later," he said, closing his eyes.

"No! Please, I need to know now," Myranda begged.

He opened his eyes and craned his long neck into a more attentive position.

"It was intuition. Partly my own, but mostly Myn's," he said before a long, silent yawn that gave Myranda a clear view of his teeth.

"Myn's?" Myranda asked.

"You claim to have been present at the unfortunate circumstances surrounding the creature's birth. After speaking with her, I believe that this is so. The fact that you are alive today speaks of something that is special about you," he said.

"Why? I thought that she had merely sought out the only thing that had a heartbeat," Myranda said.

"I am sure she did, but a dragon, even at birth, is quite capable of identifying others of its kind. There are times that a parent cannot be present at the time of the hatching. When that happens, wounded prey is left as food for the creatures. When Myn found you sleeping, this is what she should have seen you as. Instead, she saw you as a guardian. A protector, as well as something to be protected. She chose you. We dragons see more of the world than what our eyes show us. We know things. She saw something in you that day, and I see it as well," he said.

"But what? What did you see?" she asked.

"It cannot be put into words," he answered, "but I can tell you this: she sees it in Lain as well," he said. "And he too was present at her birth."

"Lain? The malthrope!? He was there!?" she said.

"Certainly. But that alone would not explain her attachment to him. He too has the spark. I can see it quite clearly. It is stronger than yours. Were he willing, I would have taken him as my pupil all of those years ago. But enough questions. Return at sundown," Solomon said, settling back down for sleep.

"Yes, thank you, I will," she said, leaving the hut.

Myranda marched out of the hut and directly to the stand of trees where she had found the malthrope the day before. He was nowhere to be found, but there were tracks from Myn, who must have checked here as well. Carefully, she followed them. They led further into the Warrior's Side.

Entering it alone made Myranda suddenly aware of how different it was from Wizard's Side. While wizards could often be found in spirited discussion with one another, that trait was compounded here. Men screamed at each other as they voiced their opinions. Here and there, students sparred under the supervision of teachers. There were archery targets and practice dummies populating sizable runs of ground. Finally, she found her way to a simple hut, smaller than the one that had been provided for her. There was not even a door. She approached the opening and was enthusiastically greeted by Myn.

"Resourceful," the malthrope's voice came from within.

"I accept your offer, and I want to begin right now," she said, entering the hut.

It was absurdly austere. There was not even a bed. A cloth was spread on the floor, upon which the creature was sitting cross-legged.

"Haven't you got previous obligations?" he asked.

"Solomon is not ready for me yet, and you are," she said.

"Very well," he said, climbing to his feet and leading her out the door.

They approached a storehouse. Her teacher entered, returning with a pair of quarterstaffs.

"Have you ever used one of these?" he asked.

"No," she said, catching it as it was thrown to her.

"Hold it with one hand in the middle, the other between the middle and the end," he began.

After a short demonstration of the correct manner to defend and attack, he instructed her to first prepare herself, then attempt to strike him. She could use whatever method or style she chose, and he would only defend, not attack. After a deep breath, she put her limited knowledge to use.

It became clear after the first maneuver that this would be a long and grueling road. The malthrope's movements were subtle and fluid. A minor shift of the foot, a tiny adjustment of his staff, and the best attacks of Myranda were thwarted. After each round of attacks, he would offer advice to improve her method. Early in the training, Myn was concerned by the fact that the two people who meant the most to her were trying to hurt each other. Very shortly, she calmed, perhaps because she understood that he was trying to teach Myranda, or perhaps because Myranda seemed unable to do any harm.

By the time the sun had set, Myranda was nearly exhausted. She had learned to handle the weapon, and understood its use fairly well, but had made no progress in successfully attacking the teacher. As the darkness of night fell about them, she knew it was time to turn to lessons in magic. Myranda took her leave and headed toward Solomon's hut.

As she walked, Myn in tow, she realized that she had yet to eat. After the exertion she had just endured, a meal would have been welcome, but there was no time now. She made a quick visit to her hut to retrieve her casting staff and stow her quarter staff before hurrying to Solomon.

The dragon greeted her and put her immediately to work. After the trance was achieved, she instructed in the method of "bending the will of the fire." The training was mercifully less taxing, calling for more detailed manipulation, as opposed to the marathon usage of the day before. She learned how to shape the fire and carefully regulate the heat and light it created.

Solomon seemed pleased with her progress. As a final task before parting for the night, Solomon had her conjure a flame from nothingness, as he had done for her previously. When she managed to do so, he informed her that her training for the night was through and that she should get some rest.

"At this rate, you will be offered the final test of fire before the week is out," Deacon said, having appeared while she was entranced.

"Thank you," she said, using her staff to get to her feet.

"I understand you and Lain have started your training. I am sorry I missed it. Have you shown the same skill in battle as you have in magic?" he asked.

"Not nearly," Myranda answered. "You called him Lain, as did Solomon. I thought that was just a title."

"It is. In the absence of a real name, it seems only fitting to refer to him by the title he earned," he said.

"I suppose I may as well do so," Myranda said.

"How is your head? Is the magic still taking its toll as severely?" he asked.

"I've still got most of my wits about me," she said.

"Splendid. Your endurance is improving. You will need that for the final test," he said.

"What is the final test?" she asked.

"Well, you see--" he began.

"Wait, I haven't eaten yet. Tell me on the way," she said.

As the trio continued on, they spoke.

"When any of our Masters are satisfied that you have learned enough, they will administer a test to be sure of your understanding. Each comes in two parts. The first is an endurance trial that will assure that you have the strength to perform the spells that are expected of a Master. The second is the dexterity trial that will assure you have the skill of mind to perform the most complex of spells. Both take place in the same day," he explained.

"Wait. You mean to tell me that the complex test will be immediately following the taxing one?" Myranda said.

"Indeed. I think you will agree that is a fine method for determining whether one ought to be considered a Master," he said.

They spoke while each finished their meal. When they were through, Deacon remarked that Myranda seemed a bit more physically weary today than she had in the past. Myranda assured him that such would be the case from now on, thanks to Lain's lessons. He escorted her to her hut and bid her goodnight.

The next day passed in much the same way. She arose before sundown, trained with Lain until night, trained with Solomon until dawn, enjoyed a meal with Deacon, and collapsed into sleep again.

In many ways, it was a far more difficult life than the one that she'd lived before she found the sword. The only trial then was finding enough food and shelter to live comfortably. Here, she was constantly being tested in both mind and body. Yet, she could not say that she was unhappy. As trying as it was to be here, it was a home--her first real one since the days when Kenvard still stood. She had a very real friend in Deacon, and she was learning things. Not simply magic or combat, either. In those times when she was too weary to undergo any of her training, she would sit among the others of the village. Slowly, she was finding that she understood more and more of what they said. By the end of the first month, she found that she could at least follow conversations in nine different languages and make herself understood in a half-dozen.

One thing burned at her. In Solomon's training, she was progressing, though perhaps not as quickly as Deacon had theorized. Such was not the case with Lain. Her understanding of staff combat was manifold what it had been when she began. She knew that her abilities had expanded vastly, but she had yet to lay a single blow on Lain. Not once did her attack even approach success. It frustrated her to no end that she could try so hard, and he could stop her so easily.

What bothered her more was how powerful her emotions became when she was attacking. She felt an intense anger that grew with every failed attempt. Lain could sense it and she knew it. There was no outward indication of it, but the warrior could feel the change in her, and he enjoyed it. She truly was sacrificing a part of herself for even a chance to learn what he knew.

Something changed one day. She had finished yet another infuriating session with Lain and approached Solomon. He had, the day before, taught her how to create different types of flame by "feeding" the fire different types of energy. The results were remarkable, ranging from a black flame that only consumed, shedding no light, to a whitish blue flame that burned cold. She was looking forward to more of the same, but it was not to be. There was a crowd again, awaiting her arrival, and the dragon had some equipment in place.

"Today, Myranda, you will be tested. Ready your staff and follow my instructions," he said.

She clutched the crystal and began to ready her mind. In the past week or so, she had found that the trance came easily enough that she could now cast spells while still remaining aware of her surroundings. She did so now, gathering her mind while looking nervously about at the onlookers. Solomon lowered a large, twisted stone into a clay stand with a hole in it. Below it was another block of clay with a hole in the top, aligned with one in the stand.

"You will focus as hot a flame as you can manage onto this piece of ore for as long as it takes to melt it entirely into the mold below," he said.

No more instructions followed. Myranda took a deep breath and began to conjure heat. She was already beginning to tire before the metal had even begun to glow. She found that she needed to double her efforts and double them again before the stone began to soften. The draw on her power, even after all of the improvement she'd had, was unbearable. She could feel the heat she was generating on her face despite the fact that she was a fair distance from the ore. Crackles and snaps emanated from the stone as it began to lose its form. By the time the first fat orange drop of molten metal flowed into the mold, she could no longer focus her eyes.

Myranda started to relent, trying to gather her mind for a renewed effort, but as soon as she did she felt the heat fade and the stone began to harden again. She couldn't rest, or she would lose ground. It had to be done all at once. Myranda poured all that she had into making the heat as intense as possible.

The second drop fell, followed by a third. Soon, a steady flow had formed, but she knew she couldn't last much longer. The stone had settled into a thick pool of bright orange glowing fluid with a ribbon of the stuff leading from the stand to the mold. A dizziness was swirling in her head that threatened to rob her of her consciousness, but she was too close to fail now.

As she turned to look at the crowd, they seemed to be moving in slow motion. She could barely muster the strength to grip the crystal. The pool of metal was now receding into the center of the stand. Just a few more drops.

After countless eternities, it seemed, the last drop fell and she released her mind's grip. The world rushed back in a dizzying swirl of awed whispers and enthralled faces. Solomon took away the stand and the mold. Had anything but a dragon done so, they would have been horribly burned. Myranda fought to remain awake as dry leaves were scattered on the ground before her. Atop the leaves there was placed a piece of parchment, and atop that more leaves were spread.

"To complete your test and prove to all that you have a masterful knowledge of this discipline, you must prove the dexterity of your mind by burning the paper without touching the leaves," Solomon said.

Knowing if she did not act quickly, she would lapse into deep and involuntary sleep, Myranda drew her mind as tightly as she could to the task. It was impossible to see where the leaves were below the paper, so keeping her eyes open was of no use. She closed them and instead looked through her mind's eye.

Slowly, she conjured a precise flame and guided its spread. Simultaneously, she kept the leaves near the flame cool. Spreading her mind in so many directions at once would have been difficult enough with a fresh start, but now it was as though she was attempting to juggle with her hands tied. The paper was steadily devoured by the flames, and as it fluttered off as ash, the weight upon her mind was slightly lessened. So little was left. Just a bit more.

At last, the final speck of paper was destroyed. She opened her eyes to find that at some point during her concentration she had collapsed to the ground without realizing. She tried to right herself, but her body would not obey. A thousand miles away, the crowd surrounding her let out a roar of approval. She was vaguely aware that Deacon was lifting her onto his shoulders as the onlookers swept in to offer congratulations. This turned out to be more than Myn could bear, and she let a burst of flame free to back the crowd away, allowing only Deacon to touch her.

He thanked the dragon for both the help and the permission and made his way to Myranda's hut. Tomorrow she would be told that she had succeeded. Today she would have a very well deserved sleep. After a trial like that, it would be a slumber from which it was difficult to awake.

#

A trio of worn and ragged forms rushed through the night toward a flimsy shack nestled in a stand of evergreens. When they reached it, the door was flung open and they tumbled inside. A lamp was clumsily lit, revealing walls covered with soggy maps and a table heaped with pages of every shade, quality, and state of repair.

The three figures huddled about the light. The first, Undermine leader Caya, cleared the table with her arm and dumped a leather satchel on the table, replacing the notes with fresher ones. Her partner, Tus, did the same. Their final companion was casting nervous glances through a slit in the door.

"Kel, don't dally. Show us what you've got," Caya said.

Kel was one of the newer recruits and had ended up as third in command fairly quickly, mostly by virtue of the rapidly dwindling ranks of the Undermine. The man dug through his pockets and deposited a few grubby wads of paper on the table.

"That's it?" Caya asked. "Why didn't you bring more?"

"That's all there was. The usual places are empty. All the drop spots. Everything. Half--half of the places aren't *there* anymore," Kel sputtered nervously. "Commander, I think I heard something."

"Easy, Kel," she said, looking over the notes.

After fumbling through the scattered pages until she unearthed a quill and an ink bottle, Caya attempted to make a mark on one of the maps, only to find the ink frozen. She placed the bottle on the lamp and looked at the map.

At its height, the Undermine had agents in nearly every city. That was when her father had been running things. In the weeks after Myranda's arrival on the grand stage, they had very nearly equaled that. Now things were falling apart. As the ink melted enough to be useful, Caya digested the pages she'd brought with her. One by one, names were crossed off. Cities, safe houses, and informants were scribbled off of the map. By the time all had been considered, there were only a handful of names left, and only two marks on the map. Caya sagged, but the eyes of the others looked to her expectantly.

"Well . . ." she began. "Between desertions, casualties, people turning rat, and all of the arrests . . . membership is down."

"How far down?" Kel asked, glancing again to the door.

"We're it," Tus stated, his eyes on the updated roster.

"Well, not quite, but soon. I suppose we only were able to exist because the Blues didn't consider us a threat . . . now they do," she said.

"About time," said Tus.

"Heh. Yes. At least they are taking us seriously now. Kel, there's too much going on now. My brother Henry is the one giving Wolloff his supplies. If the Elites are still prowling around in Ravenwood . . . I would just feel better with a hand that is a bit firmer on a sword doing the job. I want you to see to Wolloff," Caya said.

"Yes, Wolloff. Where is he exactly?" he asked.

Caya hesitated. By virtue of his status as perhaps the only white wizard not in the employ of the Alliance Army, Wolloff's exact location was a closely guarded secret. Caya, Tus, and Caya's younger brother Henry were the only ones who knew, besides those that he trained. The field healers tended to have a rather short life expectancy, due to their tendency to attempt to desert after receiving their training, and Tus's tendency to silence them when such an attempt was made. Thus it was highly likely that no one captured had been able to supply that particular piece of information. As such, someone eager to become a valued informant to the Alliance Army would be particularly interested in that fact.

"He is . . ." Caya began.

The distant thud of hooves drew her attention. Tus looked as well.

"Where!?" Kel insisted.

"Someone is coming . . . and from the wrong way. We weren't followed here. We were--" Caya said, before being cut off.

"Tell me where Wolloff is!" Kel cried.

They turned to him. His sword was drawn. Caya looked more disappointed than afraid.

"Every time . . . *every time!* You know something, Tus? It is a sad fact, but the only sort of people we manage to attract to the Undermine these days are traitors," Caya groaned.

"Tell me and I will see to it that they go easy on you!" Kel demanded.

"Tus, would you?" Caya sighed.

In a one smooth motion, Tus slapped the blade from Kel's hands, wrapped his hand around the traitor's face, and thrust his head into the rickety wall of the shack. The would-be informant crumpled dizzily to the ground and caught one final glimpse of the massive Undermine soldier before being brought to a mercifully swift end with his own sword.

Caya and Tus stepped into the cold night, the commander holding the lamp. Sure enough, in a few moments the pair was surrounded by soldiers in crisp, fresh Elites armor, but the men were no Elites. The mismatch of weaponry made it clear what they really were. Caya sighed again.

"Mercenaries? We don't even warrant the true Elites? So be it," she said, casting the lamp into the shack.

As the flames swiftly consumed the contents of the temporary headquarters, Tus and Caya drew their blades. The hired Elites closed in. The battle was spectacular, though brief. One expected strength from a man such as Tus. One did not expect speed. Thus, the massive warrior managed to drive his weapon to the hilt in the chest of a still-mounted soldier before he could react. The subsequent swings struck a more prepared soldier's shield, eventually cleaving it in two.

By the time his initial rush was through, he'd managed to shatter his own sword, killing a second soldier and its horse in the process. Caya raised her single-handed sword, prompting the man who targeted her to raise his own. A moment later, a crossbow bolt punched through his armor. Caya dropped the weapon she'd concealed in her cloak and made ready to put her blade to work, but by then the troops had recovered. Tus managed to burst between the ranks and tear free a piece of the burning shack to use as a weapon, but Caya shook her head.

She was a capable warrior, but a better leader, and as she stared at the wrong end of a trio of mercenary crossbows, she knew the fight was over. She dropped her weapon, and Tus did the same. Prison offered the chance of escape. The same could not be said for death.

#

Myranda tried to focus herself. Slowly, she felt the darkness lessen. Sensations returned to her. She opened her eyes. It was night, Myn asleep on top of her. She managed to turn her eyes to the side, where she spotted

Deacon in a chair beside the bed, also asleep. Her eyes lifted in time to see a dark form vanish from the window. Lain? She tried to move, causing Myn to stir. The dragon caught a glimpse of the girl's fluttering eyes lids and sprang to her feet, still on top of her. Myn looked to the sleeping Deacon and gave a sharp lash with her tail, jerking him to wakefulness.

"What, what?" he said, before gathering his wits enough to realized that Myranda was awake. "Thank heavens."

"What is wrong?" Myranda asked.

"We lost you for two days. I was afraid we might have another Hollow on our hands," he said.

"Two days. I was asleep for two days?" she said, scratching her head and sitting up.

"Actually, two and a half. You may have given a bit more than you should have to pass that test," he said.

"But I passed?" she said.

"Flawlessly," he remarked. "Your place is secured in our records. You have gone from zero knowledge to mastery of a magic in one month. I doubt such a feat will be matched ever again."

"I am honored," she said.

"It is I who should be honored. Stay here. I will fetch you some food. When I return, I must discuss something with you that is of great importance," he said, hurrying off before she could object.

He returned to her with a bowl of the same stew and a loaf of the same bread that she had eaten every day since she arrived, save for the days that Myn would share some of her fish. He handed it to her and pulled out a book. It was not the one he usually carried. Instead, it was much older. As she ate, he spoke to her.

"When you were telling me about yourself, I was intrigued by your mark on your hand. It was familiar to me, but I couldn't place it. When I discovered that Lain had the same mark, I decided to look into it. I would like to read you a bit of this," he said.

"All right," she said.

He pulled open the cover and carefully flipped to a point near the center of the book and began to read.

"'A matter of land. Death too far south brings war. The three lands of the north join. The line is drawn. Generations fall to the blade of the enemy,'" he says.

"Why are you reading me a history of the war?" she asked.

It was a tale known to depressingly few, but the conflict that would become the Perpetual War began when, during meeting of the continent's nobility, the infirm king of Vulcrest grew ill. It was a long-held tradition that the kings of the north would be buried where they fell. Most came to

217

rest within the catacombs beneath their palaces. On that fateful day over a century ago, the king fell on Tresson land. The resulting demands that the Tressons relinquish rights to the land beneath him would escalate into a generation-spanning war.

"A history? Yes, today this would make a fine history. But this was not written today. This was written nearly two hundred-fifty years ago, a century before the war began. It represents the life's work of our finest prophet--a man called Tober. He is the only man who ever came to this place not to prove himself, but because he knew what he would find. He spent his time here perfecting this prophecy. He believed that if he could make the development of the war clear to the finest warriors in the world, then at least we could prepare. His only fault was his completion of the prophecy so long before it was needed. By the time warriors began to enter with tales of the war, the prophecy had lapsed into legend. Upon reviewing it, many of the events he told of have come to pass already. If the rest are to be believed, then a very important time is coming. The end of an era," he said.

"The coming of the Chosen," she said.

"Precisely. I looked further, and there is a description of the Chosen. Listen to this. 'He will have the blood of a fox, a member of a creature race. His skill with all weapons will be unsurpassed in the mortal world,'" he said.

"Lain," she said, her voice an awed hush.

"Yes. And therein lies the problem," he said.

"What do you mean?" she asked.

"The prophet tells of three things that will signify the Chosen when they arrive. They will be pure of soul, divine of birth, and born with 'the mark.' The prophet speaks at length about the mark, but he could never describe it," he said.

Myranda looked to her left palm. The thin white line of the scar still remained.

"He bears the mark. We do not know about the rest, but he bears the mark. And so do you. But . . . the prophecy does not speak of you. It does speak of 'a swordsman and knight, a leader among men, who will carry an enchanted sword and bear the mark upon all his armament,'" he said.

"The soldier . . . the one in the field. I took his sword. But he was dead. How can that be?" she asked.

"The prophecy does not speak of his death. The fact that you found the knight dead can mean only two things. One, that neither Lain nor the knight are the Chosen spoken of in the prophecy, and their appearance is a coincidence. The second, and far more disturbing, is that Lain is the one spoken of, which would mean that the leader of the Chosen was the one you came upon. If that is true then . . . the Chosen will not be complete and . . . the end of the war will not come," he said.

"But how can we be sure?" she asked.

"There is a way. The other three Chosen are described as well. One is an artistic prodigy, skilled in all that she puts her hands to. Another is a cunning strategist and tracker. Finally, a mystic being of unimaginable might, awaiting the day that the words of the others coax a return to the physical realm.

"Soon there will be a blue moon. On that night the mystic energies will be at their highest. That is the night that we have made it our tradition to attempt to summon this legendary being, but without the voice of a Chosen, our attempts have always been met with failure. Lain was never made a part of the ceremony in his time here, but will see that he is this time. If he is involved . . . and we are able to summon the strength . . . the mystic creature will return. If the being appears, then we will know for certain that a Chosen is among us," Deacon said.

Myranda sat silently in the bed. She had heard the tales. The tales of the Chosen. It was a favorite bedtime story. She had pictured the Chosen as the pristine and perfect knights that populated all of the other tales. Now Lain could be one? How?

"You say if you are able to summon the strength . . . there is doubt?" Myranda said insistently.

"The night of the blue moon is a night of high magic, to be sure, and we are quite likely the greatest wizards in this world. That having been said, the mystic creature will be one of monumental strength, and we shall be tasked with creating its physical form from nothing. There is no telling if there is strength enough in the *world* to succeed," Deacon stated.

"This ceremony to summon the Chosen. May anyone be a part of it?" Myranda asked.

"Anyone may observe. In fact, the Elder specifically requested that you and the others do so--but participation is limited to full Masters of war or the elements. The rite is a dangerous one. A lesser level of training would leave one at great risk," he explained.

Shortly after, Deacon left her to get her rest, the revelations he'd spoken of churning in her mind.

#

It took another day for Myranda to recover completely from the overexertion of the test. During that time, she received several angry visits from Ayna, the air wizard who was to be Myranda's second trainer. She reminded Myranda that she had been specifically told to report to her on the day of the test, and now three days had passed. She went on to accuse

Solomon of sabotaging her so that he could appear to be the only teacher capable of producing such a pupil.

The harsh words swept over her without effect. There were more serious concerns stewing in her mind. When Myranda finally felt well enough, she ventured out to find Lain. He was outside of his hut, as usual, engaging in some manner of odd stretching exercise.

"I have been told to congratulate you," he said.

"You are one of the Chosen," she said, angrily.

"Not this again. I thought I was through hearing this nonsense when I left this place the last time," he said, readying his staff. "Prepare yourself."

"You finished your training here decades ago. You were out there, in this war, with the power to stop it. *And you did nothing!*" she screamed, lunging at him with the weapon.

"It is the dream of a child. There are no Chosen," he said, parrying her attack.

Myranda launched into an offense with a ferocity that she would have never thought herself capable of. With each block or dodge, she grew angrier. Visions of the war spurred her on. Had he done what it was his destiny to do, she would never have had to know war. Every hardship of her life would never have occurred. Suddenly, it happened. Perhaps it was the long rest, or the anger-fueled strength, or the unpredictability of her furious attacks, but a blow slipped through, passing by his block and striking him squarely in on the chest. In an instant, he swept her legs out from under her and put the end of his staff to her throat, his teeth bared.

Myn stood rigidly still, unsure what to do.

"That's . . . one," Myranda managed.

Lain removed the staff.

"So it is," he conceded.

The vicious session continued. A handful more hits slipped past his guard before the sun finally set. Myn was beside herself watching the two finally attack each other in earnest. Myranda mopped the sweat from her brow. Lain inspected the site of one of the more powerful blows for blood or swelling.

"I count six," Myranda said.

"Five. I said solid blows. The third was glancing at best," he corrected.

"Fine, five. Time for you to pay up. I know that you have not been fighting to end the war as your destiny would dictate, and I know that you are not a tournament fighter as you said you were. For my first question, I want to know what you really do," she said.

"Are you certain? I warn you, you will not like the answer," he said.

"I assure you, I like the mystery even less," she said.

"Very well. I am an assassin. As a matter of fact, you are quite familiar with my exploits," she said.

"Why would . . . no," she said as the answer dawned on her. "You are the Red Shadow!"

Lain nodded.

"That is impossible--he is a man," she said.

"A man who killed a wolf with his bare hands and wears the bloody skull as a helmet," he said. "I started that rumor myself. If I was seen, I couldn't risk being recognized as a malthrope. Your kind would more easily let a mass murderer slip through your fingers than one of my kind. So if the gossip speaks of a man with a red wolf helmet, that it what people will see."

"And the Elites were after the Red Shadow. That is why they were really after you," she said.

"They are a formidable force," he said.

"If you are an assassin, then why were you after me?" she asked.

"This is your second question. The Alliance Army hired me to locate the swordsman and retrieve both he and the sword. I was also told that I was not the only one that would be after him, and that if he was to fall before I found him, I was to retrieve the sword and anyone who touched it and lived. That was you. I was also to kill anyone who tried to stop me," he said.

"But those men who came to claim me. They were of the Alliance Army. Why did you kill them?" she asked.

"Your third question," he said. "I must first inform you that I did not kill four men that day."

"I saw you with my own eyes," she said.

"You saw me kill four soldiers, but they were not men. Not quite," he said.

"I don't understand," she said.

"Somehow, I thought that you hadn't noticed them yet," he said. "They have been around for as long as I can remember, always wearing Alliance armor. At first they looked and sounded just as men do, but even then there was the smell. It was something . . . artificial. As time went on, they began to look less and less like men. Now they must wear their helmets lest their faces give them away. I do not know what they are, but I have taken to calling them nearmen, and they have infested your army.

"It was four of those that I killed that day, because they had come to collect you for themselves. They had been sent out with the same orders as I. Had they brought the payment, I would have let them have you and the sword, but they were empty-handed and they had to die."

"Wait, wait? Nearmen? You mean that there are creatures in the army that look human but aren't?" she said.

Lain began to open his mouth.

"That wasn't for you. I will not have you wasting one of my questions by answering that. Two more . . ." she scolded.

"Very well," he said.

Myranda looked at Myn, who had finally begun to relax after the anxious battle.

"Tell me about her. She likes you, me, and no one else. Solomon tells me he is sure that you were present at her birth. What happened that day?" Myranda asked.

Lain sighed.

"When I saw the cloaks recapture you so soon after I released you, I realized I had underestimated the number of other agents that the Alliance Army had dispatched after you. If you were to remain my prize I would have to keep you on a shorter leash. I made certain that, once you left the Undermine headquarters, I did not let you out of my sight. It turned out to be a very good thing that I did, because you chose as shelter a dragon's den. Even *your* nose could have told you that.

"I followed inside, and as fate would have it, a large male had been on the way. You panicked, so I knocked you unconscious, pulled you aside. If you had only kept your head and slipped out after the male had passed, you would have been safe. The dragons had no interest in you. After the female warded off the male, I remained near. The last remaining egg hatched, the creature inspected us, and deemed the two of us family," he said.

Myranda's head reeled. There was so much she had learned, and yet there was so much more to ask. What were those cloaks that had captured her? He had spoken of them so matter-of-factly, they must be as common as the nearmen that she had only just learned of. And exactly what *was* Lain? She didn't know much about malthropes, but she knew that they didn't live much longer than humans, and yet he had been active for over seventy years. There was only one question left . . .

"I will save my last question until next time. And I intend to earn more," Myranda decided.

"As you wish. I must warn you though--thus far, I have been limiting myself. It will not be so simple next time," he said.

"And I must warn you, Lain, I will not let this pass. You are Chosen, and I will see to it that you do your duty. I swear to it. From this day forward I am dedicating myself to the task," she hissed.

Myranda marched off to her hut to retrieve her casting staff and begin her first day of training under Ayna, the wind mage. Her place of study was a breezy grove not far from where Solomon spent his time. She looked about, but could not locate the little sprite that had been taunting her so regularly.

"Hello?" Myranda called anxiously.

Myn sniffed at the air and seemed to indicate a particular tree. Myranda approached the tree and looked up into it. It had an odd rune carefully carved into it.

"Ayna?" she repeated.

The tiny, gossamer-winged creature fluttered down from the tree to eye-level with Myranda. She resembled a tiny, exquisitely beautiful woman in a shimmery, powder blue dress. Looking at her, it seemed as though she should be the sweetest, dearest creature alive, but the illusion was destroyed when she opened her mouth.

"In this world, we have a thing we call 'the sun.' It is a great ball of light, and when it is overhead we call it 'daytime.' 'Daytime' is when civilized creatures do their business!" she reprimanded in the most condescending manner possible.

The wind of the grove seemed to wax and wane with the fairy's anger. It was quite gusty at the moment.

"I am sorry," Myranda said.

"You certainly are. I want you here at dawn tomorrow. Just because you are showing an unusual amount of prowess for someone of your stunted species does not give you the right to disrupt my way of life," she said.

"Ayna, enough!" came Deacon's voice from behind.

"Oh, good heavens, another one. Do you things travel in packs?" Ayna raved.

"You know that she just got through with Solomon, and he likes to work at night," Deacon said.

"That may be so, but I could hardly be confused for that beast. Now, if you two are through irritating me, I would like to get a bit more sleep before I begin passing on real wisdom," Ayna said, whisking off before any more could be said.

"What can I say? Ayna excels at first impressions," Deacon said.

"So I see. She is quite the little tyrant, isn't she," Myranda whispered.

"Yes, and with remarkably acute hearing," Deacon said with a pained look on his face.

"That is true," Ayna said, suddenly directly behind Myranda again. "I must say, I am surprised to hear such an infuriating statement come out of your mouth. Not for the stunning ignorance behind it. That much is to be expected. I frankly am surprised that you are able to form a complete sentence, particularly after your suicidal performance of Solomon's test."

"Oh, Ayna, excuse me, I--" Myranda began.

"There is no excuse for you, and do *not* call me Ayna. I am Highest Master Ayna until I give you permission to call me otherwise. Now leave before you stick your foot further into your mouth," she said.

Myranda walked slowly away, Deacon beside her.

"Tell me when we are far enough," she mouthed silently.

They were nearly halfway to the meal hut before Deacon gave her the sign.

"What a monster!" she said.

"Don't mind her. *She* assumes that *you* assume that *she* is inferior, so she constantly affirms the opposite," he said.

"I wasn't talking about Ayna," Myranda said.

"Oh?" Deacon replied. "I'd heard that you and Lain had a rather eventful session today. What did you learn?" he asked.

"That my home kingdom's army, which is composed at least partially of inhuman creatures of some sort, hired him, an assassin, to capture me for touching the sword and surviving," she said.

"Well . . . that was . . . informative," he said.

"What am I going to do now? I only awoke recently, and now I have to show up at dawn fully rested? I would never be able to sleep with all of this swirling about in my head even if I was tired," she said.

"Well, I suppose you could cast a sleep spell on yourself," he said.

"The only sleep I know is healing sleep," she said.

"Oh, no. Never use a spell for a purpose other than it was explicitly intended. You said that you were a student of white wizardry. How is it that you do not know sleep?" he asked.

"I was taught with the explicit intention of being a field healer for a rebel group. I do not think that sleep had placed highly on their list of requirements," she said.

"Well that is folly. In the repertoire of a pure white wizard, sleep is among the only spells that may be used to defend one's self. It is also one of the simplest spells. Though, to be fair, it is far wiser to have it cast upon you rather than to cast it upon yourself, unless you have also learned how to delay the effects of a spell until it has been fully cast. Delay falls within my realm, by the way," Deacon said.

"I would appreciate it if you would just put me to sleep," she said.

Deacon agreed and the pair, as always joined by Myn, went to her hut.

"Before you do this . . . is there any way that you can . . . prevent a dream from happening?" she asked.

"I am not certain. Why?" he wondered.

"I have not been having very pleasant dreams. In fact I have come to dread them," she said.

"How so?" he asked.

She quickly recounted the dreams of the dark field, the dreams of Lain's treachery, and the darkness that spoke with her voice. All the while Deacon nodded with concern.

"I see. The dreams of Lain are understandable, but the others . . . they seem to have an almost prophetic quality to them. Were I you I would not wish to silence them. In times to come they could provide much-needed clues about . . . well . . . times to come," he said.

"Well, if you really believe that, I suppose I can suffer through them," she said.

"Oh, indeed I do," he said. "And from now on, while we take our morning meal together, I would greatly appreciate it if you would tell me any dreams you may have."

"As you wish," she said.

Deacon held out his crystal and, with a few words, sent Myranda into a deep, pleasant sleep.

#

Perhaps as a favor, or perhaps as a coincidence, her dream that night was unusually muted. It was a clash of blurred images and muffled sounds, indistinct and incomprehensible. By the time she awoke the following morning, only one image had clearly revealed itself, but it alone was enough to leave her disturbed upon waking. It had been of a man, sitting solitary on a worn chair. His beard was long, with gray strands beginning to weave through it. The light that filtered over him was striped with shadows. His clothes were little more than rags. Everything about him radiated misery--save one powerful feature. His eyes, locked on some point in the distance, had a look of unbreakable resolve.

The man was her father. Having nearly escaped her dreams unscathed, the image was doubly shocking.

She took a moment to recover before grabbing her staff and heading out to Ayna's training ground. Myn trotted happily along beside her and watched intently as the fairy fluttered about impatiently. Apparently, despite the fact that Myranda had skipped breakfast in order to assure she would arrive before the sun had even fully slipped over the horizon, this was still not quite early enough.

"Well, I am pleased to see that you are no longer nocturnal," Ayna taunted. "I do hope you brought what little mind you have to spare, because I expect a lot out of you."

"I hope I can meet your expectations," Myranda said.

"Yes, well, you completed Solomon's little test, which is usually the last one, so at least you have the strength to do what is required of you. Regardless, enough dillydally. Listen carefully. Elemental magics differ greatly in technique, so you will be as good as starting over to learn my ways," she warned.

Myranda opened her mouth to give a response, but was swiftly admonished for it.

"When I want you to speak, I will order you to do so. Now, would you like to learn this through concentration, or incantation? Speak," she said.

"Concentration," Myranda said flatly.

"Oh, you mean you have forsaken your precious 'magic words'? Surely you would rather chant them again and again like a sing-along. Oh, what fun it would be," Ayna said with mock enthusiasm.

"Do not patronize me," Myranda said sternly.

"Oh, my! Patronize! That is a big word, isn't it? What else have you got rattling about in that head of yours? Not much, I imagine. But I digress. Close your eyes and focus," she said.

"I don't need to--" Myranda began.

"*I* will tell you what you *need* to do. *Close your eyes and focus!*" she demanded.

Myranda did so.

"Clear your mind of all but my voice. Nothing else exists," she said.

Normally she would have been able to enter the appropriate state of mind nearly instantly, but her infuriating new trainer had clogged her mind with anger that had to be coaxed away. Even so, it still was not long before she was ready. As though Ayna could feel her serenity, she began to speak.

"That is adequate. Now listen closely. I want you to focus on your skin. Feel the wind. Feel how it passes over you. Raise your hand," she instructed.

Myranda did so.

"Notice how, at your merest thought, your hand moves. Notice, too, how the air moves about it. Focus wholly on the air as it swirls and whirls. Always moving. There is an energy in it, just as there is an energy in fire. Sense the energy," she said. "Keep the flowing wind at the front of your mind. Remember how you moved your hand. You simply willed it forward. Exert that same will again, but let it slowly slip from your body. Let it flow forth into the shifting air. Mix your strength with that of the breeze. It is little more than an extension of your body. Another limb. Add more energy. Give the air more strength."

The hypnotic tone of Ayna's voice slipped easily into Myranda's mind. Whereas just days ago she had passed a test infinitely more grueling than this, she found herself straining slightly. It was not like learning again from the beginning, but it was measurably more taxing to her than fire had become. Already she could feel the fatigue. What's more, the trance she was in was not nearly as sound.

In the closing days of her fire training, she could conjure and control a flame with her eyes open and mostly aware. Now even the minor distractions of having to listen with her ears and feel with her skin were threatening to break her focus. The steadily increasing breeze was, at least, more appreciable than the minor warmth that had evidenced her fire skill in the first days. That, too, was revealed to be a curse. As the wind increased, she became both more excited about her success and more distracted by the sensation of it dancing over her skin. The stiff breeze she had managed began to waver until finally the hard fought battle with concentration was lost and the world came flooding back into her mind.

"Oh, come now. You must have discipline. You nearly had it," Ayna said with a swiftly vanishing look of admiration.

"I . . . I did it," Myranda said.

"Well, in the same sense that tripping over your own feet can be called taking a step forward. Still, it would seem that vacant head of yours is quite susceptible to concentration. It stands to reason, though. You never need to clear your mind," Ayna jabbed.

Myranda stood silent. Solomon very seldom gave any critique, good or bad. As a result, what little words of encouragement he did give were truly meaningful. Ayna, it would seem, felt almost obligated to qualify any compliment by hiding it in an insult.

"Don't just stand there slack-jawed. You have got a long way to go," Ayna said.

Myranda complied. This time her anger slowed the trance even further. Over the course of nearly an hour, she cast enough of her will into the air around her to match her previous achievement.

"That will do; now, open your eyes and I will show you where to direct it," Ayna instructed.

Myranda slowly opened her eyes, but she had not attained firm enough a grasp of this new magic to permit her mind to withstand this distraction. The wind instantly subsided. The strain of flexing this new mystic muscle suddenly became apparent, as an intense dizziness took the place of focus. She stumbled forward, failing to catch herself on with her staff and dropping to the ground.

"Endurance, girl, endurance. What good does it do to take your first steps so quickly if you stop before you get anywhere?" Ayna said with frustration.

"I am sorry. Let me . . . try again," Myranda said, struggling to her feet.

"No, go. It is obvious we will not get any further today. Just be sure to be better prepared next time. Make sure you rest. I will not be so patient tomorrow," Ayna warned.

As Myranda shuffled wearily away, Ayna fluttered back to her tree, twittering in her native language. Myranda had only found a handful of people in this place who shared the language, and she had learned little of it in the month she had resided here. She did know enough, though, to know that her tone was one of quiet awe. Regardless of what Ayna may have said, she was amazed.

It was still quite early in the day, but the effort had left her with the odd, deep weariness she had come to know so well. She longed for sleep, but knew that it simply would not come until her body became tired as well. After a long overdue breakfast, she made her way to Deacon's hut. The door was open and she could see that he was at work scribing this spell or that from his voluminous knowledge. When he noticed her in the doorway, a smile came to his face and he welcomed her inside.

"I am so sorry. I had meant to meet you," he said, glancing at the position of the sun as he helped her to a second seat that had not been present during her last visit. "But I didn't think that you would have been through so soon. So, how was your first day under the tutelage of Ayna?"

"I did what she said. I managed to get the air moving, but I couldn't keep it up for very long. I don't know what was wrong," she said.

"How many times did you try?" he asked.

"Twice," she said.

"You managed results after only two tries and you are asking what is wrong?" he said in disbelief.

"Actually, I managed after only one," she said.

"I assure you. You have nothing to worry about," he said, fetching a volume from one of the shelves.

It had an old-looking brown cover bearing the same rune that had been on Ayna's tree. He leafed through the book until he found the page he sought.

"I borrowed this book from the library on the hunch that you might feel this way. When Ayna was teaching novices, which you technically are in her discipline, she did not have a single student who could manage even the slightest breath of wind for the first three weeks. You are a gifted student," he said, closing the book and returning to his seat before another book in which he continued writing.

"But she is so insulting. She said that I had an empty head and--" Myranda began.

"It is just her way. I have said it before. Just ignore it," he said. "Her greatest virtue is that she is the finest expert in wind magic that we have. Her greatest fault is that she knows it."

Myranda sat with a dazed look on her face.

"Are you quite all right?" Deacon asked as he returned to his seat.

"Just a bit dizzy," she said.

"A few minutes of meditation will take the edge off of that," he said.

"I would rather just rest for a bit," she said. "It is not very serious. I only need enough wit about me to face Lain tonight."

"Very well. You have been at this long enough to know what you need," he said, putting pen to page again at his desk.

Myranda sat silently for a bit, listening to the distant rumble of the falls.

"Deacon," she said.

"Yes," he replied, without looking up.

"You say that no one can leave because of the falls," she said.

"That is indeed true," he assured her.

"But the most skilled wizards in the world are here, aren't they? Surely someone could find a way around the waterfall problem," she said.

"Were this any other place, I can assure you that such would be so. However, the selfsame crystal that makes casting so much easier for us is present in scattered clusters throughout these mountains and all along the cliffside," he said, flipping a page.

"Wouldn't that make magic all the easier to use?" she asked.

"Not as such. You can think of a well-refined crystal as a mirror. Quite useful. A cluster of small, rough crystals is like a broken mirror. It does nothing but distort and confuse things. As a result, save for very small, simple spells, any magic directed at the mountain or in the mountain falls apart quite quickly. There are theories we have developed that could conceivably offer a solution to the dilemma, but few are interested enough in leaving this place to develop them much," he explained.

"Ah . . . What are you up to?" she asked.

"Scribing, as usual," he said.

"What exactly?" she asked.

"The analysis of an efficient method of illusionary motion synchronization and appearance duplication," he said without looking up.

"Pardon?" she said, bewildered.

"Oh, I am sorry. I am required to phrase things in that way when I record them. What it is, is . . . well, let me show you," he said.

Deacon stood and took his crystal in hand.

"Now, for the duration of this demonstration, you will be able to recognize me as the one with the crystal. Ahem . . . most wizards have at least a basic understanding of illusion. They use a method that gives this result," he said.

Beside him a second Deacon appeared, indistinguishable from the first. It began to speak.

"As you can see, this produces an admirable result. It can look like, sound like, or *be* whatever I desire," the copy said. As it mentioned the different possibilities of appearance, sound, and form, the illusion shifted quickly through a series of examples. Suddenly, it faded away.

"Such illusions are difficult to create, though," he said, recreating the first, followed by another and another.

The three spoke simultaneously. As they did, they moved about, pacing in well-choreographed circles around Myranda.

"The trouble is making more than one is difficult. Keeping the illusion intact is more so. For long term or large scale pursuits, this method will not do," they said, slowly fading away until only the voice of original remained.

"I propose we use a new method," the real Deacon said. "In my new method, similar copies are made that are based on the original. These copies synchronize their movements and appearance. As a result, no more effort is used for the tenth as was used for the first."

As he spoke, one duplicate after another began to appear. Soon the room was crowded with them, all precisely mimicking the true Deacon, who had quickly been lost among the crowd.

"Now minor changes in appearance or movement can be added to each without much more effort," the crowd said. Immediately, each of the copies took on a slight change in appearance. Some walked more slowly, others more quickly. Voices changed. And then they all vanished. All but one.

"That is what I meant," Deacon said.

"That was remarkable," she said.

"Thank you. Illusions are one of the most refined aspects of my art," he said.

"Can you make an illusion of anyone?" she asked.

"Anyone I have seen or can imagine. It actually makes it possible, with the addition of some strategic invisibility, to create instant disguises. Observe," he said.

He proceeded to transform before her eyes into a myriad of different people. Some she did not recognize, others she had seen in Entwell. She even noticed herself appear briefly. Lain, too, made an appearance before he ended the effect.

"It is such practices that gave gray magic a poor standing in the mystic community," he said.

"I don't understand," she said.

"It is used to create disguises. Therefore it is used for dishonesty. Dishonesty and treachery are among the worst crimes a wizard can commit," he said.

"Why?" she asked.

"For the same reasons anyone else might be looked down upon for lying. Of course, there is a second stigma for a wizard who lies. The spirits who we so often call upon to aid in our conjuring judge us by the purity of our soul. Dishonesty twists a soul, rendering us distasteful to all but similarly twisted spirits. These spirits tend to take a far greater and far darker toll in exchange for their aid. Hence the gnarled appearance of the darker wizards and witches we hear of in children's stories," he said.

"I see," she said. "Couldn't you solve the problem of your art seeming to be a lie by making it the truth? Couldn't actually make the things appear?"

"In theory, yes, but that would not solve our problem at all. We can change things from one form or substance to another with enough effort, but to summon objects is strictly forbidden," he said.

"Why?" she asked.

"It is fundamental to the rules that govern this place. All areas may be studied, but some may not be practiced. Chief among them are time travel and summoning or manifesting. Time travel has consequences that no one can fully comprehend, and is thus too dangerous to consider, and summoning . . . well. When you summon, you may accidentally or purposely draw something from another world. That is unacceptable. Things of this world belong here; things from elsewhere do not," he said.

"Why?" she asked.

"They simply do not. It has never been made clearer than that, but it has been drilled into us from the first day of our training. I don't question it," he said.

"No one warned me," she said.

"You haven't received any gray training. For it to become an issue for you, you would have to stumble upon the appropriate spell by mistake," he said, his mind suddenly shifting directions. "Say . . . how is that dragon of yours?" he said.

"Come to think of it, I haven't seen her all day," Myranda said. "I suppose she could be with Lain. Or Solomon. She does look forward to hunting with him."

"Well, not that she isn't a joy to be with, but I cannot say that I have missed her little reminders of when I get too close. I wish that she would learn to speak so that there could be a less painful alternative. She doesn't even give me a warning in her own language," he said. "The only time that she seemed to tolerate me at all was when I helped you after Solomon's test, and she was more than a bit reluctant even then."

"I keep telling her not to do it. It is as though she thinks it's a game," Myranda apologized.

"She is young and overprotective," he said dismissively.

"Why did you ask about her?" Myranda asked.

"You mean to tell me that you do not hear that?" he said.

Myranda listened closely. Outside there was a commotion. The voices of several excited villagers could be heard, as well as an odd crashing noise. She rushed out of the door. The eyes of the villagers were trained on a rooftop. Myranda looked to it just in time to see Myn finish scampering to the top.

"Myn! What are you doing!?" she called out.

The dragon looked excitedly to her and unfurled her wings. She leapt from the roof and flapped wildly, taking a less-than-graceful lurching trip through the air. Despite the rather abortive attempt at flight, the little creature did manage to pick up a remarkable amount of speed. Her aim was impressively accurate as well, as she covered just enough ground to collide with Myranda, knocking them both to the ground.

"Well, you have certainly been busy," Myranda managed after sitting up and looking the little creature in the eyes.

Solomon came trotting over to them, growling some throaty message to Myn.

"That is the furthest she has managed to travel," he explained.

"When did this start?" Myranda asked, climbing to her feet as Myn sprinted back to the building and clawed her way to the roof.

"This morning, after watching you and Ayna at work, she came to me, curious. I showed her how to start on the path to flight," Solomon answered helpfully in Northern.

Myn took to the sky again, flailing through the air and slamming into Myranda. This time the girl was ready and caught the dragon in her arms. The force of the landing still caused her to stumble backward. Myranda realized for the first time how much Myn had grown since the day they first met. The creature was as heavy as a child! She let her down and watched her run to another building, this one even further away.

"How long is this going to keep up?" Myranda asked Solomon as she braced for a third test flight.

"She needs to develop the muscles. To do that, she will need to practice. If she remains as enthusiastic as she is now, I cannot foresee her requiring much more than a week to fly for at least a few minutes at a time," he said.

Myranda caught her friend and released her again.

"Take a few more steps back. Make her work. It will speed her progress," he said.

Myranda stepped back. Sure enough, Myn fought harder and made it into her arms. The game continued for some time. Though it was a bit rough, Myranda found it quite enjoyable. The sun had drooped in the sky before Myn couldn't manage the distance from the roof to her friend, a distance that had grown to nearly a hundred paces. The poor little thing was exhausted. Solomon praised both dragon and girl for working together so well before retiring to his hut. Deacon, who had left to continue his scribing after watching for a time, had returned when he found that the sequence of flaps and crashes had ended.

"I trust you had some fun," he said.

"Did you see her? She practically made it halfway across the village!" Myranda said excitedly, scratching the weary creature.

"Perhaps a bit of an exaggeration, but it was impressive nonetheless," he said.

"She's growing up. I know I should be happy, but inside I'm not," she said.

"Why?" he asked.

"I don't want to lose my little dragon. She's enough of a handful at this size. Can you imagine when she is grown?" Myranda said.

"Yes, well, you've got years before that becomes a problem," he said. "As I understand it, they grow quickly at first, but it slows after the first year. Besides, I think you've got something else to worry about right now."

"What?" she asked.

"Look at the sky," he said.

The sun was nearing the horizon.

"Lain! I have to get to training!" she said.

"I'm afraid so," he said.

Myranda rushed off to her hut, with Myn trudging as quickly as she could to keep up. She retrieved the quarterstaff and hurried to where Lain was waiting.

"Myn is learning to fly. I lost track of time," Myranda explained as the tired dragon collapsed beside her.

"I know. It is a difficult spectacle to miss. Never mind the quarterstaff-- take this," he said, tossing her a shorter, stouter rod.

"What is this?" she asked.

"That is roughly what you will be given when you have finished your wizard training, minus the crystal. It is the weapon that you are most likely to make use of in the future. It is also the second weapon I have decided to teach you," he said.

"Very well," she said.

"Today, I will attack, and you will defend," Lain said.

"You will attack? I have been catching Myn all day. I am not sure I can take many hits," she said.

Lain took a wooden training sword from the rack behind him. With a swift slash, he brought the weapon to within an inch of the girl's neck before she could react. There it stopped without touching her.

"If my weapon comes as close as this, you can consider yourself killed," he said.

"And how do I earn a question?" she asked.

"If you manage to block three attacks in a row, I will allow you one question," he said.

After a brief explanation of the differences in the usage of the staff as opposed to the quarterstaff, he instructed her to prepare herself, and they began. Had she more energy, Myn would have viciously objected to the violent display. Instead, she cast a weary eye on the proceedings between dozes.

Whereas she had been slow to pick up the correct methods of attack, defense came far more naturally to Myranda. Before long, she was blocking his first attack without fail. Unfortunately, this nearly always left her weapon out of place to block the follow-up attack. Lain scolded her as she failed again and again to block his second attack.

"Your opponent may be able to attack more quickly than you can move, but not more quickly than you can think. Use your mind. Battle is more than about the body. If you cannot position a block in the time between when you identify the intended target and the moment of impact, then you must move sooner. You must know where the foe will attack next! Anticipate!" he demanded.

By the end of the session, she had only managed to block a second attack a handful of times, and never a third. Magic had forced her to think deeply. It would seem that combat was forcing her to think quickly. The two skills, on the surface, seemed practically opposite. It was clear that if someone were to possess both skills, though, there would be little that such a person could not handle.

After a few final pieces of advice from Lain, Myranda parted ways and headed for home. Myn was still quite weary and took her usual post atop her when Myranda went to bed.

#

Across the Low Lands and across the west, the black carriages rolled. Trigorah watched in cold silence as her Elites carried out their orders. Anyone who met the girl since she found the sword was found, captured, and hauled away. The orders seemed pointless, arbitrary, but they were not the first such commands to bear fruit. It was not her place to question them, only to carry them out. The other generals had managed to keep the Northern Alliance free despite a centuries-long struggle against a foe twice its size and many times its strength. It didn't matter that their methods were . . . unsettling. The only thing that mattered was victory.

Trigorah repeated it to herself during the long nights without sleep. These orders were vital steps toward victory. Victory would bring peace. Peace was an end high enough to justify any means. She repeated the words to herself as she looked into the eyes of the innocents being taken away for reasons they didn't understand. She repeated them as she heard the wails of children separated from their parents. She repeated them until the words were without meaning, until the wheels of the black carriages wore deep ruts in the roads of the low lands.

She repeated them, praying each time that she might finally believe them.

#

Myn awoke and looked upon her friend with concern. Myranda was sweating and out of breath. Perhaps through no coincidence, her dreams had been of Trigorah, of that fateful meeting in the forest before they came here. The night when she nearly killed the nearest thing she had to a living relative. In her nightmare she'd seen the face of one of the injured soldiers. It was her father. She knew it couldn't be true, that her mind was playing tricks, but that hardly mattered.

Thoughts raced through her head. Trigorah had worked with her father, and she was now an Elite. Could her father have been an Elite as well? It would explain why he was away so often . . . and since the Elites were so secret and important an organization he could still be alive today, and she would never know. A brief flash of happiness at the thought vanished when she realized that Trigorah knew her, and if her father was still alive, he most certainly have been informed. He would have come for her if he was still living as a member of the Elites. Unless he was ashamed, or . . . there was no time for such thoughts.

Myranda gathered her things and headed to Ayna's place while Myn trotted off to be with Solomon. As usual, the fairy was up and about, impatiently waiting for her student to arrive. A smile came to her face as she noticed that Deacon was there, too.

"Well, well. It would appear that my little pupil has attracted an audience once again," Ayna said.

"I missed out last time. I just want to see this firsthand. It promises to be quite a spectacle," he said.

"So is a forest fire," she said with a sneer, "but if you must stay, keep clear. I will not tolerate interruption."

"I will be a mere shadow," he said.

"Well then, get to it. Concentrate," Ayna ordered.

Myranda quickly shut off the world as she had done so many times before. When her mind was prepared, Ayna's voice sounded.

"Eyes open," she demanded.

"But--" Myranda began.

"I said eyes open. And if I have to repeat myself again, you will learn just how unpleasant being my pupil can be," she said.

Myranda opened her eyes. Set before her was an array of thin poles, each with a wooden ball perched on its end.

"Now, the purpose of this apparatus should be clear to all but the dimmest of individuals. Therefore, let me explain it to you. You will conjure up a wind and direct it at the poles. If it is of sufficient strength, the ball will fall. I will see to it that no natural breezes give you any help," Ayna said. "You may close your eyes, provided you can remember which direction is forward."

Myranda closed her eyes and tried to push away the anger Ayna had stirred up with her belittling remarks. The wind came quickly. It was only a breeze at first, but it grew steadily, and before long, she felt that it must be strong enough. She opened her eyes, managing to maintain the strength of the breeze. Of the ten poles, four had already lost their cargo, and a fifth came quickly after that.

As time went on. the strain of keeping the wind at speed became nearly unbearable, but one by one the other poles shed their contents. Finally only one remained, but try as she might she could not shake the ball free.

"Oh, come now. Just one more," Ayna said, a thin veneer of encouragement poorly masking her smug satisfaction.

Myranda redoubled her efforts, but the ball would not budge. Had she less of a task occupying her mind, she might have noticed Deacon shaking his head in disgust and casting a glare at Ayna, but all of this was filtered out in her attempts to focus her mind more powerfully. Her trainer wore a grin that widened with each unsuccessful gust. The fury within her grew and eroded her concentration. The gales began to waver, and finally she let the trance lapse entirely.

"Well, well. Our prodigy is not all-powerful after all. You have your rest, and perhaps tomorrow you can take another baby step," Ayna gloated.

"No!" Myranda proclaimed, raising her staff and trying to conjure another breeze.

"Listen to me, little girl. You have failed. Leave now before I have you removed," Ayna warned.

Myranda ignored the fairy's protests and brought about a weak breeze. She tried to strengthen it, but the anger filling her mind left no room for concentration. Ayna flitted directly in front of her disobedient pupil and continued to threaten, but Myranda heard none of it. Her fury grew and grew, like a river straining against a dam. This awful creature that took such joy in her failure would be taught a lesson. Her hands began to shake.

Finally the dam broke and the anger flooded her mind. A powerful burst of wind erupted, seemingly from nowhere, shaking her from her focused state of mind. The profound dizziness struck with equal speed. She had dropped her staff when the wind had startled her and had nothing to steady herself. Deacon was beside her in time to keep her on her feet.

"Are you all right? You shouldn't have done that. You really shouldn't have," he said.

"I did that?" Myranda said with disbelief.

Her eyes finally came into focus to see what looked to be the site of a disaster. All of the poles were shaking violently. Those nearest to the one she had been focusing on were snapped off at the base and were only just now falling to the ground yards away. The one she had targeted was missing entirely, along with a generous portion of the earth it had been anchored in. Some distance away it could be found, embedded in Ayna's tree. Ayna herself was fluttering, stunned, in front of a slight impression in the same tree where she had collided with it. She was plastered with the dirt kicked up by the wind and slowly turning to the tree to survey the damage.

"You had better move. Quickly," Deacon whispered to her as he led her away.

The fairy lifted a hand without turning. A fierce wind rushed up around Myranda, forcing Deacon away and lifting her from the ground. When she had flitted to the ground beside the flailing girl, she snapped her fingers. The wind cut off, and Myranda fell forcefully to the ground.

"That is all. You are *through!* I do not want to see you again for a year," she said.

"Now, Ayna, you cannot do that," Deacon said, trying to reason with her.

"You know the rules as well as I. That girl used a spell fueled by anger. Such an offense is punishable by whatever means *I* see fit. You should be glad I do not choose to kill her," Ayna said.

"But the rules also call for leniency for a first offense," Deacon countered.

"Leniency! I do not care if that *thing* has never made a single misstep in her life! She allowed the darker emotions to empower a spell, and did so *while* she was disobeying me, using said spell specifically to *assault* me!" Ayna raged.

"I did not--" Myranda attempted, but the fairy made a fist and she felt the air withdraw from her lungs.

"You prompted it. She was not assaulting you, she was attempting to pass a test that you had sabotaged," he said.

"How dare you accuse me of sabotaging the test!" Ayna said, aghast.

"The pole is sticking out of the side of your tree and the ball is still attached," he said.

"I didn't deny sabotaging the test, but you have no right to accuse me of it," she said.

Myranda's vision was fading as what little air she had left was giving out. As her thrashing slowed, Ayna took notice and opened her fist. The fresh air rushed back into her lungs and brought her back around. When she had caught her breath enough to climb to her feet, she did so.

"What have I done to you to deserve--" Myranda attempted again, only to receive the same treatment.

"For someone renowned for her skill in learning, you certainly are slow to learn when to keep your mouth shut," Ayna said as the girl fell helplessly to the ground.

"You are the one at fault as much as her, because you know better," Deacon said.

"Fine. Get the flute and the . . . elegy, I suppose. But I am through with her until she is ready for her exam. She is your student now. See that she drills every day," Ayna said, flitting off to her tree and releasing her grip.

Deacon helped Myranda to her feet again and the two made their way to the meal hut. As they ate, and Myranda's mind cleared, they spoke.

"What just happened?" she asked.

"Ayna coaxed you into breaking one of our cardinal rules," he said, lowering his voice to a whisper. "It was probably her plan from the start. Once she found out just how fast you were learning, her concern likely drifted to maintaining her own grip on the record for air mastery."

"What rule did I break?" she asked.

"You allowed anger to affect your casting of a spell," he said.

"Is that why it was so powerful? I don't understand. Why did it happen, and if I released so much energy so quickly, why am I not exhausted?" she asked.

"Well, magic is an expression of the soul's power. High emotion stirs the soul and boosts the power. Anger in particular has a way of amplifying the effect of any forceful spell beyond the point of controllability. That fact, coupled with the fact that one grows reliant on such methods if used too often, makes it one of the worst offenses one can commit while training. Long term uses can twist the soul far more than dishonesty and treachery," he said. "As for the reason that you are not exhausted? It will catch up with you, probably while you are asleep. Too much energy too quickly sometimes takes a few hours to take a toll, particularly on a first-time user. More experienced users feel it sooner."

"Why?" she asked.

"Magic still holds a few mysteries, even from us," he said.

"Wait. I saw all of the Masters literally destroy the Elder's hut. Weren't they breaking this rule?"

"They were angry *while* casting the spell. The anger was not affecting the strength of the spell. If it was, there wouldn't be much of a village left," he said.

"Oh. Well, what do I do now?" she asked.

"There are very few fundamentals to be taught in air magic. Two, really. You already know how to conjure wind, and the display you put on today proves you can direct it with a fair amount of accuracy. The rest is practice," he said.

"So, now I just practice until I feel ready to take some final test," she said.

"Indeed. You will be getting a flute and a tune to learn, as well. It doesn't take a prodigy to figure out what you will be doing with them for the final test," he said.

"I suppose I will be doing a hands-free performance," she said.

"Right you are," he said.

The pair finished and left the hut. Myn came trotting up and wedged herself between Myranda and Deacon.

"And where were you? I was attacked and you were nowhere to be found!" Myranda said, jokingly.

The dragon shot a vicious look at Deacon and pounced him to the ground.

"No, no! Not him. He didn't attack me!" Myranda said, pulling the creature off of her friend.

"Well, it would seem that she has gained a fairly firm understanding of the language," Deacon said, accepting a helping hand from Myranda.

The creature gave Myranda a questioning stare. She clearly was awaiting the identity of the real attacker.

"Well, I am not going to tell you who really did it because I don't want you to get me in any more trouble," Myranda said.

"And thank you so much for assuming I was the guilty one. I have got to find some way to get on your good side," Deacon said. "I am going to start bringing you gifts."

"Well, I don't face Lain again until sundown, with nothing to do until then," Myranda said.

"I wouldn't recommend doing anything mystic. Something too strenuous could certainly bring that angry expenditure back more quickly," Deacon warned.

Little did Myranda know, Myn had made the decision for her. She sprinted off to nearest building and scampered to the rooftop. By the time Myranda noticed she had gone, she was already in the air. Myranda scarcely had the time to brace herself for impact before the beast collided with her.

An afternoon of doing so left her fairly bruised, and bleeding here and there from where Myn had gotten a bit careless with her claws. It was nonetheless an entertaining time, and a few moments of a healing spell wiped away the consequences, save a bit of fatigue of both mind and body.

Lain was waiting, as always, when she approached him.

"I am sorry, Lain. I had a rather rough time of it today. I may not be at my best," she said.

"All the better. I can think of few times that I have been fully rested when I have been expected to defend myself," he said, tossing her the staff. "Now, prepare yourself."

It was her worst showing since she began. His blows were on target constantly. On the off-chance that she managed to block a shot, the force of it threw her off balance. Several times, she lost her footing and nearly fell into a handful of blows. Thankfully, Lain's reflexes were swift enough for the two of them, and he pulled the weapon away in time. By the time Lain felt she had done enough, Myranda was on the edge of unconsciousness. The outburst she'd had earlier had most certainly made its cost known.

"I sincerely hope that you improve your off-peak performance, or you will fall swiftly in a real battle," he said.

"I will work on it," she managed as she trudged off, Myn keeping a watchful eye on the teetering girl.

She made it back to her hut and fairly collapsed on the bed. With no sunrise appointment with an unpleasant teacher, her sleep was doubly deep. No nightmare came, only the dark, dreamless sleep of pure exhaustion.

#

Myranda was awakened by Myn, rather than the other way 'round, several hours later than she was accustomed to rising. Deacon hunted her down during breakfast and provided her with the flute and music that Ayna had called for. It was a simple reed flute, and the tune seemed easy enough. After spending a bit of time practicing, she felt sure she would be able to master it before long.

Myn was still eager to make her practice flights, and seemed to feel that without a teacher to steal away her valuable time, Myranda would be free to act as a landing pad for the whole of the day. The girl tried to enlist Deacon in distracting the dragon so that she could spend some time at work on her wind magic with little success. He brought a few fresh fish and the rarest of rare, a piece of red meat that he would not relinquish the origin of. The dragon snubbed them, choosing to eat them only when Myranda offered them. None were enticing enough to eat out of his hands.

A compromise was struck when Myranda aided the dragon in practicing her soaring by providing a constant breeze to fill her wings. Without a tyrannical teacher pushing her to her limit, the girl was able to cut her training off while she still had the clarity of mind to give Lain a real challenge. She found that predicting his attacks early enough to deflect them required nearly the presence of mind that magic did.

The next few days passed in much the same way, and were the most pleasant in recent memory. She found that her skill with wind was growing at about the same speed as Myn's flight prowess. At the end of the first week, the dragon could stay aloft for over an hour, and Myranda felt only the slightest strain in helping her do so. Deacon had not yet found the item that would win Myn over, and was running out of ideas.

The least improvement came in her time with Lain. Over the course of her time with him, she had managed to earn only a single question, a question so hard-won, she could not bring herself to ask it. With only two questions, she would only be able to whet her thirst for knowledge.

While Myranda was having trouble convincing Myn to allow her to practice her flute-playing one day, Deacon arrived with a dusty bag.

"What have you got there?" Myranda asked.

"I have tried everything at my disposal that a dragon might like and Myn still ignores or attacks me. Things have become somewhat desperate. Thus, I've ventured into the garden and selected one of each vegetable. Not much to appeal to a carnivore, but it is my last chance," he said.

While Myn was reluctant to treat Deacon with anything less than suspicion, she did get a bit curious each day when he brought around the latest round of gifts to reject. One by one, he offered carrots and celery and onions. Not surprisingly, the dragon sniffed once or twice and swatted them away. However, when Deacon pulled a large potato from the bag, she sniffed with a bit more interest, and finally took it from his hand, eating eagerly.

"Potatoes?" the pair said confusedly.

When the beast looked up and rooted around in the bag for another, he knew he had found his way into her heart.

"Very well, then, only I give her potatoes. She already likes you, I'm the one that needs help," he said to Myranda before turning to address the creature directly. "And as for you. For every day you don't hit me, I'll give you one of those. Agreed?"

Myn seemed to be in reluctant agreement as she licked her lips a few times and sniffed and licked at his hands in a far gentler way than he was accustomed to. The pleasant moment was cut short by a voice that they had been mercifully free from for the past two weeks.

"How lovely, the animals are getting along," Ayna said.

"Well, what brings you this far from your safe haven?" Deacon asked.

"I have been hearing the elegy wafting through the air with steadily decreasing inaccuracy. It sounds to me that the time of the final test is near," she said with a smile.

"As I recall, you were eager to postpone that date by no less than a year. Why the sudden change of heart?" Deacon asked.

"I am entitled to test my pupil when I have brought her to the proper level of knowledge," she said.

"Are you certain I am ready?" Myranda said.

"Reasonably. If not now, then in a few days. Certainly before the week is out," she said.

"Oh, I see. She will be ready before four weeks are up. That is the amount of time that she took to complete Solomon's training," Deacon said.

"What a coincidence! Well, the performance of a student speaks well of the teacher, doesn't it? It would be a shame to see that dragon's name alongside hers in the history books without mine above it," Ayna said.

"So you are willing to treat her with the respect she deserves when you have something to gain from it," Deacon said.

"If you wish to view it that way, you may. Oh, and, Myranda, my dear, be well-rested when you come to take the test. I expect to break more than one record with your help," Ayna said, slipping away.

"What do you suppose that means?" Myranda said.

"Well, the air test is largely up to the discretion of the teacher--more so than most, traditionally. It also tends to be the easiest. I have a feeling that Ayna's intention is to end that tendency, thus forcing you into a record-setting performance that she can claim responsibility for. It is her first real Master exam; she can always claim that it was her intention to make the more difficult test the standard for all of her students," Deacon said.

"Wonderful," Myranda said flatly.

"You have certainly been bringing about the most inexplicable events since your arrival. However unpleasant it may be for you, it is at least refreshing for the rest of us," Deacon offered.

"At least there is that," she said, with a heavy sigh.

After a bit more practice to assure that she was prepared to play the tune, at least, Myranda decided that if this test were to have a similar effect on her as the last, she had best put forth a considerable effort to earn a few more questions of Lain. It would be her last opportunity for a number of days.

Deacon hurried off to secure as many potatoes as he could while Myranda and Myn headed to the designated place for training. Upon her arrival, Lain offered his usual pointers and critiques of her previous performance in lieu of greeting.

"You continue to focus entirely on my weapon while defending. You must be aware of the whole of my body. My feet may be the furthest thing from a threat to you, but they tend to be the greatest indicator of where my next attack will fall," he said, tossing her weapon to her.

"I may not be able to meet you for a few days. I will be having my examination in wind magic tomorrow," she said.

"Very well," he said. "Prepare yourself."

Myranda paused. He had begun each of the sessions since they began with that simple phrase. Each day, she disregarded it as a simple warning that battle was about to begin. Perhaps it was the impending test that Ayna had sprung upon her, but when the words reached her ears this time, they seemed to take on a different meaning. After all, Lain had recently revealed himself to be a man of few words. It was unlike him to speak a phrase so frequently for nothing. Perhaps she should prepare herself as she would for one of her mystic sessions. Each day, she found more and more parallels between battle and magic; it stood to reason that this was but another. She took a moment to gather her mind. When she was focused, she opened her eyes and took her stance.

Lain's attack flashed in with its usual speed. She shifted her staff and knocked it away. His weight shifted as his weapon returned. A slight re-angling of the wooden blade betrayed his next target. Myranda quickly placed the staff between herself and the strike. His weapon pulled back with incredible speed. It was this third strike, regardless of its origin, that seemed to be far too swift to react to. In her focused state of mind, though, her thoughts could match the speed of the motion, and even get a step ahead. From his position, there was only one way to offer a reasonable offensive. She pulled herself away from the likely target and thrust her weapon toward it with as much speed as she could muster. The staff collided with the blade.

Slowly the blade withdrew and Lain looked upon her with satisfaction. She had succeeded in blocking adequately only once before, and it was clear even to her that it was more through blind luck than skill. This had been different. She had found her way to the block through careful observation. Without another word, Lain attacked again. She blocked the first two blows and reduced the third to a grazing one at best. By the time the session had ended, she had earned no less than a half-dozen questions, sometimes stringing more than six blocks in a row. These new questions, added to the two she'd saved, would put a few of her curiosities well and truly to rest.

"Eight questions. I shall ask them now," she said, catching her breath.

"As you wish," he said, gathering the practice weapons and heading to his hut to replace them. "But be warned. Your third level of training will begin with our next session. It will be by far the most difficult for you," he said.

"I had imagined as much," she said.

She pondered for a moment over how best to spend the first of her hard-earned questions. One thought pressed its way past all others.

"I have been told that you first came to this place, and spent a number of years here, over seventy years ago. Now I don't know anything about your kind, but were I to venture a guess, I wouldn't place you at a day past thirty. What's more, my grandmother used to tell me tales of the Red Shadow when I was a little girl. As far as I can tell, you have been active for easily one hundred years. How can that be?" she asked.

"I cannot answer that. I truly do not know," he said.

"Well, if you cannot answer the question, allow me to rephrase it," she said. "How long have you been alive? How old are you really?"

"I am not certain of that either. The only age I can offer you is that of the Red Shadow legend. His first victim fell just over one hundred-fifteen years ago. I cannot be sure of the number of years that passed between that day and my birth, and I doubt that there exists anyone that can offer any information to that end," he said.

"You have lived for over a century in prime physical condition, and yet you doubt that there is some higher purpose to your existence," Myranda said in disbelief.

"There are many races of this world that can claim the same," he offered, entering his hut. "And, thanks to the efforts of *your* kind and others, we cannot be sure that my brethren are not similarly blessed. I have never known a malthrope that came to a natural end."

Myranda silently considered his words before choosing her next question.

"You say that you witnessed my capture by the cloaks. What do you know about them?" she asked.

"They are present in some small way in every town I have visited for as long as I can remember. I was uncertain of their origin or alignment until the day that you were taken. They would appear to be agents of the Alliance Army. They move about at night. It is very difficult to detect them. They have no scent, they make no noise. Be suspicious of any quiet stranger. Particularly at night. Your encounter was the first real action I have ever seen them take. They have benefited from the nearly universal use of gray cloaks even more than I. I suspect that they may be the reason for it," he answered from within.

"The nearmen . . . the cloaks. What else don't I know of this world? What else should I know?" she begged.

Lain exited the hut and looked her in the eye, judging whether it was truly intended as a question. When he was satisfied, he answered.

"You grew up in a world very different from mine. You have spent your life in the cities and on the roads between. I have spent mine in the fields, forests, mountains, and plains. I have seen things that you could scarcely imagine. If you intend for me to list all of them, I haven't the time or patience to do so. However, if it is the nearmen and cloaks that concern you, I can name a few similar oddities to my world that may have spilled into your world, or may soon," he said.

"Please," she said.

"An associate of mine has collectively called the cloaks, the nearmen, and the others I may name, the D'karon. They all share a quality of imitation, in the same vein as the cloaks are suits of demon armor. They are rare, and with any luck they will remain so. They are far more hostile. In our first few meetings, I found myself ill-equipped to defeat them. There is simply nothing to attack. Only cold, empty metal," he said, recalling briefly before continuing.

"Humans and the like are hardly the only creatures imitated. I have seen stony parodies of wolves, worms, and countless others. I believe you may have seen the D'karon version of a dragon. One lay ruined on the ground beside that swordsman," he said.

"Where have these creatures come from?" she asked.

"Where do any races come from? I have lived for some time and these creatures have been lurking in the background since my earliest days. Perhaps they have been present at least as long as your kind, and have been lucky enough to avoid discovery. The only thing that I know for certain is that they are native to the north. I have spent time south of the battlefront on several occasions and found them to be absent," he said.

Myranda considered the information as Lain began stretching his legs. He showed little outward sign of the terrible state he'd been in when she found him, but slight limp still nagged him.

"How many questions have I asked?" she asked.

"Four. Unless you intend this to be the fifth," he answered.

"Of course I don't. Four left. I have strayed too far. You need to tell me more about yourself. I want you to retell the story you told me as Leo. Where you grew up, what your life has been like. Only this time I want the truth," she said.

"I had hoped you wouldn't realize your carelessness until your stockpile of questions had dwindled. Well, then. Of my earliest years, I know only what I have read. If the record-keepers are to be believed, I was found in the forest. My mother had died giving birth to me. The man who found me handed me over to his brother, a slaver. I was sold with a batch of two dozen slaves while I was still an infant, included free of charge. I was beaten, isolated, and ostracized by all who saw me. The only man who offered any semblance of care was a blind man named Ben. He was not so much fond of me as he was indifferent, but being ignored was as good as being pampered in those days. He and I had something in common. We had three stripes," he said.

Myranda gave a questioning stare. Lain rolled up his sleeve, revealing a trio of vicious-looking scars, visible even through the fur on his arm. Below it, a similar scar formed a jagged curve.

"A slave is branded once when purchased, and again when they begin to work. The bottom mark is the symbol of the slaveholder I was sold to. The three lines denote my value. One line indicates the highest value, young men mostly. A second line may be added when a slave is less useful. These are given to most women, aging or weak men, and those with permanent injury. A third is added when a slave is considered worthless. The elderly, the infirm, and undesirables such as myself.

"I was treated to the full three on the day I was deemed capable of working. Life was bad until the owner died and left us all to his son. It became much worse very quickly after that. He made a series of bad decisions that drained the coffers in a matter of years. In response, he sold all of the most valuable slaves and switched to more valuable crops. Lower quality workers coupled with crops that left the land nearly barren after only a few seasons worsened matters. Most of the two stripes were sold as well as a fair amount of the land. I was one of the only able-bodied workers left. We were all doing triple the work as in past years. I personally was doing the work of an ox. I had been lashed to a plow.

"One day Ben died at the whips of the drivers and I . . . lost control. When I regained my senses, I was standing over the new owner's youngest son, scythe in my hand and death all around me. I fled into the woods. Later, I learned he was the only survivor of the staff and family," he said.

Myranda shifted uncomfortably. She had almost managed to put aside the fact that Lain was an assassin, and had even begun to see hints of the warmth that had made her fond of him in the past. Now he sat, telling this tale of his torturous youth, followed by his unapologetic account of a murderous rampage. He was a monster, a murderer. She'd known it since her first question. Now she knew of the life that made him so. He went on.

"I found myself free for the first time. I had to find a way to support myself, and if possible, get revenge for the years that had been stolen from me. I had only two skills, it would seem. I could work a farm, and I could take lives. I swore never again to do the former, so I chose the latter. After a few years, I developed the Red Shadow legend, as well as one or two others. My travels brought me here, and I took away the knowledge and skill to continue my task with a good deal more success. Since then, life has been an endless hunt for my next target," he said.

Myranda sat silently. There was a look in Lain's eyes as though he expected this answer to be the last, at least for today. He knew that what she had learned sickened her. Perhaps it was just to avoid proving him right again, but Myranda decided to continue.

"How many questions left?" she asked.

"Three," he said.

"Very well, then. I know you are a killer. What sort of people pay you to do so?" she asked, her voice shaking a bit.

"Rich ones. Not only because they have the funds, but they tend to be the only ones arrogant enough to believe they may choose who lives and dies," he said.

"You'll have to do better than that. I want names," she said.

"Over one hundred years have brought me more employers than I can recall. It is safe to say that nearly every powerful family in the north has been on one side of my blade or the other," he said.

"I am still waiting for names," she said.

"Then you will have to be more specific. Refine your question," he said.

"Fine. But this is still the same question. Have you ever worked for anyone I might have known? Someone in Kenvard?" she asked.

There was a reason she had danced around the question. She feared the answer. Kenvard was the former capital of the nation of the same name. Every influential family in the west had a representative there, and her parents had known all of them. What she knew of them told her they were good people who would never make use of a hired blade. What she knew of the world made her fear otherwise.

"My answer remains the same. More than I can name," he said.

"Choose one," she demanded.

"Sam Rinthorne," he said.

"The Lord! You were hired by the Lord of all of Kenvard! For what? Tell me everything, and this is *one* question," she said.

"The people of Kenvard, *your* people, were taking terrible losses, disproportionate to both Ulvard and Vulcrest. Military strikes were hitting their mark with accuracy that could only be the result of a leak in the intelligence chain. I was hired to find and kill the responsible party, or parties," he said.

"Continue," she said.

"I followed the flow of the information to a messenger. To keep any more information from escaping, I killed him--and eventually followed the trail to a military headquarters in Terital," he said.

"Terital? That is the old capital of Ulvard. It's on the other side of the continent," Myranda remarked.

"Indeed. In those days, it was home to the five generals. At least, it had been until a few days before I arrived," he said.

"But the generals didn't move north until--" she began.

"The massacre happened a few days later," he said. "Since my employer was killed, I had no reason to continue."

Myranda froze as a thought passed through her mind.

"What information was the spy carrying?" she asked.

"As I recall, he was carrying orders from the general to change the patrol route around Kenvard. He also carried a letter written in Tresson detailing the unique weaknesses that the new patrol offered," Lain answered.

"What did you do with the information?" she asked.

"Nothing," he said.

"Then what--" she began.

"You have had your questions. If you want to know more, earn it," he said, turning and entering his hut.

"You had the orders. You knew there was a weakness. You could have done something, and you did *nothing!*" she cried.

Lain sat on the ground in his hut, eyes closed.

"You are a *monster!*" she growled.

Lain sat motionless. Myranda picked up the staff. Her hands shook with frustration as she stood helpless. Every hardship in her life was born that day, and he could have stopped it. The thought of it overwhelmed her. Before she knew what she was doing, she had thrust the staff at Lain. An attack with all of the force she could muster. In a blur, Lain's hand was around the end of the staff. A fast, painful twist wrenched the weapon from her grip and hurled it to the wall. His eyes never opened.

"I am proud to know that I have lit a fire in your soul. I warn you, though: do not let it consume you," he said.

Myranda stormed out of the hut. Myn, who had watched the display with more than a bit of uneasiness, followed after her. She had watched them trade blows for so long, she had learned that it was a game. There was something different in this last attack. The dragon had detected much anger between them, and it troubled her in the same way that a child might be affected by an argument between parents. She was further troubled when Myranda did not eat afterward, as she commonly did when strong enough. Instead, the human collapsed into her bed and wept.

Myn comforted her as best she could without words until both fell asleep.

#

The night was riddled with nightmares. Myranda saw images of the atrocities Lain had admitted to. She saw the day of the massacre replayed over and over. More than once during the night, she was jarred from sleep, and once gone it was slow to return. After scarcely an hour of real sleep, she was awakened by the last voice she wanted to hear.

"Oh, you and the beast share a bed. How appropriate," Ayna said.

"Why are you here?" Myranda mumbled.

"Well, the time has come for you to display all that I have taught you. I suggest you eat first," she said.

Myranda pulled herself out of bed, grabbed her staff, and trudged to the food hut. Ayna fluttered along beside her.

"You don't seem particularly well-rested. I seem to recall ordering you to have a long and full rest," Ayna muttered angrily.

"My dreams kept me awake," Myranda explained, as she tried to eat.

"That is a sign of a very weak mind," Ayna reprimanded. "And must you eat so slowly?"

Deacon entered and took a seat beside Myranda.

"Lovely, your shadow has arrived," Ayna sneered.

"Myranda, you do not look very well. Are you sure you are up to this?" Deacon asked.

"She hasn't got a choice. I will test her today," Ayna said.

"And what have you got in store for her?" Deacon asked accusingly.

"A suitable test of skill for our little prodigy," the fairy said.

"And something certain to make you stand out as a teacher," he offered.

"My mere existence is quite enough to make me stand out," Ayna said, sniffing at the air before remarking, "What is that smell? Your food? How can you eat that?"

"It is the only food available," she said.

"To you, perhaps," Ayna said. "Those with more evolved palates have alternatives."

"What do you eat?" Myranda asked.

"Nectar. It is the only proper food that nature has ever provided," Ayna said.

"Have you ever tried anything else?" Myranda asked.

"I cannot eat anything else," she answered. "Quickly--finish. I am eager for you to begin."

Myranda obeyed and made her way to the tree, which still bore a pair of scars from her last trip there. A reed flute, identical to the one she'd been practicing on, was attached to a pole beneath it.

"Now, the tasks you are to complete are rather simple. First, you will hold a single note on this flute for twenty-four hours, then you will--" she began.

"A whole day!" Myranda exclaimed.

"To state it another way, yes. And please do not interrupt me again. Following the endurance test, you will play the elegy flawlessly, from beginning to end, while standing no less than ten paces from the instrument," she continued.

"The most that a Master test has ever required before was three hours," Deacon offered.

"Congratulations, your knowledge of our history remains unchallenged. I frankly have never been fond of the fact that the test has been so . . . insubstantial in the past. This is far more fitting, I feel," she said.

"I have trouble remaining *awake* for more than a day," Myranda said.

"Well, with a spell to occupy you, you should have no trouble at all avoiding sleep. Now, no more dawdling. Begin," Ayna ordered.

It was clear that she was serious. Myranda set her mind to the task. Fortunately, it took very little effort to conjure a breeze strong enough to produce a note. Unfortunately, Ayna would not be satisfied until the note was loud enough for all to hear. Her effort had to be more than tripled before the fairy stopped badgering her to bolster her efforts. The sound was enough to gather a crowd. The strain was not terrible, but it was noticeable.

She looked over the crowd, which continued to grow as her test approached the end of the first hour. Ayna seemed to delight in informing each newcomer of the circumstances of the test.

Time passed slowly. The sun crept across the sky. It was nearly impossible to know how long she had been at it. Deacon knew this, and was kind enough to keep a running tally for her in the form of marks etched into the ground. His visits seemed to get further and further apart as the day progressed. By the time the daylight of the short day had waned, she had to devote all of her mind to maintaining the note. Most of her crowd retired for the night, including Ayna. The only ones that remained were Deacon, who spent the time between hourly updates writing in his book, and Myn, who stood faithfully beside her.

The night was a dark one, and cold. At some point a blanket found its way about her shoulders. It must have been Deacon, but she lacked the awareness to know when it had been placed there. She locked her eyes on the horizon. When the sun finally peeked over, she knew that she would be through. Her eyes closed without her noticing a handful of times as she slipped into some bizarre state between sleep and concentration. She wrestled them open each time to the same dark sky.

Around the fifteenth hour, the most curious thing began to happen. The spell she was casting seemed to have worked its way into the back of her mind. It was as though her consciousness had split. One part was devoted to the spell, the other was free.

"Deacon?" she managed to speak.

"Yes?" he answered. His voice was a bit slurred, as though he had begun to doze.

"I feel strange. I . . . I don't feel that I am the one casting the spell any longer," she said.

"Ah, yes. Your mind is becoming accustomed to casting as a whole. It is becoming second nature to you. This is a huge step toward becoming a successful wizard. Before long, the spells you use most will become reflexive in nature. Defense, healing, they will be cast in some small way on their own when needed. This skill cannot be taught; it must come with experience. What can I say? You continue to amaze," he said.

While casting the spell now seemed to take much less conscious effort, it took no less of a toll on her strength. By the time the sky had begun to redden, she was having trouble sitting up. Her mind lacked the will to control her muscles. Myn allowed Myranda to lean on her to stay upright. The hours ticked by until, finally, Ayna awoke and fluttered down.

"Well, not much longer. How is my student?" she asked.

Myranda found that she hadn't the will to blink her eyes, let alone answer. Even after the fire test she had not been so weary. At least then it was a lot of power over a relatively short time. This was more akin to a marathon to a sprint, and she was left with her reserves utterly drained.

"You should know better than to expect her to answer that," Deacon said, fighting to keep his own eyes open as he etched the twenty-third mark on the ground.

The minutes passed and the crowd reformed. The tone of the note was wavering slightly as the sands of Deacon's hourglass trickled down. As the last minute of the endurance test began, Ayna offered some advice.

"You will need to play through the elegy once. I would not lift the spell that you are casting, lest the sudden release of focus set your mind to rest. Instead, use the stream you've been conjuring to play the tune. And . . . begin," She said.

Myranda pulled the notes of the song to mind and plodded her way through them. It was not a spirited performance, by any means, but neither was it incorrect. The last note rang out, prompting a deafening roar from the crowd. The approval reached Myranda's tattered consciousness in the form of a distant whisper.

Deacon was left again with the task of bringing her to her bed, though this time with little objection from Myn, once the customary bribe of a potato was offered. Ayna deliberated over the performance, criticizing the tempo of the tune and taking full credit for the success of her pupil. As the assembled crowd lavished praise upon the fairy, Myranda was lowered to her bed and left in peace.

#

The black carriage lurched to a stop and General Teloran pushed the door open. By rights, this should have been her first destination, but she'd left it until last. The elf paced up the path to the church. Inside, a service was just ending, and the sparse congregation was rising to depart. When they had climbed aboard their meager transportation and left for their homes, Trigorah stepped inside, leaving the other Elites to guard the door.

"Father?" Trigorah called out.

"Enter, my child," came his voice from his chamber.

The general stepped inside.

"If my memory serves, I am again being honored by a visit from one of our esteemed generals," the priest said.

"I must ask you to come with me, Father," Trigorah stated.

"Much as I would like to aid you with whatever it is you seek, I am afraid my duties here forbid my absence," the priest assured her.

"It is not a request," Trigorah replied coldly.

"Not a request? Have I committed some crime?" the priest asked.

"Please, come with me," Trigorah pleaded.

She could feel something inside of her rebelling, and did all that she could to silence it.

"What have I done?" he demanded.

"You spoke with the girl, and she had the sword. I am ordered to detain all who may have touched it," Trigorah stated.

It was the first time she'd explained herself. It was the first time she'd felt compelled to. Until now, she'd been able to separate herself from her task. Now, even while his unseeing eyes were hidden, Trigorah swore she could feel his gaze searing her.

"I refuse to believe that our just and noble army would arrest an innocent man merely for having met some woman. I cast her out! She was a sympathizer, nothing more! My faith in our people and our war remains firm!" objected the holy man. "What could that horrid girl have said or done to warrant this! What could I have possibly done!?"

"I am a general. It is your duty as a subject of the Northern Alliance to do as I tell you," the general reminded him.

"It is in my nature to trust in the word of my fellow man, but there is no way that a general would do such a thing. Prove it to me. Generals carry a seal, do they not? Let me feel it!" he demanded.

Before she could stop herself, Trigorah found that she was undoing the fastening on her left arm, to reveal the symbol of service. Normally, she would have refused, but there was something about his words. They were spoken with such conviction, such strength. This was a man who knew what he believed to be true. There was no doubt. His faith was unshakable. The force of it permeated his every word. It was something that she had to respect. Finally she was able to reveal the gold band against her skin.

"The band awarded to me on the day of my selection as a general. The symbol of my rank, and of my loyalty to the Alliance," she said, guiding his hand to it.

"Yes . . . yes, I see . . . That is how it is done," he said, his voice distant. "Then you are a general after all. And you believe that it is right to take me away with you?"

"I believe it is necessary," she replied.

"That is not what I asked," he said.

"It doesn't matter what is right. What must be done must be done," she said, drawing her blade with a slow, deliberate motion to prolong its ring.

"So it must . . ." he said rising and heading toward the door. As he walked, he spoke, quietly. "That girl . . . that blasted girl . . . I hope it is worth it . . ."

#

Nearly four full days passed before Myranda's eyes opened again. Deacon visited her at meal times to help her eat until she found the strength to do so on her own. With each visit, he offered another profuse apology for Ayna's disregard for her well-being. To Myranda's surprise, though, Deacon was not the only visitor during her recovery. When she heard the familiar tapping of a dragon's claws on the stone floor, she assumed it was just Myn after a visit to Solomon or Lain.

"You bring me great pride, Myranda," came the voice of her old instructor.

"Solomon?" Myranda said as she tried to sit up in bed.

"Lay down. I come to offer congratulations," he said.

"I am sorry to hear that Ayna will now be ahead of you in the book of records," she offered.

"I have no concern for records. I am pleased that I was able to aid you for a time. I see great things in your future," he said.

"Thank you," she said.

"One more thing before I leave you to rest. You are raising a fine dragon. Myn is as bright as any I have met," he said.

"I am glad. Be sure to tell her that," Myranda said.

"I have. At length. Rest well, Myranda. The worst of your training is behind you now," Solomon said, rising to leave.

"Wait!" Myranda called out.

"Yes?" he answered, sitting once again.

"I hope you won't mind me asking, but I have been wondering since I met you. I . . . I hope you won't be insulted, but . . ." she fumbled.

"You wish to know about my size," he guessed.

"Well, yes," she said.

"There is a city on the west coast. I neither know the name, nor care to know it. Many, many centuries ago, humans there began breeding dragons for their own use. Some for size, some for strength. I was bred to be small," he answered.

"Why?" she asked.

"It is not my place to understand the motivations of your kind," he said. "Now rest."

The dragon padded out. It was another week before Myranda found the strength to walk under her own power. She likely could have benefited from another day or two of rest, but the long stay in her hut was beginning to drive her mad. Deacon caught sight of her hobbling and leaning heavily on her staff and quickly scolded her. Myn kept him at bay until he fished into a pocket of his cloak and produced the standard treat. She chomped away happily as he spoke.

"Don't push yourself! You are remarkable, but not indestructible," he said.

"I had to get out of there. I was beginning to selna porthen," she said.

"Selna porthen. You were losing your mind to inactivity? That is a rather unique phrase. Your language skills are improving," Deacon said.

"I can't help it. No one else speaks my language here. If I can't learn to communicate with someone else, I may as well lock myself in my hut," she said.

"I didn't realize it was so painful to have conversations with me. If you need some time alone I can oblige," he said, looking genuinely saddened by the comment.

"No, it isn't that. I just like the idea of learning new languages, having new people to talk to," she said.

"Well, let's hear what you've learned," Deacon said.

The pair walked through the village. Now and again, Deacon would point out a person and ask Myranda to translate what he or she had just said. Myn found the activity to be less than exciting and trotted off in

Lain's direction. Myranda was doing rather well at Deacon's random tests, until an odd commotion was caused by a man running through the courtyard screaming what appeared to be nonsense. Deacon seemed particularly affected by the repeated cry.

"This is momentous! This way, quickly! Where is that book of mine!? Here, ah!" he stammered.

"I must need a bit more practice," she said.

"Why?" he asked, fairly pulling her along.

"It sounded like 'Hollow is twitching,'" she said.

"You are not mistaken," he said.

"What does it mean?" she asked, as she realized that they were headed to the Elder's quarters, along with nearly every other resident of the village.

"Do you recall the prophecy I was reading you? How it was the life's work of Tober, our prophet? Well, all through his time here, he was constantly in search of the next thing that could enhance his already remarkable scrying skills. He drank potions, underwent treatments. Each altered his body and mind to lengthen and deepen his trances. Soon he was able to commune with the spirits for days at a time, and an army of assistants worked in shifts committing every word to writing.

"One day, he entered the trance, never spoke, and never left it. We still speculate on what precisely occurred that day. Some say he had spent so much time with the spirits that he left his body to join them. Others believe he asked one too many questions of a malevolent spirit and paid the ultimate price. All that is known for sure is that his body no longer contains a soul.

"We've taken to calling the empty shell he left behind 'Hollow.' It wasn't dead, not technically. It never ate, never moved, but continued to live. We left it in his hut. No one really knew what else to do. Then, decades later, someone heard a noise. Hollow was speaking. His body remains a superb conduit to the spirit realm. In times of incredible import, the voices from beyond speak through him. The words are impossibly cryptic, but flawlessly accurate predictions," Deacon said, lowering to a whisper as they made their way inside and took a seat on the crowded floor.

A heavy, throne-like chair was brought in by four stout young men. In the chair was a frail and ancient man dressed in a dusty, but not worn, tunic. A pair of milky white eyes stared vacantly across the room at nothing at all. His hands, gnarled like the branches of an oak, curled around the arms of the chair. When the men lowered it to the ground, others opened a chest attached to the back of the chair. Inside were chains and shackles. The shackles were clamped onto both of his ankles and wrists. The chains were attached to loops installed in the walls of the hut.

"What are the shackles for?" Myranda asked.

"Some of the spirits have never been in a body. Their actions when they find a vacant one can be unpredictable," he said.

When the restraints were in place, the handlers retreated into the rest of the crowd. No one would venture closer than ten paces from the seat. The only sign that the man who was given so much space was even alive was the subtle twitch of his fingers every few minutes. Despite this, the scene was tense. Absolute silence was maintained as the most powerful wizards and warriors of the world watched the withered old man. Minutes passed.

Finally, the silence was broken by the rattling of chains as Hollow shifted forward. He seemed to be pulled by an unseen force in his chest, and in a flash he was suspended in the air, straining at the restraints. He drew in a breath, pained and ragged enough to be his first in years, as he lowered slowly to the ground. His legs folded limply beneath him, and he lay in a pile on the ground. Words began to flow from his mouth. It was a terrifying sound. He spoke not with one voice, but with dozens, perhaps hundreds. They formed a sort of sloppy harmony, some voices lagging, others rushing desperately through the messages. There were whispers and screams alike. Some even uttered in different languages.

All who had the means to do so wrote madly. Deacon was writing, not only with his own stylus, but with three more that moved about on the page under their own power. Myranda tried to listen, but the language was unfamiliar to her. As he spoke, Hollow's body jerked and shifted, as though he was a marionette with different hands pulling at every string. As more time passed, his motions became more violent.

Nearly an hour passed without a moment of peace before, as suddenly as it had begun, the tumult ended. Hollow fell to the ground as though his strings had been cut. Fully half of an hour passed before all were convinced that the prophet had spoken his last for the day.

"Splendid. This has been a fruitful session," Deacon said, marking down notes and separating blocks of text.

"Did you understand that?" Myranda asked.

"A great deal of it," Deacon said.

The crowd was filing out of the hut. Deacon was comparing notes to those near him as the handlers began to unfasten the chains from the walls. As they did, Myranda approached Hollow. He was being loaded back into the chair. All of the chaotic life that had filled the hut was gone. She looked with curiosity at this bizarre side effect of so many mystic procedures. His wrists looked thin and brittle as twigs, yet earlier the chains had been barely strong enough to restrain him. The eyes were disturbing. There was no hint of the previous color of his eyes, and even the pupils had clouded over. She was wondering what seeing through those eyes must be like when they slowly turned, locking onto her. Myranda shook her head, not certain if she was imagining it.

A moment later, she was on the ground and the wrinkled fingers were stretching out in the direction of the wall behind her. Three chains were still in place, but one had been removed from the wall and was still in the hands of the handler. Hollow's arm hurled chain and man effortlessly through the air. He collided with the far wall. Five men rushed to the flailing chain and tried valiantly to reconnect it to the wall.

"Light! More than for one! Another still! Threads! Connections!" Hollow's many voices cried.

He was reaching out for something specific, not like before. It was as though he was looking through the wall. Beyond it. The three chains were creaking at their moorings. One leg restraint broke free and lashed across the crowd. The possessed form jerked out of the air and onto the ground with earth-shattering force. He reached out toward Myranda.

"At the meeting of light, light, light! Above the darkened door! A sacrifice! A blinding ring! The elders of the crescent made equal! All is a whimper in the shadow of the white wall! Victory is a prelude. The final struggle follows!" he decreed.

There was no denying it. Myranda was the target of this last prophecy. Once it was delivered, the shell of a man fell limp once more. The handlers returned Hollow to the chair and re-secured the restraints. White-robed healers emerged from the crowd to care for the injured. The loose chain had bloodied no less than five people. When they were satisfied that Myranda was not hurt, they helped her to her feet. Deacon helped her outside.

"That has never happened before! Hollow, once he dropped down like that, has never awoken again in less than a year. And he never, *never* addresses anyone directly," Deacon said.

Myn came sprinting to the hut. The commotion had attracted her. She surveyed Myranda for injury, and was less satisfied than the healers. She shot angry looks at all who drew near.

"Come on. I do not want her to start breathing flame at imagined attackers," Myranda said.

They had to move quickly. Already witnesses to the unprecedented event had begun to assemble around Myranda to learn more. Still not eager to be confined to her quarters again, Myranda joined Deacon in his hut. He closed the door against visitors and took a seat at his desk. All of that which he had written while watching Hollow was in the open book waiting for him. Myn set herself faithfully before the door, adopting a hostile posture each time footsteps passed too near.

"So much to be done. Translation, interpretation. But first I must ask you. In the commotion, I could not record Hollow's unexpected additions," he said.

He began to mark down the words.

"When he spoke to you, he said 'light' three times, correct?" he asked.

"I believe so. Does that really matter?" she asked.

"Not a single word is wasted when he speaks. Of course, your message and the one before it are among the most straightforward I have ever heard," Deacon replied.

"Do you mean to tell me that you know what was meant by those words?" she asked.

"Well . . . no. But the imagery was at least obvious. Most times interpreters must work for days, or weeks, to uncover something that even resembles reality. Luckily, Tober took volumes of notes before his transformation into Hollow. The spirits that choose to communicate with us through him are often the same ones that he relied upon. As a result, many of the allusions they make are documented and translated," he said, selecting a book from one of the carefully kept shelves.

"One of the shorter statements. Keltem gorato melni treshic. Now, Keltem translates literally to people--or, more specifically, physical beings. The spirits use this term most often when they intend to indicate a specific body part. An arm or a leg, for instance. Gorato is the name of a prolific gold mine of years gone by. In older prophesies, gorato has been used to imply things of virtue and worth, but mostly it refers to gold itself. Melni is the name of a specific spirit that was known for terrorizing the living. The spirits tend to use the name interchangeably with fear. And finally treshic. Treshic is the name of a fabled ancient tree that stood for so long against the forces of nature that it eventually succumbed to rot from within. This is essentially the spirit 'word' for corruption," he said, flipping constantly through the book to find his answers.

"What does it mean?" Myranda asked.

"Well. If I were to arrange these translations into a sentence as we know it, it would be . . . Beware those with golden . . . no, *virtuous* limbs, for they are corrupt," he said.

"I see," Myranda said with a smirk.

"It is not an exact science. There are other listed interpretations for each one of these words. They could even be intended literally, or some combination of literal and interpreted. It could mean to fear people who wear gold on their bodies, or simply warn against trusting the wealthy. That is why a skilled interpreter is worth his weight in gold. Right now, the best we have are the historians in the records building. When I have had my fun with my personal notes, I am to relinquish them to the experts," he said.

Myranda turned to the dragon, who had not been at ease for several minutes. There was now an audible clamor outside of the door.

"What is going on?" Myranda asked.

"I would imagine that my fellow Entwellians have finally come to see the truly exceptional person I have known you to be for some time," Deacon said.

"I really do not want the attention," Myranda said.

"I should expect you will have a rather difficult time avoiding it. Unless you sic Myn on them," Deacon said. "Besides, you were just saying that you were hoping for others with whom you could speak."

"This is rather more than I was hoping for," Myranda groaned.

When the door was finally opened, Deacon was proven to be quite correct. Her earlier achievements had made her at best an interesting oddity, admired by some, envied by others, but nothing remarkable. Now she was nothing short of a celebrity. Hollow had permanently labeled her as something of the greatest importance. For several days, while she was still recovering, she was constantly being approached by wizards and warriors alike. Some made an earnest effort to converse with her in her own tongue. Mostly, the admirers adhered to the standard policy of Entwell, speaking in the language of their origin.

Myranda was able to muddle through most conversations passably--but, in truth, she learned more from the first day's dialogue than she had in all of the time she'd been listening. The wizards who spoke to her were primarily practitioners of white and black magic. They seemed to know that she was something special, and tried their best to inject their knowledge and expertise, hoping in some way to make their mark on history though this unique girl. In the few days that followed, she was made aware of dozens of techniques in white and black magic alike, many of which were little more than theory. Warriors were more interested in learning what great deeds she had done before arriving. They latched onto her tales of the Undermine and questioned relentlessly to that end.

The attention was almost more than Myn could bear. She'd had a hard enough time sharing Myranda with Deacon. Now she had to endure dozens of people a day. The little dragon had learned restraint in her days in Entwell, but she had her limits. Each new visitor received the same harsh treatment as Deacon had when she had first met him. Even a handshake was cause enough for her to flash her teeth and lash her tail. Visitors learned quickly that a bit of caution was in order when dealing with her.

Myranda scolded her halfheartedly each time. The times that Myn chased her visitors away tended to be the only times that she was alone. It was something of a reversal of fortunes for her.

#

Nearly three full weeks elapsed before the clerics and healers agreed that Myranda was ready to continue her education. Her next teacher, Cresh, had been contacting her during the last few days of her recovery. He never met with her directly. Instead, books found their way onto the table of her hut in her absence. If the dirt smudging each page was any indication, the books were from his personal collection, and he loved his work. They were written in a language that made them incomprehensible to her.

Now the time had come for her to meet him face to face for the first time as his student. The usual crowd of admirers followed as she approached her teacher's home, with the exception of Deacon, who had taken to remaining in his own hut rather than compete with the crowd for Myranda's ear. Cresh's home was a low, unusual hut fairly buried in a jungle of plants and trees. The structure was unlike any of the others. It had no seams, as though it had been carved, or grown, from a single stone.

"I am not putting on a show. Off with you and leave us in peace," Cresh warned the onlookers as he emerged from within. He was speaking his own language. It was the same he'd spoken on their only other meeting, the same she had failed to decipher in his books.

The eager onlookers shuffled away, much to the relief of Myn. Cresh looked at the creature for a moment, then shrugged.

"A cave-dweller is a welcome visitor any day, but no one else, if you don't mind. This is serious business. Mine is the most important of magics, you know," he informed her.

Myranda took a moment to attempt to translate his words. After managing to understand only a few she requested that he address her in Northern, or Tresson. He answered with what would be the first and last word she would easily understand for the duration of her training. No. He then launched into a speech.

It was rather entertaining to watch him speak. He was fully two feet shorter than she, and perpetually encrusted with dust and dirt. In addition, he tended to gesture enthusiastically while speaking. This was fortunate, as it helped her to understand his meaning. She could tell by the chest thumping and smiling of the speech that he was bragging about himself. He gestured for her to follow as he entered his hut.

The inside was as unique as the outside. There was no floor, only bare earth. There was also no furniture to speak of, save the shelves of books and jars. Even his staff was sticking into the soft earth rather than sitting carefully in a rack, as was the habit of the other wizards she'd met. He

260

plucked it and held it in one hand while the other reached into one of the jars. He tossed a few grains of the substance within to the ground at her feet, and a few more at his own feet. A sweep of the staff sprouted the seeds instantly into stout vines that obligingly wove themselves into a rather inviting chair for each of them.

"That was very impressive," she said as she took a seat.

The dwarf waved off the compliment and sat as well. He began to talk again. It was apparently one of his favorite pastimes. After ten minutes of listening, she was able to understand enough to know that he was responsible for growing all of the food for the village, in addition to drawing up all of the crystal, metal, and stone that they might need. She had often wondered how a moderately-sized village like this could satisfy its demand for resources without any apparent source. Now she knew.

Suddenly, the time for idle chitchat was over. He first gestured at her feet, clearly indicating that her boots had to be removed. He said something about a sculptor wearing mittens, if Myranda pieced together the words correctly. She obeyed and copied him as he dug his toes into the dirt. He launched into another long speech, cupping his hand to his ear and pounding the ground with his feet. After receiving a puzzled look from Myranda, Cresh indicated that she should close her eyes and cover her ears. He then tapped the ground again. When she responded that she could feel the footfalls, he indicated that she should focus and discover what else she could find.

Focusing and searching with her mind was, at least, familiar to her. Before long, she found that she could sense the footfalls of the other people of Entwell. He seemed pleased and encouraged her to continue. More time passed and she realized that she could feel the constant flow of the waterfall. Again she was encouraged to deepen her search. It was truly remarkable the information that the earth could give her in the absence of all of her other senses. As she revealed everything from the movement of insects in the earth to the wind rustling the grass, he entreated her to speak up when she discovered something that she could not identify, rather than those things she could.

This assignment left her silent for some time. She quickly identified all of the new things she could detect, and gradually ceased to locate anything new. Her mind delved deeper and deeper. The thing that Cresh had been waiting for her to find came slowly. It was barely anything. At first, she was unsure she'd felt it at all. However, slowly she was able to push aside all else. Soon it was undeniable. There was something there. Something she'd never felt before.

"It is a rhythm. I can feel it. Like a heartbeat," she said.

Cresh nodded enthusiastically. He stood and took her outside, scolding her when she instinctively reached for her boots. She stood in front of the hut, dug her toes into the ground, and found the pulse again. Once in the stance that would be commonplace in the days to come, she was able to lock onto it and hold it in the back of her mind. In this way, she would be able to listen--or, at least, attempt to listen--to her instructor. The procedure he seemed to describe was familiar to her as well. She was to allow the rhythm to mingle with her own strength. The fire and wind methods were similar. Different, though, was the way that she was to do so. The rhythm was to ripple up through her feet, and later her staff, and into her body. Once she was a part of the pulse's path, she was to allow it to echo inside of her. It was to rebound and reverberate through her, growing ever stronger as it did.

She did as she imagined she was being told. Once the faint rhythm was coaxed out of the earth, she found it a very strange sensation. It did not feel like it was shaking her like a pounding of a drum, as she imagined it would. The pulse changed as it blended with her own strength. It moved through her as it had through the ground, but in a way that she felt in her spirit, not her body. Somehow, Cresh was able to monitor the strength of the ripple, and instructed her to release it, through the staff, back into the earth from whence it came. She did so, and was shocked by the result. A tremor, small but noticeable enough to make Myn fairly jump out of her skin, was created, with her staff at its center.

Cresh was quite pleased and declared the day to be a success. He returned her boots to her and retired.

No sooner had the dwarf shut the door of his abode than the people of the village returned to ask their questions. She was forced to tell her story again and again. She was hungry, but frowned at the thought of entering a crowded hut filled with equally enthusiastic people. Fortunately, an alternative presented itself, as Myn was already off in the direction of Solomon, who was just exiting his hut for his weekly hunting trip. She took her seat beside the crystal arena. At least here she didn't feel cooped up as the mob of people besieged her.

Myn returned, happily presenting Myranda with a pair of fish. She suddenly realized that when the time came to cook the fish, it was Deacon who always did the honors. It seemed a shame to break the tradition, particularly in light of the fine job his spell always did. Myn anticipated Myranda's plan and cleared a path through the crowd, leading the way to Deacon's hut. While the little dragon had learned to control herself in crowds, her manners left something to be desired. She pushed the door open with her head and barged in.

Deacon was at work as he always was. The door closed against the crowd once more.

"What brings you here?" Deacon asked.

Myranda held up the fish.

"Don't you know it is bad luck to break tradition?" she said.

"I suppose so. Particularly when a dragon is involved," he said, providing the treat that Myn had been anticipating since her arrival. Meanwhile, a snap of the fingers prepared the fish.

"One of these days, one of us will have to remember to bring a plate along on hunting day. Eating fish out of one's hands can get a bit messy," he said.

"Agreed," she said.

"You know, most people here don't get to have fresh fish but once or twice a year. Solomon being the only carnivore, he tends to be the only one who gets them before they get stewed," he said.

"Well, it is yet another benefit to having a dragon as a friend," she said. "But, then, you haven't been around lately."

"You are busy," he said.

"It would seem that no one here is ever otherwise," she said, enjoying a bit of her meal.

"I have been falling behind in my scribing," he said.

"You've always been able to scribe while out and about. It isn't like you to make excuses," she said.

Deacon sighed.

"Myranda. You have been here for just a bit under three months. I have been here for two and one-half decades. You have achieved more than I have, become more than I have. I have grown to the limit of my abilities while you have only begun. Look at how the others follow you. The crowds may thin after they have all heard what they seek, but they will always see you as something remarkable," he said.

"Don't tell me you are jealous," she said.

"Oh, no. To say I was jealous would be to suggest that you did not deserve all that you have. I know that you do. Fact of it is . . . well, I don't deserve to be near you. Were I not your guide through this, I would scarcely be tolerated among the other Masters. You are destined for far greater things than I. It is past time I gave you the space to grow," Deacon said.

"I don't care about any of that. Unless you have grown tired of my company, I want you to come see me whenever you like," she said.

"Well . . . thank you," Deacon said.

With that misunderstanding behind them, they spent the next few hours discussing what she could expect from Cresh. He was not the most thorough of instructors, but he had far more subjects to cover. Also, if ever she was to get on his bad side, she need only request a demonstration. He reveled in displaying his art.

Unfortunately, sundown came all too soon. The crowd had grown tired of waiting and dispersed, so she quickly set off to the Warrior's Side and found Lain waiting. As soon as she saw his face, she felt all of the anger return. He handed her a short sword. Unlike the one he'd been using, this one was steel, every bit a lethal weapon.

"You must be very brave, handing a real sword to me after telling me what you did," she said.

"I understand you've had experience with the short sword," he said.

"I have," she said.

"We will spar a bit to see how skilled you are," he said.

"And how shall I earn my questions?" she asked.

"Still interested, are we? I thought you were content to assume and jump to conclusions," he said.

"Lain, you told me you had the leaked information in your hands! You had to know what was going to happen, and you did nothing! What am I supposed to think!" she cried.

"If you thought at all, you would not be acting as you are, but that is irrelevant. Prepare yourself," he said, lifting his own sword.

"But this is not a training sword," she said.

"I will pull my attacks if they are going to land. As for you . . . I seriously doubt that you will even come near, but if you manage to strike me, I will give you ten questions," he said. "And the offer still stands that if you draw even a single drop of blood, every answer you wish is yours."

"But--" she began.

"Begin!" he said.

He attacked slowly at first, one at a time. Her blocks were a bit sloppy, as she hadn't practiced with a sword in years. Worse were her attacks. The weapon was quite a bit heavier than the staff.

As she began to recall what her uncle and father had taught her, her performance improved. Lain noticed it and increased his attacks in both rate and intensity. The attacks were followed by a pause for her to attack. She was holding him off well enough, but her attacks were still slow. The clash of steel against steel was unnerving. Perhaps that was why he had chosen not to use the training swords. He was toying with her.

Anger had as powerful an effect on combat as it did on magic, it would seem. She fought back harder and faster. As she did, her defense suffered. More than once, an attack slipped through. She didn't even pause when it did. Lain pulled his attacks so effortlessly his flow of attack and defense was not even interrupted.

Despite the accelerating attacks, Myranda never came close to landing a blow. After a few minutes, Lain called the sparring to an end.

"You are not a cold beginner, but you can benefit from practice. A bit of discipline is in order as well," he said, not a hint of fatigue in his voice.

"Oh?" she remarked, trying to catch her breath.

"You fight as though I am trying to teach you," he said.

"Is that wrong?" she asked.

"You should fight as though I am trying to kill you," he said. "Those strikes that you trusted me to pull would have been enough to end your life. A bit more care is in order, even when the weapons aren't real. We will be switching back to training swords for the rest of the training, but I will not be pulling my blows quite so far anymore."

"You are planning on hitting me!?" she said.

"This is combat training. You need to learn about consequences," he said, tossing her the replacement for her weapon.

It was lighter, but solid. She would be able to swing it faster and more easily, but the thought of being hit by a blow as powerful as Lain was capable of was not appealing.

"We will dispense with the offense and defense drills. This will now be proper sparing. Attack or defend when the opportunity arises. Until now, you haven't had to consider counterattacks, so that is how you will earn your questions. You will earn one question for each counter you land. I will not throw any until you have thrown your first. A counter is quite different from a normal attack, so I will demonstrate the times when they are appropriate," he said.

Myranda thought she'd had enough to think about before--trying to identify when to attack, when to defend, and whether a counter was possible was like playing a game of chess in a heartbeat. The position of limbs, the distribution of weight, the speed, direction, and location of the weapon . . . she could take an hour to consider each one and still be wrong.

All too soon, the demonstration was over and the sparring began. She quickly found that during an attack or while defending, things were clear. The tenseness came in the moments when she and Lain were between attacks, quietly measuring each other, deciding what would happen next.

Finally, it happened. Myranda had leaned in for a downward strike. Her arms were raised, leaving her abdomen undefended. Lain struck with what looked to be one of his slower attacks. It most certainly did not feel like one. Myranda cried out, dropped her weapon, and doubled over. In an instant Myn was between them, desperate to stop them from fighting. The pain shot through her. It was a moment before she could regain the wind that had been knocked out of her.

"That was a kill," he said, as though his point had not been made clear enough.

She managed to recover after a minute or two and tried to continue, but Myn would have none of it.

"That is all for today. I imagine that Myn will be cutting our next few sessions short. But if she can get used to your attacks connecting, she can get used to mine," he said.

"Don't be so sure. My attacks were not as cruel as yours," she said.

"Oh, no? You were swinging with all of your might. You came near to breaking a rib once," he said.

"Impossible. You didn't make a sound," she said.

"In my line of work, it is wise to keep silent," he said.

"I don't care how disciplined you are, you would have doubled over, too, if I'd hit you as you did me," she said.

Lain dropped his weapon to the ground and grasped his right little finger with his left hand. With a sharp twist and a horrid snap, he wrenched the digit out of place. The merest flutter of his eyes was the only indication he'd felt anything. He took his hand away. Myranda cringed and turned away. When she heard a second snap, she knew that the finger would at least be where it had started.

"Why didn't you tell me? I wouldn't have struck so hard," she said.

"You will never learn to fight properly if you are pulling your attacks. I want you to fight as you had before, or I will never answer another question," he said.

A terrible guilt filled Myranda.

"Let me see your hand," she said.

"No need," he said.

"Just let me see. It is swelling already," she said.

A whisper of a thought was enough to heal the minor damage he'd done. While she was at it, she healed the blow she had taken.

"Unlike you, I can't stand idle while someone suffers," she said.

"Sometimes standing idle is the best course of action," he said before retiring to his hut.

Myranda gritted her teeth in anger as she walked away. Myn canted sideways behind her, trying her best to keep an eye on both of them. Past sundown, it would seem that the throng of admirers had better things to do, as she was not assaulted by them as she headed back to Deacon's hut. Myn barged in as before, and rushed over to him to start sniffing at his tunic's pocket.

"Stop. I said one per day. You've had yours," he said, protecting his pocket from her search long enough for her to give up and retreat to Myranda for a scratch on the head.

Deacon could see that something was on Myranda's mind.

"I suppose that things didn't go well today," he said.

Myranda fumed for a moment before she could answer.

"Deacon. Lain . . . he could have done something about the massacre," she said.

"What massacre? Ah! The one you told me about, at Kenvard. He could have prevented it? How?" he asked.

"He found the person who leaked the information! He knew it was going to happen!" she said.

"What did he do with the information?" he asked.

"Nothing!" she said.

"Well, that was decent of him," Deacon said.

"Decent of him!? I cannot think of something worse he could have done!" she cried.

"He could have sold it to a higher bidder, or delivered it himself to receive the payment intended for the man he killed," Deacon said.

Myranda paused for a moment. Each was admittedly far worse than doing nothing at all.

"But still--he could have warned them!" she said.

"Well, I suppose you are right," he agreed. Almost immediately, a confused look struck his face as a thought came to mind. The same thought struck Myranda as well.

"Why would he need to?" she realized. "If the intelligence never got delivered, the Tressons couldn't have known about the weakness . . ."

"Indeed. One wonders how the massacre could have happened at all. That is, if Lain's word can be trusted," Deacon said.

"I don't think Lain cares enough about what I think to lie to me anymore. And after how I have acted, I don't blame him," Myranda said.

After having a late meal, Myranda retired.

#

The days to follow began a new routine for her. She awoke, had breakfast, and played with Myn for an hour or so. The little dragon was now quite the flier. Once airborne, she could stay aloft seemingly indefinitely, and before long, she was able to take off from the ground rather than a rooftop. Once the flight was over, either through the fatigue or choice of Myn, Myranda would stop by Deacon's to look for any tips before venturing to Cresh's hut.

Once there, she would learn the next step in a long string of earth magics. Despite the language barrier, Cresh was a very good teacher, managing to coach her through refining the size and direction of her tremors, identifying the qualities unique to each type of earth, and even coaxing plants to grow faster, larger, and stronger. This last topic was the most difficult, and required nearly three weeks to complete. In this time, Myranda found that she had come to understand his odd language well enough to not rely so heavily on the gestures.

Her time with Lain was the most trying. Over a week of battle was needed to finally convince Myn that Lain and Myranda were not fighting out of anger again. This, however, was not completely true. Myranda's apology for her behavior prompted no response at all from Lain. He fought in almost complete silence each day. She managed a pair of well-placed counter attacks, several days apart, but they differed from her other achievements. She stumbled upon them less in a moment of epiphany, and more through some new instinct that she was developing. They were almost mechanical in nature. Lain's only words on the topic were to remark that such was as it should be.

Further trying was the fact that, with each passing day, sparing with Lain was becoming more difficult. A bit more speed and a bit more accuracy found their way into his maneuvers every time they fought. He was keeping his skill level just beyond hers. Before long, the clear openings for her to attack vanished, and the split-second openings for counterattack were shaved thinner and thinner.

Five weeks after starting her work with Cresh, the dwarf indicated that it would be a fine time to offer her the final test. There had been no warning that the end was near until now. At least, none that she'd managed to understand. He produced an apple from his pocket, proclaiming it to be, apparently, the last fresh one to be had in the village. Myranda wondered where the others had gone, and how many there had been, considering in all of her time in Entwell she'd seen neither an apple nor an apple tree. The latter fact, it would appear, would soon be remedied.

Cresh took a bite of the fruit, dug his fingers into its core, and retrieved a seed. The dwarf launched into a speech that was apparently very amusing, as he punctuated it with stifled laughter. A quick tremor churned up the earth beside his hut enough to yield to the seed when he dropped it. After pushing it into the soil, he requested that Myranda replace the lost apple, as well as supply the pantries of the whole village. Her success would hinge upon how the apples tasted. He expected to be sinking his teeth into one by sundown.

"Sundown!?" she objected, hoping that perhaps she had misunderstood him.

The dwarf replied with the beginnings of yet another long-winded exposition on one subject or another, but the vigorous nodding that preceded it was all the answer she needed. Had Myranda known that the test would be on this day, she would have arrived earlier. The sun was only a few hours from the horizon. She set to work immediately. The method was one she had practiced time and time again. She would mingle her energies with those of the seed, coaxing it to sprout. Once the growth had begun, she would provide for its every need from her own strength. Until now, she had only done so with weeds, and in some occasions, flowers. The tree required far more nurturing than any of the previous plants.

Halfway through the first hour, the sapling of the tree had emerged from the ground, and leaves were beginning to form. This test was unlike the others. Whereas the fire and wind were enormously taxing to keep fed for the appropriate amount of time, they required only one type of energy. The tree's needs were many and varied, requiring her to call upon nearly all of what she knew of earth magic to meet them. The elements in the soil had to be drawn into the still-growing roots at many hundreds of times the speed that nature would have allowed. Similarly, Myranda's spirit took the place of the sun as the source of energy for the leaves to feed on. Only water was provided by Cresh, as water was not the point of this test.

Another half-hour saw a tree as tall as she.

The task of growing the tree, while growing in intensity, decreased in complexity as the end grew near. Though dizzied by the energy she'd spent, Myranda was able to push enough of the spell to the back of her mind to be able to appreciate the completion of her handiwork. It was a sight to behold as new cracks in the bark appeared. The leaves shriveled and dropped away onto a growing mound beneath the tree. Almost immediately, the greenish brown leaf-buds reappeared, followed in turn by the brilliant white apple blossoms. A breath of wind that she conjured pollinated the flowers and the resultant fruits plumped before her eyes. She cut off the flow of energy just as the last of them reddened.

Through the virtue of her magic, she had brought this tree through two dozen seasons in the space of an afternoon.

The sun had, by rights, set a few minutes prior, but as the sky was till rosy with its light, Cresh decided that the time requirement had been met. He reached for an apple, but found the lowest of them just be out of reach. He raised the crystal-tipped root he used as a staff. The tree lowered its branch as though it had a mind of its own, and shook an apple free into his hand. The dwarf sniffed the fruit thoughtfully before taking a bite, considering the flavor as a connoisseur might sample a fine wine. Finally, he declared the endurance test to be complete.

Myranda heaved a sigh of relief, as she had far more strength and clarity left now than she had entering into any of the other tests of dexterity.

Myranda was led inside of his hut, and the door was shut behind her. A table was in the middle of the room, and a chair had been grown before it. Atop it was set a bowl filled with gray sand. A pair of empty bowls was set beside it. Cresh spread a pinch of the sand on the palm of his hand to reveal that there were actually fine grains of black and white mixed thoroughly enough for the bowl's contents to seem uniformly gray. He then produced a blindfold, which he secured over her eyes. She was to separate the black and white into the separate bowls without the use of the eyes or her hands. With that, Cresh retired to another room.

She reached out with her weakened mind. The differences in the energies of different types of earth were difficult to detect in the clearest of mind. Despite her many impairments, the black grains were soon clearly unique enough in her mind's eye to separate. The spell to manipulate earth was one she had learned well, but with so much of her concentration devoted to keeping the two types distinct, when the time came to move them, they seemed as heavy as lead weights. Moving them more than a few at a time seemed impossible, but she pressed on. By the time the last white grain found its way to its own bowl, she felt as though she'd moved a mountain.

Cresh pulled the blindfold from the weary girl's head and patted her on the back, chuckling. She opened her eyes to the light of a torch and smiled weakly at the reason for his laughter. While she had succeeded in separating the sand, she had been less precise where the sand landed. Rather than in the respective bowls, she had managed to scatter the sand anywhere but. The only clear spot was the bowl that the sand had formerly occupied. Fortunately Cresh was satisfied. He handed her an apple and helped her to her feet and out the door.

The hour was late. None of the admirers and well-wishers were awake--save Deacon, who had remained despite being required to wait outside of the hut. He helped her to her hut and set her on her bed.

"Well, this is a refreshing change. You finished a test and did not need to be carried home," he said.

"A personal best," she said, lying down. Myn hopped atop her immediately.

"Sleep well. When you recover, you shall begin work on the final elemental magic," he said.

Myranda likely hadn't been awake long enough to hear the end of the sentence.

#

She awoke after a black, dreamless sleep, and stumbled forth groggily. Myn led her to Deacon--who, in turn, led her to the food hall. As they ate, and she shook off the last of the sleep, they spoke.

"How many days has it been this time?" Myranda asked.

"Only single night has passed. Another personal best for you. Here, have one," he said, placing another of her apples before her.

"Ah, yes. The fruits of my efforts. I still have the one that he gave me last night," she said, taking a bite. The flavor was familiar, but different. It had a hint of something that made it unlike any apple that she had ever tasted. Her face betrayed her thoughts.

"Curious? The apple tastes different because you grew it. When a person prompts a plant into being, the result is a fruit slightly different from any grown before. You leave your mark. What's more, any apple tree grown from a seed from this one will bear fruit with the same quality. You have given birth to a new breed," he said.

"I like it," she said, munching happily.

"Are you quite rested? Calypso has already been told of your completion and is eagerly awaiting you," Deacon said.

"I feel well enough to do a bit today. Calypso . . . I haven't met her yet," she said.

"No, I don't believe you have. Well, we shall remedy that soon enough," he said.

After the meal, Myranda fetched her staff and was taken directly to her next trainer. At least, she was told so. When she reached her destination, she found it to be the small lake near the edge of the village toward the sea. Myn sniffed at the water and immediately retreated. She seemed terrified of the stuff, and adamant that Myranda not go near it. Apparently, the circumstances of their arrival in this place had taken their toll on the poor creature.

"Calypso!" Deacon called out.

They waited a few moments before he called again.

"I know that I learned my fire magic from a dragon. Does this mean I will be learning my water magic from a fish?" Myranda asked.

"Well . . . I suppose that would be half correct," he said, picking up a small stone and skipping it across the surface.

The ripples spread across the top of the lake. Among them was a small, more stable ripple that ran steadily toward them. It grew stronger as it approached. Through the water, something distorted could be seen beneath the ripple. When it had made it to the water's edge, the disturbance finally emerged. It was fantastically beautiful woman. She was wearing a shimmering bodice and had long golden hair. Around her neck hung a pendant that contained her gem. Whereas most had been as near to clear as possible, hers was a deep blue. Just visible beneath the water was an exquisite emerald tail, like that of a fish, that was the precise color of her eyes. She was a mermaid. Her voice had such a pristine clarity that she seemed to be singing every word.

"Deacon! Always a pleasure! And this must be Myranda! I have heard some very impressive things about you, my dear. These next few weeks will be a treat!" she said.

"I am quite sure that you two will have a fine time together--but remember that Myranda is still unaccustomed to the whimsical attitudes of wizards. Please treat her gently," Deacon requested.

"Deacon, I am shocked that you would think that I would treat my guests with anything less than complete and utter civility. Now come on, we've so much to do!" Calypso exclaimed.

With that, she grasped Myranda's hand and pulled her into the water. Before either she or Myn could object, the helpless girl was dragged swiftly to the bottom of the lake, near the center.

"There. That is so much better. Out of that hot sun and harsh breeze," Calypso said, turning to her guest.

Myranda was floundering and struggling to keep her breath. The trip to the bottom had been so sudden she hadn't even the time to take a deep breath.

"Oh. Silly me," Calypso said, touching her fingers to the amulet.

Myranda dropped to the lake bed and took a long, wracking breath. Her panic turned to confusion as the cool water filled her lungs and she no longer longed for air. She stood and tentatively took a second "breath," if such a word could still be applied. Her clothes and hair billowed about her as the slight currents swept past her, while she felt as steady on the pebble-covered ground as if she were on dry land.

Now that she was able to relax, Myranda looked at her surroundings. The light danced on the ground in the most beautiful way. The slight blue tint of the water seemed to highlight the green of the algae on the rocks. In the distance, what must be Calypso's quarters stood majestically, a hut just like the others, though a bit larger. It seemed frightfully out of place at the bottom of a lake.

"What did you do to me?" Myranda asked.

"Oh, that little spell? I merely swapped the roles of water and air for you. It is rather simple; every mermaid and merman knows it. If we didn't, we would hardly get any surface visitors at all, and those we did would be holding their breath. Not that I mind, of course. If you want to hold your breath, that is your business, but it really cuts into conversation," she said.

Calypso spoke with a speed that was almost disorienting, yet with perfect diction and tremendous expression. Cresh had spoken volumes at a time, but the few words she had understood made the conversations, at least manageable, albeit one-sided. The mermaid grinned at the bewildered look on Myranda's face.

"I apologize in advance to for my tendency to ramble. You see, I am the one and only water-dweller in the whole of this wonderful little village. As a result, I am seldom blessed with visitors, and when anyone *does* come down here, it is always strictly business. I suppose that is why you have come here as well, but what I have heard of you tells me that you are *very* personable. I mean that, of course, in the sense that you have a fine personality, rather than the meaning that you are attractive.

"Which is not to say that you are not attractive. Quite the opposite. I merely intend to imply that attractiveness is not the quality that I was looking forward to. Deacon told me. He is a dear, and he thinks the world of you. Always raving about you, your mind, your skill. I've never seen the boy more excited. It does him good, though. I do hope you feel the same about him," she said.

"Oh, I do. I only wish that I could learn a bit of what he has to teach. It seems interesting, but we haven't had the time," Myranda said, after her mind had managed to catch up to the question. The brief silence seemed unusually long in light of the torrent of words Calypso produced.

"What he has to teach? Oh, yes, you mean his magic. I'm sorry, dear, but I wasn't concerned about what you thought of him as a magician. Although you are, of course, correct. Quite staggering, the knowledge he has. And there is so much of it in the spells that we elemental wizards use. I tell you, it is a wonder that he isn't more respected than we. But, then, that is politics for you. No one had ever expected there to be a Master who specialized in gray, and so is no place for one in the old ways. Antiquated, I say, but still we cling to them. Oh, there I go wandering again. The subject was Deacon. Yes, I was rather more concerned about what you thought of him as a person," she said.

"He is a fine person. He is most certainly my very best friend," Myranda replied.

"Excellent! It does my heart good to meet someone with a bit of life left in her. I honestly cannot say that I have heard the word 'friend' used here since my arrival. It is always 'colleague' or 'associate.' Lifeless words.

"Most that come here have already rendered themselves down into little more than a repository of information about this or that. These people can scarcely open their mouths without a statement about magic or battle spilling out. They forget that there is a life to be lived, but not you. And, since you have arrived, not Deacon. Doesn't spend nearly the time in that dusty old hut keeping those books. You know, before you showed up, he hadn't come to see me in over two years?

"I tell you, you have been a tonic for him. As a matter of fact, I would like to see more of the two of you together. After we get the preliminaries out of the way, I say we bring him down here. He can assist me. Better yet, he can distract you enough to keep you down here a bit longer, and I'll have more company. However, before we can put that plan into action, there is the small matter of giving you the basics of my art. You know the procedure by now. Ears and mind focused, everything else ignored. Didn't you have a staff when you came here?" Calypso spouted.

Myranda had become so lost in her words that it took her a moment to realize that she had been addressed.

"Oh, yes, I did bring my staff. Where has it gone to?" Myranda wondered.

Myranda looked around her feet. Calypso, more accustomed to the environment, looked in the other direction.

"Ah, there we are," she said, spying the staff that was now bobbing on the surface of the water.

With a speed and grace that made her seem as fluid as the water around her, Calypso darted up and snatched the staff, returning to the waiting student.

"Hold on to that, or else I'll let *you* get it next time," she said playfully.

Myranda swiftly entered the focused state of mind.

"Very good. Now, I suppose I really haven't much to say, though that is not to say that I will not be saying much. You see, save the specific mystic quality of the element, dealing with water is identical to dealing with air. They are both fluid. Water is thicker and heavier than air, of course. This will require a bit more energy to work with it, but the principles, at least in the beginning, are the same. In a way, Ayna has done my work for me.

"First, I want you to get a feel for what water 'looks like' mystically," Calypso said.

Myranda looked through her mind's eye, reaching out with her spirit into her surroundings. The water around her was something of a cool, feathery feeling in her mind.

"Once you have it, move it about. I want to feel the current," Calypso said.

Myranda did as Ayna had taught to this new element. It was indeed much more difficult to move. She felt as though she were pushing on a wall. Regardless, after a bit of effort, the mass of water around her began to shift.

"Fine. Fine work," she said. "Now, just for the practice of it, cast the spell."

"I *am* casting it," Myranda said.

"Oh, I am sorry. Terminology has never been my strong suit. You see, the word cast, as in 'cast a spell,' is used to mean the same as throw or some such. When I use it I think of it as 'form the spell' or 'shape the spell.' I don't recall what the word is that we have decided upon to mean what I mean. Set the spell, I suppose. Oh, whatever the others called it," Calypso said.

"I am afraid I don't know what you mean," Myranda said.

"Honestly? Well, then the others have been remiss. It is a very useful thing to do. I would wager to say that it effectively doubles the usefulness of a spell. You see, what I want you to do is to allow the spell to continue in the absence of your concentration. It is quite simple. Just increase the amount of force you are using to create the effect, but do not increase the effect. Think of it as, say, clenching your fist about a handful of wet sand. When you relax your hand, it keeps its form. The energy in the water will do the same thing, staying in the excited form you had coaxed it into," Calypso said.

Myranda tried, but it was not immediately apparent how to do so. Refreshingly, Calypso watched and coached her as she went. This was something that, owing to Ayna's attitude and Cresh's language, hadn't happened properly since Solomon had taught her. It took several tries, but finally she loosened her mind and, lo and behold, the current she had conjured did not weaken for nearly a minute.

"Remarkable," Myranda said, feeling the fruits of her labor without the veil of concentration for the first time.

"I agree. And there is so much more to show you," Calypso said.

As the light filtering through the water waned, Myranda learned how to draw air from the water, eventually creating a bubble the size of her head. Calypso assured her that in no time she would be able to create one large enough to stand in, and after a bit more education, large enough to ride in.

All too soon it was time for her to leave.

"Well, I will see you tomorrow," Calypso said, holding her hand as she whisked the girl back to the water's edge.

"I look forward to it," Myranda said.

She walked a few more steps, emerging from the water. There was an odd sensation of heaviness. Myn, who had been watching anxiously and waiting for hours, sprang to her feet and tried to usher her away from the water.

"It is all right, Myn. There is nothing to be scared of," Myranda said, or tried to at least. Instead water poured from her mouth. She took a breath of air, and found it worthless to her. Realizing what was happening, she turned and plunged her head back into the water. After a long breath, she opened her eyes. There before her was Calypso. She was lying on the floor of the bank, just below the surface of the water, smiling. Her face was so close their noses were practically touching.

"Something wrong, dear?" she asked innocently.

"I can't breathe up here," Myranda said.

"Is that so?" Calypso asked.

"And I can barely move," she said.

"I suppose you would like me to undo that little spell I cast," she said.

"I would appreciate it," Myranda answered.

"You know, you could stay down here, if you like," Calypso offered.

"I would love to, but I have another trainer to see," Myranda explained.

"Who?" Calypso asked.

"Lain. Do you suppose you could undo the spell and finish this conversation on the surface? I feel a bit odd with my face plunged down in the water," Myranda said.

"Lain? I cannot picture him . . . never mind, bring him down, too! The more the merrier," she said, hopefully.

"Ouch!" Myranda exclaimed.

"What is it?" Calypso asked.

"Myn is trying to pull me out of the water. She is terrified of it," Myranda said.

"Well, well. We are just full of excuses, aren't we? Very well. I shall see you tomorrow, bright and early. And do bring Deacon!" she said, touching her fingers to her pendant.

In a typically playful fashion, the mermaid neglected to allow time for Myranda to withdraw her head from the water before undoing the spell. The result was a fit of coughing and sputtering as she hoisted her head up and took her first real breath of air since she'd gone below. She was soaked to the bone, and though it was far warmer here than it should have been for winter, she was beginning to shiver. As she began to walk away, she heard her teacher surface.

"Here, just to show that I am not all bad," she called out.

Myranda heard her snap her fingers sharply and instantly the water fell away from her like a sheet, a good deal of it splashing on Myn. With the water gone, she immediately felt more comfortable.

"I will be sure to teach you that one. It tends to be rather handy," she said, leaping up and splashing down gracefully in the water.

Myn shook off the water and looked scornfully at the lake.

"Don't be too hard on her, Myn. She is just lonely. It makes people do strange things. I can vouch for that," Myranda said as she headed to the dining hall.

Deacon had apparently retired to continue his scribing, as he was not about. She enjoyed a meal, and headed to Lain. In keeping with the recent trend, he seemed to be fighting faster and harder than any day before. It was a struggle to keep up with him, and as his attacks landed more and more frequently, Myranda slowly began to treat their encounters as real battles. She found herself fighting not to learn, but to win.

There was a feeling. It wasn't fear, or anger, or hate. It was something deeper. It stirred her to swing harder and move faster. She felt it more strongly every time she landed a hit, and found herself longing for more when the training was done. At the end of the day, she retired to her bed, hardly aware of any blows she had taken. By morning, there would be no sign of a bruise, as that which Deacon had spoken of was beginning to happen. Her mind began to work at a healing spell instinctively after an attack, and continued to work in some small way even while she slept.

#

Trigorah stood in the throne room, her eyes scanning tapestries and portraits. Her elfish lineage had afforded her a very long life. She turned her eyes to the portrait of King Erdrick II. It was under his rule that she had begun her military career. He had blessed the creation of the Elites. He had even been the one to promote her to the level of general. He had been a great man. Trigorah had seen his son grow, and was present at the coronation. That was many years ago.

There were footsteps behind her. Trigorah turned, and swiftly dropped to one knee, head bowed.

"Your Imperial and Royal Majesty," she uttered.

"Rise, and dispense with the titles," the king replied wearily.

General Teloran stood. There was a time when it would have been unthinkable to be surprised by the appearance of a king. He should have been preceded by fanfare, by a royal procession. In the beginning, he was. Alas, as the years passed and the war marched on, the king had become less and less a leader. It was as though he shared the plight of his land. The decades of war had steadily drained them both of life and spirit. Now he was a withered husk of a man. When not attending to the affairs his people, King Erdrick III paced the halls of his nearly empty castle. His eyes had a faded, distant quality. The eyes of a man who had done things that could not be undone.

"Awaiting General Bagu, no doubt?" the king asked as he settled down into the throne.

"I am," the general replied.

The king nodded.

"He has this conflict firmly in hand, it would appear," he said.

"Not as firmly as he might, but surely you are aware," Trigorah answered.

"Bagu has not seen fit to involve me in his actions in some time. Even my seal and signature, which he had so meticulously seen applied to each order and dispatch, has not been requested in months," he explained. "It was my hope that perhaps his--"

The door to Bagu's chamber opened and his voice issued forth.

"General Teloran, step inside, please," Bagu requested.

"General, the king was speaking," Trigorah stated.

"Your Majesty, the matter is of great importance," said Bagu.

"Go. The war comes first. Always, the war comes first," the king said.

Trigorah reluctantly stepped through the door and closed it behind her. Bagu was seated at his desk. His normally calm and collected expression was tempered with the tiniest hint of impatience and concern.

"I must object to your behavior in the presence of the king," said Trigorah. She was in no position to issue a reprimand, but nonetheless her tone carried a sting.

"Noted. What news have you of the girl?" he demanded.

"She has not left the cave of the beast, but I am confident that she is still alive," Trigorah explained.

"What possible source can you have for such confidence?" Bagu asked.

"She has shown herself to be resourceful, intelligent, and resilient. Furthermore, the assassin is with her. If he wishes her to be alive, she shall be alive," Trigorah explained.

"Epidime has been unable to detect her. He has been known to track targets to their graves and beyond," Bagu reminded her.

"Epidime is skilled, there can be no arguing that. However, he is not infallible. With all due respect to him as a fellow general, he is blind of his own shortcomings," she replied.

"And the sword?" he asked.

"The Red Shadow would not have been so foolish as to bring it with him. He knows we seek him, as well as the girl and the sword. The scoundrel is wise enough not to place all of our targets such that they may be gathered in a single stroke," she reasoned. "No, he would have concealed it. That said, if he does not wish it found, it will not be found."

General Bagu steepled his fingers once more and pressed them to his lips.

"You found the assassin's go-between once. You shall find him again. When you do, you will secure the sword and bring it to me," he decreed. "I sincerely doubt that this Myranda still lives, but see to it that your men are vigilant. Important times are at hand and we cannot afford to be caught by surprise."

"General, if I may make a suggestion . . ." Trigorah attempted.

"You may not. You have your orders. If you wish ever to be returned to battlefront command, I suggest you follow them," he hissed.

"As you wish," she replied.

General Trigorah bit her tongue and pulled open the door of the office. As she marched through the throne room, she looked to the king one last time. The old man's gaze, a knowing look of defeat, caught hers briefly.

Trigorah looked away. She had a task at hand. However difficult, however misguided, she had a job to do. It was her duty to succeed. And succeed she would.

#

The next day, Myranda awoke to her normal routine. Deacon, while having breakfast with her, was thrilled to hear that Calypso intended to involve him in the training. He raved for a time about what gray magics he could teach that would mesh perfectly with water magics. His enthusiasm was contagious, and by the time the two had set off for the lake, she was more excited about learning the things he had spoken of than the things Calypso had in mind.

Myn, however, felt differently. She was no fool, and when it became clear that they were headed back to that wretched lake, she leapt in front of them, spreading her wings to block their way.

"What is this all about?" Deacon asked.

"Ever since we had to make it through that waterfall, she hates the water. She is trying to protect me from it," Myranda said.

"Oh. Well, that is quite noble, if perhaps a bit misguided. You really have nothing to worry about. It can't hurt you if you don't let it," Deacon said, directing the final comments at the dragon.

"I think that is what she is trying to do. She won't let the water hurt me," Myranda said.

"Ah, yes. Well, let us just go visit Lain, then," Deacon offered with a strange tone and a wink.

The two walked toward Lain's hut. Myn followed for a few steps, but paused.

"Come on! Let's visit him. I promise, we won't even fight," Myranda said.

Myn looked questioningly at Myranda. The dragon then turned back to the spot at which they had been standing. She sniffed curiously.

"This way!" Deacon urged.

Myn lashed at the empty space with her tail. After the whip crack of it striking something, the veil of invisibility, as well as the pair of illusions, dropped away. Deacon was hopping painfully on one leg and Myranda was laughing.

"Clever little thing, aren't you. Practically any other animal would have followed the illusions. I suppose that I had best look into both covering our scent and producing a false one. I ought to thank you for illustrating a weakness in my methods," Deacon said.

With a bit of effort, the trio managed to make it to the lake again. Myranda tried her best to convince Myn the water was safe.

"Permit me to demonstrate," Deacon said.

He waded out into the lake until he was waist-deep. Myn watched cautiously.

"There, you see? Nothing has happened!" he said.

"Myn, watch me. I promise you that nothing bad will happen. And when I am in the water and you can see that it is safe, you can come in, too. Then you will know that there is nothing to be afraid of, we won't have this problem anymore," Myranda said.

Myn, with the utmost of reluctance, stepped aside to let Myranda wade in beside Deacon. She stood, chilled a bit, but unharmed. When a few more moments passed with no ill effects, Myn began to edge closer to the water. She touched the surface and leapt back at the sudden cool feeling. After building courage again, she ventured back to the water's edge and dipped in a single foot. It had no sooner broken the surface than Myranda and Deacon suddenly jerked beneath the surface.

Myn sprang backward. When her friends didn't reappear, she panicked, finally taking to the air and gliding across the top of the water. She could see the two humans streaking along the bottom of the lake, being dragged by the mermaid from the day before. When the center of the lake had been reached the water creature touched her pendant and the pair of humans dropped to the lake floor.

"Why did you do that!?" Myranda scolded.

"Well, you were just standing in the water. There is only so much daylight, we've got to use every drop of it," Calypso said.

"But Myn was just starting to trust me that the water was safe. You may as well be a sea monster, pulling us under like that. I promised her that nothing would happen!" Myranda said.

"I think she knows nothing is wrong. Look," Calypso said, pointing up to the surface.

Myranda looked up. Through the rippling surface they could see Myn skimming just above, looking down longingly.

"Oh, drat. My potatoes," Deacon said, realizing too late that the pair he had brought along as anticipated rewards for good behavior floated to the surface.

Myn skillfully snatched them.

"You didn't earn those!" he cried after her.

"She'll get tired and land eventually. Now, before we get too deep into our studies, I think that we three are long overdue for a chat. Learning magic is a fine way to spend a day, but a good conversation is food for the soul. I find that after a spirited exchange, I am far more prepared to do my casting, and I think you will feel the same. So, where to begin? Have you any questions for me?" Calypso asked.

"Well, I had been wondering . . ." Myranda said, looking worriedly at Myn as she made another pass.

"Yes, what is it?" Calypso asked.

"How exactly did you get here? I know that the rest of you were either born here, or entered through the cave. You couldn't have," Myranda said.

"Oh, couldn't I? You are no doubt aware that the cave is mostly filled with water for the vast majority of the year. While it is draining, some of the water finds its way to the mouth of the cave in the form of a stream. Most filters through a honeycomb of tunnels and caverns that are full of water year 'round. At least one such cave connects with the ocean on the landward side of a *very* treacherous rock formation that runs nearly the entire coast.

"I was busy exploring said cave and I found my way up into the then-flooded main section. It didn't stay flooded long enough for me to find my way out again. As the water drained away, I was forced further and further along until I slipped into that smooth little bowl the waterfall has carved out. To my surprise, I was helped to this lovely little lake and here I have lived, quite happily, ever since. I can't say I don't miss the other merfolk, but I wouldn't trade all that I have learned and seen here for anything," she said.

"Really? Remarkable," Myranda said.

"Oh, but I always do the talking. I can hear my own voice anytime. Let's hear about you!" Calypso said.

Myranda proceeded to retell the story of her life for what seemed like the hundredth time since her arrival. Deacon continually reached for his book to find his notes on the subject. Even in the water, he kept it by his side, casting a half-dozen spells to protect it from any damage it might take for the time being. When the tale worked its way to her arrival, Deacon did more telling than she, so excited was he. It was just as well. Myranda could never manage to tell of her own accomplishments without feeling she was boasting. Deacon concluded with a very detailed account of the Hollow incident.

"Hollow. Quite a creepy fellow. Come here, Myranda. Let us see this mark of yours," the mermaid said.

Myranda showed the thin white scar that had begun this bizarre journey of hers.

"Ah. Yes. It is just as I had imagined it. Simple, elegant. The work of the spirits--or the gods. Tell me, Deacon, do we know yet what it means that this girl has the mark, but was not born with it?" she asked.

"There were a number of phrases we've been able to translate from Hollow's latest speech that seem to allude to it," Deacon said, flipping to a seemingly random page in the book. "Yes, right here. 'A mark both fresh and faded belongs to the carpenter'; 'A label of white adorns that which will see each.' Things of that nature."

"I see; well, that certainly answers that." Calypso snorted. "Honestly. The spirits could be a bit more straightforward in their messages. If they truly wanted us to know what they were saying, they would say it more clearly. Well, regardless of what that mark means, we had best be sure you become what you are capable of. Let us begin the lesson," Calypso decided.

The routine that formed that day would prove to make the next two weeks the most pleasant since Myranda's arrival. Aside from having to practically plead with Myn for permission to enter the water each day, and the inevitable pranks that Calypso would play, she had a glorious time. In the early lessons, Deacon and Calypso were equally involved in teaching her--though, as the days progressed, Calypso allowed Deacon to do as he pleased, preferring to watch and offer comments where needed.

Each lesson would end at the water's edge, where Deacon would really shine. He taught her to levitate the water by filling it with her energy as she might slip her hand into a glove. As the time went on, she found that she could will the elevated water into simple shapes. Each day, of course, ended with her sessions with Lain, which continued to grow more challenging and frustrating with each fruitless battle, but even the sparring matches were not wholly unpleasant. They at least proved to her that she could hold her own with a gifted warrior--who, by this time, could not have been holding much back.

The end of the second week marked the beginning of the lessons that would have to be done entirely on the land, as she would be doing the reverse of what she'd done before. Instead of drawing air from the water, she would be drawing water from air. Myranda was having great trouble with it. Calypso sat on the shore, instructing Myranda and allowing Deacon to be her hands.

"I don't see why you don't give yourself a pair of legs for the time being. That is what you had done for all of your other students," Deacon said.

"Yes, but I feel this is easier. No, no. Myranda, that is not quite right. You need to hold the staff lower; the energy will flow more smoothly. Deacon, show her," Calypso said.

"She is right; it needs to be a bit lower, and your other hand a bit higher. You have to leave room for the ball of water to form. Later, you can twist the magic any way you wish, but right now you should be focusing on the spell, not the energy it takes to cast it," Deacon said.

"*I* can tell her. I asked you to show her," the mermaid said.

Deacon stood beside Myranda and guided her hands. He was fairly shaking as he touched her, taking his hands away quickly when her hands had reached the correct position.

"There, I, uh . . . that is approximately where they, uh, ought to be," he said, stumbling over his words and seeming slightly out of breath.

It was the first time since she'd met him that he had been anything but eloquent. A blush came to his cheeks. Myranda realized that she was blushing a bit, too. Calypso noticed it and grinned. The girl tried the spell again, but found that she couldn't manage it. She was having trouble concentrating. The grin on the mermaid's face turned to a smile. She beckoned for Deacon. When he waded over to her, she whispered something into his ear.

"But why?" Deacon responded.

"Well, you agree, don't you?" she asked.

"Of course I agree, but I cannot imagine that she wouldn't already know," he said.

"Well, don't you think it would be best to be sure?" she asked.

"I suppose," he said, turning to Myranda. "Myranda, you are, um, very lovely."

Myranda could feel the warm blush fill her face.

"Thank you," she said.

"Oh, there is no need to thank me. I am merely speaking the truth. I frankly do not see why Calypso thought it needed to be said," he said.

The mermaid laughed.

"You know a great deal about a great many things, Deacon, but you still have a few things to learn. That is enough for today. There is plenty of time to get it right," she said.

"Oh, no! I had forgotten until this morning. We may not have the time we thought," Deacon said.

"Why wouldn't we?" Calypso asked.

"The full moon came on the first day of this month," he said.

"Did it!? I hadn't been paying attention. How exciting!" she said.

"What do you mean? What is this all about?" Myranda asked.

"There will be another moon before the month is out! A blue moon!" Calypso said.

Deacon answered Myranda's questioning look.

"I've spoken of it before. I must have. It is a night when mystic energies run higher than any other. Acts of magic impossible on any other day can be done when the moon reaches its peak on that night. It is a tradition that on such a night we attempt to summon a being described in detail by the prophecy. This being is born of the elements themselves, and it is most assuredly one of the Chosen, and represents the sole exception of our rule banning summoning. However, it will not arise unless the mystic power used to conjure it is influenced by the strength of another Chosen.

"For as long as this place has existed, it has been used as the test to see for certain if one of the Chosen is among us, and it would be a crime if you were not included in the ceremony," Deacon said.

"And I need to be a Master of the elements by then, if I am to be a part . . ." she recalled.

"Indeed. You will need to finish your training with me and have your overall exam by the end of next week. We will indeed need to hurry. Oh, curse it all. I finally get student with a personality and I have to push her through faster than any other. Someone up there is toying with me," Calypso said. "No matter, though. Myranda, you ought to get a bit more rest than usual tonight. We will need to push you harder tomorrow. Enjoy. Deacon, would you remain for a bit? I need to discuss something with you."

Myranda headed off while Deacon lingered.

"What was it you needed to discuss?" he asked.

"In a moment," Calypso said, waiting until Myranda was well out of earshot. When their privacy was assured, she continued. "You like her. As more than a colleague."

"Well, I . . ." he began.

"It is an observation, not a question. She likes you as well. I know that you aren't going to confess your feelings so easily, so let me just give you a word of advice. If you feel that you wish things to move forward between the two of you, invite her with you to watch the opening of the cave when the falls relent. There is something about that place. It is where your parents met. It is where many parents met," she said. "Now go. Think about it."

#

The training continued the next day. The feeling was far more serious now. The days that followed were filled to the brim with education. The gray magic expertise that Deacon offered sped her progress markedly, so much so that there was a bit of time at the end of each day to slip in some pure gray magic, particularly illusions. By the time the end of the following week had drawn near, Myranda was deemed ready for the final exam.

A large bowl with a hole in it was placed on a stand, just as Solomon had done in his test. However, this one was far larger, and the hole was smaller. She was charged with filling it with water by conjuring it from the air. The task would have been a simple one if not for the drain. Now she would not only have to not only conjure up enough water to fill it, but she would have to do it quickly enough to do so before it poured away.

Myranda set her mind to work, reaching out and drawing in all of the moisture she could muster. It came in a tiny trickle into the bowl, and flowed out just as quickly. She would need to do much better. Her mind fanned out, reaching in all directions to try to find more water. The trickle increased, but not nearly enough. There must be enough water somewhere. She was not permitted to draw it from the lake or the sea; it had to be from the air. Finally, her mind happened upon what appeared to be a monumental mass of water suspended on its own. She began to draw it forth, but it must have been very far away, because she couldn't hear the trickle increase. She opened her eyes to see all in attendance looking up.

"You didn't warn her about that, did you?" Deacon said.

"Neither did you. This is going to be entertaining," Calypso said with a grin.

Myranda wanted to crane her head and see what had attracted their attention, but the strain of concentrating was growing greater, as though she were pulling an ocean, yet nothing came. Then, in a tumult so sudden it nearly tore her from her focused state, the water came all at once. It was like a torrent coming down--not only where she intended, but everywhere else. Myranda guided as much of the water as she could manage into the bowl, not daring to open her eyes until she was finished, fearful of what she might see.

"Enough! Well done! On to dexterity," Calypso said joyfully.

The girl opened her eyes to see that, despite the fact that she was no longer drawing it forth, water was falling like a savage rain. She had reached forth and drawn down the very clouds, and what she had begun would have to continue until the storm had run its course. The people watching her scattered for shelter. Myn, who was just getting over the shock of being doused so suddenly, returned to Myranda's side. Now, all who remained to watch her were Calypso, quite at home in the rain, Deacon, drenched but unwilling to miss the spectacle, and Myn, faithful as always.

"Just draw up a bit of the water. Heaven knows there is enough of it about. I want an ice sculpture of . . . oh, how about little Myn there. I want every detail. Shape it and freeze it. Begin immediately," Calypso instructed.

Myranda obeyed. She drew up the water from the soaked ground until it seemed like a rippling mound. Her energies filtered through it, forcing it to change its shape to match that of the little dragon. The basic form was simple, but as the details came to be formed, Myranda could feel the strain of stretching her mind in so many directions at once. Nostrils, scales, teeth--each had to be crafted and held. It was difficult to tell how quickly the time had passed, but finally she found herself staring at a near-perfect replica of her dragon, sitting on its haunches, mouth open a bit and tongue protruding slightly.

Myranda applied the reverse of one of the spells that Solomon had taught. A wave passed through the water, leaving all behind it solid ice.

"Excellent. Wonderful job! Deacon, tell me, do you remember that foolish spell Gilliam used?" Calypso asked.

"Of course," he said.

"Well, cast it on this work of art. It needs to be saved in a form a bit more enduring than ice," she said.

Deacon raised his crystal and closed his eyes. The spell must have been a mighty one, because even in her drowsy, weakened state, Myranda could feel the power of it flowing. A less distinct wave of light began to pass over the surface of the ice statue. It rippled slowly along like a dozen grasping fingers creeping up. Behind it, the ice was turned to stone. When it reached the nose of the statue, his work was done. It was solid rock, saved for posterity. Deacon gave a sigh of relief as he finished.

"Well done, both of you. It has been a pleasure working with you, Myranda. Don't think that just because I am no longer your teacher that you can just stop visiting me. Deacon, you get her to Azriel. I have got to get this lovely thing down below," Calypso said.

"What? Azriel? Isn't she the founder?" Myranda asked, still dazed from the effort.

"Yes, you need to be declared a Full Master," he said, walking her in the direction of the crystal arena. All the while, the rain she had caused was hammering down.

"But I have been. Calypso said it," she said.

"No, no. You have been declared a Master of four separate disciplines. Now you must prove just how capable you are in their practical use. Then you will be a Full Master," he said.

"I don't understand. There are that many different levels of Master?" she said.

"Oh yes. We have nine main levels of mastery in magic alone. There is Novice, Journeyman, Master, Full Master, Highest Master, Grand Master, Archmage, and Elder. Aside from that we have Battlemages, Specialists, Seers . . ." he said.

"What? I have been through four full disciplines and I am not even half of the way up the hierarchy?" she said in disbelief.

"Well, with any luck, after today you will be halfway," he said.

"But I can barely think. How am I going to pass another test?" she asked.

"Don't worry about that. In fact, you had better give me that staff. You are likely to break it," he said as he led her onward.

They approached the crystal arena. When she had first seen it, Myranda had been struck by the beauty of the place. Now, with rain pouring down from a darkened sky, it was the size that seized her mind. The spires around the perimeter looked like the teeth of some horrible creature. Myn scampered up beside them, familiar and quite fond of the place that now seemed so ominous. They stopped at the base of one of the carved columns. There, Deacon laid the staff on the ground.

"Now, before we enter, I cannot stress this strongly enough. You absolutely must take this seriously. The danger will be real. She will try to trick you. Her purpose here is to test your mind. She will not relent. I have seen the strongest men and women I have ever known enter this place to face her and leave changed. My own experiences were mild, and I must say they still have a place in my nightmares. This is likely to be the most trying experience you've ever had," he said.

"What will she do?" Myranda asked.

"I don't know. She seldom repeats a specific test. Are you prepared?" he asked.

"How can I be?" she asked.

"Then let us begin," he said.

The three stepped across the border. It was the difference between night and day. Once inside, her head was as crisp and clear as it had ever been, the sun was shining, the clouds were gone, and instead of the cold, hard crystal that she knew to be beneath her, she found downy, soft grass. It was uncannily similar to her image of what the south must be like. Ahead there was a wholesome-looking thatched cottage.

As they approached, a woman appeared before them. She seemed to materialize, like a cloud of smoke that wafted together rather than away. Draped about her graceful form was a black cloak with white, flame-like patterns rising from the hem that flickered and twisted as though they truly burned. She stood a few inches taller than Myranda, older, but the picture of elegance. Her hair was a glorious white and hung well past her shoulders.

The dragon showed her usual suspicion, becoming defensive at the woman's arrival, but upon recognizing her as the mealtime host, she relented.

"Welcome. I have been waiting for our prodigy. By the grace of your own skills, I have not had to wait long. And, Deacon, I understand that you have been this young girl's steward. Splendid, please come inside," she said in a voice that radiated civility.

She led them inside where a trio of overstuffed chairs surrounded a table set with the most sumptuous feast that Myranda had ever seen. All manner of meats, cheese, and bread covered it from end to end. The four sat--Azriel at the head of the table, Deacon and Myranda at each side, and Myn upon the floor beside Myranda. The chair was impossibly comfortable, and the food was something out of a fantasy. The wine was nectar. The meat fairly melted as soon as it touched her tongue. The atmosphere was so warm and inviting, Myranda couldn't feel more at ease.

The same could not be said of Deacon. He sat rigidly in place, eating slowly and sparingly, as though he did so only because of what might happen if he did not. The fear rolled off of him as palpably as the grace flowed from Azriel. When they were through, their host spoke again.

"Now, I have been blessed with the honor of treating your little Myn to her meals. She is as fine a beast as I have ever seen. Treat her well and she will serve you well. Of that much I am sure. As for you, Deacon, am I to take your presence as an indication that Myranda has had a dose of gray magic as well?" she asked.

"Just a touch, your grace. A spell or two," he answered quickly, hesitating to even look Azriel in the eye.

"Well, every little bit helps. Gray magic is a favorite of mine. It is possible that I shall have something of a challenge from this one. I relish the thought. I also understand that Hollow had a word with her. Quite the unique occurrence," she said.

"We believe that she may have a connection to the Chosen. She even has a semblance of the mark," Deacon offered timidly.

"Might I see it?" Azriel asked.

"Show her. Show her the mark," Deacon whispered insistently.

As Myranda revealed the palm of her left hand, she couldn't understand how this motherly woman could be making Deacon so uneasy.

"Yes, yes. It is not a birthmark, but no ordinary person could bear such a mark, if it truly is that of the Chosen," Azriel said.

"That is why it is very important that we get her to the ceremony just as quickly as we can," Deacon said.

"Well, that is hardly any concern of mine. I shall test her as I would any other. She will decide if she is ready," Azriel said, the tiniest hint of annoyance in her voice.

One would have thought that she had lashed out at Deacon, so quickly did he retract himself.

"Oh, your grace, I meant nothing by it. I am certain that you will be fair, and that Myranda will succeed," Deacon said, brushing sweat from his brow and releasing a shaky sigh.

"Perhaps, though, it is best that we do not dally. Now, now. What test is best for a prodigy? I believe that I will administer the escape test. That seems appropriate," she said.

Myranda nodded, curious as to what the test entailed. Deacon shook as if struck when he heard the words.

"W-what duration . . . if it is not too forward of me to ask?" Deacon nervously inquired.

"I believe, for this occasion, ten minutes seems long enough," she said.

"Oh, well, that doesn't sound so--" Myranda began.

"Ten minutes! You must reconsider. She has only just finished her water training today!" he objected, his fear for Myranda overcoming his fear for himself.

"I have spoken. I will not be dissuaded," she said.

Suddenly, Deacon vanished, wafting away just as Azriel had appeared. Myn was similarly swept away, leaving Myranda alone with her examiner.

"What have you done with them?" she asked, slightly taken aback by the action.

"They are still about. Myn is with him, but she cannot see any of this. She and I have a fine relationship, and I would hate to spoil it by upsetting her. Deacon is somewhere where he can watch without becoming a nuisance to either of us. Ah, that boy. His concern for you is rather charming, and perhaps not out of place, but so irritating. Nevertheless, we've a task at hand. First, allow me to expand the field of play," she answered.

Without any outward semblance of effort, the sorceress began to reconfigure their surroundings. The walls pushed away and turned from warm, inviting wood to cold stone. The table lengthened, and as it did, new food sprouted up to occupy it. The doorway gaped massively and chains sprang forth to connect to the door, which fell away with an earthshaking crash to bridge a moat that had formed outside. The fire from the hearth shot to the center of the room and scattered, lighting a dozen or so torches dotting the walls, as well as countless candles and a massive chandelier that dropped down from the now-towering ceiling.

In the space of a few moments, she had come to be standing in the great banquet hall of some ancient castle.

"There. I would say that this is a far more fitting venue. Now for the rules of the game. This hourglass will run through after five minutes," she said.

An hourglass appeared, floating above the center of the table.

"After that, it will be turned over, such that it may run back. Now, while the sand is in motion, I will endeavor to capture you, and you will endeavor to escape me. You will be designated a failure if you remain captured long enough for me to mark you down in a red book of failure with this pen," the wizard said.

A case of books materialized behind her. Out from it slid the last in a very long line of red-covered books. The bottom shelf was the only one not fully occupied by the books of failure, as two white books occupied it, and one conspicuous black-covered one.

"Now, if you pass, you will be marked down in the white book. The trial ends when the last grain of sand has returned from whence it came, or when your name has been marked down," she explained. "Have you any questions?"

"How can I expect to resist you? Look how powerful you are. I have only begun my training," she said.

"You have reached a level of mastery in the elemental arts. That is quite enough. As for power? In this place, you are as powerful as I. So long as you know how to cast a spell, you shall do so without effort and without delay. You are being tested only on your knowledge and ingenuity. Now-- begin," she said.

"But I--" she began.

Her words were cut off by a bizarre sensation as the room, and all that filled it, seemed to grow to many times its size. A second odd feeling came as she was drawn into the air by some invisible force and dropped down into a red liquid. It stung her eyes, and when she surfaced and looked about, her view of the massive room was wavy and distorted. She had been shrunk and dropped into a wine bottle! The cork worked itself into the opening as Azriel walked the short distance to the pedestal, having already willed the pen into her hand.

Myranda cast her strength into the air around her. Instantly it swirled into action, bursting the cork from the bottle with such force that the bottle tipped. After sloshing violently about, Myranda squeezed from the mouth of the bottle. She had to find somewhere to hide long enough to figure out how to undo the spell. Deacon had yet to teach it.

She ran further among the place settings of the table, crouching behind a folded napkin. Her mind swiftly analyzed her body, quickly happening upon an odd twist of magic that seemed to be wrapped about her. She made ready to levy her own strength against it when a shadow appeared.

Looking to the source, she saw, towering over her, the form of a cat. It was pure black with white flames flickering in its dark eyes. Myranda tried to run, but the cat swatted her painfully to the ground and held her there. In a flash, the cat was turned to stone, pinning her to the ground. Azriel appeared beside the table and headed in the direction of the book again. Myranda finished her work against the shrinking spell, restoring her size quickly enough to hurl the statue away and clear a good portion of the table she was laying on.

"Really, now. Must you make such a mess?" Azriel complained as she turned to watch Myranda sprint out of the banquet hall and down one of the adjoining halls.

Myranda found herself in a long hallway, lined with doors on either side. The doors began to slam, working their way toward her. The girl dove into a doorway containing an ascending staircase before the door could close and climbed it. There was another hall at the top, and she quickly entered the nearest room. It appeared to be a bedroom with a narrow window and posh furnishings. Azriel couldn't have made it out of the dining hall yet. With any luck she still thought that Myranda had been trapped in the first hallway.

"No such luck, I am afraid," came a second voice in her head.

The door slammed shut and locked. Myranda struggled against it, but the heavy wooden door would not budge. It would be a fool's errand to search for a key. Thinking quickly, her mind turned to one of Deacon's spells. Outside of this place, she found the manipulation the spell to be a clumsy and imprecise procedure, but here things might be different. She cast her mind into the lock, manipulating the individual elements directly. Within a few moments, with a satisfying click, the door popped open.

After a moment of relief, she tried to leave the room. The door was opened barely halfway when it slammed shut again, hurling her backward. Before her eyes the wooden door turned to a heavy iron cell door, and the lock vanished entirely. Soon the door was just a barred portion of wall. It could not be opened. Myranda scrambled out the window onto a thin ledge. The window sealed up behind her, as did each other one along the ledge.

"Well, now. Trapped on the ledge? That is a capture as well," Azriel's voice echoed in her thoughts.

Again Myranda's mind raced. She combed her thoughts for any foreign presence. Finding one, she forced it out. That was how Azriel was reading her thoughts. Now, perhaps, the wizard would not be so certain of her location. With one problem solved, Myranda had to now escape the ledge. The solution was obvious, but unpleasant. Without delay, the girl leapt into the frigid water of the moat below. She resurfaced, gasping for air, only to find Azriel peering off of the drawbridge with a grin.

"I may not be able to detect your mind anymore, but a deaf man could have heard that splash," she said.

In an instant, the water around Myranda began to freeze. She tried to scramble up the edge of the moat, but her foot was locked into the ice. Azriel chuckled lightly to herself as she walked leisurely toward the pedestal to mark down her victory. Myranda listened closely to the footsteps recede. In a flash, enough heat was conjured to free her foot. No sooner had the girl scrambled to freedom than the teacher stopped. Myranda acted fast--before her return.

"You know that I will always know when you are captured and when you are free. There is nothing you can do about that," Azriel informed Myranda.

The girl, now on the drawbridge, tried to rush silently past her. Once the student had made it inside the castle, Azriel willed the individual stones of the floor to rise up as bars to form a cage. Myranda stopped abruptly. Azriel opened her mouth to gloat, but stopped. Poking her hand through the bars to grab the girl, her fingers passed right through.

"An illusion! I didn't expect to see any of those out of you," she said.

The teacher ran outside and forced away any illusions that were not her work. Clinging to the wall were a number of bars of ice, forming a crude ladder leading to one of the first floor windows that had fortunately not been willed away like those of the second floor. Azriel rose into the air and approached the window. It widened to allow her through easily, but Myranda could already be heard hurrying down the hall. Azriel made her way out of the room just in time to see an image of Myranda rush into every open doorway and slam it.

"What fun, a student with creativity," Azriel said.

The powerful wizard touched her fingers to the wall and the stone became as transparent as glass. The effect spread until each and every block that composed the castle could be seen through. One by one, the illusions of Myranda were dispelled, but finishing was not necessary. The change that came over the castle startled the true Myranda, who stumbled backward, knocking over the bookshelf.

When her eyes met Azriel's, and a wicked grin came to her instructor's face, the girl sprang to her feet and ran toward the hourglass. Only a minute or two had passed, and the rules said that the test would be ended when the last grain returned from whence it had come. If she inverted the glass now, she would need to last only a minute or two more. Azriel was moving quickly toward her, unimpeded by the walls and floor, which separated like curtains at her approach. Just as the teacher's feet came to rest on the floor of the banquet hall once again, Myranda grasped the timepiece. With any luck she would be able to invert it and lock it in ice until the last few grains fell.

Luck, alas, was not with her. When the floating hourglass was tipped to the side, the whole of the castle seemed to lurch in the opposite direction. She lost grip on the glass and slid along the floor, colliding painfully with the wall. Nothing else seemed to be affected by the bizarre shift, which was a mercy, as were the furniture similarly affected she would have been crushed beneath it.

"Surprisingly, you were not the first to attempt to exploit that little technicality. As a result I have assured that, regardless of which way the hourglass is pointing, the sand continues to fall in the appropriate direction. Just for fun, I have seen to it that *you* fall in that direction as well, no matter which way I turn it," the devilish instructor said.

As she spoke her last sentence, she turned the hourglass in a random direction, sending Myranda sliding or falling in that direction. She concluded by flipping the hourglass over. Myranda held fast to the table, which she had become pinned against. It was heavy enough to keep her down.

"Well, if that is how you want it," Azriel said. Suddenly the furniture, with the exception of the pedestal, the book atop it, and the hourglass, plummeted upward. In a thunderous crash of splintering wood, the contents of the room collided with the vaulted roof.

Myranda struggled to move, a good portion of debris having landed atop her. Many bones were broken by the crash, but no sooner had she realized this than they were repaired. As she pulled herself from the rubble, Azriel floated "down" to the ceiling and flipped upside down to survey the damage.

"Still able to move about, eh? Very well. We shall have to restrain you," she said.

The sorceress's eyes wandered as she tried to think of something creative to torture her student with. They came to rest on the chandelier, which was hanging "up," unaffected by the shift. She smiled, and the leg-like candle holders twitched to life, scurrying up its chain and across the ceiling like some ornate spider. Everywhere the candle-tipped feet touched took to flame. Myranda freed herself and moved as quickly as she could across the rubble-strewn ceiling, but the animated candelabra moved across debris as though it was born to do it, which of course it had been. The pseudo-creature tore its chain from its mount and threw a loop of it around the hapless girl. In a twinkling she was wrapped tightly in the chain, and the fire was pooling around her.

"Right. I am rather proud of that one." Azriel beamed as she moved to the pedestal and took up the pen.

Myranda used her mind to gather up as much of the fire that surrounded her as she could and focused it around the chandelier spider. The automaton melted immediately, dripping in bright orange blobs to the floor below, but the chain cocooning her remained taut. With the utmost of care to protect herself, as she had the leaves in Solomon's test, she sliced the chains with the fire.

"Your resourcefulness is remarkable. I may have to redefine the word capture," said Azriel.

Approaching the hourglass again, she gave it a twirl. Instantly, Myranda found herself falling, jerked this way and that as "down" perpetually changed. It was disrupting beyond belief. She could barely think. She certainly couldn't move, as each time she approached something that she could grab onto, she fell away from it again. She was trapped in mid-air. Another smile of satisfaction came to her instructor's face and the pen was once again in hand.

Myranda's mind searched for something that might free her. The only thing that seemed to have a chance was levitation. She had never managed it on anything but water before, but Deacon had assured her that the same technique needed to be changed only slightly to levitate anything. Myranda consciously took hold of the mystic energy inside of herself and commanded it to be still. Her uncontrollable flight through the room came to a swift end. A second thought brought the spinning hourglass to a halt, this time properly oriented. As she lowered herself to the ground, Azriel gave a smug smile.

"I must say, you are driving me to new heights of creativity," Azriel said.

Myranda opened her mouth to reply to the compliment, only to be stopped by an odd sinking feeling. She looked down to discover that the floor beneath her had turned to quicksand. She sank swiftly to her waist before she once again put the levitation spell to work. The sand held firm, but slowly she was beginning to pull herself free.

"Sandstone," Azriel said audibly.

Instantly the sand was stone once more, and straining against it felt as though her legs, still encased within, would give far before the stone did. Azriel still had the pen in hand and approached the book to mark the failure. Myranda needed time. She threw up a wall of flame between Azriel and the pedestal. Azriel smirked and undid the spell, barely missing a step. Myranda focused her mind on the tremor spell. A few moments of shaking that threatened to turn her bones to powder shattered the stone of the floor. The pieces of rock fell away, as there was nothingness beneath them, but Myranda levitated herself up.

"Right, that is quite enough levitation for one day," Azriel said.

Myranda dropped, grabbing onto the edge of the hole she'd made. She tried to levitate again, only to find that some spell--an enormously complicated one--was blocking her from doing so. Though she knew that with time she could break the spell, she had more pressing matters at hand.

The girl pulled herself out of the hole in the ground and bolted for the doorway. The chains of the drawbridge pulled taught as she approached, and the stones of the floor began to shoot up in front of her, forming bars as they had for her illusion earlier. She dodged some and cast a quick tremor to shatter others. She was determined to escape this castle. Azriel's spells were becoming more potent by the second, and there was no doubt that she was not far from discovering one that would stall Myranda long enough to mark her failure. She simply *had* to get as far from the book as possible to maximize the time she had to escape.

The drawbridge was nearly halfway shut by the time she had fought her way to it. As she climbed the steep wooden incline, the surface turned into a checkerboard of fire and ice. Was Azriel trying to catch her or kill her? She swept the fire away with her mind and managed to leap from one piece of charred wood to the other until she pulled herself onto the nearly vertical end of the bridge. With a mighty leap, she came crashing down on the outer bank of the moat. The drawbridge sealed shut and for a moment there was peace. Myranda breathed a sigh of relief, but it was cut short by the creaking of the chains. A moment later they snapped and the drawbridge began to fall open. The terrified girl rolled frantically away, narrowly avoiding being crushed beneath the massive door. So narrow was her escape that, when she tried to move, she found that the hem of her tunic was pinned beneath the bridge.

The shadowy form of Azriel was approaching through the doorway. Myranda pulled desperately at the pinned cloth until it tore free. First, she rekindled the blazes on the bridge. In an instant smoke, fire, and steam concealed the outside world from anyone within. With the modicum of time she'd bought, the girl scanned the horizon. There was a scattering of trees and bushes dotting the open field before her. She conjured a wind to rattle the branches and prayed that her idea would work.

Azriel walked across the flaming walkway utterly unaffected by the flames. She reached the other side of the moat a moment before the tattered wooden door fell into the water. An unseen force made her twitch. Turning to look through the steam rising from the moat, she saw that the first five minutes had elapsed. The hourglass inverted itself, foregoing the gravity reversal that generally would accompany it. Her purpose here was to be tested against as many situations as possible, not the same one over and over again.

With the approaching deadline renewing her resolve, Azriel turned back to the field. Myranda had been busy. She'd managed to shake free the seeds from the trees and bushes and grow a veritable forest to hide in. It was far too dense to see through, and the girl was still able to thwart her detection spell.

"Clever girl, but there are more ways than one to track prey," Azriel said.

She began to stalk forward, seeming to waft away and back again as a pitch-black wolf with the same flickering white fire in her eyes. The air carried the scent of her target as clear as day. As she followed it, the trees nearest to her withered and died.

Far ahead, Myranda moved--unseen but not unknown--through the thick woods of her own creation. Precious little sun made it through the leaves, a fact that made her feel all the better. As a minute ticked by, then another, the tiniest hint of a feeling of safety came over her. It was a feeling quickly dispelled when she heard the quiet swish of grass beneath feet other than her own. She looked about, trying to spot her hunter, but Azriel made the very sun in the sky sink below the horizon, replacing it with a moon with hardly the strength to allow more than a few rays to peek through the thick canopy. Silently, Myranda managed to climb the nearest tree.

In a lone spot of moonlight, she saw the flicker of a black lupine form, and she realized how she had been found. She conjured a wind from behind her hunter to carry the scent away, but it was too late. The branches of the tree closed in around her like a cage. The moon seemed to brighten, lighting the cleared path leading to the castle.

Something, moving fast, came bursting out of the distant doorway toward them. It was the pedestal, book and pen perched firmly on top. When the pedestal was beside her, Azriel resumed her proper form. She took up the pen. Myranda drew all of the heat she could from the branches. They stiffened, crackling and flaking as the cold rendered them fragile. The desperate girl lashed out against the embrittled wood. The limbs gave way far more suddenly and fully than she had expected. Every last branch and much of the trunk collapsed into large, icy chunks.

Myranda landed amid the rubble and scrambled to her feet. The bulk of the pieces had dropped atop Azriel herself, as well as the pedestal. There was a powerful aura emanating from beneath the pile. If the fury of one was ever strong enough to be felt by another, then this surely was it. Myranda sprinted away, terrified of what may happen next. After a few moments, Azriel exploded from beneath the pile. The sky turned blood-red, glowing with a light that permeated all beneath it.

"No one--*no one*--attacks me. You little witch. This is no longer just a game," her voice thundered as she floated high above the tree tops.

With a thrust of her hand the trees were spread with such force that some were torn from their roots. Myranda was knocked to the ground by the force of the energy. The ground beneath her began to rumble. A vast rift split the ground, large enough to swallow trees whole. Myranda clung to the edge, but was suddenly wrenched into the air. She fought hard against the force that held her, but it had a grip on her that she could not break. The ground below her began to glow almost white hot.

"What are you going to do?" Myranda cried.

As an answer, the molten ground swirled up around her. The heat was unimaginable as she found herself concealed in a void of the swirling ball of liquid stone. As it cooled, it became clear, and she saw Azriel with a look of satisfaction on her face. Myranda was lowered to the still-scalding hot floor of her glass prison.

"Now. To mark my success," she said.

The pen came to her hand and she turned to the book. Dipping the tip of the quill in the ink, she pressed it to paper, or at least tried to. With a waver, the pen passed right through the book. Azriel clenched her fist and whisked the illusion away.

"Where is it!" she demanded.

Myranda answered only with a cold, silent stare. Azriel turned and held out her palm toward the castle in the distance. The entire contents of the bookshelf, as well as the hourglass, streaked across the ground to meet her. A wave of the same hand flung all of the books open at once. The pages fluttered, each revealing itself to be completely filled. She turned viciously to Myranda. The girl removed the red-covered book from her tunic and grinned. Azriel wrenched it from her hands, clinking it against the wall of her transparent cell.

Myranda snatched it back and protected it with all of the strength of mind she could muster, which in this place was more than considerable.

"Release it, girl. There is precious little air in there, and it grows more precious by the moment. It will not last you until the time runs out. I will make sure of that," Azriel said.

"You cannot win. If you break this to have the book, I will be free and you will not be able to sign it. If you don't, I will last the time limit. If I meditate, I will hardly have to breathe at all," Myranda fairly taunted.

Azriel gritted her teeth. The world around them was crumbling in the wake of her anger. Myranda clutched the book and turned away. The mystic pull on the book relinquished just long enough for a small opening to appear in the side of the capsule. Myranda turned to the blast of cool air, holding the book in front of her. Azriel tore it from her hands and whipped it open. Myranda grabbed it and struggled to pull it back, but Azriel had it in her hands now. Myranda pulled and pulled with her mind, and the book constantly threatened to slip from the teacher's grasp, but she managed to produce the pen and, in a very unsteady scrawl, mark down Myranda's name.

With the deed done, the sky resumed its azure hue, the faults in the ground sealed over, and the capsule containing Myranda vanished. She lowered gently to the ground. The delightful little cottage that served as the start to the trying ordeal seemed to form again around them. A moment later, while she was still dazed from the sudden and complete change,

Myranda's friends reappeared. Deacon rushed to her, having seen all that had happened. Myn scampered over, happy to see Myranda again, but stopped suddenly to survey her friend.

Myranda looked ragged and worn out. She was drenched with sweat. Vast patches of her clothes were scorched. Myn glanced first at Deacon, then at Azriel, eager to find someone to blame. The decision did not take long, as she gave Deacon a quick series of lashes with her tail as punishment.

"Ouch. I was beside you the entire time! I couldn't have done this," he said, reaching down to help Myranda up.

"She should be very proud of herself. It was a tremendous showing. I dare say she figured a spell or two out for herself while she was being tested. The mark of potential to be sure," Azriel remarked, once again fully composed and matriarchal. She was busy arranging the red and white books again, a look of mild confusion on her face. She was having trouble fitting them on the appropriate shelves.

"You certainly outperformed me on my first failure. I required no less than three attempts to complete it," Deacon reassured her. "I shudder to think what would have become of me had I put up half of the resistance you did. I was a bit worried toward the end."

When Myranda stood, a book slipped from her tunic and dropped to the ground. The rogue book, a red-covered one, drew the attention of all present. Azriel knelt to retrieve it, placing it on the table beside the one in which she had just marked Myranda's name. They were identical. The teacher silently waved her hand over the first book. The red color faded to white.

"Clever, clever girl," she said quietly.

Deacon's jaw hung agape as Azriel flipped to the last occupied page of the newly-white book, where Myranda's name could be clearly seen.

"Well then. I would not say that it was the most straightforward method, but a technicality is nonetheless a victory in this case. It would appear you have passed after all. I wonder--when did you steal the two books?" Azriel asked.

"While you were dispelling my illusions one by one," Myranda said, lowering herself shakily to a chair.

"And you stumbled into the bookcase to cover your tracks. Brilliant!" Deacon said.

"You certainly fought valiantly to keep hold of that book, despite the fact that it was the one you had wanted me to sign all along," Azriel said.

"I thought you might suspect something if I didn't. Not to mention I was not certain it would work, and I was afraid of how you might have reacted had you discovered what I'd done," Myranda said.

"You could have been killed for the sake of a ruse!" Deacon said.

"Well, I don't think she would have killed me," Myranda said with a weak smile.

"I most certainly would have. What do you suppose the black book is for? It contains the names of those whose ambition overcame their resourcefulness. Lucky for you, I was able to wrestle the book from your grip before I wrestled the breath from your lungs," Azriel said. It was unnerving how nonchalantly she was able to seem when speaking about her willingness to kill.

Myranda swallowed hard as the realization of her situation swept over her.

"Well, I would so love to chat with you, but I simply must improve my spells. I still cannot believe you managed to keep me out of your head. That is a rather rare feat. Off with you. Go do some well-deserved bragging," Azriel said.

Myranda and Deacon quickly obeyed. Suddenly, Deacon's fear of her seemed entirely justified. They kept a rather brisk pace, with Myn trotting behind, until they came to a seemingly arbitrary spot in the field surrounding the cottage.

"Wait here, would you?" Deacon said.

"Why here?" Myranda asked.

"We have reached the edge of the arena. I must retrieve your staff," he said.

He leaned forward, the very air in front of him seeming to ruffle like a curtain as he vanished, first to the shoulders, then to the waist. When he stood again, his upper body reappearing, he held the staff. He was also dripping wet.

"There. You will need this if you hope to make it back to your hut," he said.

"Why? I feel quite well. A bit shaken, but aside from my poor heart, I don't believe I am any the worse for wear. I feel better now than when I entered," she said.

"Yes, and you will lose that benefit when you leave," he said, handing her the staff. "Now, watch your step."

Myranda took a few steps forward. As soon as her head left the boundary of the arena, she felt as though all of her strength had been sapped from her. She leaned heavily on the staff for support. It sunk partway into the muddy ground. The downpour she had inadvertently caused was still raging. In some places the water was ankle-deep. When she had taken a moment to adjust to the state of mental drain she once again found herself in, she spoke.

"Why hasn't someone stopped this rain?" Myranda asked.

"There is your answer," Deacon said, pointing to an odd sight at the edge of the lake in the distance.

"What is it? My eyes won't focus," she said.

"Ayna is arguing with Calypso. This happens every time a storm must be stopped. Storms are all wind and water, so it falls to either Ayna or Calypso to manage them as our resident experts, but Ayna will not let Calypso do so. While Calypso does not care about the storm, one of her favorite things in life is torturing Ayna, so she categorically refuses to allow Ayna to do so either. More than once, the argument has outlasted the storm. Forget about that, though. Let us get you to bed. Tomorrow night is the blue moon and you must be at your best," he said.

The words barely filtered into Myranda's head. She stumbled and sloshed her way to her hut, closed the door, changed into dry clothes, and collapsed. Myn took her usual perch atop her, and the pair drifted off to sleep.

#

Myranda did not so much as stir until midday, when Deacon reluctantly woke her and informed her that the ceremony would be starting soon. When she left her hut, there was a feeling of anticipation permeating the village. People rushed to and fro. Deacon led her to the courtyard where the Elder's hut had been. It was now conspicuously missing, and in its place, there was a rectangular marble altar.

In any other place, she would question how an entire structure could have vanished overnight and be replaced with something else, but here she merely admired the altar. At each side of it, there stood a smaller one bearing a bowl. People had begun to join hands around the ring that Myranda and Deacon had retreated to when she first came here. On the edge of this ring, nearest to the mountains, was a tall post topped with a hoop. Below it was the chair of the Elder.

"We will begin shortly and continue until the last of us drops, so I had best give you your instructions. We will join hands around the central altars. When we begin, the elemental Masters will provide a mystically pure sample of their respective element. We will then focus all of the strength that we can muster into your neighbors. In this way, all of the energy that the Masters need will be available. Once the ring as a whole has reached a state of focus, we shall begin to chant 'Earth, fire, wind, water.' Whatever language you wish. With a blue moon in the sky, the spirits will hear," he said.

"How will we know when it is working?" she asked.

"You will know. Now, until the moon rises, it is very important that the ring not be broken. If you feel that you cannot go on, join the hands of your neighbors before you pass out. Once the moon is at its height, though, you need not worry. Let us begin," he said.

Myranda was led to her place on the circle. The Elder was at the north end of the circle. Calypso was present, once again displaying a pair of legs. She and Ayna, Solomon, and Cresh were spaced regularly about the circumference. Deacon was at the south end. Myranda found herself on western side, and soon she discovered that Lain was situated directly across from her in the distance. All of those who formed the circle were at least at the level of mastery that she had reached, leaving apprentices and other low-level students scurrying about, attempting to prepare the ceremony. Azriel was absent, either unwilling or unable to leave the arena, so the task fell to her to occupy Myn for as long as necessary. After what she had been through, the thought made Myranda more than a bit uneasy.

There was little time to think of that, though. She joined hands with those beside her, a pair of warriors she had spoken with several times in the days following her encounter with Hollow. Cresh approached the central altar and poured a sample of rich brown earth into one of the bowls. Ayna followed and conjured a burst of wind that swirled against the bowl, somehow persisting and rotating within it. Solomon cast a tongue of flame into another bowl and it burned brilliantly without fuel. The final bowl was filled with water drawn from the air itself by Calypso.

Soon the magic began to flow. It was the most curious feeling. She focused and spread out her strength, only to feel more than she'd contributed flowing through her. For a long time, she felt no stress or fatigue at all. The same could not be said of the warriors. Before the sun had set, half of them had reached their limits. By nightfall, she was holding hands with Solomon and Cresh, and the circle was slightly more than half of its original size.

As the moon began to peek over the horizon, the chanting began. It was curious to hear all of the different voices and languages chanting in bursts of sound. The power flowing through them was noticeably increased, and it grew stronger with each passing minute as the moon climbed higher in the sky.

The last of the warriors--with the exception of Lain--and the first of the wizards began to fall, and Myranda could feel the strength draining from her. The magic had grown so intense that it was visible, racing about the circle as a pale blue filament of energy. Holding hands was no longer needed, and the elemental Masters separated to focus more intently on their tasks.

As the moon climbed even higher, the purpose for the hoop at the end of the pole became clear. The shadow cast by the supernaturally bright moonlight was approaching the altar. When the moon reached its peak, the altar would be entirely within the circular shadow. A pair of the younger wizards collapsed and were dragged away by apprentices. Myranda struggled to maintain her concentration. The task at hand was an odd one. She had to keep the power she was immersed in moving, despite the fact it was more than she could handle if it was still. It was oddly like juggling.

The big moment was only a few minutes away. Of the dozens that had started, only eight were left. The Elder stood firm, with the four elemental Masters showing signs of fatigue. Both the white and black magic Masters had just fallen, and Deacon looked ready to break. Lain, somehow, was as steady as ever. Myranda could feel herself wavering. Then the moon made its last shift. Time seemed to slow as the thin filament of energy swelled to a thick band, then practically a wall that blocked out the outside world.

Each elemental wizard struggled forward. A portion of the energy was pulled away and forced into the pure essences at the altar. First, the wind swirled savagely, moving slowly over to the earth. Instantly, the earth was caught up in the breeze. The water came next, whirling up into the powerful mix. Finally, it approached the fire. Rather than the wet mixture hissing into steam or extinguishing the fire, the flames seemed to mix with it as smoothly as the other elements had. What was before them was a spinning mass of all of the elements, here red as fire, there brown as earth. Here thin as wind, there thick as water. The unique mass swirled atop the central altar, basking in the most direct rays of the blue moon.

Ayna suddenly lost consciousness, the force of the magic in the air hurling her through the glowing wall. A moment later, Calypso dropped, her legs shifting back to the emerald tail. She was quickly carried away by apprentices brave enough to enter the ring of magic. Deacon was next, dropping to the ground. Cresh dropped to his knees, consciousness leaving him more slowly.

Myranda, too, reached her breaking point. Unable to pull her mind to this task or any other, she crumbled to the ground, just barely able to keep her eyes open to take in the spectacle. Solomon, Lain, and the Elder remained. The dragon fought valiantly, but the energy was far too much. He dropped down. As the swirling mass of magic and elements seemed to concentrate, the Elder lowered herself slowly to her seat. She seemed to know that her strength would not last a moment longer, as when she finished sitting, her eyes closed and her head bobbed limply to the side in deep sleep.

Only Lain remained, yet the magic continued to focus. Whatever it was that they had been working to create, it had mind enough of its own to sustain itself. An ember of light formed at the base of the altar and slowly circled upward. When it reached the bottom of the mystic elements, it seemed to ignite a thin band of the material into white hot flames. The fire worked its way up the mass. What was left behind was a pair of tapering columns of wind swirling so forcefully and tightly that they were clearly distinct from the air around them. The fire continued its path, revealing a roughly female form composed of the very wind.

When the white hot flames flickered out, twin almonds of golden light opened on what would have been the face of the form. These "eyes" swept coldly over the small portion of the courtyard within the wall of light. Quickly they came to rest on the figure of Lain--from Myranda's point of view, merely a silhouette against the wall. The windy creature lowered to the ground.

The instant that its feet touched the earth, a second wave of white flames swept quickly up the form, leaving behind a sandy gray statue that walked purposefully toward Lain. He had dropped to one knee, a hand on the ground to steady himself. The being that they had fought so hard to bring into existence lowered a hand and cradled the chin of the weary creature, tilting his head up to gaze briefly into his eyes. With a slight nod, the being took its hand away and turned to look about one last time. Through Myranda's rapidly fading vision, she could just make out the very same mark that Myranda bore on her hand and Lain bore on his chest inscribed on the forehead of this new being. It returned her gaze for a moment, then was swept over by a final band of white flames, leaving behind a brilliantly glowing version of the same form that seemed to be composed of the fire itself.

In an instant, the fiery form streaked upward into the sky and out of sight. The world darkened as Myranda's tenuous grip on consciousness finally slipped away. The darkness of unwanted sleep came.

#

Scattered across the Northern Alliance, minds became alert. It had been a night of high magic. Full moons often were. Blue moons more so. Those with even the most rudimentary mystic training had, unknowingly, felt the summoning ceremony in Entwell as a dull pressure in the back of their minds. Its result, though, was not so easily missed. A smoldering ember of intense magic streaked a searing line across the minds of every wizard, witch, seer, and shaman the world over. It burned brightly, but briefly, like a shooting star in the mind's eye. Most dismissed it. Others took note of it. Some, though, were deeply affected.

In his office in Northern Capital, General Bagu sat forward in his chair. He held his eyes tightly shut and trained his mind on the fading glint of power. Hungrily, even desperately, he focused on the distant power. It had a quality--some texture or color--that he knew all too well. Years of searching had sensitized him to it.

One of the long-sought Chosen was awake. While the detection was fresh in his mind he tore a book from its shelf and threw it open to a well-worn page. Five brief descriptions were there, only one of which did not have extensive notes beside it. The shadow of a smile flickered across his face. The moment of truth would soon be at hand.

#

Myranda's eyes wrestled open and she gazed weakly about. She was in a room with other beds. Most were vacant, but a few still had occupants. The blurriness of fatigue and sleep obscured her vision too much to tell who it was that surrounded her, but her ears worked well enough. Distantly, she could hear the ever-present voice of Deacon arguing weakly with someone.

"Yes, I know I must rest . . . I really feel that I could speed my recovery if I had something to occupy my mind, or my hands . . . It would be more soothing than taxing . . ." Deacon said, continuing to argue in as polite a way as was possible.

"Deacon?" Myranda called in barely a whisper.

Her friend was too busy attempting to persuade one of the white wizards to allow him his book to hear. There was someone, though, who heard very clearly. With an unexpected pounce, Myn was on top of her. She must have been lying beside the bed. The dragon dragged her rough tongue all over Myranda's face, but the weary girl was too weak to object. The commotion did not go unnoticed. A trio of white-robed healers converged on Myn and grabbed her. She was far too intent on letting Myranda know how she felt to pay any attention to them. When she had been carried far enough that her tongue could no longer find its mark, she struggled free and leapt atop Myranda again.

"Never mind. Leave her be," Myranda said weakly.

The commotion was enough to attract the attention of Deacon.

"I don't even need to see the book. I could just hold it. Wait, is that Myn? Is Myranda awake?" Deacon asked.

When he was informed that she was, he requested to be taken to the bed to her right for the remainder of his convalescence. The attending clerics relented. The moment he was properly placed and tucked in, he turned to Myranda. The healers left him, heading purposefully out of the room.

"It has been five days. They are off to get you some food. You may not know it yet, but you are starving. They say you lasted right to the end. Tell me, did you see it?" Deacon asked.

"The . . . thing?" Myranda said, unsure of what to call it.

"Yes, yes! Fire, water, earth, air! In the shape of . . . was it a man or a woman?" he asked insistently.

"It was certainly a woman," Myranda said.

"Really. I would have expected a man. No matter. It came! You saw it! You are certain of that, yes?" he said, leaning toward her so suddenly that in his weakened and dizzy condition, he nearly toppled from the bed.

"Don't think I will ever forget it," she said.

"Tell me, was there anyone else awake?" he asked.

"Lain," she said.

"And the creature. Did she approach him?" he asked.

"It did," she recalled.

Deacon leaned back against the pillow, dazed more by the news than his condition.

"Then it is proved. He is one of the Chosen. Lain is one of the five!" he said.

Myranda took in the information as best she could in her weakened condition.

"I must speak with him. I cannot believe I have not spoken with him already. He spent all of those years here, and it was only when he returned that the truth could be known . . ." he rambled.

As he spoke, a tall, white-robed gentleman approached. He had been watching sternly from one of the corners of the room. His hair was as white as his robe, though his face was clean-shaven. He was followed by a younger man and woman, each with arm loads of potions, crystals, and medical tools.

"Deacon . . ." he said. His voice had a practiced steadiness about it. It was the voice of a man who had learned patience.

"Vedesto! Did you hear? You have, right here in one of your beds, one of the five!" Deacon said, sitting up.

"Yes. I also have an overexcited gray wizard who will not allow himself, or anyone else, to rest," Vedesto said.

"How can anyone rest? This is the most monumentally important thing that has ever--" Deacon began.

"I do not care if all five of the Chosen have selected this very building for the great convergence. My sole concern is restoring these brave young wizards and warriors to health, and I cannot do that with you raving and screaming. And what is this I hear about you bothering my people about your book?" he asked.

"Yes! Yes! The book!" he practically yelled.

"Deacon," Vedesto said with forced gentility.

"Oh, Vedesto, you know as well as I that people as psychologically weakened--" Deacon continued, ignoring the objection.

"Deacon," Vedesto said again, the anger beginning to show in his face.

"--as we are tremendously likely to forget what we have seen and done recently. I simply must have my book to record--" he continued.

"*Deacon!*" Vedesto shouted, pushing the babbling young wizard to the bed again. "Stop talking, stop pestering my apprentices, stop pestering Myranda, and do not pester the malthrope. If I hear your voice again for the rest of the day, no one will hear it again for the rest of the week. I will put you to sleep until every last one of these patients is out of bed. Understood!?"

Deacon nodded.

"Excellent," he said, returning to the calm, patient demeanor he'd shown before. "Now, Myranda, show me your hand, if you would."

Myranda opened the hand with the mark, assuming it to be the one he wanted to see. Vedesto put his hand out to the side without looking. One of his subordinates handed him a hazy gray crystal. He placed it in Myranda's open hand. A dim light flickered within it. He nodded thoughtfully and removed the crystal, holding it out in front of the other apprentice. It was swiftly replaced with one of the many bottles that each was weighed down with. After glancing at the contents, he shook his head and held his hand back out. The bottle was replaced with another one. This he was satisfied with. He opened the bottle.

"Open your mouth and put out your tongue," he said.

Myranda obeyed, only to have a drop of the most intensely foul-tasting liquid she had ever encountered placed on her tongue. It was very much like the flavor of the tea Deacon had once brought her, but far worse. As she swallowed the stuff, it seemed to get warmer. By the time it reached her stomach, she could feel the heat throughout her body. The warmth seemed to boil away the fog in her mind.

"There. Until that wears off, you should feel like yourself. That should give you enough time to get some food inside of you without having to worry about choking to death. Once you've eaten, I want you to go back to sleep. Another day and you ought to be able to walk out of here unaided," Vedesto said, turning to Deacon. "You, on the other hand, will require at least two more days, because you couldn't simply rest like a good patient."

Food was given to Myranda, which she ate eagerly. Deacon sat, sulking but quiet, while she ate. Myranda glanced around her with her temporarily clear vision.

In one of the corners, furthest from the door, Lain lay asleep in a bed. It was only the second time she had seen the creature in any form of rest, and once again it was through no choice of his own. She couldn't help but look at him in a new light. It was certain now. This was a divinely anointed being. He could be the savior of all of the people of the continent, plucking them from the jaws of the war once and for all. Myranda would never have imagined someone like him as a Chosen a few years ago, yet now that she knew the skills he had, she wondered if there was another in the world better suited.

Shortly after she finished her meal, the warmth that kept her mind clear faded and she, quite against her will, drifted again into sleep. This slumber was not so deep. Simple dreams came in the form of brief glimpses of what was to be. She saw Lain, the bizarre creature she had helped to create, and three hazy forms standing before a grateful city, accepting the praise due to them for ending the war and bringing the soldiers home. The scene repeated itself in varied forms through the night. By the time her eyes opened again, she was convinced that such a sight must come to pass, no matter what. With the end of the war now a very real possibility, she simply must make sure it occurred.

True to the white wizard's word, Myranda felt strong enough to stand. Myn was nowhere to be seen, and Lain's bed was empty. Deacon was still asleep, and when Myranda asked Vedesto where Lain had gone to, he seemed quite dismayed that the bed was empty. It should not have been a surprise that Lain had let himself out of the chief healer's care.

After the news had spread that he was a Chosen, though, there was little doubt that he would be easy to find. All that she would have to do was look in the center of the largest group of people around. Or perhaps not. Upon being officially discharged from Vedesto's care, Myranda found that the people outside, many still mildly under the effects of the ceremony, were unaware Lain had slipped out. She headed quickly to his place on the Warrior's Side. There, inside his simple hut, she found him sitting with his back against the wall. Myn was curled up on his crossed legs.

"I am surprised you are not inundated by well-wishers and admirers," Myranda said.

"I value my privacy. The people here respect boundaries when you set them," he said.

"You know you can't ignore it now. You are one of the Chosen. It is not a theory. You and I have seen proof," she said.

"So it would seem," he said calmly.

"I suppose you will leave this place soon to perform your duty to the world," Myranda said.

"You may believe what you wish," he said.

Myranda paused.

"You do intend to stop the war, don't you?" she asked.

"Is that to be one of your questions?" he asked.

She only had two, and there was little hope of any new questions anytime soon. This, though, was quite worth it.

"Yes," she said.

"Absolutely not," he said.

"What!? You cannot be serious! Lain, it is your purpose! You were born to do it! You owe it to the world!" she said.

"I have not finished forcing the world to pay the debt owed to me. I am in the business of killing. I depend upon feelings of hatred and loathing, and deeply-seated longings to end the life of another. Such feelings are not forthcoming in a time of peace. War is my livelihood," he said.

Myranda was frozen with rage. She could feel the hope of an end slipping away because this short-sighted, greedy, heartless *thing* that sat before her refused to use the power given to him for the one and only truly good purpose in the world. Her hands trembled and tears formed in her eyes. The stand that held the training swords they had been using stood to the side in the room. She grasped her weapon and, shaking, held it up.

"Outside, now!" she demanded.

"I am not prepared to train you now. It is not yet sundown," he said.

"Lain, damn you, if you will not do your duty for this world, then you will keep your promise to me! On your feet!" she shouted.

Myn, who had been roused from a light sleep by Myranda's entrance, watched in a pleasant daze. When the girl began to speak her harsh words, the dragon snapped quickly out of it. Lain grasped his training sword and hoisted himself to his feet. The pair left the hut, with Myn keeping a close and watchful eye. She could feel that there was something different about this fight.

Myranda was hardly at her best. She had only just regained the strength to walk. She wouldn't be able to fight nearly as well as she normally would, which wasn't nearly well enough to exact the revenge she so desired. It didn't matter. She wasn't in control of her own actions any more. Lain lasted even longer than she, and he was unaccustomed to the mental fatigue that she had come to expect at the end of a training day. Perhaps, just this once, the balance would be tipped in her favor.

The first blows began to be exchanged. Myranda was slower and sloppier than she had been in weeks. Lain's speed was not what it had been either, and his movements were, for the first time, less than graceful. Still, he managed to raise his weapon to block each attempt. As Myranda's anger stirred, she got sloppier. Soon she was paying no attention to anything but attacking. Lain landed punishing blows, hammering her ribs and legs--but in her mind, the pain was nothing. He had done more through his single decision to forsake his purpose and allow the war to continue than he ever could with his weapon.

Myranda put every ounce of strength she could into each attack. Either through fatigue or lapsed concentration, Lain's weapon was only barely able to block them after a time. Then came the moment. Myranda managed a single sidestep to take her out of range of a mighty swing by Lain. The force of the attack took him off balance, and there it was. Her chance. Time seemed to stop. Her weapon was ready and his was not. Before she could even think, she had struck. With a force that could only be mustered by rage, Myranda's weapon crashed with a sickening snap into Lain's jaw.

All at once, time came rushing back. Lain shook from the force of the attack. His face turned away, but his body remained planted. Myranda dropped her weapon and gasped, shocked at what she had done. Regret instantly replaced the hate in her heart. She wanted badly to rush to him, to see if he was badly hurt. A part of her, though, held her back, fearful of the consequences of her action. Myn shot between the two, a look of pure betrayal in her eyes. Lain's face turned to her. He wore the same stony expression that he always had, but his eyes spoke volumes. There was respect, pride, and perhaps a bit of pity, but no anger. A trickle of blood crept from the corner of his mouth, staining the cream-colored fur red.

"If that were a proper blade, I would be dead. You have learned all I can teach. When you came to me, you would not draw a drop of blood from my arm," he said, spitting a gob of blood and a tooth to the ground. "Now you are capable of taking my life. The fire is burning inside. You are every bit a warrior. The rest will come with time."

He knelt and picked up the tooth.

"Here," he said, stepping around Myn and placing it in Myranda's hand. "Keep it. It will be a reminder of the day you proved that you were no worse than I . . . and no better."

Myranda stared at the bloody thing for a long time. Lain returned to his hut, leaving her to her thoughts. Her eyes wandered to the practice sword, a stain of blood near its tip. A deep, dull pain burned in the palm of her hand. The sight of the stained sword turned her stomach. Myn settled to the ground, her eyes a window to her conflicted soul. The girl couldn't stand the questioning stare and turned away, heading slowly toward her hut.

The walk back was a long one. The distance was short, but burdened with the reality of what she had done, and what she had said, it was almost too much to bear. She tried to remind herself of the anger, that what she had done was justified. It did little good. As she walked, she slowly became aware of each and every blow she'd let slip by. Her mind was too taxed to heal them by itself. She could have gone back to the healers, but deep down, she knew she deserved what she had received. The fact that she had let hate turn her into exactly what she hated warranted every lump and bruise she had and more.

She had not killed him, but the fact that she could have, the fact that she wanted to, burned her mind.

She entered her hut. Myn was with Lain. The dragon would need some time to forgive her for what she had done. The room seemed too empty. Myranda was tired. She should sleep but . . . no. She couldn't. Not now. The dreams. Silence and solitude were all she wanted now. A knock at the door broke the silence, and the man on the other side broke the solitude. She opened it to find Deacon leaning heavily--*very* heavily--on both the door frame and a staff. It was clear that the chief white wizard was right. He'd needed at least another day. He managed a weak smile.

"Hello. May I come in?" he asked.

Myranda would have said no, but he clearly had put a lot of effort into the trek to her hut.

"Please," she said with a rather unconvincing attempt at joviality.

He hobbled in, dropping heavily to a seat.

"My goodness. I haven't had to use a staff in ages," he said.

"Shouldn't you still be in bed?" she asked.

"Vedesto evicted me. He caught me trying to convince one of the apprentices to sneak a book in for me. Again," he said.

"I see," she said.

"So, I thought . . . the falls. The falls have stopped while we were sleeping, and the water in the pool beneath is gone," he began, his voice wavering a bit. "The way is open again, and will be for a day or two more. We post people in shifts to watch for newcomers. In groups of two. I thought maybe that you and I could . . . is something wrong?"

Myranda shook as she remembered what she had done, and then she slowly shook her head.

"What is it? I can help, I assure you," he said, nearly falling over forward in an attempt to place a hand on her shoulder.

"Nothing, I . . . I passed Lain's test," she said.

"Perhaps my mind is a bit more addled than I thought. I would have imagined that was a reason to rejoice," he said.

"I tried to kill him," she said.

"Did you succeed?" he asked.

"No, but I wanted to. I really did. I couldn't control myself. I just . . . I hated him so much. I knocked out his tooth. I may have broken his jaw. He *gave* me the tooth. He wants me to remember. He wants me to remember that I wanted to kill," she said.

"What did he do to make you feel this way?" he asked.

"He won't do it, Deacon. He *is* one of them! He *can* stop the war, but he won't! He would rather go on profiting from murder than end all of this!" she said.

"Myranda, no, no. You mustn't trouble yourself over that. Listen, it does not matter what he says. This is a matter of fate. What must be done *will* be done," he said.

"I know him well enough to know that when he gives his word, he doesn't break it, and he promised to answer my questions truthfully. If he said he doesn't intend to, then he won't," she said.

"You don't understand. It doesn't matter. Myranda, the future is not so fragile as to be broken by a simple decision. The future is *made* of decisions. The spirits speak not to tell us what to do, but to tell us what will be done. Something will change his mind and he will rise to his proper place. Until then, just leave him be," he said.

"I just don't know," she said.

"Well, I do. That's the wonderful thing about the future. All you ever have to do is wait for it. It will come to you," he said.

Until the sun set, Deacon kept Myranda company. He then hobbled slowly home as Myranda went to sleep without her friend Myn to keep her company for the first time in ages. The time had not protected her from the dreams. Morning couldn't come soon enough. When her eyes opened shortly before sunrise, she made a decision. She would convince Lain to do what he must, even if it took years. But not today. She could not face him after what she did yesterday, after what he made her do. For now she needed something to occupy her mind.

She left her hut, with her mind fully recovered and her bruises mostly healed. The thundering of the falls had indeed stopped, Myranda finally realized for herself. It was odd. The sound had been so constant in her time her that she had accepted the low rumble as silence. Now that it was gone, the quiet seemed unnatural. It felt as though there was something missing. The feeling was deep in her soul. It must be the missing sound. What else could it be?

She had a meal before seeking out Deacon. It was odd not being hurried by an impending training session with an impatient teacher. She supposed that black and white magics would be next, and she wondered what sort of things those Masters would have in store for her. No. Gray magic first. She owed it to Deacon to finish his training. After knocking at his door, she heard bumping and thumping, as well as a rather insistent voice telling her to wait. Finally the door opened, revealing Deacon looking a good deal more disheveled than usual.

"Did I wake you?" she asked.

"No, no. Not you precisely. The door did. When you knocked on it," he said, trying to set her mind at ease without really lying.

"You can go back to bed. I know you need your sleep," Myranda said.

"Not at all. Not at all. I am quite well-rested," he said, struggling valiantly to hold back a yawn. "I haven't slept so deeply since I was an apprentice. What brings you here?"

"I haven't slept so poorly since I was a frightened little girl. Myn isn't about. I just need some kind of distraction. Something to pluck up my courage before I speak to Lain again," she said.

"Well, if nothing more than distraction is required, I can most assuredly oblige. Please, come in," he said.

She closed the door and took a seat in the second chair while Deacon went about pulling books from shelves. When he had a fair amount, he pulled his chair to the desk and opened one or two of them.

"If you like, I will teach you a bit more gray magic. You may have your choice of lessons. Whatever interests you," he said.

Myranda scanned the books. The names were not in her tongue, but thanks to a whispered enchantment by Deacon, the lines and letters twisted and turned themselves as her eyes swept over the pages. In a few moments it was all quite legible to her. Eventually she found the most recently scribed of the enchantments.

"What about this one?" she asked, placing her finger on a spell marked "Gilliam's Folly."

"Trans-substantiation. That is a rather advanced one, but nothing beyond your ability, I am sure," he said.

She had not brought her staff, but Deacon allowed her to borrow his crystal. Gray magic tended to be quite different from the elements. Each spell that the fire or wind Masters taught was much like the first. Gray magic was wholly different from spell to spell. It was like learning a new discipline each time.

The pair decided she would begin by turning a piece of clay into glass. The two substances were fairly similar, and thus the change would be simple. Myranda worked at the spell with Deacon's coaching, but it wasn't easy. The sight of the spell at work was quite unique. Faint waves of energy swept through the clay, leaving thin bands of glass that faded quickly back to normal. After an hour or so of unsuccessful attempts, they decided to rest.

"Well. The falls are quiet today. For now, at least. Calypso indicated that they would give way sooner than expected. Perhaps by the end of the day. Nevertheless, that still leaves time for a shift or two at the fall's edge. It is quite peaceful there and you and I might--" he began. He was interrupted by a thunderous slam on the door.

"What was that?" she cried, startled.

"I seem to have a rather insistent visitor," he said.

A second crash nearly knocked the door from its hinges, and a third succeeded where the last had failed. Atop the fallen door stood a dizzied Myn. She had a desperate look, catching the edge of Myranda's tunic and pulling her forward.

"What is it? Calm down. What is it, little one?" she asked.

Myn looked desperately to the base of the temporarily quiet falls and back to Myranda.

"What about the falls? I don't . . . Lain. Lain went to the falls," she said.

She knew from the dragon's eyes that it was so. He had gone.

"Then we must follow," Myranda said, walking resolutely toward the falls.

"What!? No! You--you need to stay here! There are ceremonies, there are tests. You've so much more you can learn! You haven't even been inducted as a Full Master yet! Your Master crystal will not be forged for another month, at least!" Deacon said, rushing out the door behind her.

"I've learned enough. I need to see Lain," she said.

"The falls could start at any moment. You'll never make it! You don't have any supplies! You need to stay!" he pleaded.

"No!" she said, turning to him. "Lain has left this place to go back to killing. He has turned his back on his purpose. I will not rest until he faces it again!"

"Myranda, that is a job for fate, not for you," he reasoned desperately.

"What if fate means to do it through me? I have been thinking. That nonsense you said that Hollow had said about me. A label of white adorns that which will see each. I have seen the Swordsman," she began, holding up her white scar of the mark. "I have seen Lain. I have seen whatever being we summoned in the ceremony. What if it is my purpose to seek out the Chosen? A mark both fresh and faded belongs to the carpenter. What if carpenter is not meant to be taken literally? What if he meant that I was to be the one to join the members of the Chosen five together as a carpenter joins wood? Doesn't that explain why I have the mark? Doesn't that explain why magic comes so easily to me?"

"Perhaps, perhaps . . . But perhaps not! You are reaching, Myranda. You are twisting the words to fit your purpose," he said. "The prophecy is clear about mere mortals who try to help the Chosen. The trials that the divine ones must face would destroy anyone else. To offer aid where it is not needed is a death sentence!"

"Then so be it. If I must die so that the world may be spared of this war, let it be done," she said.

"No, Myranda, I--I . . . Five minutes more, I beg of you!" he said.

"I must--" Myranda tried to answer. Before she did, Deacon was gone. He disappeared inside his hut.

Myranda hurried along. She simply could not be delayed. A terrible din came from Deacon's hut. He sprinted out after her a minute later.

"Wait please!" he said, running in front of her. He carried a bag and an armload of books. The precious tomes spilled to the ground as he finally found the specific one he was looking for. He riffled through the pages and tore one out.

"Here! Take it! Have you the tooth still? Good. With this spell, and that tooth you can track him wherever he goes! And the bag! Take the bag! It contains some necessities, an old staff and crystal. Better than yours, but not nearly what you deserve. Oh, if only you would wait until the next time that the way opens. We could give you a crystal worthy of your skill," he said.

Myranda took the bag and the page, stuffing it inside. Tears were welling in her eyes. As they approached the base of the falls the mountain seemed to shudder. At any second, a column of water would come crashing down.

"Myranda. Take care. Please, come back to m--us," he said.

"I swear to you. If I can, I will," she assured him.

Myranda rushed to the edge of the waterfall basin. Those keeping watch claimed that neither they nor their predecessors had seen anyone enter the mouth of the cave, but considering the fact that Lain had managed to sneak out of his own hut without waking Myn, that meant little. The dragon leapt down into the basin, while Myranda lowered herself as gently as she could down inside. With much difficulty, she managed to reach the mouth of the cave. She fought the urge to have one final look at those she was leaving behind, for fear of changing her mind. Instead, she hurried as quickly as the slick floor of the cave would allow.

Ahead lay darkness, danger, risk, and war. All of this Myranda knew. But somewhere there were two creatures, two creatures she'd seen with her own eyes, which could change the world. The mountain groaned, filling the cave with echoes. At any moment, an icy wall of water could drop down, robbing her of the haven, the wonder, the paradise that was Entwell. Her every desire, save one, lie in that fair village. Her greatest desire, though, lay ahead.

Lain carried with him the shining gleam of hope for peace, and she would follow that dying light in the darkness to the ends of the world. Now she knew the truth. She would show Lain the error in his ways. Now she understood her purpose. She would find the other Chosen. Now she had the power. She would see the war brought to an end, or she would die trying. Around her the mountain gave a groaning roar. Squeezing her scarred left hand tightly, she climbed on, toward her destiny.

#

Important though it is to tell the tale completely, the enormity of the task was not clear to me at the onset. Much as it pains me to leave you in the grip of so tense a moment, the hour is late and my hand grows unsteady. For now I must rest, and begin anew when I am able. I can only hope that the volume to follow finds its way to your eyes as well, as the tale is not half told, and I know all too well what incomplete knowledge can bring. Until then, let me leave you with an assurance. The tale does not end here. Indeed, this is merely the beginning.

Made in the USA
San Bernardino, CA
04 December 2015